LUCIANO S WARD

LUCIANO'S WAR

Untold stories of the liberation of Sicily

DAVID WESTON

*To Nicholas,
with many thanks,*

D J Weston.

July 2017.

THISTLE
PUBLISHING

First published in 2016 by:

Thistle Publishing
36 Great Smith Street
London
SW1P 3BU

www.thistlepublishing.co.uk

To
PRRJ
and Dora, who went with me to Villalba and beyond

Author's Note

According to legend the notorious gangster, Lucky Luciano, was secretly released from Great Meadow Prison in 1943 and accompanied Patton's army in the invasion of Sicily. He was reported as having been seen in the port of Gela, where the US Seventh Army's first headquarters were established, and to have ridden on the first tank that drove into the town of Villalba, the home of Don Calo Vizzini, the *Capo dei Capi*, the Boss of Bosses, of the Sicilian Mafia. This has always been vehemently denied by the US Government and Armed Forces. The following is a conjecture of what might have happened. I have chosen to tell the story through a variety of voices and factual and imaginary diaries and reports. Danny Crivello and Frank Dunford and their immediate associates are fictitious, although based on a variety of real-life characters; I have no evidence Luciano was in Sicily during 1943, but the greater part of the events described are true. What can never be questioned is the heroism and sacrifice of the Allied forces, the tenacity of their German opponents, and the indescribable suffering of the Sicilian people. This has been a largely forgotten campaign, but the struggles and incredible sacrifices at Piano Lupo, Etna, Troina and Brolo deserve to be commemorated alongside those in Normandy, Arnhem and the Bulge. I am all too aware that I have ignored the great and valiant contribution of the British and Canadian Armies. That is another book.

The establishment of a just democracy after military victory is a conundrum we have yet to solve.

Europe had been fighting since 1939 but 1941–1942 was America's first winter of war and it was a bitter one for the three great tribes of New York City. On Brooklyn Heights, Jews lamented the suffering of their brethren under Hitler's persecution. In the Irish bars along Ninth Avenue old-time supporters of the IRA stared into their stout, finding the fact that the hated British were now the US's strongest allies hard to swallow. Up in the Bronx and down the lower East Side, Italians agonized that Mussolini had joined Hitler and Japan, and that their folks in the old country were now officially sworn enemies of Uncle Sam.

The Japanese attack on Pearl Harbor on 7 December 1941 shattered the illusion that America could remain safely outside the wars in Europe and Asia. The battleship **Arizona** *and five other first-rate warships, together with 2,310 dead and 946 wounded, paid a heavy price for that complacency. In January 1942 German U-boats began operating unhindered virtually within sight of the skyscrapers of Manhattan and torpedoed nearly a hundred ships, seeming to have an uncanny awareness of the movements of their prey. Spies were suspected everywhere. Allied ships were being sunk faster than they could be replaced; vital supplies to beleaguered Britain and Soviet Russia were in danger of drying up, whilst thousands of merchant seamen were meeting terrible deaths in the icy waters of the North Atlantic.*

1

SABOTAGE

Danny Crivello:

Most guys can remember a certain day that changed their lives and I suppose February 9, 1942 had to be mine. Light snow was falling as Uncle Tony and I made our way along the banks of the Hudson towards Pier 88, where the smokestacks of the *Normandie* towered above us like skyscrapers. She'd been berthed in New York Harbor when France fell and was now in the protective custody of the United States. Even at this godforsaken hour she was swarming with stevedores, loaders, fitters, and all ranks of Navy personnel, striving frantically to complete her transformation into the USS troopship, *Lafayette*. With her speed of over 32 knots they claimed she could outrun any U-boat and would safely transport GIs, an entire Division at a time, across the Atlantic into the European war.

I shot a look at Uncle Tony as we drew near the pier gates. I'd been up half the night trying to persuade him, but his dark face betrayed nothing. It was only to be expected; he was a damn Sicilian. He'd sworn he'd never set foot on the Waterfront again after the Mob killed his pal, Pete Panto; but that had been three years ago – three long years during which he'd just sat silently in our small cold-water apartment on the Lower West Side, staring at the wall throughout the livelong day. Uncle Tony had been a fervent Communist all his life, and when Stalin signed his pact with Hitler in 1939, things got even worse. Ma and me had begun to fear for his sanity; but now the Nazis had broken the pact and invaded Russia, things had to be different.

We passed white-helmeted Navy guards and merged with the noisy crowd swarming past innumerable snow-covered pallets, crates and bales, stacked up under the shadow of the giant liner. Winches snarled and clanked overhead as loaded slings swung towards open hatches. The air was heavy with the stink of bilge and diesel, mingling with the stale sweat on the clothes of the men around us. They were nearly all Italian, even in war you needed a ticket to work, and only Albert Anastasia's International Longshoremen's Association could give it you. The guys were in good humour – they'd be on overtime until the ship was ready, even after they'd paid their kickbacks to the ILA, the money would be good. I was only here for the dough. If war work continued at this rate, in six months I'd have enough to see me through college at Notre Dame. I'd become an engineer, like Ma had always wanted me to be.

Uncle Tony had remained silent, but as we neared the foot of the gangway he caught sight of a fat guy sprawling in a chair and stopped abruptly, blocking the flow of longshoremen pushing behind. "It's no use. I can't do it. I swore I'd never give those *bastardi* another nickel."

"We've talked it through, Uncle Tony. You agreed. You'll be fighting the Fascists, same as you've done all your life. Besides, Ma could use the extra dough."

"Get a move on. Some of us wanna work." A heavy longshoreman shoved him in the back.

"Lay off, will you?"

As I turned, fear raced across the guy's face. He stepped back apologetically. "Sorry, kid. I didn't know he was with you."

Fats Florino, hearing the altercation, looked up from the racing page. I quickly stepped in front of Uncle Tony and waved my ILA membership card under his swollen nose. Fats ignored it and smiled.

"Hi there, Danny boy. How you doing?"

"Fine. How about you?"

I was always uneasy with old hoods like Fats. Pa had provided muscle for Joe Masseria's organization before he'd been gunned down in Benito's restaurant with four bullets in his back. I'd often wondered if the Mob expected me to prove my Sicilian blood and seek out the guys who'd shot him. I could remember Pa telling me: "Never let the smallest wrong or insult go unavenged". But that terrible night they brought his body home, Ma had made me swear, on my father's eternal soul, that I'd never go back to the ways of the old country: I was an American.

Fats held out a metal ticket. "Easy job for you, Danny, *materassi* – mattresses. You'll find 'em on the top deck. Don't sleep all day; they say there's a fuckin' war to be won." His smile faded when he saw my uncle. "Jeez, if it ain't Tony Lorenzo, the Commie agitator. Decided to help Uncle Sam now that bastard Stalin needs him to save his rotten neck?"

Tony gnawed his lip. "I'm a better *Americano* than you'll ever be." He held out his worn membership card. "Just give me a ticket."

Fats snatched Tony's card and examined it intently, his dark eyes, squeezed almost into slits by podgy cheeks. "Looks as though you're behind with your dues." He looked up and smiled malevolently. "No problem – I'll tell the office to put you on half pay till you're up to date. Unless of course you'd like a union loan? They'd be happy to fix you up with one."

"At twenty-per-cent a week interest? Anastasia can lick my ass. I'd die sooner than let him suck me dry..."

I cut in quickly. "Come on, Fats, give him a break. He's Pa's brother-in-law."

Fats picked at his teeth with a dirty finger. "Yeah, that's the only fuckin' reason he's allowed round here." He flicked a ticket towards Tony, deliberately aiming beyond his reach. It clunked like a dud nickel as it hit the snow-covered ground. Some of the men behind laughed. Tony's hand instinctively went to the clawed baling hook hanging from his belt, but he caught my eye and reluctantly took it away. He flushed with humiliation, but bent down and picked his ticket out of the snow.

"Remember, start shooting any of that Red shit propaganda, and you're out," Fats continued. "The men are happy. They just wanna work." He returned his attention to the form of the ponies.

I pulled Uncle Tony up the gangplank and into the *Normandie*'s bowels. We pushed past sailors painting white walls grey, and fitters dismantling the ornate panelling that decorated the public saloons. Longshoremen were rolling up thick expensive red carpet, exposing the bare wooden deck. The ship was like an elegant dame being stripped to her underwear. My uncle still seethed with anger. "Pete Panto was the only man with the guts to stand up to Anastasia. Pete wanted to put the union into the hands of the men. Have fair elections, fair hiring, stop the kickbacks, beatings and bribery. Give the union's money to those who need it – not for silk shirts for *camorristi* – gangsters..."

"Give it a rest, Uncle Tony. I've heard it all before."

"*Pregare Dio*, that you should never stop hearing it. Else Pete died for nothing."

"What did my pa die for? Some bastard shot him when I was a little kid. I'm still trying to learn to live with it. Don't you think I've wondered every single day of my life who killed him, or who gave the word? I swore to Ma I'd have nothing to do with the Mob – so how will I ever know? If I can live with that so can you."

Tony's anger left him abruptly and his eyes filled with pain. He turned and led the way up the stairs out onto the main deck, which towered above the dock below. The west side of Manhattan and the Waterfront were spread out pure white through the snow. The air was cleaner and Tony filled his lungs before taking his pipe out of his pocket. "My sister is right. Have nothing to do with hoodlums. It is not the work for an honourable man."

"Pa said anything was better than working in the sulphur mines in the old country. He travelled across the world to escape it."

"That was true. The mines were like the Inferno of Dante – the heat, the smoke, the stink. Your father was a different man then. We thought alike. We both hated the *Fratellanza* and the *Fascisti*. We fought against them together; we were comrades, brothers. But he came here, met Luciano, and became a different man."

"Pa had no choice; you know that. He arrived in New York with no money and no work. He couldn't speak a word of English. He had Ma and me to feed."

Tony pondered for a moment then gazed at the piles of mattresses, stiff and white with the cold and snow. "*Freschi materassi*, for virgin boys to sleep on." He looked westwards into the biting wind. "Even now, they are coming on trains and buses from every State: boys from school, from farms and the prairies. They know nothing about war and are being sent to fight the most powerful army ever created by man. I hope they will enjoy many warm and tender beds and not be virgins when they die." He knocked out the smouldering bowl of his pipe against his foot, took out his baling hook, swung a bundle of mattresses over his broad shoulders, and carried his load towards the stairway.

I followed thoughtfully. So far, I'd never got round to dames.

Room 402,
Taft Hotel,
152 W 51ˢᵗ St.
Ensign Frank Dunford, US Navy:

I lay and watched the weak winter sun slowly steal across the bed and onto the golden downy hairs on Sue's shoulder. It had been my first weekend in New York on this my first posting. Sue had taken the train from Cleveland on Friday to spend two nights with me here at the Taft. She'd be travelling back that evening at six, and at the bottom of my gut, in the words of Clark Gable, I frankly didn't really give a damn. I was twenty-one, a newly commissioned officer in the Navy, at loose in the Big Apple for the first time for Chrissake! I'd seen how the smart young secretaries of Manhattan appreciated my blue uniform with the golden star and single stripe on my sleeve – I wanted to lay as many of them as possible. I'd volunteered for Naval Intelligence partly because no one else seemed to want to and the pass mark would be low, but mostly in the hope of getting a posting like this. Even so it hadn't been easy, I'd been lucky that foreign languages were at a premium and the Italian I'd learned from my mother had carried me through. Now all I wanted was to have a good war and keep out of harm's way. Yet what did this posting entail? I still hadn't the faintest idea. On Friday afternoon I'd reported to Room 196 at the Astor and had met my new boss, Lt Commander Haffenden, a burly old Navy hand, who was forming a new section within Third Naval District. I didn't think the bastard liked me: implied I'd only got the job because I spoke Italian. I was to report back to him this morning. That was all I knew.

I gazed at Sue's dark nipple resting just above the sheet and my small town morality gave me a twinge of guilt. As a good Catholic, I should never have used the rubbers the Navy had so thoughtfully provided. Mother would be hurt if she knew. I'd better go to confession sometime at St Patrick's, which I'd passed yesterday on Fifth Avenue. But what would I confess? Sue had done things to me last night that were certainly beyond the comprehension or imagination of a priest. At least I would hope so. She was no longer the girl I'd dated at high school; Ohio State had a lot to answer for. Who the hell had taught her those things? I felt jealous of the jerk, whoever he was.

The sun stole up to her eyes and wakened her. She looked up at me, smiled, and ran a pink tongue around her lips. I only had to look at that tongue and soft mouth and the sheet in front of me rose like a snow-covered mountain.

"I'll die if I don't get a cup of coffee, Franco."

Only my mother called me Franco: it didn't sound right coming from Sue. I telephoned room service and ordered coffee and cookies for two.

Sue stretched out her arms, provocatively: "I'm going to enjoy your new assignment if it means I can go shopping in New York every month."

I looked across the room, strewn with our hastily discarded clothes, to the pile of purchases she'd be taking back and forced a smile: "I don't reckon my Navy pay will be able to cover it. Bloomingdale's must have laid on that sale especially for you." I knew all about stores – father ran a grocery shop in Millersburg, Ohio. "Anyway, I've no idea how much free time I'm going to have."

"Franco," she reached up and kissed me on the cheek as her hand fumbled for my rigid pecker, "you've been very quiet about this posting. What is it you're actually going to do?"

"You may not have noticed it but there's a war going on." She stroked me with her thumb and forefinger as my blood throbbed. "The Navy has been given responsibility for the security of New York Harbor. You've no idea how many ships we're losing every day. Third Naval District Intelligence has formed a special section ... F Section ..."

She laughed sexily. "If 'F' stands for what I think, Franco, they couldn't have picked a better man."

"It's for counter-espionage ..."

There was a sharp rap on the door. Sue pulled up the sheet to cover her breasts and I hurriedly crossed my legs. A good-looking dark-haired waiter entered. He gave Sue's naked shoulders a lingering look of approval as he put the tray on the table beside her. He was about my age and had the natural ease and arrogance of all Latin waiters. I slipped a quarter into his hand. He looked at it disdainfully, gave Sue a final appraisal, and went out softly closing the door.

Sue put her hand back under the sheet. "If you didn't have that naval uniform, I could go for him."

"His cousin's probably in Mussolini's navy. Every Italian in Manhattan could be a spy. It's going to be a hell of a job."

She squeezed me harder: "As I said, F Section couldn't have picked a better man."

Danny Crivello:
We staggered down the stairs with our first load of mattresses. A guy was working in the corner cutting away at a

bulkhead with a blazing blowtorch. He was wearing a protective mask and I couldn't see his face.

Uncle Tony gave the stranger a wide berth. "I never like acetylene" he grumbled as he threw his load onto the wooden deck. "It was acetylene lamps that caused the fires in the sulphur mines: fires so terrible that they burnt out your guts. The owners were supposed to provide miners with safety lamps, but lamps were expensive and miners' lives were cheap."

I nodded wearily: I'd heard it all before.

We worked throughout the morning, heaving more and more mattresses below until they formed a soft, sweet-smelling wall. I acknowledged the stranger on the odd occasion our eyes met behind the glass of his mask, but received nothing in return. I knew most of the guys who worked this shift but had never seen this one before. He didn't look Italian. Was he Irish?

The hooters blew for a break; I threw down my load, rubbed the damp patch in the small of my back and ambled over to him: "Cheer up, pal. I know it's Monday and we're at war, but at least the Depression's over. Think of all the dough you're earning with that torch." The man pulled his mask up to his brow and wiped the sweat from his face with the back of his hand. I tried again: "The PX is serving free coffee and doughnuts on the main deck." The guy nodded but said nothing. I noticed his watery, baleful eyes before he looked down to inspect the metal he'd been cutting. I shrugged and gave up. "OK Pal. See you up there." As I clambered up the stairs behind Uncle Tony's broad hips, some odd premonition made me look back. I caught a glimpse of the stranger taking his bag towards the mattresses.

A few minutes later, we stood on the deck dunking our doughnuts in paper cups, gazing through the snow towards the Cunard Building on the other side of the dock.

Uncle Tony sipped a mouthful of coffee and grimaced. "Americans make the finest automobiles and radios and refrigerators, but can't make a decent cup of coffee. Maybe they will after the war, if they get to Italy." He thought for a moment. His brow creased with frowns. "All wars are bad, Daniello, but this is going to be the worst. I don't want to fight against Italians, but the world will be a better place without that bastard, Mussolini. *Il Duce* he calls himself – The Leader. All he's done is to lead Italy up his fat ass." He searched vainly among his pockets for his pipe. "He swaggered down to Sicily after the earthquake at Messina in 1923. We were living like dogs in shantytowns. He swore he would not sleep until we were all living in dignity. He swore, he would not make such a promise unless he knew he would keep it. The people believed him; but nothing was ever done. The people still live in squalor. Their life will get no better while that vain fool and his *Fascisti* are in power."

I looked at my uncle and knew I loved him more than any other man alive. "You've had a tough life. I'll always be grateful how you took care of Ma and me after Pa was killed."

Uncle Tony nodded and pursed his lips. "It wasn't easy. But at least we didn't accept a single nickel from the Mob." His blunt, scarred fingers made a final check of his pockets: "I must have left my pipe below. Go get another cup of that godawful coffee while I go down and find it."

Ensign Frank Dunford:

The coffee had been weak and tasteless: I'd screwed Sue yet again before falling back into a sweet sleep of exhausted satisfaction. I woke to see her gazing lovingly at me from her pillow. She'd always had a crush on me – even at High School when I'd been a solitary half-Italian Catholic boy mocked and bullied by the WASPs. She brushed away the lock of hair that had fallen over my face:

"I don't have to go back you know. We could easily find an apartment here and live together. It won't be hard for me to get a job."

She waited for a response, but I couldn't think of anything to say. I slipped out of bed, wrapped a towel around my waist, and went into the bathroom.

Danny Crivello:

I was talking baseball with a group of longshoremen, discussing the form of Joe DiMaggio and the prospects of the Yankees in the forthcoming season, when I realised the coffee in the paper cup was cold. I made my way back along the crowded deck to where I'd left Uncle Tony. He wasn't there. I got two fresh cups of coffee and went below. I opened the heavy iron door and was immediately engulfed in a whirl of choking smoke. Fire! I could see orange flames coming from the mattresses. Why no alarm? Why hadn't the sprinklers come on? Where was Uncle Tony?

I raced back up the stairs and yelled for the Fire Watch, and then plunged back down below.

Ensign Frank Dunford:

I stood under the shower, collecting my thoughts in the soft, warm, steaming water. I hadn't bargained for Sue offering to stay. I liked her: she was fantastic in the sack, but I wanted to play the field. Besides, Sue was Protestant, my mother would never approve. I wrapped the towel back and went into the bedroom. She was flicking through the pages of *Life*, but I knew she was waiting for my answer. She'd tied a ribbon round her blonde hair and looked like Betty Grable – although her legs weren't in the same class. I'd always gone for slender ankles and Sue's were decidedly thick. I could sense her watching me as I walked across the untidy room towards the window. I gazed out towards the Hudson, over the flat tops of the lower buildings. The round wooden water tanks with turreted tops reminded me of European fairy-tales. They looked incongruous in this, the most modern city on earth. I couldn't help but feel guilty – to be here, having such a good time.

"Cat got your tongue?"

"I was thinking of Henry Linville and George Kelly. They were my closest pals at Annapolis. They passed higher than me and got postings at sea."

"That shouldn't bother you. I know you've no intention of being a hero. You only enlisted for the free college education at Annapolis."

"I was envious when they wrote me about the sunshine in Honolulu."

Sue laughed, "And the girls."

"They were both at Pearl Harbor when the Japs attacked. Henry went down with the *Arizona*; George is dying from his burns on the *Raleigh*. I had a letter from his mother."

Her smile vanished. "My darling, I'm so sorry."

To my surprise, there was a tear in my eye. I didn't want her to see. I turned back to the window. It took me a moment to register a pall of black smoke that was being blown by a southwest wind across the lower part of Manhattan Island. The Empire State, the Chrysler and their neighbouring skyscrapers were already obscured.

Something really big was burning on the Waterfront.

Danny Crivello:
I tried to peer through the smoke. My eyes were streaming.
I could hardly see. The alarms were already ringing on the
deck above as I made my way along the wall towards the fire.
Against the glow I made out a bulky form, lying face down
on the deck. It was Uncle Tony. His coat was burning I tore
off my donkey jacket and frantically beat out the flames.
Then, with gasping lungs, I bent down and struggled to
get him across my shoulders in a fireman's lift. I turned
to retrace my steps to the stairs, but a fresh sheet of flame
burst from the mattresses. The whole of the wooden deck
was alight: we couldn't get out that way. A foul stench came
from the burning horsehair. Pa's tales of the sulphur mines
raced across my brain. This was another Hell. But there had
to be a way out. I'd too much to live for, too many plans – I
wasn't going to die like my forebears in terrible fire. Then it
came to me. When I'd gone to the john, I'd noticed a small
service staircase at the far end of the saloon. The fire wasn't
so fierce in that direction. I turned around and staggered
forward, doing all I could to keep Uncle Tony's head from
the flames licking hungrily at my ankles.

Ensign Frank Dunford:
I'd hastily pulled on my creased uniform and was running
down the wharf past open warehouses towards the stricken
ship. My heart was pounding and my mouth was dry with
panic. I'd no idea what I should do. I looked up at the

ferocious flames leaping amid the thick smoke from the forward holds. I'd never seen anything so huge and terrifying. I was still looking upwards when something hard thumped into my chest. I fell backwards onto the smoke-blackened snow. In the shock, I was just able to make out the back of a man in woollen hat and dark blue jacket, running rapidly towards the dock gates. He had a bag on his shoulder. I tried to yell after him, but the wind had been knocked out of me. I got to my feet brushing snow from my uniform and gazed, mesmerized at the stricken *Normandie*. The huge vessel was already listing towards port as endless streams of water poured into her from the fireboats bobbing around her, like fretful ducklings about a dying swan. Sailors and dockworkers were pouring down the gangways, pushing and cursing; some were carrying casualties, choking with smoke. The sirens of ambulances screeched in competition with fire trucks and police cars. Everywhere was chaos and confusion.

Some raucous bellowing rose above the din. I pushed towards it and was relieved to see that my new chief, Lt. Commander Haffenden, was already on the scene. He turned his bull neck and nodded implacably at me, showing not the least surprise at my arrival. "This is a hell of a mess. So are you. Your uniform is a disgrace and you need a shave."

"How did it happen?" I asked blandly, rubbing the stubble on my chin. I was shivering despite the proximity of the fire.

"You tell me. It could have been a fifth columnist, or else some damn fool dropped a cigarette. Half of them are Italians; they want Mussolini to win for Chrissake..." He turned to see a dark-haired kid struggling down the gangplank carrying a badly burned man. "Don't just stand there, like a useless prick, Ensign. Go and give that young fella a hand."

I had barely made a reluctant step towards the gang-plank, when an explosion on the deck above sent mattresses soaring into the sky. Shards of burning horsehair rained down. I screamed and covered my face with his hands, certain I was about to be burned to death like George Kelly. I cowered for a moment before forcing myself to look up. To my profound relief, the young guy had managed to stagger down to the dockside. I hurried over and struggled to extract the man from his shoulders. He was older; his dark hair was streaked with grey

"Be careful. His back's badly burned." The young guy was near exhaustion and his hands were red raw from the fire.

Haffenden spotted some sailors approaching with stretchers: "Let's have one of those over here!"

Two sailors hurried to my aid and helped me lay the older man face down on the stretcher. His breath was coming in agonized rasps. His rescuer slumped to the ground and plunged his burnt hands into the fresh cold snow. Other workmen and sailors from the ship mingled around, attracted by the authority of Haffenden's uniform.

"Does anyone here have any idea what fool started this?" he demanded.

A fat guy pushed his way through the crowd with gravy on his chin. The fire had obviously disturbed his lunch. "They were working with acetylene torches and there were thousands of bales of mattresses. I guess a spark must have hit one of the bales and smouldered, but the stupid fuckin' idiots didn't notice."

"I saw a guy acting suspiciously just before we broke for coffee."

Haffenden turned and looked down at the young guy sitting in the snow: "Suspiciously? What d'you mean?"

"He just didn't seem right. I'd never seen him before; wouldn't answer whenever I spoke to him. When we went up on deck at the break he was still down there with his acetylene torch."

"You talking baloney, kid," The fat man seemed anxious to avoid any accusation of dereliction of duty. "I handed out the tickets. No fucker got past me."

"There was somebody there." A medic had gently turned the older man over. He winced with pain as he looked up at the Lt. Commander, his voice scarcely more than a whisper: "I went down below and saw the fire. It had just started. I thought at first it was my fault – perhaps my pipe was smouldering when I put it down. I went to get the extinguisher from the wall but someone hit me with a blackjack or something like it; knocked me cold. Feel the bump on my head."

The medic examined the back of his skull and nodded affirmation.

The old guy began to cough violently. "That was worse than the sulphur mines of the old country."

Haffenden sucked on his pipe: "Italians, of course."

The kid shook his head proudly: "No sir, we are *Sicill*... Sicilians."

"What's your name, young man?"

"Danny Crivello, sir."

"Would you recognise that guy if you saw him again."

"I'm not sure. He had his mask on most of the time."

"Haffenden took a gold embossed card from his billfold. "If you think you see that guy again, you ring me at once on that number. That's an order. Don't forget."

The kid took the card painfully between two fingers and slipped it into the pocket at the back of his pants. At the medic's nod the sailors gently lifted the stretcher and began to bear the casualty to the nearest ambulance. The kid followed by his side, still holding snow to ease the agony in his hands.

"Take him to Mount Sinai. Make sure he gets the best treatment possible. The LSA will pick up the bill."

I turned to see a thickset man in his early forties. He wore a grey trilby, a smart double-breasted overcoat and polka dot tie. He was surrounded by a group of menacing-looking hoods.

The newcomer held out his hand towards Haffenden. "Albert Anastasia, Commander. This is a terrible tragedy, but something's gotta be done. My members are at risk. We never had trouble on the Waterfront until you Navy guys took over."

There were general grunts of agreement from the men around.

"Are you accusing the US Navy of incompetence?"

Anastasia gave an ingratiating smile. "I wouldn't dream of doing that, Commander. I'm a patriotic American. I know you guys know how to fight a war, but you know nothin' about the Waterfront. Those guards you put on the gates have no fuckin' idea who belongs here and who doesn't. Leave it to the LSA, or things will get a helluva lot worse." There were more growls of assent. Anastasia touched the brim of his trilby before sashaying towards a warehouse that was rapidly being converted into a casualty clearing station. His entourage followed dutifully behind. Haffenden watched them go thoughtfully, as if an idea was forming at the back his mind.

My mind had wandered back to sex. I decided I'd ask Sue to stay for a couple more nights, but there was something I really wanted to know: "By the way, Commander, what does 'F' stand for?"

Haffenden took the pipe from his mouth: "Ferrets, son; ferrets. We will be vicious and will go down any hole to get what we want."

I wasn't quite sure what the Commander meant.

2

A LITTLE HELP FROM
MY FRIENDS

February 12, 1942
Ensign Frank Dunford:

I was sitting at a long polished table with an assortment of naval officers, police, customs, and civilian officials, feeling wrung-out after another heavy night in the sack with Sue. Admiral Andrews had summoned us all to an emergency meeting at the Port Authority Building to discuss subversive activity on the New York Waterfront. The mood was grim: reports had just come in that U-boats had sunk five more ships that very morning. I glanced across the table to Commander Haffenden, gazing thoughtfully out of the window at the burnt-out wreck of the *Normandie*, which was lying helplessly on her side in the dock below. I'd sneaked a look at his record and now knew more about the old sonofabitch. He'd joined the Navy in the Great War as an enlisted man. His captain had somehow perceived certain abilities in him and had recommended him for a commission. He'd been fiercely proud of it and throughout the Twenties and Thirties, in a series of mediocre jobs and failed businesses, had held on to his place on the Navy Reserve. He was fifty-one, and I guessed the old fool was hoping another war would finally give him a chance to fulfil his potential.

We rose to our feet with a scraping of chairs as the Admiral entered, silver-haired, neat and handsome in immaculate blue uniform. He took his place at the top of the table and motioned us all to sit. We waited apprehensively as he took a sip of water before speaking. "Gentlemen, in the words of the President of the United States, something must be done. Churchill has said the Battle of the Atlantic is the most vital battle of the war, and the U-boats are winning it." He got to his feet and went to the huge map of the Atlantic that hung on the wall behind him. "They wait in packs all along our eastern coast, from Maine to Florida, and seem to know exactly when and what to strike. Nearly always the most vital cargoes get hit. Someone must be supplying them with the information." There was a general murmur of agreement around the table. The Admiral waited for it to subside before continuing. "The enemy appears to be getting help in other ways. Even with the greater range of their new IX-C U-boats and their new bases in Brittany in north-west France, it is impossible they can remain at sea so long without being resupplied and refuelled offshore." He returned to his seat and took another sip of water. "A few survivors have been taken aboard the U-boats for medical treatment before being put back in their life rafts – thank God, there are still some humane officers in the German Navy. Some of these survivors have stated that they saw clearly marked US supplies on board." There were gasps of disbelief and dismay around the table. The Admiral registered them before continuing. "And then three days ago the *Normandie,* one of the largest objects ever set in motion by man, was destroyed here in New York City before our very eyes. The FBI has found traces of highly inflammable material placed under the mattresses where the fire originated. The sprinklers on that deck had been turned off. It was an obvious case of sabotage. If we want to win this war we cannot allow this state of affairs to continue. The Waterfront and the entire eastern seaboard must be made secure." He swept the table with an imperious eye: "I am open to suggestions."

A swarthy-looking guy with receding black hair rubbed the dark stubble on his chin as he spoke. I recognised Frank S. Hogan from the newspapers: he'd just been appointed New York District Attorney following the resignation of Thomas Dewey, who was going to run for Governor. "I can promise you that anyone caught in the act of sabotage, or passing information on to the enemy, will be prosecuted for treason for which I will demand the death penalty. The NYPD have promised more men to guarantee total security."

An overweight cop, NYPD Chief George O'Reilly looked at him gloomily and seemed to agree.

"Gentlemen, I've heard this before but the leaks have continued. The Waterfront appears to be a law unto itself." The Admiral studied his well-clipped nails. "I'm considering declaring martial law."

Haffenden cleared his throat and took off his horn-rimmed spectacles: "If you'll permit me sir, I don't think that'll do any good." All eyes around the table turned to him; even I knew it was unusual for a Lt. Commander to question an Admiral.

"Well, what would you suggest?" Captain Roscoe C McFall, the District Intelligence officer, was clearly irritated that his subordinate had spoken before him.

"There's only one authority controlling the Waterfront. We don't want to admit it, but we all know who they are: the Mob, Cosa Nostra, the Mafia; call them what you will. But we share one thing in common – a hatred of Mussolini. Most of them are Sicilians; he's been cracking down on them there with an iron fist for the past twenty years. In some parts he's wiped them out completely."

"Some would suggest it was the only decent thing Mussolini's done. Are you suggesting we do a deal with pimps and murderers?" Hogan sounded as if he was back in court.

Haffenden leant forward with his hands clasped before him and ploughed on with a passion I hadn't noticed before: "If they hate Mussolini at least we agree about something. What's that expression? – 'My enemy's enemy is my friend?' We've got to keep the lifeline to Britain and Russia open until we're ready to join in. We're losing ships faster than they can be built. I'd say we must use any means to safeguard the security of the United States."

McFall, clearly furious that Haffenden had taken over the meeting, raised his hand as if to make a point, but the Admiral turned to O'Reilly: "What d'you think? You know these hoodlums best."

O'Reilly shifted his heavy bulk on his leather seat, making a noise like a fart; perhaps it was. "Sure we've done deals in the past. Sometimes you have to if you want to get things done..."

Hogan broke in: "But we are representing the people of America: God-fearing, law-abiding people, in a crusade against the most evil powers on Earth. Are we seriously proposing an alliance with the Devil?"

Haffenden looked him straight in the eye. "If you want to put the Devil on trial, you have to go to Hell for your witnesses."

"I wouldn't bet money that those hoodlums didn't set fire to the *Normandie* themselves to push us into this sort of unholy deal." Hogan responded.

Admiral Andrews puckered his brows and pondered. Haffenden watched anxiously before the Admiral turned again to O'Reilly.

"Whom should we talk to?"

"Well there's Joe 'Socks' Lanza – he's head of the United Seafood Workers Union. He runs the Fulton Fish Market on Pier 18 under the Brooklyn Bridge. You can't buy a piece of fish in New York unless he's touched it."

"His hands must stink." My attempt at humour was squashed by Haffenden's frosty stare.

"Why do they call him 'Socks'?" the Admiral inquired.

"He's a big heavy guy and he socks anyone who opposes him."

"He's got a record as long as my arm," Hogan hadn't given up. "He gets $5 from every boat that docks and $15 from every truck that takes the fish away. The Court of General Sessions has currently an indictment for extortion and coercion against him; he's awaiting sentence,"

"But he controls the fishing fleets," O'Reilly persisted. "The lobster boats and the mackerel fishers know every inch of the coastline. Socks used to be a rum runner during Prohibition; if any supplies were being run to the U-boats he'd know about it."

Hogan was adamant: "I will make no deals with him. If he does help it will make no difference to the indictment."

The Admiral nodded: "Anyone else?"

O'Reilly thought hard, which he seemed to find painful. "Well, Socks has no power on the wharfs. You need somebody with connections in every dock and union, with the ILA, and the longshoremen. Lucky Luciano controlled them all before Dewey put him away on a fifty-year stretch."

Hogan broke in: "Too right he did. That shitheel is in solitary in Dannemora, toughest prison in the State." He smiled maliciously: "A Russian inmate swore it was worse than Siberia."

The Admiral wasn't amused. "Anyone else?"

O'Reilly shrugged: "You could sound out Meyer Lansky. He had a Jewish mother but they say he sure sucked on a Sicilian tit. He grew up with Luciano. He was his pal: ran the mobs with him before Lucky went inside. We've never been able to pin anything on him. He's too smart; they say the little bastard can see round corners. He's now in the jukebox business. Officially he's clean."

"If you sleep with dogs, you get fleas," Hogan said almost to himself:

Haffenden was confident now, almost contemptuous. "If I could help save one American ship or even the life of one American sailor, I'd sleep with Satan himself."

The Admiral's mind was made up. "Chief O'Reilly, arrange for those two gentlemen to meet with Commander Haffenden, Captain Roscoe and myself as soon as possible. That is by two o'clock this afternoon." Haffenden had a self-satisfied smile as we rose. The Admiral stopped us with his hand: "Nothing we have discussed will be mentioned by any of you outside this room. If I hear of any leaks or information passed to the press I will have the person responsible charged with treason. I kid you not."

Appetising smells were wafting around me, as I waited outside the Astor's kitchen entrance in my sports jacket and slacks. It was just after lunch and I hadn't had any. At five minutes to two an unmarked Navy limousine drew up with its blinds down. Two men stepped out. One was large and unkempt, looking ill at ease in his suit and soaked in cheap cologne, which couldn't quite hide the smell of fish. His fleshy lips turned down at the sides of his chops, which gave him a look of perpetual gloom. The other was small, spruce and tidy, with a cigarette hanging in the corner of his thin lips. His eyes were cold – like small ponds of ice.

I nodded and led them silently up the service stairs to the mezzanine floor where F Section occupied three rooms. Two naval typists in civilian dress looked up as we passed through. I noticed the white flesh of Yeoman Mary Hampton's thighs above her stocking tops and stole a look at her trim ankles. She was Haffenden's secretary and I meant to get into her sometime during the duration. She looked at me admiringly as I knocked and opened the door to the inner sanctum. The Admiral, in grey lounge suit, flanked by McFall still in Navy uniform, and Haffenden wearing Prince of Wales check, were waiting to confront their visitors. I ushered them in, closed the door, caught the Commander's eye and took my place in the corner of the room.

The Admiral got down to business immediately: "Gentlemen, it was good of you to come. Please sit down." Lanza and Meyer eyed him incredulously as they took their seats. The Admiral cleared his throat and automatically put up his hand as if to smooth the medals he usually wore on his breast. "In case you are wondering why I have summoned you here this afternoon, it is because the United States is urgently in need of your assistance. I am responsible for the security of New York Harbor, and I need allies to help me defeat the deadliest enemy in our history. I know of both your reputations, but I will ignore any moral and ethical considerations if it is in the best interests of the American people. I can offer you no deals. I will be blunt and I want an honest answer. What are your feelings about this war?"

Socks wiped the greasy sweat on his forehead with the back of his hand. He glanced at the impassive Meyer before replying: "We're, er...businessmen, yes, but we're loyal Americans first."

Meyer stubbed out a cigarette in the Coco-Cola ashtray on Haffenden's desk and lit another: "I'm a Jew. I was born in Poland; I have family being slaughtered there right now by those Nazi bastards. This country has been good to me. What do you want us to do?"

The Admiral scrutinised them carefully before continuing: "I want you to talk to your friends. I want you to ask them to eliminate all sabotage and subversive activity on the Waterfront. I want no strikes and the maximum effort to ensure the rapid and safe loading of convoys. I want no more careless talk and leakage of classified information. I need to know if, when, and how the U-boats are being re-supplied at sea. Who are Nazi sympathizers or agents? I will ensure your friends are given carte blanche to act as they think fit, but I want results immediately. We are losing this war."

Socks stole another glance at his companion, whose stone features had remained impassive.

The little man inhaled deeply before he spoke: "Socks can get you information about the ships and the coastline; but he has no sway over the LSA on the Hudson, or Cockeyed Dunn, who runs the West Side, or Mickey Lasceri over in New Jersey. Lucky Luciano is the only man who has the authority to control all the families and all the unions, and you've locked him way out of reach upstate…" Meyer's face broke into the faintest hint of a smile, "But if you were to transfer Mr Luciano closer to New York City, and put him in a more hospitable establishment, I'm sure we could do business."

The Admiral had been studying his nails and looked up. "Luciano is one of the most vicious and bloody killers in the history of crime. I doubt whether even my powers will be able to prevail on the authorities to sanction any easing of his conditions."

Meyer fixed him with his eyes of ice: "Tough shit. If you want a deal it'll have to go through him."

TOP SECRET.

February 16, 1942.

Verbatim report of meeting between Prisoner 4322, Charles Luciano (Salvatore Luciana) with Meyer Lansky and Joseph Lanza at Great Meadow Prison.

Recorded in secret by Warden Vernon A. Morhous.

Sound of door opening. Luciano enters the room.

Silence.

Luciano: What the hell are you doing here?

Noise of some sort of physical contact.

Meyer: I've brought you your favourite sandwich from Rosen's: Jewish salt beef, with pickle on rye.

Noise of rustling paper.

Luciano: Smells good. You remembered how I always loved Jewish food.

Crunching noise.

Meyer: That pickle was from the top of the barrel. You're looking pale; we'll see you get some fresh air and better food from now on. I hear Dannemora was a terrible place.

Luciano: Nothing's as bad as the sulphur mines of Lercara Friddi, little man. But what the hell! I'd never have guessed even you could pull off a stunt like this. We're in the Warden's fucking office for fucks sake!

Meyer: It's the most secure place in the entire fucking establishment, and no fucker will disturb us until I pick up that phone.

Luciano: Don't you believe it. The bastards listen in even when I shit. What the fuck is Lanza doing here? It's the closest I've been to fresh fish for five fucking years."

Meyer: We've got a proposition for you.

Slight pause.

Lanza: It's like this Lucky; the authorities think the Waterfront's swimming with Fascist agents and sympathizers. They say information's getting out to the German subs. The US is losing ships faster than they can be built. Work gets done very slowly, accidents seem to happen all the time – and now – you must have read about the fire on that French ship, the *Normandie* – millions of Government money went up in smoke ...

Luciano: What the fucks this to do with me?"

Meyer: Lucky, the Navy has asked for our help, in exchange they'll back off and leave things to us. Socks can deal with the fishing boats and the fish market, but he has no power on the wharfs."

Luciano: I still don't see what you're getting at."

Meyer: Lucky, your country needs you.

Luciano: Country. I've got no fucking country. Sicily was my country but it wasn't fit to live in. That bastard Mussolini has made it worse. I never became a US citizen because those government guys were always out to get me. I never fitted in. They didn't want to see an immigrant spic wearing smart suits and silk ties, so they fixed me up with a bum rap. That fucking Special Prosecutor, Thomas Dewey set me up, swung the jury against me, and then made sure the judge gave me fifty years. Fifty fucking years for running a whorehouse, for Chrissake! I've had five years contemplating my sins. Sitting on my butt in that stinking cold cell for sixteen hours every day and then working my ass off in that scalding laundry for the other eight. I owe nobody nothing.

Meyer: "Listen to me, will you? We can get a special deal if you co-operate. You'll have anything you want – booze, good Italian food. Someone's got to talk to Anastasia and the Longshoremen's Association, the Camarda Brothers, Sullivan, Lascari, and Joe Adonis in Brooklyn. They'll only listen to you.

Silence

Meyer: As far as countries go, Lucky, this is a good one. At least it's been good to me. It gave me refuge in 1911 from the pogroms in Poland. I'd do anything to see that sonofabitch Hitler gets his ass kicked. If you give the word, all the families, all the unions will come on side.

Luciano: Why should I stick my fucking neck out? I've a deportation order hanging over me. Who says the US is going to win this war? I could be sent back to Italy and shot by Mussolini as a fucking collaborator.

Silence.

Meyer: If you think you know about killing Lucky, you know nothing as far as those Nazis bastards are concerned. They're wiping out thousands of my people, women, children ..."

Noise of nose blowing.

Meyer: I can remember back in Poland when the Cossacks were raping our women and killing the men; the whole community had a meeting in the synagogue. The kids went, even me. Some said we should go east, some said west, the Rabbi told us to pray, but one old guy, I can still see him now, told us that Jews had suffered enough and should fight like other men. I've fought ever since and I want to help fight those Nazi bastards now."

Silence.

Luciano: Maybe you're right. Go and see Adonis and Frank Costello and all the rest. Tell them I sent you. I give my word New York Harbor will go all the way for the Allies."

End of Recording.

16 March, 1942.
Danny Crivello:
It was mid-March before I was able to get back to work. My hands still hurt like hell in spite of the lotions Ma had applied – old remedies she'd concocted from back home, from the herbs of Sicily – and I had to wear protective gloves. Uncle Tony was still in Mount Sinai Hospital. Anastasia had been as good as his word: the Longshoremen's Association was taking care of the bill.

As I approached the gates into the piers I saw at once that things had changed. The men were quieter, more solemn, and seemed to have a purpose and determination about them. ILA officials in dark overcoats were everywhere, directing and overseeing the bustle and activity. Even Fats seemed to be concentrating on his job as I approached.

"Hi there, Ciro's boy! How's your uncle? Hope the old bastard appreciates how well the Union's taking care of him." He didn't wait for an answer. "There ain't no soft jobs now. We're going to win this fuckin' war and whip those fuckin' Nazis. We're loading ammunition for those limeys in London and your uncle's Commie comrades in Moscow. No coffee breaks. Big convoy leaves tonight." He tossed me a ticket: "Load on deck three."

I took the ticket carefully in my gloved hand, boarded an ancient British merchant vessel and went below. It was dark and smelt of bilge. The noise was deafening as crates of anti-aircraft shells came hurtling down the metal rollers of the chutes in never-ending lines, to be heaved up by waiting longshoremen and stacked in the vastness of the hold. I took my place at the end of one of the chutes and began to work. It would have been hard and backbreaking at the best of times, but each grip I took on a box of shells sent a spasm of pain to my hands. I gritted my teeth and worked mechanically, thinking of the future. Many of my old school pals had received notice of the draft, but my place at Notre Dame would keep me out of the war for at least three years. Ma was happy: it would be all over by then. Everyone, apart from Uncle Tony, said as soon as the Americans got to Europe it would be a piece of cake. Part of me regretted missing out on a great adventure.

I lifted yet another crate of shells up to the guy above, who was bending down to grab it and stack it on top of an ever-growing pile. I'd looked up to check he'd got a firm grip, when an open hatch threw light onto a pair of cold, inexpressive eyes. As the guy took the crate and swung away into the darkness I remembered where I'd seen those eyes before. I ran back to the chutes and told the foreman I had to go to the john. I rushed up the stairs, pushed past the shabby British sailors, repairing tracer damage to the superstructure, and went ashore. I found Fats in the union office eating a hamburger and reading the funnies.

He looked up in annoyance. He never liked being disturbed whilst he filled his face: "I told you kid, no breaks today. That ship's got to sail tonight. I can't show you any favours"

"The guy that set fire to the *Normandie*: I've just seen him loading ammo in the hold."

Ensign Frank Dunford:

I was back in Room 196 at the Astor ready to take notes as Socks Lanza made his latest report. He'd come direct from the Fish Market and was wearing a jacket over his greasy, stinking overalls. He eased himself into his chair and pushed a bag across the table to the Commander.

"Thought you might like some fresh lobster. Those are the best, there's half a dozen there."

"Thank you, Mr Lanza." I reckoned Haffenden had never eaten so well. He poured two shots of iced vodka from the thermos jug on the table and pushed one towards Socks. The tight-assed old bastard never offered a drink to me. "Have you any news?"

"I've got word out all along the coast. I've got my people on every boat, even on the mackerel fleets, which are full of Italians and Portuguese. If they see or hear anythin' they'll let me know."

"What about supplies? Any ships taking on extra fuel and food?"

"Don't worry about a thing, Charlie Goldberg runs the supply house on South Street. As a personal favour, he's gonna inform me if any captain makes any large purchases and then heads out to sea. My boys are everywhere."

Socks was probably feeling like a useful citizen for the first time in his life, and Haffenden was as happy as a pig in shit in his new-found authority: "I wonder if you could do me a few more favours. There must be records of every boat's engine horsepower and fuel consumption. If my people had access to those, we could judge if any vessel was refuelling the U-boats from its own tanks."

Socks laboriously made notes with a well-chewed pencil.

The Commander sipped his vodka; "It would also be more effective if I could get some of my men on the fishing boats. They'll need union cards of course."

"No problem. Leave it to me."

Haffenden hadn't finished: "New York is full of foreign embassies, legations, trade missions. There are also headquarters of hundreds of firms from neutral or near hostile countries. I want to get people in those buildings as cleaners, telephone operators, liftboys, janitors, and night watchmen. I want waiters, hat-check girls and toilet attendants, in every goddamn restaurant on Manhattan."

Even this didn't seem too much for Socks: "Joe Carter owes me a favour. He controls the International Brotherhood of Building Trades, all the office cleaners and porters are with him. I know the superintendents of most of the buildings downtown; I'll get your men wherever you want. I've got the Elevator Union too."

Haffenden smiled complacently: "Socks, I don't know how I'd fight this war without you."

Sweat was forming in greasy spots on Sock's brow. He twisted his weight from one side of his huge ass to the other: "I was wondering Commander if you could do something for me?" He downed his vodka in a noisy gulp. "I can't put off that indictment for ever. It would help if you could put in a word for me when the time comes. I've been inside once; I don't think I could take it again."

Haffenden swallowed the remains of his drink: "You get me some firm information about those U-boats, Socks, and I'll see what we can do."

Danny Crivello:

I led Fats and two other union men back into the hold. They watched silently in the shadows as I scanned the faces up above. I could sense Fats fidgeting irritably by my side.

I became anxious; had the guy gone? I didn't think he'd recognized me when I'd passed him the crate – I'd been beneath him in the dark. Had I made a mistake? There was a movement above. In the glow of the arc light an immobile face was bending down to heave up yet another load.

"That's him; the guy on top now. See, he's just moving away."

Fats nodded and immediately his two heavies climbed up the ladder and disappeared from my sight. A moment later they were coming back with a figure slumped between them. One of them was carrying the stranger's bag.

A few heads turned. Fats was anxious to avoid any suspicion of trouble: "Make way there. The guy's fainted: must have been overcome by the fumes."

I followed as they carried him down the gangplank, past the guards and the piles of ammunition on the wharf, to the union office. Fats pulled down the blinds then leant against the door, as his aides threw the stranger in a chair and roped him firmly to it. He was still unconscious; his head hung over his chest and blood was dripping from his ginger hair. Fats put his fleshy hand under his captive's chin and forced his face up into the light from the fly-blown shade: "You're sure this was the guy?"

I was completely sure. It was the face I'd seen that morning on the *Normandie*. I nodded.

"Good work kid. Get back to work. I've gotta phone some important people who'll want to talk to him." Fats led me to the door.

"I must phone that Commander guy. I promised to tell him if I saw this guy again."

"Don't worry kid – it'll all be taken care of. Don't mention this to anyone. Not even your uncle. Understand?"

There were many questions I wanted to ask, but Fats was already picking up a baseball bat as his pals locked the door in my face.

18 March, 1942
Ensign Frank Dunford:

So far my war had been a piece of cake, consisting of daily trips on the Subway to the fish market under the Brooklyn Bridge, classifying the information flowing into Section F at the Astor, and taking notes of Haffenden's mundane meetings. I'd every intention of keeping things that way. The past few days I'd been taking increasing notice of Mary Hampton's ankles, but it was the promise of what lurked between her thighs that had finally persuaded me to send Sue back to Ohio. Thankfully Sue had listened to my excuses in silence and had agreed to go without a fuss. She'd been so decent about it – I felt a bit of a heel. It was like being in a movie when we walked down the staircase into the great hall of Grand Central Station. Sue had tears in her eyes, like many of the women in the crowd below. Mothers, wives and sweethearts were bidding farewell to hundreds of young guys like me, leaving for destinations unknown. I squeezed Sue's hand and tried to sound affectionate.

"I'll write as soon as I sort things out. This is top-secret work I'm on now. I can't have any distractions."

I could tell she didn't believe me. She avoided my eyes and scanned the departure board for the platform of the Cleveland train, as tears trickled down her cheeks. I watched a young soldier gently kissing his bride goodbye. She was carrying the nosegay from their wedding that morning; confetti was still in her hair. I looked at the guy's loving face and wondered if I'd ever feel emotion like that. I guessed I'd always be selfish and greedy.

"I'll go see your folks if you like and tell them you're well."

I didn't reply. I wasn't sure how my mother would react if she knew Sue had been with me in New York.

"You will write, won't you?"

"Of course," I lied.

We walked down Platform 11 as black smoke from the engine drifted up to the glass roof high above. As she got into the train I noticed how pretty she was. Her neat behind looked good in her tight skirt and I remembered, very fondly, the firm white cheeks beneath it. Even her ankles didn't look so bad. She closed the door and leant out of the window, taking a golden crucifix from her pocket. "I don't know what a good Protestant gal like me is doing giving you one of these." She slipped the chain over my head. "Wear it for me, will you? I've had it engraved. I really love you, Franco. Do you know that?"

I kissed her but couldn't think of anything to say.

She was still crying as the train pulled slowly away.

I immediately called Mary Hampton from a phone box in the Great Hall and asked if she fancied a movie. She came from good English stock, and said there was a British film about the Royal Navy showing at a small cinema in the Village that she was desperate to see. Later, I sat holding her cold hand in the dark as I watched some prissy English guy, who spoke as if he'd a cucumber shoved up his ass, pretending to be captain of a destroyer. The crew all spoke with incomprehensible British accents, but I wasn't bored. I found myself admiring the heroism of these men and the pride they had in their ship and their loyalty to each other.

Somehow I felt ashamed.

Extract from private diary of Lt Commander Haffenden, U.S. Navy:

March 19, 1942. Luciano's edict appears to be working. So far there's been no more sabotage and a quicker and more efficient turn round of the convoys. Worked late at the Astor, entering coded information into my little black book. Supposed to channel all information through my direct superior McFall, but it takes too long. Besides McFall is a pain in the ass. Constantly complains I'm no team player. Says I'm a loose cannon who cuts across rules – that's what an Intelligence officer is supposed to be, goddamit! McFall resents the growth of my operation and questions every damn expense sheet I put in. But have to admit things haven't gone as well as I'd expected. Latest secret figures show that U-boats are inflicting heavier losses than ever. Up till today have received little useful information, but have just had a call from my new friends. Claim to have picked up someone who may be able to help. They are questioning him now and hope to have valuable information by morning. Certain we've made a breakthrough at last.

Danny Crivello:

I scanned *The Daily News* every morning, expecting to read of the capture of a saboteur. All I could discover was that a badly mutilated body had been dragged from the Hudson.

3

STRATEGY

From private diary of Lt Commander Haffenden U.S. Navy:

March 27, 1942. Frustrating month so far. Lanza's last consignment of shellfish gave me a bad case of the runs. Pity Anastasia's guys were too heavy on the saboteur. Pity the motherfucker had a weak heart. Had hell of a job getting it hushed up – especially when the police found traces of gunpowder beneath the sonofabitch's fingernails. But that was nothing to the shit McFall threw at me when German agents landed by submarine on Long Island – a coastguard found their rubber boat and oars. They'd apparently sailed unnoticed through all my fishing fleets. To make matters worse, despite all of Lanza's supposed contacts at filling-stations, the trucking industry and the railway system, the Krauts passed through the entire breadth of Third Naval District undetected. Even more humiliating is the fact they've been arrested in Chicago, by that bastard Hoover's FBI, complete with a large quantity of explosives and $170,000 in cash. That faggot McFall has been crushing in his scorn. Almost makes me wish I was back home in Flushing with Betty and the kids.

Ensign Frank Dunford:

I'd been bored to the seat of my pants all morning: making my usual rounds at the fish market, gathering the pitiful scraps of information that were offered. I was beginning to hate the entire experience – the cold, dead eyes of thousands of fish gazing up balefully from their boxes, the slime that stuck to my shoes, and most of all, the smell that hung upon my clothes for the rest of the day. I was fed up with people turning and sniffing me on the Subway. I returned to the office, hoping to spend an hour or two looking out of the window, hoping to catch sight of a girl in some state of undress in the apartment building opposite, but Mary purloined me into helping her get some order into Haffenden's ever-burgeoning files. The old buffer had a crazy system: the scale A-E was supposed to mark the reliability of the informant; 1–4 the supposed value of the information. On top of that he had devised a colour code: white for routine information; yellow dangerous; blue dangerous and urgent. Needless to say all the stuff I'd gathered that morning was white, 3F. Mary had the curse and was even more ratty than usual. I'd had more than enough of her. It took me weeks to get her into bed, and then I discovered she was frigid. She refused to do any of the things Sue had taught me.

The bitch even accused me of being a pervert.

From private diary of Lt. Commander Haffenden, U.S. Navy:

April 6, 1942. Received coded message: *Be at the western-most bench by the boating lake in Central Park at 10.00 hrs.*

Wear civilian clothes. Arrived five minutes early. Fine spring morning. Watched the ducks. Didn't recognise P.R.R.J at first. He's got old and was wearing a trilby hat and sunglasses. Put a receipt in his wallet to claim for his taxi. He's as tight as a racoon's ass-hole. Don't ever remember him buying me a drink. Offered me a Lifesaver before telling me there'd been a big turn round in Washington. The War Department has formed a new operations division under someone called Eisenhower. Things seem to be moving at last: Major General Strong is now in charge of the Intelligence Division. P.R.R.J. reckons he's a real live wire and he's been granted huge funds to establish a really professional intelligence network. We've years to make up: the Nazis, Soviets, even the bloody Limeys have had them in place for decades. The new policy is to urgently find men capable of operating anywhere in the world. P.R.R.J. informed me they are very impressed with what I've achieved here in New York. Said he didn't know anyone else who could've done such a good job. New York Waterfront now seems more or less secure. But he reckons we've a helluva long way to go to win this war. There are still a hundred U-boats in the Atlantic and we've lost over a million and a half tons of shipping in the past two months; nevertheless, he thinks we'll turn that around by the end of the year. We're developing long-range fighters and bombers and building hundreds of cheap escorts for the convoys. But sooner or later US forces will have to fight on land, and if they are to win, we must provide them with the best and most accurate information. We won't be ready to invade Europe until late next year at the earliest, but apparently there's some talk of a landing in North Africa, perhaps on the Atlantic coast to get up behind Rommel. The British don't seem to be able to beat him on their own – the plan is to crush him between us. Once we've secured North Africa and the southern half of the Mediterranean then where would we go next? Sardinia? Greece? Southern France? Nobody knows. P.R.R.J. believes we must be ready for any possibility. His personal hunch is Sicily. It is the nearest landfall to North Africa – the stepping-stone to Europe. It's been invaded more than practically anywhere else on earth. The Greeks, the Romans, Vandals, Goths, Normans and Saracens – you name them, they were there. Sicilians are practically a different race to the rest of Italy. They've their own language; most of them are supposed to hate Mussolini. But the top brass in Washington know hardly anything about the place; haven't even got a decent map for Chrissake! P.R.R.J. then threw his arm around my shoulder and told me he wanted me to use all my sources to find out information about the island: the layout of the ports, coastal defences, and the state of civilian morale. More importantly, he wants me to recruit some Sicilian-born Americans for Navy Special Service, just in case we end up going there. He's sure my friends will be able to find some reliable volunteers. Told him about my problems with McFall: that he would insist everything went through him. P.R.R.J told me not to worry. Said he'd cover my back. From now on I'll be reporting directly to the Operational Division. P.R.R.J.'s money is on us going to Sicily.

Life begins to feel good again.

Ensign Frank Dunford:
I was toying with the idea of asking for a transfer, trying to convince myself I had the guts to leave New York for the open seas, when Lt. Commander Haffenden threw open

the door, looking as mean as Charles Laughton's Captain Bligh on the *Bounty*. He ordered me to go at once to the Waterfront and find Daniel Crivello, the young Sicilian we'd met on the morning of the *Normandie* fire.

I'd waited by the dock gate for three hours before I found him, and was tired and very hungry when I ushered the kid into Haffenden's office.

❧❧❧❧

Danny Crivello:

Commander Haffenden stopped talking into the mouthpiece of an old dictating machine and looked up at me through the fug of his pipe: "Good, he's found you. How are you Mr Crivello?" He turned to my companion before I could reply. "What took you so long? You may as well stay, Dunford; you'll be involved in this." He motioned me to the chair on the other side of his desk: "May I get you some coffee, Mr Crivello?"

"A cup of coffee would be great."

"Dunford, go and tell Miss Hampton to make a pot, and then come back with it."

The young ensign was not looking very happy as he left the room. The Commander stared at me in silence. I was worried. I was sure he was about to question me about the guy they'd dragged out of the river.

Haffenden relit his pipe: "You told me you were Sicilian? Why are your eyes blue?"

"My pa always said it was the Norman blood in my veins. The Normans occupied Sicily for hundreds of years."

Haffenden nodded approvingly and sucked on his pipe. "May I ask what your feelings are about this war?"

"I know very little. Mussolini drove my uncle from Sicily. He says the Fascists must be defeated."

"Excuse the question but did your uncle belong to the Mafia?"

"No sir, he was a Communist."

"That's no problem now. The Russians are our allies."

There was a knock at the door and the ensign re-entered with a tray bearing coffee pot, sugar and cups. At Haffenden's nod he proceeded to pour.

"Do you know anything about the Mafia in Sicily?"

"Only what my uncle told me."

"And what is that?"

I found myself concentrating like a kid in school. "It's a word that comes from the Arabs and I think it means skill and protection. Some say it's a state of mind, a philosophy of life, a sort of moral code ..." I paused but the old guy nodded for me to continue. "In the old days the men of honour pro-tected the peasants from their foreign masters. The poor could never get justice unless the *Fratellanza* gave it them. My uncle says it only exists because the Sicilians have always hated authority."

The ensign handed the Commander a cup of coffee, spilling much of it into the saucer. Haffenden frowned with irritation but continued to look at me intently: "That's a pretty good definition. You seem a very intelligent young man. When are you going to enlist?"

"I've got a place at Notre Dame in the fall," I sipped the weak American coffee, so unlike the strong, smooth stuff Ma made. I'm going to major in engineering, I'll get defer-ment from the Draft."

"What would you say if I offered you a guaranteed com-mission in a new Navy Department? You could take up your place at Notre Dame after the war, and naturally there'll be generous educational grants for all ex-service personnel, especially officers."

I stared at the burly man with his noxious pipe and found it hard to believe it wasn't all a joke: "But you know nothing about me. What makes you think I could be an officer?"

The old guy stole a disdainful glance at the ensign who had now spilt coffee over his uniform: "It don't take much these days, I can assure you."

"But why me? You only saw me the once."

"I'm going to bind you to secrecy. I'm told Sicilians are good at that. I'm forming a special squad of Italian and Sicilian Americans in case we invade Europe. There are no plans as yet, but it's my job to ensure that we have a team in place should that eventuality occur. You'll be sent to a special outfit near Washington, where you'll undergo an intensive course of training in the latest intelligence procedures. You're bright and fit and seem ideal for such an operation."

I thought long and hard. "There's something you should know. When my father came here in the twenties he had no money and no job. He ended up with the Mob, working for Joe Masseria. He was gunned down in 1932."

"I know all about your pa." He sounded almost paternal. "He knew about explosives didn't he?"

"Yeah." I was stunned. The old guy seemed to know everything. "He learned all about them in the sulphur mines in the old country."

Haffenden leafed through the papers on his desk. "I see. He blew a few safes over here as well. He must have been a pretty useful recruit for the Mob." He looked up and stared me straight in the eye. "Did he teach you to make bombs?"

"I was the only kid on the block that made his own fireworks."

He laughed: "A straight answer. That's what I like. Don't worry, young man, I've run a full security check on you. We'll take anyone who'll help us win this war."

I was nonplussed. "What would the job entail?"

"Nothing arduous: interviewing Sicilians, grilling prisoners of war when we get them, gathering information – learning how to analyse it."

I still couldn't believe it. "My mother and uncle, I'd have to talk it over with them."

"Naturally, I'm a family man myself." He pointed to the framed photographs of his wife and children on the table behind him. "But in strictest secrecy of course. By the way, when did your uncle leave Sicily?"

"I'm not sure. Around 1930, I think."

"Tell him to come in to see me when he's got the time."

The ensign attempted to stifle a yawn but failed to escape the Commander's notice.

"Dunford, I almost forgot. That course I mentioned; when he goes you're going too. It's about time you began to earn your pay."

Ensign Frank Dunford:

I walked down Fifth Avenue in a state of shock, cursing the old fool. An intensive fucking training course! I thought I'd finished with that crap. I'd been certain I would remain in New York for the duration. The only consolation was that I'd get away from Mary; she'd hardly looked upset when I'd told her I was being posted. The bitch was useless – couldn't even make a decent pot of coffee. I noticed a phone box and decided to ring my parents in Millersburg, then remembered Sue in Cleveland. There was only one nickel in my pocket. I couldn't decide whom to call. I tossed the nickel. It came down heads: I rang my mother.

⚜⚜⚜

Danny Crivello:

My mother was dressed in her usual black. She'd worn black every day since Pa died. Her eyes filled with tears as I told of the Commander's offer.

"But Daniello, this is not your war. It's nothing to do with you. Don't throw away all I've tried to give you."

We sat with Uncle Tony, who'd been discharged from Mount Sinai, around the small table in the parlour of our apartment, which also served as my bedroom. It was a nothing but a cold-water apartment on West 16th Street, but meticulously clean, despite the soot that was constantly emitted from the stove. The simple furniture and ornaments shone from the endless polishing that Ma lavished upon them. It was only to be expected, she was a professional; she'd been a cleaner almost from the day she landed in New York.

"I can't tell you much about it, Momma, but it's not dangerous," I tried to reassure her. "It's a great opportunity; guys like me don't usually become officers. A commission will help me no end when I become an engineer."

"If you live to be an engineer. For ten years I've worked and fought for only one thing: that you would have a life your father and uncle never had. You swore on your father's soul you would never join Luciano and his murderers."

"Ma, I'm joining the US Navy not the Mob."

"I prayed every night God would give you an education and security. I hoped one day you would marry a good Italian girl and give me many grandchildren. You will ruin my life as well as your own." She put her head into her hands and began to sob.

I looked towards my uncle. "What do you think?"

Tony rubbed his chin. "I fought for Italy against the Austrians in 1917. I will never forget the faces of the young boys who died and the pain they endured. And for what? Things were worse when it was over, even though we were supposed to have won." He could never resist a political diatribe: "Then the industrialists and large landowners became terrified of Communism and allowed the rise of Mussolini and his thugs. The fools thought they could control them. They must regret that now. The same thing happened in Germany and they have even more terrible monsters there ..."

"But what should I do?"

"For once all the good guys seem to be on the same side." He lit the new pipe I'd bought him. "The Democrats here, the Communists in Russia, even that old guy Churchill don't seem so bad. If they can defeat the *Fascisti*, even though at the moment it looks far from easy, perhaps we will be able to make a better world. If you want that better world, you should go."

I could only think of adventure: Washington, the gold stars on my shoulder. The money I'd earn without having to hump crates. "What about Momma?"

"Is she not my sister? I will take care of her."

April 7, 1942
Top Secret.
Verbatim report of meeting between Lt. Commander C. Ratcliffe Haffenden and Mr Joseph Lanza. Transcribed by Yeoman Mary Hampton.

Not to be forwarded without ratification of Lt. Commander C. Ratcliffe Haffenden.

Mr Lanza entered the room at precisely 11.47 hours.

Lanza: Sorry about those clams, Commander. They sometimes have that effect on me.

Haffenden: It was a very uncomfortable couple of days.

Lanza: I've brought you some good Sicilian olive oil today, it's the best. You'll have no problems with that.

Haffenden: Thanks, Socks. My wife will appreciate it.

Lanza: My pleasure.

(Commander Haffenden ran red pencil through the above exchange)

Lanza: How are you doing?

Haffenden: Well, Socks, everything seems to be going according to plan. Your fishing fleets are now fully incorporated into the intelligence system and, thanks to Mr Meyer's visit to Great Meadow, the unions are fulfilling their obligations on the Waterfront. You were born in Sicily, weren't you Socks?

Lanza: That's right, Commander. Born in Palermo, don't remember much about it though. Came here as a kid.

Haffenden: Good. You see the map of Sicily on the wall behind me. I'm afraid it's rather out of date: charted long before Mussolini came to power. We have hardly any current maps. That's why I've called you in. We are going to have to improvise and resort to unconventional methods. I want you to put out the word. Get me any postcards, travel leaflets, books, charts, holiday snaps, and of course maps, that any of your associates have had sent or have brought back from Sicily, or any other parts of Italy in recent years. Find out information about the Italian Navy, the capabilities of the ports and docks, the locations of coastal gun emplacements. In fact bring me anything or anybody that could be useful."

Lanza: Does that mean that you're thinking of invading?

Haffenden: Nothing has been decided. But we need information for effective planning, so we make the correct decision.

Lanza: OK, Commander, leave it to me. There's one other thing Commander. That indictment is really wearing me down. That sonofabitch Hogan has even bugged my office at the fish market. I was thinking I would plead guilty and get it over with. You will mention the assistance I've given?

Haffenden: Don't worry, Socks. What are friends for?

(The Commander ran red pencil through last two exchanges)

Various entries from private diary of Commander Haffenden

9 April, 1942: Information trickling in. Lanza found two Italian sailors working on a pier in Brooklyn who purported to have an intimate knowledge of the Sicilian coastline. Covered my map of Sicily with an overlay of strong tracing paper and duly entered their extremely limited knowledge upon it.

10 April, 1942: Socks brought in Vincenzo Margano, an ex-confidence trickster, who imported Sicilian wine, cheese, olives and olive oil before the war, and claimed to have contacts with the Sicilian Mafia. Noted down the names and businesses he gave, together with complete list of all his relatives.

15 April, 1942: Socks produced a waiter from Palermo, who claimed his brother worked in the harbour. Offered no worthwhile information.

23 April, 1942: Socks is determined to create a good impression. Brings in a stack of old holiday snaps, postcards and newspapers. Some date back to 1900. What the hell am I going to do with them?

27 April, 1942: Large lady from Clancy Street barged into my office, demanding I bring back the Sicilian sonofa-bitch who left her daughter with three young kids and ran off to Palermo with a hat-check girl in 1940.

4 May, 1942: Meyer Lansky arrived unexpected at 8.15 a.m. inviting me to accompany him to Great Meadow Prison, where Lucky Luciano wished to make me an offer. Immediately dropped all plans for the day and went with Lansky on the train to Albany, then drove sixty miles to Comstock. Phoned ahead and on arrival we were shown directly into Warden Morhous's office. Luciano already there. First time I'd encountered the greaseball in the flesh. Face still badly scarred from the effects of that ride they took him on in 1929. Cheek muscles severed. Right eyelid droops. Dark wavy hair; well-groomed, but turning grey. Seems fit. His prison clothes appear to have been cut by a bespoke tailor. Forced myself to offer my hand and said I hoped the authorities were looking after him well. The bastard grinned and looked as cunning as a snake. Said things were better than they were and had the goddam gall to hope that his boys were running things OK for me. Guard brought in a tray of coffee and sandwiches I'd ordered – there'd been no diner on the train. Meyer put out his goddamn cigarette for the first time all morning, but after examining the contents of a sandwich complained it was ham. Called the guard an ass-hole and accused him of doing it on purpose. Luciano found it amusing. Said it wasn't kosher but the finest Parma ham. Claimed he gets a haunch of it sent in every month, would you believe? Have to admit it was an excellent sandwich. Waited for guard to go before asking Luciano why he wanted to see me. Said he'd heard about me wanting information on Sicily and concluded we were planning an invasion. Told him it was just routine: we wanted information from all over occupied Europe. He shook his head and said he'd been reading newspapers and studying maps – he's no dumb-ball. Said he knew how the boats were being loaded and where they're headed. Knows we're going to North Africa to help the British push out Rommel. After that Sicily is the only logical place to go. Ham very tasty after all that seafood. Put slices Meyer had discarded into my own sandwich. Told Luciano he was barking up the wrong tree. We could go to Sardinia, or the Balkans, or just sit tight and save ourselves for the big invasion into Northern France – the easy route into Hitler's backyard with no mountains in the way. Meyer hadn't eaten a thing but lit another cigarette. He said he didn't fucking care how we get there as long as it's soon. Claims to have information from Europe that the Nazis are beginning to send thousands of Jews east in sealed cattle trucks. Don't know where he got that crap from. Assured him we're moving as fast as we can. Damn civilians have no idea how long it takes to build planes, tanks, ships, and landing craft and, more importantly, train men. Pointed out the US Navy is fighting a two-ocean war with half our fleet out of action. Luciano didn't seem impressed; said if we take Sicily we'll knock Mussolini out of the war. The Italians despise the ass-hole. They're just waiting for the opportunity to blow the bastard away. I played cool and helped myself to another sandwich before asking him what it was he had to offer. He replied: "Get me out of here. Get me to Sicily and I'll make sure you'll have an easy ride when you get there." Even I was taken aback. Told him he couldn't be serious. It was impossible. The bastard then had the cheek to ask if we really wanted to win the war. Claimed if he was there he'd save thousands of lives. Proposed that we fix him up with fake papers and fly him to Portugal or Spain. Said he'd make his own way from there, or we could get him to Sicily by submarine, like those Nazi spies on Long Island. He had a malicious glint in his one good eye as he said that. Even offered to go by fucking parachute if we taught him to jump. Said he had contacts with all the Mafia Dons on the island. Said he would organise an entire network, like he did on the Waterfront. Said he would radio out locations of the strongest defences, the best places to come in. Said when our boys hit the beaches they'll have no idea what they are up against, unless someone is there showing them the way. Said he could raise a whole army behind Mussolini's ass. I began to see the possibilities, but told him he was talking crap. Meyer had been quiet for a while. The little bastard stubbed his cigarette in the last sandwich, which I was about to eat, and said that Luciano could do it. He was the best soldier he'd ever seen. I lit up my pipe and blew some smoke over Meyer for a change. Hid my excitement and made every effort to appear detached. Said I'd see what I could do, but it would be a hard sell. Luciano became angry. Said we'd had our pound of flesh. He'd been locked away for five fucking years and had paid his dues and expects consideration for all the help he'd given us. Told me to tell my boss, if we want his further co-operation we'd better listen to him. The guy certainly has nerve.

5 May, 1942: Arranged to meet P.R.R.J. under the arch in Washington Square. Arrived first again. Watched young soldiers and sailors on furlough, mingling with New Yorkers exercising their dogs. A small terrier came up and sniffed my carefully polished brogue. Thought it was about to pee on it. Kicked it away. Always been particular about my shoes. Then saw it was attached to a leash. Holding the leash was a familiar face. P.R.R.J. had borrowed the mutt from a nephew, to blend in more easily with the surroundings. We walked to an isolated bench. P.R.R.J. unleashed the pooch and took a chewed-up ball from his pocket. He threw it to the other side of the square; the little dog crapped just in front of me before chasing after it. We sat down. I came straight to the point. Told him of Luciano's proposition. P.R.R.J. whistled and said he'd got to be joking. If Luciano were to be released we'd never get it past the press. Anyway the DA's office would never allow it; they were seething already at the special treatment the bastard was getting. I said if we kept it top secret, the press and the DA would never know. Told him that Luciano thinks he's paid his dues and expects something in return. P.R.R.J then became testy. Pointed to two young GIs, sitting on the bench opposite, hoping two attractive girls would pass by. Said that those boys, and thousands like them, would soon be sent into the line of fire. Why should hoodlums be rewarded for what everyone else is doing? I said I thought Luciano could be very useful over there. He'd done a good job here. P.R.R.J. replied that Luciano has his contacts in New York – but he was a kid when he left Sicily. He knows no more about it now than the rest of us. I told him Luciano could stir up a hell of a lot of trouble – like Lenin did when the Kaiser turned him loose in Russia in the last war. If we dangled the prospect of an early release, I was certain we could control him to our advantage. Dog returned with ball after sniffing a poodle's ass. P.R.R.J. threw ball again before asking if anyone else knew of this. Told him only Lansky, but was sure he would keep schtum. I could see P.R.R.J. was taking the hook. He pondered before asking if I'd heard of the OSS – Office of Strategic Studies – the new organization that Bill Donovan is trying to establish. His mandate is to raise a special force, like the British Commandos, to conduct special operations not assigned to other agencies. Donovan's got Roosevelt behind him so he can do almost anything he wants. P.R.R.J said he'd pass Luciano's offer on to him. In the meantime, he instructed me to string Luciano along. Tell him we want firm information. We need to know which Italian units will fight and which will come over to us. We need to know the details of every goddamn beach, every hill, and every road in Sicily.

P.R.R.J. is pretty certain we'll end up going there.

⚜⚜⚜

During that summer of 1942, the US Navy won its first victory over the Japanese in the Battle of the Coral Sea, but on all other fronts Germany and the Axis forces held sway. The first Allied raid on mainland Europe by the Canadians was repulsed with heavy losses at Dieppe. In North Africa, Rommel advanced towards the Nile, hoping to link up with Hitler's legions on the Russian front, which were thrusting deeper into the Caucasus. If Rommel succeeded, a German victory would be almost certain.

Luciano took the bait and put out the word that all information pertaining to Sicily should be made available to Haffenden. Soon high quality intelligence began to flow into Room 196: details of the tides, the slope and texture of the sands. The state of the roads leading from the harbours and the height of the hills that dominated them; the dimensions and weight capabilities of wharfs and piers, and the names of the leading members of the Sicilian Mafia, many of who were languishing in the high security prison at Termini Imerese.

On July 24 Churchill and Roosevelt finally resolved to proceed with the planning of an invasion of North-West Africa with an Allied force of all arms, under the command of the yet untried General Eisenhower. On August 12 Churchill appointed a new general to reinvigorate the dispirited British forces in Egypt. His name was Montgomery.

4
EMBARKATION

August 12, 1942.
Ensign Danny Crivello:

I fingered the gold star and single stripe on the sleeve of my uniform, not quite believing it was there. But I'd the proof in my pocket: a report stating I was resourceful, intelligent and displayed great practical skills, particularly in the use of explosives and detonators. I'd learnt the intricacies of radio and codes, and how to kill with a knife, garrotte or my bare hands. I'd been duly commissioned and recommended for instant assignment.

I checked my watch: "We're on time. Not long to Grand Central."

Frank Dunford grunted and continued to stare morosely at the flat New Jersey landscape hurtling past the window. Although we'd spent several months together at a secluded naval base overlooking Chesapeake Bay, we'd hardly had a proper conversation. I think he resented the fact that I'd just walked into the Navy on an even footing with him: an Annapolis Academy graduate. We'd little in common apart from our Italian blood.

"Are both your parents Italian?"

"Only my mother." I thought he would clam up as usual but I must have hit the right spot. "She came with my grandfather from Turin in 1907. My grandmother died in childbirth and my grandfather wanted to make a fresh start. He drifted across to Ohio and ended up in a dump called Millersburg. The only job he could get was a cook in the town's only diner. He died in the influenza outbreak in 1919. My mother was just a girl, alone in the middle of America. The diner took her on as a waitress though she was under legal working age. I've often wondered how she survived."

"What about your pa?"

"He's Middle-America through and through. Very shy and reserved. My mother served him breakfast practically every day for five years before he asked her out."

"What does he do?"

"Runs the local hardware store. Millersburg's the pits – I couldn't wait to get out."

"How come you speak such good Italian?"

"My mother missed the old country so much; made sure I knew all about it, including the language. She always intended to take me back one day for the vacation of her life – but I suppose the war's put paid to that now."

"I wonder what Haffenden's got planned for us? Do you think we'll be posted abroad?"

He shook his head disdainfully: "Not me. I intend to stay in New York for the duration. Stay where the real action is. I purposefully did badly on that crap course. Those with the highest marks get sent on the toughest assignments. Besides, I don't see any point in acquiring skills I won't need." He proffered me a stick of gum. "You got a regular girl?"

I felt my cheeks flush. "No. Have you?"

"Had one back home. Wasn't sure if I wanted her, but during all those weeks without a woman in that asshole of a camp, she's got sexier by the day. I phoned her last night, wanted to ask her to come to New York, but her mother answered the phone: seemed quite pissed off when I told her my name. She told me Sue's volunteered for the Army Corps of Nurses and is in training at Fort Meade, Maryland. I'm going to ask that old fool of a Commander for some leave. I've got some due. I'm going to take myself off to Fort Meade for some serious rest and recreation."

The train had steamed into Grand Central and we walked down West 42nd Street towards Broadway and the Astor, our holdalls slung over our shoulders. I noticed our smart uniforms turned the heads of several pretty girls. It was a new sensation; girls had never noticed me before. We entered Times Square and I remembered the evenings my father had carried me on his shoulders, showing me the bright, magical lights; but now the neon signs had gone, revealing the shabby buildings and dirty windows behind. Sailors were lingering outside the Astor looking for girls, or just looking. It sure felt strange when they saluted as we passed. We found Haffenden in Room 196, in a fug of tobacco smoke, surrounded by sheaves of information, which were being pored over by three attractive secretaries. He looked up at us through his horn-rimmed spectacles and immediately waved the girls out. He made sure the heavy door was firmly closed before taking the pipe from his mouth.

"Welcome back to F Section, gentlemen, albeit you'll not be staying here long." He rearranged some papers on his desk, "I have received both your reports and Dunford, you sonofabitch, your performance was a disgrace to your uniform. In normal circumstances I would consider you not fit to serve as an officer in this Navy; but these are not normal circumstances. The Navy is forming a task force, destination unknown, and needs every godforsaken man it can get – even you, Dunford." He took off his glasses and studied Frank as if he were something unpleasant he'd scraped from his shoe. "You'll be leaving for Cape Cod on the afternoon train to attend a ship-shore liaison gunnery course. You'll also be practising beach landings from LCIs – Landing Craft Infantry, in case you're not familiar with the term. I hope you've a strong stomach; some poor devil died of seasickness in one of them last week. Go and get your travel voucher from Miss Reeves, and get your stink out of my office. Remember, every day hundreds of better men than you are dying bravely in the Pacific. Good luck."

Frank was about to protest but thought better of it. He saluted, turned on his heels and went out without saying a word.

Haffenden relaxed and smiled at me warmly. "Please sit down, Ensign." I slid onto the polished leather of a well-worn seat. Haffenden smiled again: "Young man, you've completely justified my faith in you. You passed with flying colours. The war is moving very fast and so are the Navy's requirements. You're also going on the task force, but you'll be attached to Vice Admiral Hewitt's staff, assigned for special intelligence duties." I was astounded by the ease which Haffenden could send my life spinning in directions I'd never imagined. I opened my mouth but the Commander silenced me with a wave of his hand. "What I'm going to tell you now is top secret. Any loose talk can cost thousands of lives, perhaps even the success of an entire invasion. Do you understand?"

All I could do was nod.

"Although the first destination of this force will be an invasion of North Africa, we can't rule out the possibility that an invasion of Sicily will follow. If, and when, that happens, you'll be required for those special duties." Haffenden refilled his pipe and lit it. "Could you kill a man?"

I found myself voicing the standard response, "If it was necessary to the success of the operation."

"It may well be." He stared at me intensely. "You've heard of Lucky Luciano?"

"Of course; who hasn't?" I paused: I wasn't certain how much Haffenden really knew. "He was an associate of my father's: helped him get into the Mob."

"Well, he's been helping us with the planning of this operation. In fact, there's a particular mission he wants to do himself, but, as yet, the authorities don't deem it fit to allow him to go." Haffenden fixed me through his horn rims: "Would you mind accompanying me tomorrow to Great Meadow Prison? I'd like you to meet him. Don't wear uniform and don't breathe a word of this to anyone."

My mother wept with relief and I suspect a little pride when she saw me standing on the threshold. Uncle Tony nodded with pleasure at her shoulder. The small apartment was filled with the aroma of my favourite dish: oven-baked tuna with tomatoes, capers and pale olives. On the table was a bottle of Ciclopi, Uncle Tony's favourite wine, from grapes grown on the volcanic soil around Mount Etna. It was the perfect welcome home.

Later, after we'd eaten and drunk most of the wine, out of the small glasses my mother polished until they shone like crystal, we sat around the table clasping each other's hands. Everything was good; at that moment, we were happy. I dreaded having to break the spell and was relieved when Uncle Tony did it for me.

"I went to see your boss at the Astor, he asked me many questions. It was lucky for him I could get no work before I left Sicily. I tried all the ports around the coast – Palermo, Messina, Catania, Syracuse, even smaller ones like Gela and Licata. He wanted to know a helluva a lot of things. I tried my best: I wish I could have remembered more." He shot a look at my mother before continuing: "They will be invading sooner or later – I am sure they will want you to go if they do."

My mother's face told me they'd discussed this many times: "You are a man now, Daniello. You have made your decision. I will say no more."

I was overcome with love for them both, for the first time since I'd been a kid, salt tears ran down my cheeks.

The Commander had outlined his plan on the train, and my heart was pounding as I looked out of the window in the Warden's office onto the grim exercising yard below. I turned as the door opened and a middle-aged guy dressed in well-cut prison clothes came in. He stopped abruptly, blinked his eyes in the sunlight streaming in from the window, as a look of astonishment spread across his face.

"Who the fucks are you?"

I stared back, uncertain what to say.

Haffenden, sitting behind the Warden's desk, broke the silence: "Lucky, I've brought along the son of an old acquaintance. May I introduce Ensign Daniello Crivello of the US Navy?"

"Jesus Christ! I thought I was seeing a ghost. I could've sworn Ciro Crivello was standing by that fucking window."

I held out my hand tentatively, but Luciano, after a moment's hesitation, threw open his arms and embraced me, kissing me on both cheeks. "Your father was a good man. I'm proud to meet his son." I stiffened and he felt it.

He seemed embarrassed and broke away. He looked around the room before demanding of Haffenden: "Where's Meyer?"

"This doesn't concern him. The fewer people that hear what we're going to discuss the better."

Luciano frowned. "Meyer's about the only guy I've ever trusted. This had better be something really big."

"It is. Have a cigarette. They're your own brand." The Commander threw Luciano a packet of Lucky Strike.

"I wish I had a dollar for every time I've heard that shitty gag. I prefer Camels." Luciano pulled a packet from his breast pocket, lit a cigarette and sat down opposite Haffenden at the Warden's desk.

The Commander relit his pipe: "We've found you a new attorney: Mr Moses Polakoff. Meyer says he's more kosher than what you've had in the past – been a member of the New York bar since 1912. He's putting a motion to the New York County Supreme Court to modify your sentence. There's no chance of release at present, but I'm sure that if you continue to co-operate we'll get you out by 1946. You'll have served ten years by then and Mr Polakoff is certain he'll be able to convince the authorities you've paid the price for the convictions against you."

"He'd be a dope if he couldn't. Nobody in the whole history of the United States ever got a sentence of fifty fucking years for running a whorehouse, for Chrissake!"

"Anyhow, he's going to stress your exemplary conduct in prison, your affirmative indications of a repentant spirit, and your invaluable contribution to the war effort."

"Like fuck he will. What if they decide to deport me back to Italy? How am I gonna explain that to Mussolini, if you stupid motherfuckers lose the war? I've told you a thousand times, if you want Sicily send me ahead on my own. I'll serve it up to you on a plate."

"That's another thing I want to discuss with you." Haffenden motioned me to join them at the desk. "If we go to Sicily, and it's by no means certain that we will, we're thinking of adopting some of your advice. I'm still trying to persuade my superiors to let you go in first. If it happens it will be in the strictest secrecy – no one will know – not even the guy in the next cell. And if you go, we will take every measure to ensure that you come back as soon as your job is done. If you disobey an order or try to escape, you can forget any hope of a parole. Ensign Crivello will go with you."

Luciano started at this. "Like fuck he will. If I do this I'll do it on my own. I ain't going to be keeping some kid's ass tidy. I'll have enough to do looking out for myself."

"I repeat, Ensign Crivello will go with you. He'll be closer than your shadow and will ensure that you come back, dead or alive. He knows the Sicilian dialect, and if anything happens to you, or the authorities decide they cannot allow you to go, he will be fully trained to perform the tasks in your place."

"Are you guys nuts? He's still a fucking kid. He has no name, no respect."

"He would if he went in your name."

"The Dons would only deal with a *consigliore*; he's not even a soldier."

"I'm an ensign in the US Navy." I spoke for the first time. "I'm as old as you were when they took you on that ride."

A glint appeared in Luciano's hooded eye. I suppose he wasn't used to being answered by a kid. He turned back to Haffenden. "Without me, how the fucks will he know where to go when he gets there?"

"He'll have studied maps, same as you would have done. He'll pass as a Sicilian, he'll find his way, make the contact. You've given us the names; all he'll need is something from you to convince them he's the real thing."

Luciano appraised me again. "Don't think I'm doing you any favours, kid. Have you any idea what Mussolini's police, or even worse, the Gestapo, will do to you if they catch you? It takes a special sort of man to take that much pain. Do you know what Maranzano's shitheels did to me in '29? When they took me on that famous fucking ride? Maranzano wanted me to come in with him. I told him to go fuck himself. So his goons hung me from a beam in a shed on Long Island and pummelled me with pistol butts and clubs for hours on end. They cut my face to pieces with a razor, but still I wouldn't give in. The bastards left me for dead on the beach. D'you think you could take that?"

"They won't catch me alive." My mouth was dry.

Luciano pondered for a moment then shrugged reluctantly: "OK, it's your funeral, kid. I hope it ain't a painful one. This is the plan. Go to the north-west of the island, to Palermo and the towns in the hills behind: Lercara, Prizzi, and Corleone. That's where our people were always strongest. That's where they've survived, despite everything Mussolini's thrown at them. But only one man has the respect: only one man can do for you there what I've done over here: Don Calo Vizzini. He's boss of a crappy little town, not more than a village, but he's the *Capo*. He hates Fascists more than I hate cops or those smart ass DAs that fixed me up in here. Just give him this." He took a yellow silk handkerchief from his pocket. It had a large C embroidered in blue in one corner. "He sent it me when I did him a favour a few years back. Had it specially embroidered in my honour. Tell him I gave it to you. That'll be enough." I took the handkerchief and examined the delicate needlework. I was about to put it into my inside pocket when Luciano snatched it back. "But you won't need it because I'll be coming with you." He turned back to Haffenden: "When you invade it's gotta be in the north: the bay of Castellamarre, just west of Palermo. Don't try the south or the east; Don Calo has no influence there. Whatever you do, keep away from Etna, if it's defended you'll never get round it."

"Thank you, Lucky. Your comments will be duly noted. I'll pass them on to my superiors and do what I can to persuade them. Nevertheless, in the interim I must insist on having that handkerchief in my own care. It is too valuable to risk being lost in prison. There are too many thieves about."

Luciano did not find this funny. "It's mine. Nobody takes it from me."

"I would hate to order the guards to confiscate it. It would be painful, and you would forfeit all your privileges."

"Do that and I've only to give the word and all the co-operation goes down the can. Your fucking war effort will be poleaxed."

"If you should be foolish enough to do that, Mr Luciano, you will be committing sabotage and treason, a capital offence, and I will make it my duty to ensure you go to the chair."

Luciano glowered at him before grudgingly tossing the handkerchief over. Haffenden folded it carefully into his briefcase. He made some notes with his pencil in a small black leather notebook before nodding me to leave, but something was gnawing at my gut.

"Can we have a few moments alone?"

Haffenden hesitated. "This is most irregular."

"Please. There's something I must ask about my father."

The Commander nodded reluctantly: "OK, but make it brief. I want to catch the 3.30 train." He went out, intending to leave the door slightly ajar, but caught Lucky's eye and closed it firmly.

Lucky was still smarting. "Without that uniform he'd be nothing but a pile of shit." He looked at me inquiringly: "All right, you can say what you like. The room's clean; it's not bugged."

"Who killed my father?"

Lucky was taken aback: "You know the rules, kid. All that stuff's dead and buried. When I took over the organization I ruled there would be no more revenge hits. The slates were all wiped clean."

"But I'm not part of your organization. I'm his son; I've a right to know."

Lucky shook his head: "Sorry kid, I can't break the faith. I gave my word."

"He was my father. I loved him. I can still remember the stories he told me about the old country and what it meant to be a man. Is it not a son's duty to avenge his father? In a few days I'll go to the war, I may never come back. This could be my one and only chance."

Lucky drew on his cigarette: "It was a bad time. Orders were given within families that had to be obeyed. It was a clean hit, quick; not like the shit they gave me. Believe me, there are some things it is better not to know."

"Wouldn't you expect your son to avenge you?"

His eyes softened before he stubbed his cigarette into the Coca-Cola emblem in the centre of the Warden's ashtray. "OK, I'll tell you, but I advise you with all my heart to let it go. Let it rest with your pa."

"Who was it?"

He sighed and stared at me with his dark, unblinking eyes. His voice was barely a whisper. "Tony Lorenzo."

I shook my head with horror and incredulity: "My Uncle Tony? That's a dirty lie. I'll never believe that in a thousand years."

"I warned you, kid, not to ask me. The truth's often the most painful thing."

"But why? He loved us and was never involved with the organization; he hated all it stood for. Why in God's name should he do such a terrible thing?"

"Because he's a no good Commie bastard. Your pa was my pal. When he was shot, I made it my personal business to take care of whoever had done it. I couldn't understand it; there were no contracts out for him. I thought at first it might be something else." His scarred face gave the hint of a smile. "For God's sake don't tell your mother, but your old man always had an eye for the broads. Some guys don't like it if you fuck their old lady. I put out the word, but there was nothin'." He reached into his breast pocket and put an unlit Camel into his mouth. "Then one day a waiter from Benito's, the restaurant where your pa was shot, called me; he'd been too terrified to speak to the cops. He told me he'd seen the killer for an instant before he ran out. All he gave me in way of description was that he was a stocky Italian type and he thought he'd seen him around. I offered him a hundred bucks to tell me if he saw the guy again. He called back, a week or so later, and said that he'd seen the same guy on Houston Street and had followed him to a tenement on Essex. I went there with him and we waited outside all night. Just before dawn, as the men were beginning to make their ways to the Waterfront, he came out. I couldn't believe my eyes: it was Tony Lorenzo. The waiter swore on his mother's life it was the same guy that shot your pa. I went to your old lady and told her. I asked what she wanted me to do. I couldn't believe it. She just stood there and screamed. She was like a crazy woman. I thought for a moment she was gonna die. She said she'd come to America to get away from guys like me. She said I'd corrupted your father, turned him away from God. She then went on her knees before me and pleaded for your uncle's life. She said she'd persuaded him to kill Ciro; it was a family matter – settled in blood in the way of the old country. I didn't know what to do. I thought for a moment there might be something funny going on between them. Know what I mean? I didn't know what your pa would have wanted. I put my marker on Tony Lorenzo but decided to let it rest. I'm sorry kid, I told you to let it be."

"We Sicilians are taught in the cradle or are born already knowing, that we must fight the common enemy even when our friends are wrong and our enemies are right. We must defend our dignity at all times and never allow the smallest wrong or insult to go unavenged." I recalled my father's words as I sat across the table watching my uncle eating his pasta. What greater wrong could anyone suffer than the murder of a father? Yet what if the murderer had become another father? Uncle Tony looked up and smiled at me. I looked away and saw the anxiety in my mother's eyes. I'd seen that same look throughout the years and understood it now for the first time. She carried the guilt of the greatest of sins, the fear of God's eternal punishment, and would carry it to her grave. Had she ever confessed to her priest? The same priest, Father Angelo, who'd always befriended me. And Uncle Tony, who until that day I'd loved with all my heart, how could I face life if I killed him? Until that morning my life had seemed simple, ordained. Now everything had fallen apart and turned to shit.

The meal finished and even with a block of ice by the electric fan, the night was hot and sultry, as only hot August nights could be in the tenements of New York. Tony lit his pipe and rose to sit in his chair by the radio. He turned it on and we listened to the news: another big naval battle was being fought in the Solomon Islands. There'd been heavy losses. Ma picked up her embroidery and busied herself, trying to eradicate thoughts of young men burning and drowning.

"I'm hot. I'm going to throw some cold water over my face."

I went into the kitchen not knowing what I should do; and there it was, my father's knife, lying at the bottom of the sink, as if it were a sign. Ma had been using it to gut the tuna. It was now gleaming, clean, and razor-sharp. Pa had brought it with him from the old country; when I was a little kid I'd always admired the handle with its pommel like a leopard's head. I looked at it tenderly, remembering the evenings I'd watched Pa using it to carve my boat: the little Sicilian fishing boat he'd painted in traditional bright colours which was still on my shelf. I fondled the knife, feeling the handle that had rested in my father's grip; looking at the dark stains of his sweat. I wrapped the knife in a cloth, put it in my pocket and went back into the parlour.

"I'm really thirsty, Uncle Tony. Whaddya say if we go and have a beer?"

Ma tutted: "Only away for a few weeks and already he's drinking beer."

"He's a man now. If he's old enough to fight for his country, he's old enough for a beer."

We descended the stairwell, past the reeking communal privies, and went out into 16th Street, passing the group of women sitting on their chairs at the top of the stoop. I nodded but they stared coldly in reply. They didn't like Ma. They thought she was above herself; she never came down to sit and gossip. I guess they didn't think much of me or Uncle Tony either. I ignored their frowns and stepped onto the sidewalk.

"Let's walk a while."

I led the way across 10th Avenue. It was dark and cavernous: the shining strings of streetlights and brazen electric signs were all turned down because of the war. My mind was still in turmoil as we meandered our way down to the Hudson along shadowy sidewalks. To our right the Empire State Building still towered above Manhattan, but it was no longer a light-drenched honeycomb. The moon above was brighter than I'd ever seen it, giving the bricks of the tenements a blue-red hue and throwing sheets of shining white satin across the river. We walked silently down past the gates of the piers, full of ships waiting for the morning's loading. Ships bound for perilous voyages to the ends of the earth, carrying vital supplies to fight the evil that was threatening to engulf all of mankind. We continued up river to where the streets gradually became more deserted and the warehouses formed dark pools of shadow. The hot damp air was causing a mist to form above the surface of the Hudson, transforming the dirty waters into a luminous skirt that seemed to encircle the entire isle of Manhattan. Now and again I brushed my hand against the hard knife in my pocket, checking it was still in place. I led the way on to a deserted pier thrusting out into the river. Across the water, we could just make out the giant statue of Liberty, silhouetted against the dark sky. Her torch shone feebly: the thirteen powerful 10,000 watt lamps had been reduced to a couple of very weak ones.

Tony took out his pipe. "That's what you will be fighting for, Daniello. Nowhere else on earth is there the liberty that we have here. Everyone has a chance to make his way to a better place. It was never like that in Sicily. For thousands of years we had Greeks, Romans, Normans, Turks and Spanish oppressing us, working us to death. Then the *Fratellanza* came, claiming at first to protect us, but they only kept us poor and made themselves rich. Now we have the *Fascisti* and the Germans. What we have here in America is worth dying for."

"Is it worth killing for?"

Tony turned to me. A look of terrible sorrow crossed his face.

"I killed only once. I think it was worth it."

There was now no going back: I'd been taught to use the knife, where to stab, the river was waiting, dark and deep: "Who did you kill?"

My uncle sighed deeply. "I intended to tell you one day, I did not expect it to be so soon, but it is best you know before you go to war." He wiped his mouth with his hand. "When I first came to New York, I found your mother, my sister, in utter despair. In the old country your father had always hated. *Cosa Nostra. La Piovra,* we called it then, the octopus. It spread its tentacles everywhere, and it choked everything to death. In the sulphur mines, the owners paid the *Fratellanza* to increase production; the miners paid the *Fratellanza* to get a job, even though they were worked to death. Your father tried to organize a strike against them, but it came to nothing: the miners were afraid. It was then your mother persuaded him to leave Sicily and begin a new life here. He worked day and night in the mines for months on end, to get the money for the ship. His eyes were still red and swollen from the sulphur on the day you were supposed to sail from Palermo. The ship's doctor would not let him aboard; he thought he had some sort of infectious disease." His voice softened to a whisper. "You were too young to remember, but it was terrible for your mother. Your father insisted she take you and he would follow as soon as he was better. She arrived here with you on Ellis Island not knowing a soul. The *Unione Siciliano* put you both in a hostel, and she could do nothing but wait for Ciro to come. I think something happened to Ciro in Sicily at that time. Your mother told me when at last he found her in New York he was a changed man. He did not look for work but went at once to Luciano. *La Piovra* had finally caught him. Within weeks, he was so tightly bound he could not free himself. Your mother begged him to stop during the years before I came, when you were a little boy. By the time I arrived, he was deep into narcotics – some nights he came home angry and violent and beat your mother. She thought the only chance for you to have a decent life was to cut the tentacle; I was her brother, mine was the only hand she had. For many months she begged me to kill him, and for many months I refused; but I watched you idolizing him, and I could see one day you would follow his path. The tentacle was reaching out for you; I had to free you and give you a chance."

"So you shot my father in the back?"

The knife was out now, shining in the half-light.

Tony turned and looked at me without fear. "I did, Daniello. I had loved him once too. I could not do it to his face. I bought a gun, and one night I followed him to his favourite restaurant. I was going to make one last effort to persuade him to give up the Mob. It was early in the evening, and the restaurant was empty. I waited outside and watched through the window until the waiter was in the kitchen. Then I went in and walked to his table. He looked up as he sipped his wine. His eyes were cold. I begged him to become again the man we had loved, to give up the rackets for the sake of you and your mother. He laughed and said he had only just begun. He was going into a new business with Luciano; they were going to run whorehouses. He would earn more money than I could ever dream of. He said it without shame. He then told me that he was going to leave your mother and take you with him. Your mother was making you soft. He wanted you to be a man. He had a girl he kept in an apartment off Seventh Avenue. He was going to take you there. I pleaded with him to think of your mother. He could not take her son to live with a whore. He became angry and said your mother was nothing to him. He had never loved her: he had only stayed with her because of you. He said all this to my face – and she was my sister. He then told me to get out; he said his pasta was getting cold. I went to the door – I felt the gun in my hand. I fired into his back."

My hand tightened on the handle of the knife. I braced my arm ready to stab. The sharp point was inches from Tony's heart.

"Don't kill me, Daniello. Don't suffer the guilt and remorse that will follow. I know too well the pain you will bear. I killed your father, although the real Ciro Crivello had died many years before. If you want to avenge him, give me the knife and I will cut my own throat, or throw myself in the river – whatever you wish. Promise me though, that you will look after your mother. She only wanted it done for you, and she was right. You have become a fine man."

I glanced down at the knife enclosed in my hand. It looked savage and alien. I knew at that moment I couldn't kill him. I threw the knife deep into the Hudson and walked away. Golden stars had come out and winked down at me, like watchful, uncomprehending eyes.

❋❋❋❋

Friday: August 14, 1942.
To Office of District Attorney Hogan.

Transcript of wiretap between Lt. Commander C. R. Haffenden and Mrs J. Lanza.

Haffenden: Hello?

Mrs Lanza: Is that the Commander?

Haffenden: To whom am I speaking?

Mrs Lanza: It's Mrs Lanza, Socks's wife. I've just come from the court. That bastard judge gave Socks seven and a half to fifteen years, for Chrissake.

Haffenden: He's thrown the book at him. That's a damn shame.

Mrs Lanza: You're telling me it is.

Haffenden: I spoke to the Judge myself. I told him what Socks had done for me but it seems to have made no difference.

Mrs Lanza: No, he couldn't have given him any more than he did. Socks told me he couldn't face a long sentence. He's such a good father; he'll never see his kids growing up."

Haffenden: I'll write to the Governor in Albany.

Mrs Lanza: You do that. Tell him Socks is a good man. He has a family; all that other stuff is way behind him now. He really thought you'd help him after all he's done for you. The poor sap even told me to tell you how very grateful he is for all you tried to do.

Haffenden: Well, if I'm here seven years from now, I hope I may be of more help to him then.

Mrs Lanza: I'll tell him not to bank on it.

❋❋❋❋

October 22, 1942.
Ensign Frank Dunford:

Throughout the late summer and early autumn, I'd been tossed and buffeted to hell and back, practising amphibious landings with the 45th Division off Cape Cod. I wanted to pour out my sorrows to Sue, but every time I rang her outfit, they said she was unavailable. At first I sulked and fretted. I cursed that old bastard Haffenden time and time again for taking my soft posting away from me, but after a while, to my surprise, I found I was gradually becoming interested in what I was doing. In the planning of the seaborne invasions, which the Allies would have to undertake to liberate half the globe, it had become obvious that before heavy artillery and tanks could be got ashore, infantry would have to rely solely on air support and naval guns. Naval officers would go in with the very first waves to direct fire by radio contact. It was a highly complicated process, involving bearings, calculation of speed of target, movement of ship, and the effect of wind and temperature. I'd always had a natural aptitude for math and realised I could do it. I rapidly learnt how to read bearings, operate ship-shore radio, dodge live machine gun bullets among the sand dunes, and call down supporting fire. This time I passed with creditable marks and was assigned for embarkation, destination unknown.

They gave me a week's leave, a travel pass, and told me to report back to the 45th's temporary depot in New York the following Sunday. I rang Sue all morning but there was no reply. There was nothing else to do but go home to Millersburg. As the bus made its way to Boston along Massachusetts Bay, past the tall grass of the sand dunes and the small colonial towns, I remembered my friend George Kelly at Annapolis, telling me of the happy summers he'd spent sailing along this coast, and the soft-crab dinners in Plymouth and Barnstable with the daughters of the rich and sophisticated in their elegant holiday homes. How I'd envied George's privileged life then, but George was dead having lost his battle with his terrible burns. Through the bus window the leaves were beginning to turn into the flaming colours of the New England fall. Beautiful, but all too soon they would be dead and blown away, forgotten. Like George? I'd written a letter of condolence to his mother and remembered she lived in Boston.

When the bus reached Boston, I found I'd a couple of hours to kill before my train. I hadn't had sex for months and I had a pocket full of rubbers. The Navy obviously expected me to use them, but there'd be little opportunity in Millersburg. I noticed a few tired-looking whores hanging round the bus station. I had walked past them several times, trying to decide which one to have, when a group of Marines barged past me and swept up the lot. Like the fox and the grapes in the old fable I convinced myself that I hadn't wanted any of them. I found a phone booth, took out my address book, and called George's home. As the phone rang I watched the swirl of uniforms pass and re-pass on the busy street outside. Like me, young men were going home, perhaps for the last time.

"Hello?" The voice was soft and educated.

"Mrs Kelly? You may remember me. Frank Dunford? George's roommate from Annapolis? I'm passing through and I wondered if you would like me to visit? I've got a couple of hours to spare between trains."

There was a pause before she replied: "Frank, how kind. That would be wonderful. Please come; I'll make us some tea. Where are you now?"

"Just outside the State House."

"That's great. Nothing could be simpler. Just keep walking down Beacon Street until you hit Dartmouth. It's three blocks once you pass the Common. Our house is a brownstone, number twenty-two, on the left hand side."

As I made my way along Dartmouth Street I remembered that George, like me, had been an only child, and that his father, a professor at the Massachusetts Institute of Technology, had died a few years before the war. Mrs Kelly had had a rough time.

I found twenty-two; a three-storey attached row house, with ornate ironwork and steps leading to white columns on each side of the door. The lace curtain moved in the bay window to the right, and I caught a glimpse of red hair. I rang the bell and it was instantly opened by a smartly dressed, attractive woman in her early forties. She stared at me incredulously, whilst nervously fingering the pearls around her neck. I thought she looked a bit like Greer Garson in *Mrs Miniver.*

I took off my Navy cap. "Mrs Kelly?"

"Forgive me, in that uniform and short hair you look so like George." Her blue eyes filled with tears. To my surprise she pulled me inside, closed the door and hugged me close to her for fully a minute. Her scent overwhelmed me. It was like nothing I'd ever smelt before: exotic and pure.

"I'm sorry." She released me and led the way into the sitting room where tea was waiting. The furniture was expensive and antique, in keeping with the house. Oil paintings of old sailing ships hung from the walls, shelves were full of leather-bound books, silver shone from the sideboard. I'd never been in such an elegant home.

"Do you take sugar and cream?"

She sat on the sofa opposite me pouring tea into a delicate china cup; I noticed what fine legs and ankles she had.

I could see her breasts were still firm beneath her white silk blouse. "It's lucky that I had baked some of George's favourite chocolate cake." She put a slice on a plate with a delicate silver server.

"Yes I remember, every month you sent him a cake in a tin. I used to look forward to it." I ate my cake and drank my tea searching my mind for something to say.

"You spent a lot of time with George whilst you were at the Academy?"

"Sure. We shared a room."

"You got to know him well?"

"We used to talk through half the night?"

"Was he happy? I've often thought it was all my fault. Richard, my husband, wanted him to go to Harvard, but I insisted on the Navy. I come from an old Navy family, you see. He'd be alive now if it wasn't for me." She dabbed her eyes with a small lace handkerchief.

I tried to say something appropriate. "George was so proud to be in the Navy. He told me it was the best time of his life."

She looked up. If anything, she seemed even sadder. "Wasn't he happy at home?"

"Oh, sure. He loved you so much…said you were the best mother in the world." I don't think he'd ever said it, but I sensed it was what she wanted me to say. It worked. She smiled sadly and reached out and took my hand and led me over to the grand piano by the window, which was draped in Stars and Stripes.

"This is the flag which covered his coffin. I've made a little shrine."

On the flag were framed photographs of George. His freckled face and red Irish hair grinned at me in Boy Scout uniform, Confirmation suit, Graduation gown and finally as Naval Ensign.

She contemplated them lovingly. "That was his life. George lived, had friends and died, but what trace will he leave behind once I've gone? Sometimes I hope that maybe there's some girl in Hawaii, some nurse perhaps, who might be carrying his child." She stared at me intensely: "Do you think it's possible? Did George ever talk to you about sex? Did he ever make love to a girl? I hope he did. I'd hate to think he'd died without ever experiencing love."

Again, I didn't know what to say. I looked at my watch. "I'll have to leave if I'm going to make my train."

"Will you write to me? I'd feel I'd be sharing the danger with you, as I would have done with George. You're the nearest thing I've got to him. It would mean so much."

I hardly ever wrote to my own mother, writing letters bored me, I could never think of anything to say; but I looked into her pale blue eyes, watery again with grief, and found myself promising that I would. I felt her knee pressing against my own. She began to sob and something moved me to kiss her tenderly and hug her again, even closer than before. To my amazement she returned my kiss passionately, and began to undo the brass buttons on my tunic. Before I realised what was happening, her arms were around my back and pulling the shirt from my pants. Her soft hands quickly ran up and down my flesh. I was even more astonished to find myself responding to her touch. I fumbled with the small pearl buttons on her blouse and then reached behind and unhooked her brassiere. Her firm breasts hung free, bright nipples erect. She reached down and undid my fly and held my hard, throbbing flesh as she fell backwards onto the Chesterfield taking me with her, easing me inside, as I kissed those red nipples and drank in her exquisite perfume.

When it was over we lay together silently. I think neither of us believed it had happened.

I left hurriedly and caught a cab to South Station.

Ensign Danny Crivello:

I'd left for further training the morning after I'd thrown my father's knife into the Hudson. I'd left without speaking to Ma. I could not. I didn't care then if I saw either her or Uncle Tony ever again. But when it came to my final leave before embarkation, I forced myself to go home. I still didn't know what to say, or if even if my mother knew I knew her terrible secret. She received me with a look of intense anguish and went immediately into her room. I knew then she knew everything. There was no sign of Uncle Tony. I could hear her crying as I packed my few belongings. I tried to summon up the will to comfort her, but still couldn't find the words. I was torn apart. I loved my mother but she had caused the death of the father I'd adored. I remembered evenings in this shabby little room, sitting on his knee, listening to his stories of the old country. I would always love him, no matter what he'd done; but there were still so many things I didn't understand. I decided to wipe them from my mind and concentrate on the fearsome tasks awaiting me. My life had no value to me now, and I was more than willing to give it in a worthy cause.

I couldn't bear being in the apartment, there was nobody else in the whole of New York for me to say goodbye to. I decided to report back to base early, leaving a note: '*Dear Ma, I love you, but I will always love Pa. Pray for me. I will pray for you.*' I descended the familiar old stairs, past the stinking lavatory, out on to the stoop. I stood still and breathed in the stale city air. In the shadows, on the other side of the road, a soldier was watching me. I stared back at him. It took me a moment to recognise Uncle Tony. He'd lost weight and his hair was trimmed and darkened. He slowly crossed over and looked up at me.

I broke the silence: "You're too old to enlist."

"There are no birth records in Sicily. Besides, the Army needs every man they can get. I will die taking a few Fascists with me. I have no wish to live."

"You must live. My mother needs you."

We continued to stare at each other. Vainly striving to rekindle what we had lost.

"You are going to Sicily?"

"I cannot tell you."

"I know you do not wish to see me again, but there is something I have remembered. That is why I have come. It may not be important, but it is something. One night, your father talked to me about his last days in Sicily – after you and my sister had left for America. The time he was alone. I think he said he went to Villalba. It's a little town to the east of Lercara Friddi. I do not know why he should have gone to Villalba. Perhaps it was there, that something or someone changed him."

GREAT MEADOW PRISON.
October 28, 1942.
TOP SECRET.

At 6.20 pm Prisoner 4322: Charles Luciano became violently ill in his cell. The prison doctor was not available. His replacement's prognosis was acute peritonitis. Urgent operation necessary but beyond the capabilities of the prison infirmary. Accordingly the prisoner was

heavily sedated and taken for surgery by armed guards
in an unmarked ambulance.

Warden Vernon A. Morhous.

**From private diary of Lt-Commander Haffenden. U.S.
Navy.**

October 29, 1942:

Arrived early morning at US Atlantic Fleet Base in Norfolk,
Virginia. Piers and wharfs full of frantic activity and noise.
Bands played *Yankee Doodle* and *The Yanks Are Coming.*
Watched line after line of young soldiers, fully equipped
with heavy packs, entrenching tools, bayonets, cartridge
belts, and brand new semi-automatic M-1 rifles, embark-
ing into troop ships. For the second time in history, an
American Army was heading east. Carefully scrutinised the
flood of men marching up the gangplank to board Admiral
Hewitt's flagship, USS *Augusta.* Eventually spotted a soldier
with his greatcoat collar pulled up around his ears. Helmet
too large for him. Came down almost to his eyes. Walked
with his head slumped forward as if he'd drunk too much
the previous night, and was firmly held by the two men
either side of him. One of the men turned and caught my
eye. Ensign Crivello's features betrayed nothing. He'd been
well trained. I envied him – he was going where the action
would be. I've had my fill of espionage. Hogan's office is
proving to be a pain in the ass and things haven't turned
out quite as I'd wished. Maybe over fifty, but I'm damn sure
I've still got plenty to offer. There'll be invasions all across
the Pacific. Island after island has got to be wrenched back
from the Japs. Every beachhead will need a Beachmaster –
an experienced man who won't lose his head. As soon as

this mission is accomplished, going to apply for combat duty with the Amphibious Forces.

USS *Augusta*.
Ship's Log: October 29, 1942.
Captain's Orders: The occupant of the brig has been placed in the strictest solitary confinement. Only Ensign Daniel Crivello USN is allowed access to him.

USS *Brooklyn*.
Ensign Frank Dunford:
I watched from the quarterdeck, as the Boatswain's Mate blew two whistles and the crew manned the rails on the portside to render honours to the cheering crowds. I'd left my parents in Millersburg the previous morning. They'd both aged since I'd seen them last. For two boring days I'd tried to be a good son; tried to reassure them, sought to say appropriate things. My father had hoarded some of his precious gas, and we'd all driven to the station in the old Ford. Past the white clapperboard buildings of Main Street, the Baptist church with its wooden spire, the schoolhouse, the drug store, and the cinema – my boyhood palace of dreams and adventure. Bob Hope and Bing Crosby were starring in *The Road to Zanzibar*. Which road would my destiny take me? Would my journey be as brief as George's? I found it hard to think of George without thinking of what I'd done to his mother. Had it really been so bad? It could be the last time I'd ever make love.

My parents had been waving yesterday as the train pulled away, the bright sun shining on the white head of my father, towering over the diminutive figure of my mother, despite her wearing a new high hat in her favourite blue. The last thing I'd seen was her white handkerchief fluttering in the wind. Thousands of handkerchiefs were waving as we made our way along the shores of the James River; like flocks of white birds about to fly. Thousands of eyes were weeping; thousands of hearts were praying that God would protect their son; were certain that God knew their son was special.

I was glad I wasn't God – I didn't want to decide.

I turned my head and looked fearfully towards the Atlantic.

5

BEHIND THE LINES

23.00 hrs. July 4, 1943.

HMS *Unbeatable.*

Lt. Danny Crivello:

It was a cloudy night and the moon was hidden, as our small submarine surfaced in the dark waters off Capo delle Correnti, the south-eastern toe of Sicily. Her watertight hatch wound open and I followed Lieutenant Frazer up the iron ladder on to the deck, still awash with the sea. I could smell Luciano's quick breath behind me, laced with the fumes of 140-proof Royal Navy rum we'd been offered below. I'd declined my tot but Luciano had noisily swallowed both. I could make out in the dark the white-sweatered submariners putting two small collapsible canvas canoes into the water. Other sailors began to strap a heavy waterproof pack, containing a radio and explosives onto my back, a small fortune in Mussolini's lire and other necessities were in a pouch around my waist. Luciano with nothing but a life jacket tied firmly about him, kept to the shadow of the conning tower. We were both unshaven and dressed in the clothes of Sicilian peasants.

Frazer pulled a woollen hat over his auburn hair and zipped up his black wet suit before making a final check.

He'd had done this many times in the past months. Working at night, he'd swum ashore whilst his companion waited in the fragile canoe. Frazer had observed shore batteries, beach defences, minefields, searchlight locations and port facilities, throughout the 105 miles of Sicilian coastline the Allied chiefs had chosen for their invasion, code-named Husky. The Royal Navy had gathered invaluable information, but at a price. Of the thirty men trained for these missions, eleven had been lost. Last week, off the port of Syracuse, an Italian searchlight had picked out Frazer's companion, Leading Submariner Bates, as he waited for Frazer's return. The big naval guns on the Castello Maniace had blown Bates to pieces. Tonight, a fresh rating was waiting stoically in the second canoe.

Frazer turned back to me: "Ready?"

I nodded. I checked to see Luciano understood, but he was already moving unsteadily towards his canoe. So it was happening at last, the fruition of long months of training with the newly established OSS, in Algiers, and in the barren dust bowl of Oudjiida in Morocco, which General Ridgway had thought best resembled the Sicilian interior. I had wiped all other thoughts from my mind, whilst, to my other skills, I'd added parachute jumps, glider landings, battle training with live ammunition, and more exhaustive physical endurance exercises in the desert heat. I was as fit and ready as I'd ever be; I was worth the extra hundred bucks a month the Navy was paying me. I wasn't so sure of Luciano's fitness: he was forty-five and had spent many weeks in the sweltering prison the OSS had requisitioned in Algiers.

The first part of the mission was simple: to land at the headland east of Correnti, bury the radio and explosives and make for the town of Ispica about twelve miles inland. Luciano, having been convinced he'd be released as soon as the circumstances were right if he gave his full co-operation, had provided an ancient code, which he claimed was known only to the Dons of Castellammare. Throughout the past month the BBC's broadcasts to occupied Europe, beamed from their new stations in Tunisia, included a message in this cryptic code, stating that a friend wished to return a handkerchief belonging to Don Calo Vizzini of Villalba. The friend would seek him in Ispica, in the back pews of the north side of the Basilica di Santa Maria Maggiore, every afternoon in June between noon and one. If the code was genuine and contact was made, I had to gather vital intelligence as quickly as possible. Although the Allies now knew much about the coastal defences, they were still largely ignorant of the troop dispositions and fortifications inland. It was hard to believe, but the map Admiral Hewitt used dated from 1873. Prisoners taken in North Africa had given some indication as to the state of Italian morale, but how would they react defending their homeland? What support could the Allies expect? How many German Divisions were on the island? What strength were they and where were they stationed? I had to obtain this information and radio it immediately to Admiral Hewitt's headquarters, before Husky was unleashed.

My heart was pounding between waves of courage and trembling, as we paddled silently towards the shore. A merciless enemy occupied the vast landmass of Europe, from the English Channel to Moscow. The only Allied foothold was tiny Gibraltar, surrounded by Fascist Spain. My sole companion was a public enemy, for whom, after months of close contact, I now felt a keen animosity, and whose loyalty and good faith were highly dubious. The dislike was mutual. The strict discipline I'd enforced had evaporated any affection Luciano might have felt for Ciro Crivello's son. I was as isolated as if I were landing on the moon.

To the left, on the small Isola delle Correnti, a searchlight stabbed intermittently into the comforting darkness. I made my mouth wet and checked with my tongue that the cyanide pill was securely in place in the specially made gap between my back teeth. My orders were to bite into it if captured. The Nazis had drugs that could make you talk even if you could withstand their torture. Even my limited knowledge was too valuable to give away. It could be the deciding factor that brought an extra Panzer Division to the invasion area. Luciano hadn't been given the choice of a pill: if we looked like being captured, my orders were to shoot him immediately.

Frazer paddled silently but powerfully, occasionally checking our course with the compass he wore on his wrist, and ensuring the other canoe was keeping up. They were a strange breed these British sailors: awkward, stiff, shy men; hidebound with tradition, seemingly frail, but with a core of steel. In the few days I'd spent with them I'd learned to respect them and marvel at their endurance. The shoreline was already appearing through the gloom. A stretch of sand with dunes behind: a perfect landing place. Frazer turned and nodded, lifting his paddle from the water to hold the frail craft steady. My heart beat faster as I leant forward and tapped Frazer's back, it could be my last ever contact with a friend. Then, following the procedure I'd practised many times, I leant backwards and slid headfirst into the warm sea. The pack was heavy and for a moment pressed me down below the surface, but my back was strong and in a trice I'd lifted my head above the gentle swell. Luciano was still in his boat. I waved him in but he shook his head, seemingly frozen with fear. I swam over and again beckoned him to join me in the water.

"I told ya. When I was a kid, there was nowhere to swim on the Lower East Side. I never learnt how."

"Come on. Lean backwards as we practised. The life jacket will keep you afloat. I'll pull you ashore until we hit the beach." Luciano looked at the sea then shook his head again. "Get in the water. That's an order. I'll have you sent back in irons."

Luciano glowered angrily, took a deep breath and threw himself backwards. I caught his head almost as it hit the water and pushed him upright, but he splashed his arms frantically.

"Relax. Take it easy. I'll tow you in." I reached for the straps, securely tied around his chest and began to strike out for the shore. I turned once to catch a final glimpse of Frazer and his companion, silhouetted against the night sky above Luciano's dark bobbing head. They were watching until their charges were safely ashore.

After a few minutes, I felt firm sand under my feet. I nodded to Luciano and we began to wade and then run. The water splashed up noisily around us, with every fresh step I expected to hit a trip wire or mine, but we were quickly onto wet sand and rushing across the exposed beach. We were halfway across when the moon broke from behind a bank of clouds. Its beams were feeble but I felt as vulnerable as if we were caught in the most powerful searchlight. I ran even faster towards the safety of the dunes. My lungs were bursting as I flung myself onto the soft sand. I recovered my breath, and looked up to see Luciano lying face down beside me, his teeth chattering with cold or fright or both.

I tried to forget my own fear. "Get up. Bury the life jacket."

"The sea always scared the shit out me. It was a piece of cake practising in the pool."

"Why didn't you say you had a phobia? You could have ruined the whole operation."

"No way. The dumb assholes would have stopped me going." He began to dig a hole with his hands in the sand. "What a fucking way to celebrate the Fourth of July."

I tried to get my bearings from the few stars I recognised. "There's a little fishing village called Portopalo just a mile or so to the north. From there the only road leads north-east to Pachino, and Ispica is a few miles beyond." I put on my cap and brushed the sand from my wet clothes. "We've got several hours of darkness to hide the equipment. We should be able to reach Ispica by midday."

Luciano pulled on his cap and tied the yellow handkerchief, which I had returned to him the night before, around his neck. He watched mutely, as I took the Beretta automatic pistol from its waterproof case and strapped it firmly to my leg, just above my boot.

"I hope you can use it, kid. The stupid pricks should've given me a gun."

I ignored him. "OK. Let's go."

We crept northeast through the dunes, which gradually gave way to scrubby vegetation, then broad-leaved shrubs, bushes and small trees. The scent of mint, laurel, and myrtle reminded me of the herbs Ma used at home. I'd tried to wipe all thoughts of home from my mind, but the scent of the herbs brought it all back. A sharp pain in my hand brought me back to reality. Cacti were everywhere, springing out of the earth like jagged-edged machetes. We passed through them warily until we came to a road, little more than a rough track, white under the moon. I turned to Luciano, who was looking around incredulously, like an escaped animal unable to comprehend his new-found liberty.

"We'll follow the road north. Keep in the shadows. We've got to bury the radio and the explosives. If we're caught with them in Ispica we'll be dead. Look out for some landmark, some place we'll be able to identify again easily."

Luciano grunted.

Isolated buildings began to loom out of the darkness, sheds, fishing nets hanging from poles like shrouds. I could hear the sea to my left: we had reached Portopalo. Small painted boats were bobbing empty in the little harbour. I pulled Luciano down behind a low wall and scanned the boats fastidiously, looking for any sign of life.

"My pa carved me a boat like that when I was a kid. I've still got it on my shelf at home."

Luciano's bravado had returned. "I wouldn't bet on it. That old lady of yours probably has it in the garbage by now."

I cursed myself for lowering my guard. "Shut your mouth! Never mention my mother again."

"Don't push me too hard, kid. Show me some respect. That officer crap means fuck all here ..." He was cut short by the drone of an aircraft approaching from the west.

I looked up to see a seaplane silhouetted against the moon, with a superstructure so elaborate that it hardly seemed possible that it could fly. I identified it as an Italian Z501. An airman was perilously climbing the exterior ladder from the main body to the gun turret above.

Luciano was gawping upwards in amazement. "Only Italians could design a plane like that. Looks like a fuckin' Christmas tree."

"Keep in the shadow of the wall. Look down. Hide the white of your face."

We crouched in the dirt as the drone of the engine passed slowly overhead. It took an eternity. It didn't make sense, but I was certain they'd spotted us and the guy was about to fire. At last, the noise began to fade. We raised our faces and watched the plane's odd shape disappearing into the twinge of dawn coming out of the sea.

"Come on. We've got to stow the stuff soon."

We made our way carefully through a maze of thickly hung tuna nets. Not even a dog noticed as we crept through Portopalo and took the road to the northeast. The heavy radio was chafing my back by the time we came to a high stone wall a mile or so outside the town. I hugged its shadow and led the way to an ornate iron gate. I peered through and in the faint grey light, saw what appeared to be a miniature city made up of intricate marble monuments and square stone sepulchres.

"Wait here. If any one comes, whistle."

"Whistle? What the fucks the use of that? The dumb bastards should've given me a gun."

I climbed the gate, finding footholds on the filigree cherubs and flowers, and jumped down into silent darkness. Tombs towered above me; grandiose tombs worthy of great and famous men, not the local landowners or petty bourgeoisie I guessed they probably contained. I made my way cautiously along an overgrown path. Some tomb doors were hanging half ajar, as if the occupant had risen from the dead. I was creeping past one when suddenly something soft flew out of the blackness and brushed against my face. A scream was halfway up my throat before I realized it was a bat. I scurried to the far north-eastern corner, where the path was most overgrown, and sought out the most neglected grave. I found it by the side of an ancient olive tree, gnarled and distorted, with branches that reached out threateningly as if to push me away. The stonework was chipped and overgrown with creeper. I brushed it off and struck one of the Italian matches I'd been provided with. A faded photograph of a pretty girl smiled at me: *Orsoline Pancrati: 1901–1918*. Why had she died so young? The lock of the gate to her tomb was rusty and fragile; I picked it easily with my knife. A coffin lay on a shelf a few feet from the ground. She'd been short, her coffin was small. I lifted the lid, struck another match and stifled another scream, as a lizard scurried quickly out through the thick cobwebs and disappeared into the gloom. My heart was pounding as I peered inside. A small form was wrapped in a shroud. I slipped off my pack and took out the radio in its waterproof container, together with my explosives and detonators, and put them into the void at the girl's feet. I then gently pulled back the cobwebs, forced the lock back into place, and arranged the creeper to its previous state. I murmured a prayer for this long forgotten girl and asked her forgiveness for my intrusion. I retraced my way along the path, sweeping out my footprints with a sprig of broom, before climbing back over the gate to rejoin my sullen companion.

Dawn had fully risen. There was a grey, mysterious look over the whole countryside. Bald, barren mountains rose in the sky all around us, their peaks tinged with pink. The sun was already shining bright as gold when we saw the white crenellated towers of Pachino, surrounded by vineyards and fields of small red tomatoes. Luciano stopped and stuffed a handful into his mouth. "*Pachini!* I'd forgotten how sweet they taste. That's how the town got its name – Pachino – named after fuckin' tomatoes…Jesus! Look at that!"

On the white cliff above, nestling among the small trees and bushes, was the beehive-like dome of a concrete pillbox. The sun glinted on the metal barrel of a machine gun covering the road. The enemy was probably watching us this very moment. I tried to still my beating heart.

"So what? To them, we're just a couple of Sicilians looking for work. Act natural. Come on." I pulled off a bunch of tomatoes and continued along the road towards a wayside shrine, surmounted by an eroded statue. I had no idea what saint it was, but I made sure I muttered a few 'Hail Marys' as we passed by.

The sun grew hotter. Workers were making their way from the sanctuary of the bleached hilltop towns to labour, as their fathers and grandfathers, in the fields of the great feudal estates all around. The men passed with barely a nod. They were morose and withdrawn, as if their minds and bodies had been entirely subjected to their life of unending toil. A dead dog lay in the road. Flies were drinking the dusty blood seeping from its mouth. The land became harsher: clumps of olive trees in fields of arid earth, littered with white stones and boulders. Sunshine, reflecting off the rocks, made them look like dried bones. Stone walls, easy for infantry to defend, enclosed each and every field. To the right, the hills stretched as far as I could see, and blending in with the honey-coloured earth, were more pillboxes, observation towers, blockhouses and strong points. A frontal assault would be lethal; the hillsides would be strewn with the bodies of young G.I.s. My mouth was dry. I reached up and picked a lemon from a tree, bit on it and sucked out the juice. It was as bitter as the land from whence it had sprung.

It was almost noon, when we saw Ispica sitting securely on top of its hill. I quickened the pace as the road wound and climbed through olive groves and well-ordered lines of almond trees. We passed another shrine, where I mumbled a couple more 'Hail Marys'. I'd been perfecting my Sicilian accent for months, interrogating prisoners of war. My instructors had told me I was perfect, but I knew a mere word or inflection could give me away. I caught Luciano's eye.

"Remember, act dumb. Let me do the talking."

We entered Ispica. It was bigger than I'd imagined. The streets were surprisingly broad and laid out in a grid like New York, with smaller streets leading off, but the ornate, sun-bleached buildings gave off an air of abandonment and decay. Some had been palaces of noblemen. Impressive stone coats of arms remained over the doors. As we approached the centre the town, the streets became full of soldiers, sitting on benches in the shade with their tunics undone. Some were wearing the distinctive black leather helmets of tank crews. The blue insignia on their shoulders told me they were from the Livorno Division, one of the crack units in the Italian Army, but there was a sullen air about them. A bell tolled noon. I looked up to see the tower of the basilica over the rooftops to our right. I nodded to Luciano and led the way into the piazza, which was crammed with military vehicles. Their markings were also of the Livorno. Most of them were old and ill-maintained. The black-painted tanks were small, their armour looked pitifully thin. I made a mental note of a dozen ten-ton Renaults, five three-ton baby tanks, and several ancient Fiats that somehow had survived the Great War. If this was the best they could offer, I felt less afraid. I was so engrossed; I didn't see the sergeant bending over the engine of his tank until I'd bumped into his ass.

"Look where you're going, idiot."

I struggled to find my voice. "I'm sorry; I was looking at your tanks."

The sergeant looked at Luciano, who was attempting a vacant grin. "Why aren't you two in the army?"

I searched for the papers in my inside pocket. "We've got exemption. My cousin and I work in the port at Catania.

We've been unloading ammunition every day for the past month."

The sergeant held the papers in his oily hand and gave us both a cursory glance. "What are you doing here?"

"We've got two days off. Our grandmother lives near here. She is very ill."

"Your cousin doesn't say much."

"He's not very bright but he's very strong."

Luciano smiled and nodded in agreement.

The sergeant handed back the papers. "Get back to Catania quickly. We'll soon need all the ammunition you've got."

I attempted the Fascist Salute, but the sergeant didn't respond and had already returned to his engine. We crossed the piazza, turned a corner, and went through an impressive gateway into the enclosed courtyard before the Basilica di Santa Maria Maggiore. Saints and angels gazed down serenely from every niche, as if to give us their blessing.

Luciano whistled in appreciation. "Jeez, those Sinatras, sure get around."

"What the hell are you talking about?"

He pointed to a plaque on the wall. "It says this heap was built by Vincenzo Sinatra. My pal, Willie Moretti, discovered Frankie singing in a two-bit joint in New Jersey. Thought the little runt had a voice like the smoothest olive oil. Willie sent me all his records when I was in Great Meadow." He went to climb the steps into the church, but I pulled him back.

"Wait here. Remember, nobody must know who you are. Only identify yourself to Don Calo. If anything happens to me, find him."

Luciano was about to protest before he nodded and sat morosely on the bottom step. I passed through huge wooden doors into the welcome chill of the interior. The ceiling and walls and side chapels were painted in the most brilliant colours, contrasting with the black dresses and veils of the women who were dotted among the benches like hooded crows, praying for the souls of the dead or the lives of the living. I looked around, trying to look unconcerned. It took me a moment to register a solitary, broad-shouldered man, sitting in the shadow of a pillar with his head bowed as if prayer. I checked no one was watching before easing into the row behind him. I licked my lips and whispered the agreed message: "I have come to return a handkerchief to a friend."

There was silence. I could hear an old woman chanting on her rosary. Fear rose from my stomach and left its sour taste in my mouth. Was it a trap? Had the Nazis deciphered the message? Had we been betrayed?

The head nodded at last. A husky voice whispered: "I am going out. Wait five minutes, go to the gateway. If it is safe, you will see me by the statue of Garibaldi. I will lead you to where we can talk."

Twenty minutes later, I was sitting with Luciano at a wooden table in a plainly furnished room in a dilapidated house on the outskirts of the town. The stranger hadn't uttered a word since the basilica. He was quite short and squat but extremely powerful, with dark curly hair and thick moustache. I guessed he was in his late twenties. He said nothing as he poured three glasses of red wine. Luciano grabbed one greedily and swallowed it in a single gulp. The stranger held his own glass up to me by way of a toast and looked deeply into my eyes. His own eyes were of the darkest brown. They reflected no emotion. He drained his glass before speaking.

"My name is Giuseppe Falco – some call me *Jencu* – Little Bull."

"Doesn't look like a fuckin' redskin."

Luckily the Sicilian didn't appear to understand Luciano's English. "I know what you want, but you have come in vain. My uncle, Don Calo, has been in hiding, waiting for you to come. When he heard of your message, he summoned other capos to a meeting in Palermo. But the *Fascisti* have spies everywhere. A traitor – we don't know who – betrayed him. Don Calo is in the top security prison at Termini Imerese. Without him, we are powerless."

"I've names of other capos. Take us to them." Luciano spoke in Italian.

The Sicilian eyed us both warily. "Many were arrested with him. The rest will not move without Don Calo."

I sipped the rough wine and tried to think. "Termini Imerese is on the other side of the island? On the north coast, near Palermo?"

The Sicilian nodded.

"Our orders are to stay here in south."

"You will do nothing without him. He is the *Capo dei Capi*."

"Can you get us there?"

"It would be difficult. To go by truck or car would arouse suspicion. Further north, the Germans and the Gestapo are everywhere." The Sicilian wiped his moustache with the back of his hand and spat on the floor: "What could you do if I got you there?"

"I could get him out. I have explosives. You show me where he is, and I will break in."

It was late afternoon, when the three of us rode down the hill from Ispica back towards Pachino on three ancient bicycles. Cycling was another activity Luciano had neglected in his misspent youth. It took him quite a few kilometres and several falls before he mastered a basic proficiency. Dusk was falling as we reached the *cimitero*. The others loitered outside whilst I re-climbed the gate and disturbed the girl for a final time. She'd guarded my treasures well. I made sure that the lock of her tomb was secure before joining my companions outside.

I handed the radio to Falco. "You'd better carry it. It's fragile. I don't trust my friend on a bike. I'll take the explosives."

Falco slipped the radio into the large bag slung across his back. "It's less than an hour's ride to Marzamemi. It's a fishing village. I have someone there who will take us in his boat."

We reached Marzamemi and waited in the shadows while Falco went into a small stone house by the shore. He returned in a few minutes, followed by an ancient toothless fisherman. Falco gestured us to wheel the bicycles into a shed, where the old man covered them with nets. We then followed him down to the beach and waded out to a small decrepit fishing boat, bobbing at anchor a few yards from the shore.

Luciano's right eye drooped even more pronouncedly, giving him a look of abject misery. "First you make me swim, and I nearly fuckin' drown. Then you put me on a fuckin' bike and my ass is as sore as hell. Now you expect me to sail in this death trap. I wish I'd never left Great Meadow."

Falco looked at him uncomprehendingly. He took off his bag and gestured to me to do the same. The radio and explosives were still securely wrapped in waterproof. The old man put them in a sack and tied it carefully to a line that trailed behind the boat.

"If we're stopped by Germans or the *Fascisti*, he will have to cut them free. We will tell them we are his sons. We are fishing for tuna." Falco climbed into the little boat and began to unfurl the sail. "We have a motor, but not much gasoline. We are going to Syracuse. I have friends there. We will follow the coast."

We clambered aboard, Luciano choosing to squat gloomily alone among the lobster pots towards the prow. The old fisherman pulled up the anchor and the tide and a faint wind began to take us out into the Ionian Sea. He waited until we were out of earshot of land before starting his ancient motor. We then chugged northwards along the Gulf of Noto, the old man, an unlit pipe clamped between his gums, keeping vigilant watch at the tiller.

Falco gazed at the coastline, barely visible under the moon. "Our people were never strong here in the south. Mori, Mussolini's prefect, wiped them out. He tied women to their beds and poured sea water down their throats to make them betray their men. The men had electric cables tied to their balls to make them speak. Whole villages were surrounded and starved to submission. We survive only in the north-west, around Palermo and in the hill towns of Castellammare."

Luciano nodded dejectedly. "Didn't I tellya the same thing? We should've gone there in the first place."

I ignored him. "What do the people of Sicily feel about the war?"

Falco spat into the sea, "Mussolini does what Hitler tells him. There is a death penalty for defeatist talk, even for hoarding food. The people are half starving – even here in Sicily where we get four harvests of wheat a year. Everything is sent to Germany. Before the *Fascisti* we were a nation of beggars, now we are poorer than beggars. Most Sicilians pray the *Inglese* and *Americanos* will win ..." He broke off and frowned as if he'd revealed too much.

"If we get to Termini Imerese can you find the exact location of Don Calo? Can you make sure he is in a cell near the outer wall?"

"Of course." Falco let out some nets over the side in pretence of fishing.

I lay in the bottom of the little boat, gazed at the stars, trying to take stock of the situation. My reverie was broken by a distant rumble in the sky. It took me an instant to realise it was the throb of aircraft engines; hundreds of aircraft engines, creating a man-made thunder that filled the night. We looked up in wonder as wave after wave of bombers began to pass overhead. Falco nodded approvingly: "It is the British, from their new bases in Tunisia. They are on their way to bomb the docks at Avola and Syracuse. They will make a good diversion."

The old man gave the engine full throttle as the sky ahead burst in explosions and flames. Avola was burning as we passed, the anti-aircraft guns firing futilely at their tormentors above. Just over the horizon, the flames in Syracuse were creating an early dawn.

Syracuse was still an inferno as we approached the Pontile di Sant'Antonio. Freighters and transport were ablaze and listing into the water. The sea itself was burning as leaking oil caught fire. Soldiers and carabinieri, silhouetted against the flames, shouted and screamed as they vainly tried to control the firestorm with their puny hoses. Blasts from the ammunition stored in the burning warehouses lit the night sky, showering debris upon the hapless men beneath. The big naval guns on the ramparts of the fortress of Castello Maniace were smashed and burning; no one noticed our little craft sailing beneath. I remembered Lieutenant Frazer and wondered if his dearly-bought information had caused this havoc. We passed through the thick smoke towards Ortega, the Old Town, built on an island separated from the rest of the city by a solitary bridge. Falco piloted the old man to a dark jetty on the eastern side, where some stone steps were built into the sea wall.

"Get the stuff out of the water and follow me."

I dragged the sodden sack aboard and passed the radio to Falco, who slung it on his back and began to make his way up the slippery, seaweed-covered steps. I took my precious explosives, nodded thanks to the old man, and pushed Luciano up before me. At the top of the stairs was a bomb-cratered road. Falco made sure all was clear, pointed to an alley on the other side and led the way across. I brought up the rear as we twisted left and right through a warren of little lanes, the upper stories of the houses almost touching above. Everywhere was poverty and decay. Pantiles were slipping off the roofs, plaster crumbled from the walls, revealing the stone beneath, and paint had long peeled off the doors. The smell of sewage reeked up from the ancient drains. As part of my training, I'd been briefed on Ancient Sicilian history by a professor from Yale, and could hardly believe that this slum was Syracuse, one of the masters of the ancient world; the home of Aeschylus and Archimedes, the city-state that had destroyed the power of Athens.

The alley led finally into a narrow street. Falco motioned us to wait in the shadow and then crossed to the other side. He rapped lightly on a door and whistled softly.

"Jeez, what a stinking dump." Luciano studied the street name, etched above us on an ancient piece of white marble. "Via Giudecca – street of the Jews – no wonder Lansky and his other buddies chose to go to New York."

A faint light shone from the door. Falco beckoned; we crossed the road and crept inside. We followed a feeble oil lamp up a sour smelling stairway into a room above. The door closed and revealed the bearer of the lamp, a gaunt-looking woman in her mid-forties.

Luciano gazed at her approvingly. "With a good wash and some decent clothes, she wouldn't be all that bad."

She regarded him coldly.

Falco slipped the radio off his shoulders: "Stay here with her. You will be perfectly safe. I must go and arrange how we get to Termini. I will be back by midday."

He glanced at the woman who nodded her assent and was gone.

I took off my pack. The woman pointed to a large mattress with a flea-bitten blanket in the corner by the window. I fell on it, and was soon in an exhausted sleep.

July 5, 1943

Someone was shaking me awake. I was relieved to see Falco's thick moustache.

"The Nazis need sulphur. They are grabbing all they can, before you Americans and the English arrive. We will travel on a truck that is authorized to go north to the mines and take sulphur to Messina. I have our papers."

The woman came out of the inner room pulling her shabby clothes in place, followed by a satisfied-looking Luciano. I understood immediately. While the woman busied herself at a primitive stove, and Falco carefully put the radio and explosives into two dirty canvas bags, I dragged Luciano to the far side of the room.

"The Italian money you were issued with is only to be used in emergencies."

"It was an emergency, sonny. I haven't had a piece of pussy in years."

"I'm your superior officer and you'll obey orders. If you step out of line again I'll make sure it goes on your report."

"Who cares a shit about your fuckin' report? Loosen up willya? What you need is a good fuck yourself."

I smarted at Luciano's words. They were partly true. Before I could reply, the woman handed us both a cup of bitter chicory coffee. I sipped it gratefully. Falco had finished packing and laid the bag containing the radio at my feet.

"We are workmen with our tools. I will show the papers if they stop us; but I don't think they will. They are still busy with the air raid. You have a gun?"

I lifted my trouser to reveal the Beretta as Luciano shook his head in frustration.

"Good. Only use it as a last resort. I have friends shadowing us who will cause a distraction if there is trouble."

The woman who'd been watching out of the window, turned and nodded. Falco took the other bag containing the explosives and went down the stairs. I picked up my bag and pushed Luciano before me. Luciano waved farewell and winked at the woman with his good eye. Her eyes were filled with repulsion.

We came out of the ghetto's maze of little streets and entered the Via Maestranza. People were going dejectedly about their business; mostly women with empty baskets searching for food, speaking in low voices and gesturing hopelessly with work-worn hands. Thin, bare-footed children played in the gutter. The houses had once been rich and grand, but were now poorer than any tenement I'd ever seen in the meanest slum of New York. Some doorways were open, revealing litter-strewn courtyards with sweeping, dilapidated, stone-chipped staircases, and elaborate balconies with rusting ironwork. Syracuse was a destitute old lady without a trace of her former splendour. In the middle of the Piazza Archimede was a broken fountain of a horse and naked goddess. Falco stopped for a moment, surveyed the scene, gave us the nod and began to cross. We were halfway over when two German officers came out of the Banca Sicilia and stepped directly in our path. They were in earnest conversation, probably discussing the damage caused by the previous night's raid. Falco continued to walk coolly towards them. I was bringing up the rear, my heart beating fast. As we drew near the younger officer, an Oberleutnant looked idly at me. I avoided making eye contact and dropped my head.

"Come here, you!" The German was making towards me. I kept on walking.

"Halt!" His Italian was heavy with German. "I said come here! What is in that bag?"

I stopped and turned, desperately debating whether I should reach down for my gun, but the Oberleutnant's pistol was already out of his holster. Falco had stopped as well, whilst Luciano was shuffling uneasily towards the safety of the shadows.

The second German, older and stouter, a Sturmbannfuhrer, had also drawn his Mauser. They were less than ten yards away. "Come here and open that bag!"

I turned fractionally towards Falco, but he was looking towards an open doorway on the far side of the piazza.

"Open the bag!" The Oberleutnant's pistol was pointing at my heart. "I won't tell you again. Open the bag!"

At that moment a burst of automatic fire rang from the open doorway. The Oberleutnant fell backwards into the empty basin of the fountain, his blood and brains splattering over the goddess's stone thighs. The Sturmbannfuhrer immediately crouched by the rim of the basin and began to return fire across the piazza. More automatic fire came from the doorway. Two men dressed in civilian suits emerged from the bank and began to fire their machine pistols in the same direction as the Sturmbannfuhrer. At the same time, two carabinieri ran from a side street, blowing their whistles and drawing their revolvers. Falco raced towards an alley on the south side of the piazza like a quarterback heading for a touchdown, with Luciano and me in hot pursuit. Bullets ricocheted off the paving and sent chips of stone flying in the air. More shots rang out and the whistles blew ever louder, as Falco veered left and right, hoping to distract the line of fire. We were almost there. We had almost reached the sanctuary of the alley, when a bullet hit Falco's bag and sent it spinning from his grasp. Luciano, the least fit, staggered on; Falco stopped momentarily to retrieve it, but I'd already scooped it up.

"Keep going. I'll follow you."

We raced down more dark, dank lanes, under countless lines of washing. Emaciated dogs and cats fled from our path. More whistles began to sound to our left. The weight of the two bags was slowing me down. We burst into an enclosed courtyard. Children looked up from their games with frightened faces, before we plunged back into twisting alleys once more. Sweat poured into my eyes and there was a sharp pain in my chest. I could see Luciano was about to collapse in front of me. I wasn't sure how much further I could go, when Falco abruptly swung right and leapt up on a wall. He leant down to haul up Luciano, then the bags, and finally me. We dropped into a cool garden where a small fountain was gently playing. A grey-clad nun, of indeterminate age, was sitting in the shade, and looked up from her book as Luciano retched up his coffee on the flagstones. The sister said nothing but motioned us to follow her. She opened a door and pulled aside a curtain to reveal the white interior of a church and the outstretched arms of a large wooden Christ. It was as if he were bidding us welcome. She led us beneath the Saviour's forgiving gaze to a door on the opposite wall, and then along a white-washed corridor to a small cell. The nun left without saying a word. Luciano looked after her lasciviously. My loathing of him increased.

Falco took control. "The Sisters of Saint Ursula are our friends. We will wait here until things become quieter outside. You'd better check the radio."

I'd already opened the bag. A bullet had passed through the middle, shattering valves and transmitter. It was past repair. I sunk despondently to my knees. "It's useless. The mission's finished. My orders are to gather information about the projected invasion areas and radio them back. Even if I had the information, how can I do that now?"

Luciano sneered. "You're the fucking officer. That's your problem,"

Falco shrugged. "Get the Don out of jail and maybe he will think of a way." He kicked the radio. The clunk of boot on metal echoed round the stone cell. "We must get rid of it. If the Germans found it here they would shoot even the sisters."

We sat and waited for an hour before the nun returned bringing us each a glass of cool lemonade. Lucky gulped it eagerly then drew his mouth away spitting out the acidic liquid. Falco smiled bitterly: "We haven't had sugar for three years. The Nazis take it all for themselves. They take everything."

The nun watched us drink then led us, through more cool corridors, to a small door that opened on to yet another dark alley. Falco, with the bag and smashed radio, leant forward, looked right and left, sniffing the air like a dog. We followed him out noiselessly as the nun locked the door behind us. Falco led us stealthy through another labyrinth of alleys until, like hunted deer emerging from the safety of the forest, we stepped into the brilliant sunlight of the Via Trento. The massive ugliness of the Riva Della Posta, Mussolini's gift to the city, towered over us, bearing fresh scars from the previous night's bombs. The air was heavy with cordite. We could still hear the crack of gunfire, piercing whistles and screaming sirens, where Falco's friends continued their diversion.

Falco nodded towards a bridge, shrouded in the smoke of burning ships. "That's the only way out of Ortega. The truck is waiting on the other side. An ammunition ship is still smouldering from last night's raid. We must hope all their attention is on that."

He began to cross the bridge. Luciano and I followed a few paces behind. In the middle, where the smoke was thickest, Falco reached over the balustrade and dropped his bag. There was a loud splash beneath; the lack of visibility increased the sound. As if on cue, an Italian sentry loomed out of the smoke.

Falco waved a casual greeting: "I have just buried my dog. Those English bastards killed him with their bombs. Best dog I ever had."

The sentry nodded understandingly. "I miss my own dog. I'm a shepherd from the hills around Agira. I wish I was there now." He continued on his patrol.

We crossed over to the mainland, to a ramshackle truck outside a warehouse in the Via Malta. The driver was already in his cab. The street was empty. Falco took the explosives and stowed them under a tarpaulin in the back. Luciano and I climbed up and sat on the tarpaulin, while Falco joined the driver in the cabin.

The old truck shuddered and misfired its way out of Syracuse. Past the ruins of the ancient city, past the theatre where Aeschylus's plays first preached against the wickedness and folly of war, and past the stone quarries where Athenian prisoners had been worked to death as slaves. I prayed the soldiers of the impending invasion would not suffer such a fate. The broken rocks of ancient Syracuse looked little different from the broken stones of last night's bombing. Ruins are ruins in whatever age they're made.

We quickly became hot and thirsty as the truck laboured up the east coast to Catania. There was no shade and the sun beat down upon us mercilessly. As we passed beneath the smoke clouds of Etna, we could see swarms of grey-clad German engineers building gun emplacements and digging trenches on its slopes. Luciano spat contemptuously, "Didn't I tell you? You should land in the north. This is the only road this side of the island. It'll take fucking weeks to get round that."

I could not but believe that Luciano was right.

After another hour the truck stopped and Falco got out and passed us a bottle of oily- tasting water. Luciano drank it greedily. "Jeez! This place is hotter than Manhattan in August."

"This is nothing. We are going to cross the centre of the island which will be hotter than an oven."

"What about something to eat? All I've had today is a lousy cup of coffee and some lemonade that tasted like piss."

"In Sicily you will soon learn to be hungry." Falco turned to me, "We will pass General Guzzoni's headquarters at Enna. There are roadblocks all around it. If they stop us, don't say anything. The authorisation I have should be enough."

"I sure fuckin' hope so." Luciano growled.

As we approached the mountain fortress of Enna, we vainly sought refuge from the pitiless sun by crawling under the tarpaulin. Several times the old lorry juddered to a halt. We heard police or soldiers demanding papers, each time my finger reached down to my ankle and touched the trigger of the Beretta, but each time Falco's papers quelled suspicions. The troops sounded uninterested, as if they'd had more than enough of Mussolini's war. In the late afternoon, as the heat cooled, we crept out from our cover and took in the cruel, sunburnt landscape. Mountains rose around us: bald and barren apart from a few scattered brown patches. Now and then I noticed lone men watching from the mountaintops, as if monitoring our progress. Lucky observed them with lizard-like eyes, occasionally wiping dust and sweat from his face with the yellow handkerchief. The noise of the engine and our solitary position in the back of lorry persuaded me it was safe to talk.

"What gives with the handkerchief? What was the favour you did Don Calo?"

Luciano held the yellow silk in his hand and momentarily watched it flutter in the flaccid breeze, then felt for the blue embroidered C and rubbed it between his fingers. "One of his guys had to get to the States – he'd bumped someone off, in such a bloody and stupid way that even the Don couldn't get him off. If the guy had taken the rap, Calo would've lost respect, so he did a deal with an undertaker in Palermo. They put the guy in a specially ventilated coffin on a ship bound for New York for burial at sea. As soon as the ship was outside Italian waters, he rose from the fuckin' dead, like that guy in the Bible, but he didn't have no Jesus to help him. All he had was my name and this handkerchief the Don had given him to give me. When he arrived stateside, I got him the right documents and gave him a job. Didn't last long though," his face broke into a malicious smile, "the New York cops shoot straighter than they do over here. When I give this back to Calo it'll be favour for favour – that's the rule."

We reached Termini Imerse in the early evening. Falco deposited us in a mean tenement by the harbour, whilst he made necessary arrangements,

To Luciano's chagrin, an ancient flatulent woman attended our needs.

⚜⚜⚜

Termini Imerese

"Don Calo's cell is behind here. Fifty paces from the south wall."

It was a hot and humid night; I was sweating beside Falco in a small sidestreet in the middle of Termini Imerse, surveying the massive stones of the back wall of the prison. I checked that the two armed men, who had appeared as out of nowhere, were keeping watch at each entrance of the alley. I nodded to Falco to turn on his flashlight, and then began to feel the crevices of the wall for any weakness. My fingers probed and dug until I found a slight fissure. It was enough. Calmly, as I'd been taught, as if on an exercise, I began to expand the crack into a hole with my knife and chisel. Suddenly a soft whistle came from the left. Falco switched off the light and pulled me down into the darkest shadow at the foot of the wall. A police car with darkened headlamps drove leisurely along the Via Massini. Another minute and a double whistle told us the danger had passed. I returned to my task. Soon it was deep enough. I calculated the amount of explosive needed and forced it tightly into the hole. I hoped Falco hadn't seen that my hands were shaking as I attached the detonator and fuse.

"It's ready. Warn your people. I'll light the fuse in five minutes. It'll blow two minutes after that."

Falco looked at his watch. "When it blows we'll go in and get him. They'll be a car at the corner with your friend, get in and wait for us." He melted into the darkness.

I watched the luminous hands of my own watch as the minutes ticked away. It was all happening so fast; things had spun beyond my control. Admiral Hewitt was waiting for details of minefields, strong points and the state of the roads behind Gela and Licata, whilst I was on the other side of the island without a radio, facilitating a jailbreak with Luciano in the getaway car. I checked my watch again. Five minutes had passed. I lit the fuse, sheltering it with my hand. It sknuttered for a few seconds before it took hold; the fire slowly eating its way along the cord. I double-checked I'd done all that was necessary, gathered up the rest of my explosives into the pack and ran back down the alley to take cover beside Falco. I could see the other two Mafiosi were at the far corner. I crouched, sweating and shivering at the same time. Had I judged it correctly? Had the explosives been damaged in the sea? Would the detonator work? According to my watch there was still a minute to go. I tried to control my breathing. Falco mustn't sense my anxiety. Thirty seconds. Falco had somehow acquired a M38 sub-machine gun. I heard him ease the safety catch. Sweat was pouring into my eyes. Ten seconds. My mouth was dry; my tongue licked the salt sweat around my lips. Five seconds. I found myself silently mouthing yet another 'Hail Mary'. I vowed I wouldn't look at my watch again until I heard the explosion. I waited – nothing happened. Falco was stirring impatiently at my side. I was about to break all the rules and poke my head back around the corner, when the blast almost blew us to the ground. A huge shower of stones rained down through a thick cloud of dust and smoke. In an instant, Falco and the others were racing towards the newly made gap in the wall. I clambered to my feet and staggered across the road with the pack to where a car had appeared, seemingly out of the blue. It was an ancient Fiat Sedan, just like the getaway cars in the old-time gangster movies. The driver, whose face was covered by the peak of his cap, gestured me to climb in the back alongside a nail-chewing Luciano.

Through the sirens, the bark of rapid gunfire came from within the prison. Another minute, and then Falco came out of the smoke with a large, fat, dishevelled man in late middle-age. Falco pulled him across the road and pushed him in beside me, then jumped into the front seat as the car raced away. More shots came from behind, as more men ran out of the ruptured wall and made off in all directions. Fire was coming from the surrounding rooftops as other gunmen covered our escape. The car raced down dark streets as a searchlight swept above from the prison roof. The Fiat may have been ancient but it still had a kick in the engine, and the driver was an expert. He knew every bump in the road. He hardly lost speed as we spun left and right, making for the blackness and safety of the countryside. I was squashed, clasping my explosives to my bosom, between the fat sweating man and the hard body of Luciano, who seemed unwilling to concede an inch of space as a matter of principle. I began to feel nauseous; I wasn't sure if it was the excitement and tension, or the rank odour that oozed from the body of my new companion, who was staring silently ahead into the night. We began to climb a road that twisted and turned almost back on itself, as it made its tortuous way up into the hills.

Falco glanced behind: "They have not followed. We are safe."

Still Don Calo remained silent, as did Luciano; it was as if neither wished to diminish his status by being first to acknowledge the other. We drove ever higher, on rougher and ever rougher roads, until finally we drew up outside a lonely farm. Falco leapt out and assisted Don Calo from the car and led him to the farmhouse, where a woman and a mangy-looking dog waited at the open door. Luciano had got out and was walking towards the house with as much dignity as his shabby garb could muster. I gathered my pack and followed. The driver immediately swung the steering wheel around, and the Fiat disappeared into the warm Sicilian night.

Twenty minutes later, we were eating around the rough table in the main room of the house. It was smoky from the fire on which the woman had cooked a hare, flavoured with onions, bay leaves and rosemary. Coarse bread and jugs of heavy red wine accompanied the meal. Don Calo ate in silence, occasionally giving scraps to the dog, which sat with its muzzle resting by his crotch. The dog was of uncertain breed with long straggling grey hair. Its most distinctive attribute was its eyes – one blue, one hazel – which looked up lovingly and devotedly at its unsavoury master. Luciano, who also had remained silent, sat in the place of honour at the other end of the table. Each man was still reluctant to make the first move, in case it lessened the respect he considered the other owed him. The woman stood in the shadows by the fire. Once, when I looked up from my food, I caught her staring at me intently before nervously lowering her sad eyes. She was in her late thirties, a troubled life had aged her, but traces of beauty still remained. The Don was first to finish. He pushed his plate away and wiped his mouth with the back of his hand. He glanced at the woman, who immediately went upstairs. He then turned and looked questioningly at Luciano, who returned his gaze before untying the handkerchief from his neck and placing it on the table.

"I'm returning this."

Don Calo picked up. Feeling the texture of the silk with his fingers and examining the embroidery with dark, flickering eyes. "Salvatore Lucania." His voice was deep and unctuous. "Your name in Sicily is honoured like a king. Why has it taken you so long to come home?"

Luciano chewed his lip before replying, "I've been in jail same as you, but I did a longer stretch."

Calo's face broke into a malevolent grin, "Yes, I remember. But I was in jail because a traitor betrayed me – you dealt in whores. In Sicily we consider that *infamata*. It is dishonourable to our women, our daughters, wives and mothers."

"I never used Sicilian women. Only foreigners – they were animals."

They fell silent and eyed each other like poker players.

Don Calo broke off and looked at me for the first time. "Why are you here?"

"I am an officer in the US Navy, an emissary from Admiral Hewitt. He requires information and your help."

"He has wasted two months. The *Fascisti* have been in a muck sweat since the surrender at Tunis." He began picking his dirty teeth: "Are you Sicilian?"

"My father was. He is dead."

"Was he a member of the *Fratellanza*?"

I looked at Luciano before I nodded. Calo took a mouthful of wine and swirled it around his cheeks. He turned and spat it into the fire. "You did well tonight. You know your business. What information does your Admiral require?"

"He wants to know details of the inland defences behind Pozella, Gela and Licata. He wants to know how many German Divisions are on the island, their strength and where they're stationed."

Calo began to fondle the ears of his dog. "There are two: the Hermann Goering and the 15th Panzer. The Hermann Goering is not up to full strength. It is made up largely of Luftwaffe recruits or ground personnel, but they have some giant tanks, more powerful than any you have, mounted with 88mm guns." I knew what he meant instantly. Panzerkampwagen VI – the fearful Tigers; I'd seen the carnage they'd caused in Tunis. As far as I knew, nobody expected them to be in Sicily. "Both Divisions are being held in reserve around Caltanissetta and Agrigento," Calo continued. "The plan is the Italians will hold you on the beaches, and then the Panzers will fall on you before you link up and form a bridgehead."

I was impressed: "How did you manage such detailed information?"

"We have friends everywhere. Even in the command headquarters at Enna."

"You're sure there are only two German divisions?"

"I do not give false information. It is my business to know everything."

"Will the Italians fight?"

"There are still Fascists and traitors, a traitor betrayed me, but we will find him soon," Falco looked up from his food and nodded. "But the core of the Italian Army has been destroyed: in Russia, in Greece, and in Africa. As you must know, Mussolini lost 180,000 men in Tunisia alone. Much of the army here is made up of local conscripts, Sicilians. They have no desire to fight Americans. They will go home at the first opportunity." The Don unbuttoned his pants and began to scratch his belly. "There were fleas in that shit house of a jail. My friends in Sardinia tell me a German Division has been transferred there from Russia. They think you will invade Sardinia as well."

His crafty eyes sought affirmation. I shook my head. "I know nothing about that."

"You should invade in the north-west: in the bay of Castellamarre. You could take Palermo in a matter of days."

"That's what I told the stupid motherfuckers," Luciano attempted to re-assert himself. "They wouldn't listen to me."

I shrugged, "I only know about a landing in the south-east."

"Then why do your American Flying Fortresses bomb Palermo?"

"It could be a diversion. To make them think we are coming that way."

"The people of Palermo are paying a bloody price for your diversion."

I changed the subject: "How can I report what you have told me? My radio is smashed."

"When is the invasion due?"

"I would say any day now. It's a matter of the tides."

"I could put you in a fishing boat, but it is unlikely you would make it across to Tunisia."

"I've got to try. It's my duty."

"The Luftwaffe patrols night and day. They sink any boat going in that direction."

Luciano guffawed scornfully, "You're telling me they would. You won't catch me in one of those fuckin' death traps again."

I looked at him coldly. "Wherever I go, you go too."

Luciano glared back. "I told you not to push me too hard kid."

Don Calo relished Luciano's humiliation before saying softly: "Yes, young man, you too have your honour; your *omerta*." He turned to Falco, who was still mopping his plate with bread: "I owe him my freedom. Get him to his Admiral."

The fat man rose and climbed the stairs to join the woman above.

Luciano, flushed and angry, poured himself more wine and drank morosely. Falco stared into the fire. The wooden floor above creaked as the weight of Don Calo got into bed. Luciano came out of his reverie and looked up at the ceiling longingly. A minute or two passed, and then the creaks grew louder as the bed shuddered with the force of Calo's lust. I thought I heard the woman crying.

Falco drained his glass. "We'd better get a few hours' sleep. We leave at first light."

It was still dark and the embers of the fire were glowing red when I was unwillingly dragged out of my exhausted sleep by someone shaking my shoulder.

Falco was looming over me: "Your friend has gone."

"What?" I was awake in a second. "How do you know?"

"About twenty minutes ago he got up and went outside – I heard him and awoke – I thought he was going to have a shit. I waited, but he never came back. I searched outside and the bicycle is missing."

In fury, I reached for my revolver, which thought I'd stowed under my pillow. I fumbled and reached beneath it. It was not there.

"He's taken my gun."

Falco shrugged "The Don will give you another. Let him go: we can travel faster without him."

A few minutes later Calo was rummaging about in a battered chest beneath his bed. The woman watched in a dark corner, a stained sheet wrapped around her still-firm body.

"He has dishonoured my hospitality. He has stolen from my guest." Calo handed me a well-used Beretta.

"It's my fault. I should never have trusted the bastard. My orders are to bring him back dead or alive. I'll shoot him on sight." I took a clip from my pouch and slid it into my new weapon.

"But that will take time: a day at least. You say my information is crucial to the invasion, leave it to my people: they will track him down in a few hours."

I looked at Falco, who nodded affirmation.

"Your Admiral Hewitt should know the new giant tanks await him." Calo laid a fatherly hand on my shoulder. "The lives of your soldiers are more valuable than the freedom of an outlaw."

The sun was lightening the eastern sky beyond Mount Bosco when we hitched the thin old horse to the wagon full of potatoes, under which were hidden the explosives together with Falco's M38, and began our journey down the mountain. The wagon like the horse had seen better days, bearing traces of the bright coloured patterns, with which it had once been painted in traditional Sicilian style. I was smarting with humiliation and seething with anger. Luciano had made a dupe of me. Had he gone over to the Fascists and was even now warning them of the impending invasion? My mission was becoming an utter failure. I cursed him and the broken radio again and again, but was determined to get my information through, whatever the cost. We followed cart tracks across open fields until we joined a rutted road and then travelled along it throughout the morning, as fast as the old horse could go. Occasionally, a German or Italian plane flew overhead, their shadows joining those of the few clouds forming drifting patterns on the mountainsides. Now and then, the sun glinted on the metal of anti-aircraft guns, sited amid the cloud-topped peaks. The lower slopes looked arid and dry, almost like steppes. Wheat had been grown here since Roman times, when the island had been the breadbasket of Italy. The latest harvest was already on its way to Germany, and small red poppies stood alone amongst the grey stubble. Once we were overtaken by an Italian staff car, which raced past in a cloud of dust. The General in the back, resplendent in gold braid and fancy uniform, was fast asleep. Apart from that there was no sign of the war which was about to fall on this savage but strangely beautiful land.

Just before noon, we came to a rundown farm outside a small village. At the sight of strangers, thin, scrawny chickens ran clucking with alarm from beneath an ancient, red-painted Fiat truck. An emaciated dark-haired peasant was waiting with his daughter: an attractive girl whose firm breasts thrust through the threadbare fabric of her shabby dress. Falco leapt from the cart, retrieved the explosives from beneath the potatoes and flung them to me, as the man led the horse into a barn and the girl closed the doors behind us. Falco then joined the man at the far end of the barn and began to burrow into a great pile of hay. They quickly uncovered two motorcycles and a kit bag, which Falco threw to me.

"You'll find two Italian uniforms in there complete with boots. Take off all that other stuff. Give it to the girl, she'll burn it."

Falco and the man began to make the bikes ready whilst I undressed under the girl's watchful gaze. She held out her hand as I undid my belt and let the baggy old trousers fall to the ground. Underclothes would have been an absolute give away if we'd been caught, and the girl surveyed my drooping manhood with a smile. It was the first time I'd exposed myself before a woman and there was something about her smile that told me she knew it. I stepped out of my trousers and gave them to her and then pulled off the shirt, rancid with the sweat of the past days. She appraised my naked body and giggled provocatively. I threw the shirt at her. Falco had finished with the bikes and began to strip beside me. The girl continued to stare as if comparing our equipment. The man had gone onto the road to keep watch, while we put on grey-green knickerbockers and then struggled to stuff them into leather leggings.

When I had buttoned up the tunic and put the *bustina* on my head, the girl stepped forward and kissed my cheek with unexpected tenderness: "I will pray for you."

Falco, his sub-machine gun slung on his back, was already astride his machine, kicking it into life: "*Avanti*. If we are stopped leave everything to me."

I returned her kiss: "I will pray for you too." I felt an uncontrollable desire to give her something. I knew it was contrary to orders, but what the hell? I reached into my pack of explosives and grabbed a fistful of lire. "Take this. Buy yourself a new dress." I strapped on the pack and felt the engine surge between my thighs. The man swung open the barn door. We were away. I turned back to see her gazing after me, holding undreamed wealth in her hand.

We kept to dirt tracks at first. We had passed Marianopoli before Falco decided to risk taking the road to Santa Caterina. We then sped along it to a pass, winding like a black snake, through lowering mountains bathing us in welcome shade. The road became a series of corkscrew bends as it rose higher and higher. We'd just rounded one such bend when Falco braked in a swirl of dust. I halted beside him and looked to where he was pointing. A quarter of a mile ahead, the black mouth of a tunnel gaped in the side of the mountain. A German checkpoint was clearly visible at the entrance: I could see silver on grey uniforms sparkling in the sunlight. A gun emplacement was nearby. Falco inclined his head to the left and careered off the road. I followed as best I could, exhilarated as I'd never been before. We raced through groves of poplars, dodging tall rocks with jagged, teeth–like edges, and splashed through mountain streams. Hares ran startled from our path and crows rose croaking into the clear air. Despite the danger, despite Luciano, I was glad to be alive. Our petrol gauges were hovering near empty as we rejoined the road on the other side of the mountain. We continued east for a few more miles before the engines began to splutter. Falco's was the first to die. I came to a halt beside him. He pulled off his cap and wiped the sweat from his brow.

"The ride round the mountain was longer than I expected. The tanks were only half full. I thought we had enough to get us to Santa Caterina. We'll just have to push."

We took turns at pushing and riding on my puttering bike, until that too gave out. Then we both pushed and sweated throughout the heat of the afternoon. I began to feel weak as we laboured higher and higher into the thin air. The uniform was thick and heavy and the pack on my back was chafing my skin. We were still some way from the top of the pass when we heard the roar of a heavy engine below us. We pushed our bikes into the trees and walked back to the last bend. An Italian truck was making its painstaking way up towards us.

Falco made a decision. "Give me your pistol. Go behind the trees and cover me." He unslung his sub-machine gun, took a spare magazine from his pocket, and gave them both to me. I unstrapped the Beretta from my ankle. Falco stuck it into the back of his belt as I took cover by a group of pines. Falco then ran back and wheeled his bike to the side of the road and waited beside it. The noise of the truck grew louder and louder as it laboured ever upwards. I crouched behind a tree, eased the safety catch off the M38 and squinted down its cheap, unsophisticated sights. I'd practised with this Italian weapon during my training in North Africa. Accuracy was never its forte, but provided it didn't jam, it could produce a rapid rate of fire. The top of the truck appeared through the trees beneath us; it had one more turn to go. Falco pulled down his tunic and adjusted his cap, trying to look soldierly, before the truck lumbered round the final bend. Falco then stepped into the middle of the road, waving his arms. The truck came to a juddering halt before him. The driver was a middle-aged soldier. He had the look of a conscript from the poor quarter of a large city. Beside him sat a young sergeant who frowned irritably as Falco gave a very unmilitary salute.

The sergeant stuck his head out of the window: "I am not an officer. You do not salute me. You should have learnt that in the first week of training."

Behind the driver's cab a soldier, little more than a boy, poked his head from the tarpaulin that covered the truck. He raised his rifle and pointed it at Falco, who put on a most stupid grin.

"I am sorry sir, I mean, sergeant. I have run out of petrol and I have an urgent dispatch for the General, and I guess I am nervous. Can you spare me some? I have to get to Caltanissetta; it is a most urgent dispatch."

The sergeant regarded Falco suspiciously. "What unit are you with? I do not recognize the insignia on your shoulder."

Falco was taken aback. He'd no idea what regiment he was supposed to belong to. "I am with a special attachment on security duties for the General."

"Which General?"

"I cannot tell you. Orders."

"We are going to Caltanissetta. You had better come with us. You can deliver your orders to your General in my presence." His revolver was already out and aimed at Falco's chest.

"I assure you my orders are top secret. You will be in trouble if you do not give me every assistance."

"The insignia you wear is of a regiment that was lost at Stalingrad. I know it well. It was my brother's regiment." He turned just a fraction and barked at the driver: "Get out. Make sure he has no weapon."

The older man slowly, almost reluctantly began to obey. As he did so Falco flung himself forward, pulling the Beretta from behind his back and shooting upward at the sergeant, whose brow exploded in crimson as his head was blown back inside the window. The young soldier fired his rifle. Falco rolled over in the road. The bullet kicked up dust by his shoulder.

I fired automatically. My first burst went through the young soldier's heart. The boy slumped forward. His helmeted head bounced on the cabin's metal roof.

The driver was already standing with his hands above his head. "Don't shoot. I beg you!"

I rose from behind my tree and passed beneath the dead eyes of the boy, staring at me accusingly from the roof of the cabin. It was my first kill. I felt sick.

Falco prodded the driver with the pistol: "What are you carrying?"

The man was terrified. "Shells for the batteries along the south coast. I have no quarrel with you. I only want to go home."

"Give me his orders."

The driver opened the door of the truck and the sergeant's body slithered out. Falco turned it over with his boot, and signalled to the driver to take the papers that stuck out of the dead man's breast pocket. The driver obeyed, wiping off some of the blood splattered over them. Falco read them carefully while I watched the driver, who in turn watched Falco anxiously, as if the documents were deciding his fate.

"Very well; we will take over this detail." Falco put the papers in his pocket. "You will drive us to the coast as if nothing has changed."

I kept the M38 trained on the driver, while Falco took off the sergeant's tunic and belt and dragged the dead boy from the roof.

"Put on his uniform."

I took off my own tunic and began to put on the boy's. It was tight and still warm and wet with blood. Everything was becoming surreal. I shook my head vehemently: "No. I will not wear this." I threw the sodden garment into the undergrowth and put on my own tunic again.

Falco shrugged. He motioned the driver to help drag the bodies behind the trees.

The driver was in tears. He clasped the young sergeant to his chest as he lugged him from the road. "He still believed in Mussolini's promises. His father is a Party Deputy in Milan."

I shook my head reproachfully as I pulled the boy towards the undergrowth. "They were both so young."

"Blame Mussolini." Falco was already pulling his bike towards the back of the truck. "Let's get them aboard."

We loaded both bikes; I took the rifle and clambered into the back among the crates of shells. Falco picked up his machine gun and got into the cab with the driver. As we drove away, the flies were already buzzing. They had discovered fresh blood.

When we neared Caltanissetta, the road gradually became thick with German and Italian troops and guns heading for their concentration points. We mingled with the traffic, attracting little notice amid the thousands heading for battle. We moved slowly through the outskirts of the town before grinding to a halt. The air was hot, full of fumes, which made my eyes water. Engines were overheating and their exhausts belched black smoke. Horns blared in a cacophony of anger and frustration, accompanied by the shrill bleat of the whistles of the military police. I climbed on the roof of the cabin and looked up the narrow street to see what was causing the jam. Ahead was a mass of huge, black, cruel shapes; I realised with a catch in my heart, they were the dreaded Tigers.

They were massive and looked indestructible. The streets of Caltanissetta were not wide enough for them, and they were knocking down stone buildings with the fury and strength of huge prehistoric beasts. I stared at them and was afraid. I knew an airborne landing would precede the invasion. Against such monsters the lightly-armed parachute troops wouldn't stand a chance. I looked at my watch. It was half past seven. I banged on the roof of the cabin. Falco stuck out his head.

"We are taking too long. I must report they have Tigers. It could save thousands of lives."

Falco nodded and glanced up the road towards the mass of stationary traffic. I watched his reflection through the driving mirror. He nudged the driver with the muzzle of his gun: "Take the next turning on the right." We turned into a narrow street where washing hung across the road. It appeared to be a dead end. "Drive to the bottom." Falco's finger tightened around the trigger. We drove through the washing to the far end where rubbish was piled in a stinking heap. Falco motioned to the driver to turn off his engine and threw me up a length of hosepipe he'd found in the cabin: "Get the bikes down and siphon off petrol from the tank."

I did as I was told. The driver watched nervously. Little beads of sweat sprung along the lines on his brow. I unscrewed the cap on the truck, inserted the hosepipe and sucked with all my might. The odour and taste of the gasoline made me nauseous. I sucked again until I almost feel the liquid in my mouth, and then quickly inserted the hose into the tank of my bike. Gasoline began to flow into the void. I let it flow until it was full and spilling over. I repeated the process with the other machine, before going back to the cabin where Falco waited with the driver.

"I've done it. They're both full."

Falco took the Beretta from his belt and began to wind a piece of cloth around the muzzle. The driver guessed his intent. "Please let me go! I have a wife and three children. I swear I will not betray you." He tried to open the door but Falco had the revolver at his temple.

I shook my head: "Don't shoot him!"

The driver, sensing a weakening on my part, turned back to Falco and desperately began to pull a wallet from his breast pocket: "Please, I beg you. Look, I have a wife and little children."

Falco pulled the trigger. A dog-eared photo of a plump, smiling woman and three children in their Sunday best fluttered down amid the refuse of the alley. The driver slumped over his steering wheel. Blood and bone spilled on his uniform.

Falco shrugged his shoulders: "We cannot take the risk. He would talk to the first Gestapo or *Sicurezza* he saw."

I stared at the dead man. We had killed three men and made three children fatherless. I vainly tried to find solace in the doctrine that had been rammed into me so many times: 'A *few lives can save thousands. You must never lose sight of the major picture.*'

Falco was already out of the cab, his gun over his shoulder, kicking his bike into life. I took the rifle, threw on my pack, and followed him out into the traffic. We wove in and out of the frustrated trucks, then through a passageway between foul tenements, as old women implacably watched from their balconies. We followed an alley reeking with sewage before coming out onto a field dotted with broken goal posts where soccer had once been played. German soldiers were pitching their camouflaged tents in orderly lines. In contrast to the Italians, they appeared arrogant and confident. Their propaganda had told them how easily the Wehrmacht pushed invaders back into the sea: the British at Dunkirk, and only last year, the Canadians at Dieppe. We kept our heads down as we drove through their camp and then headed for the coast.

In the early evening, we stopped for more fuel at a lonely hovel, nestling against a mountain slope. Wisps of smoke were seeping from its poorly thatched roof. It did not boast a chimney.

Falco surveyed it grimly. "*Pagliari.*"

"What?"

"The poorest of farms. They live like animals and share their dwelling with their beasts."

A few scrawny goats, pigs and half-feathered chickens wandered about as a young man, with a face of a hungry eagle, dragged a jerry can from a hole in the ground beside the outhouse. Some of the chickens and a few goats followed us inside the hovel, where a woman, with whimpering child suckling her withered breast, poured wine and served us *maccu*, a soup of beans flavoured with wild fennel, which she'd cooked in a battered old tin on the tiny stove set in the earth floor. The smoke made my eyes water and its fumes seeped into my clothes. There was no furniture. We sat on two blocks of stone. Two thin-faced children watched hungrily as we ate.

"You haven't told me where we're going. I must know in case we lose each other."

Falco dipped a hunk of bread into his dish and sucked the liquid through it: "We're heading back to Marzamemi. Our old friend there will get us across in his boat." He wiped the remains of his soup around the dish with his bread then crammed it into his mouth: "*Avanti.*"

I looked at the emaciated children and hoped the orphans of the dead driver would not go as hungry. I broke the remains of my bread into two and threw it to them. They'd devoured it before I remounted my bike. A brief nod of thanks to the young man and his wife and we were away again. I felt a strong wind springing up from the west and was relieved; no airborne landing would be attempted in such conditions. There was still time to give warning of the Tigers. The weather worsened as we came through the mountains around Giarratana and continued south towards Noto. Only a few more miles to the sea – we'd have a rough crossing, but the storm would cover our escape.

It was shortly after ten o'clock, when the coast ahead erupted. We both skidded to a halt. The sky was almost as bright as day as tracer and anti-aircraft shells exploded in a mass of destructive power. It was almost beautiful: the tracer went from white, to green and then red; the shells burst in yellow and orange. Through the inferno, flew wave after wave of C-47s, interspersed with RAF Halifaxes and Albemarles. The pilots were attempting to take evasive action, breaking their formations as the fragile and ungainly Horsa gliders, the so-called 'Flying Coffins', they were towing, swung wildly behind them in the gale. The British Red Devils were heading for Syracuse.

Falco shook his head in disgust: "They are throwing away their bravest men."

From Private Diary of Commander Haffenden.
July 8, 1943. 17.00 hrs. Eastern Time:
Just heard from Washington. Colonel Gavin's 505th Combat Team have taken off from their bases in North Africa to parachute into Sicily. First US Airborne troops to see action. Jumping into an area south of Niscemi with orders to block any enemy movement towards Gela and the beaches. The poor saps have no idea Tiger Tanks will be waiting for them. The British at Bletchley Park cracked Enigma, the secret German code, weeks ago. P.R.R.J. says we have full knowledge of the German Order of Battle in Sicily, even though we've landed agents thinking their main purpose is to discover it. In the long term it is imperative the Nazis continue to believe their code is secure. Beginning to think this is a dirty business. Be glad when my transfer comes through. If I were a religious man I'd say a prayer for those young guys about to drop into hell. As I'm not religious, I'm going to get drunk.

Lt. Danny Crivello:
A terrible drama played out above us in the sky. Several gliders were hit by tracer fire and crashed into the sea like

gigantic dying birds. Others passed overhead in flames. They made no noise, which made the suffering within seem more terrible. I made a decision. It was time to assume command. There was now no point in sailing to Tunisia.

"We'll go to Gela. I'm certain the main invasion will be there. That's where Admiral Hewitt will be."

Falco didn't argue. We turned our hot and travel-stained machines southwest. Falco found a narrow road, too small for military vehicles, and we followed it for almost two hours. The engines of our bikes drowned the drone of the Allied bombers passing overhead, but the red glow of their bombs made us aware of their presence. We felt less alone. It was midnight when we came out of the mountains and looked down towards Ragusa and the sea beyond. Heavy concentrations of anti-aircraft fire were firing incessantly at another armada of aircraft, tearing the night in shreds. A pall of smoke hung over the land like fog and into it were dropping hundreds of parachutes, blown about like seeds in the strong wind We watched helplessly as one plane was hit and parachutes continued to disgorge from its sides. Some planes were flying low to dodge the fire of the guns, too low for all the men to land safely. It would be impossible for the troops to land with their units in their designated areas.

Falco began to unbutton the tunic of his uniform: "Let's go and give a hand."

"We would make no difference."

"The poor fools don't know where they are. At least I could show them the way."

"We must get the information to the Admiral – we will go on to Gela."

6

INVASION

July 9, 1943: D-DAY
Lt. Frank Dunford:

We were part of a fleet of 3,200 ships – the greatest fleet in the history of mankind. That didn't seem to be helping us as we battled through a fierce forty-mile-an-hour gale. We were making little more than two knots and waves were breaking over the deck. I leant over the side of our LCI and spewed into the whitecaps crowning the churning sea.

"You OK, sir?"

I wiped my mouth and turned to the anxious young face of my radio operator, Able Seaman Wilson. "At least we had a calm sea at Casablanca."

"Yeah, but the Vichy French sure gave us a hell of a welcome."

I smiled wryly. That was not strictly true. The French had had no tanks to speak of, and we'd come in with the third wave when most of the resistance had ended. This time we were leading the assault in point position alongside Darby's Rangers, part of the 1st Division, the Big Red One. The Rangers had distinguished themselves in North Africa at the Battle of El Guettar, where US forces had defeated Rommel for the first time. Patton had specially asked for them to lead the assault on Gela, and it was just my stinking luck I'd been assigned to them. This would be the real McCoy. I did my best to hide my fear. "If Germans are waiting for us it'll be hotter this time."

As if in reply the wind swirled around and drenched us both in a flurry of salt water.

Wilson shook the sea from his head like a dog. "The guys call this the Mussolini wind. It's keeping us away."

"But not for much longer. Look."

The coast of southern Sicily began to emerge through the spray. As we watched, great coastal guns ignited in fury, illuminating dark hills and mountains rising up behind white sandy beaches. Huge shells crashed into the sea, sending up spouts of water, more powerful than a hundred whales. Thunder erupted all around us as the great guns of the fleet returned fire. The two hundred Rangers, squatting steel-helmeted in full battle order in our open LCI, had begun to cheer, when as if on cue, the terrifying scream of a Stuka came out of the night. I looked upward at our only protection, the silver barrage balloon, straining at its tethered cable from the stern of our ship. I was about to crap my pants, but the Stuka screeched past overhead like a banshee. A moment later a great blob of light appeared, reddening the sky, marking the end of at least one of our ships.

It took away what remained of Wilson's confidence. "The motherfuckers told us we had air superiority. Where the hell are our fighters?"

I didn't answer. On top of my gut-churning fear, I'd other worries. I'd visited a whore house in Oran a week or so back. It had been beyond my wildest fantasies. Girls of all types and sizes had been sitting around naked apart from silk knickers. The madam, French, fifty, with white face and scarlet lipstick, had seen my excitement and, for an extra charge, had led me to her special girls upstairs. She'd assured me the girl I'd chosen was young and fresh, and I'd decided to go bareback and forsake my regulation-issued condom. I'd regretted it ever since. I noticed a yellow discharge in my underpants yesterday. If I lived through this I'd go to the MO for a check-up; take some of those new M&B pills I'd heard the guys talking about. I studied their young faces; the black boot polish they'd daubed on their cheeks couldn't hide their anxiety. Like me, they knew some of us were about to die.

Lt. Danny Crivello:

We crouched low over our machines with tracer bullets cracking above us, and sped westwards along the main road to Gela. The hills to our right were illuminated by exploding bombs and the retaliatory fire of anti-aircraft batteries. To our left, on the storm-tossed sea, a separate battle was being waged between the salvos of the battleships and the guns of the coastal defences. We were still several miles from Gela, approaching some trees at a junction, when suddenly I hit something tight and unyielding strung across the road. It lifted me clean from the saddle. As I flew through the air I momentarily caught sight of Falco, suffering the same fate. The breath was knocked out of me as I hit the hard tarmac; the impact softened somewhat by the pack on my back. I struggled to reach for my gun, but found myself looking up at a folding-stock US Army M1 carbine. I could see the silk emblem of the Stars and Stripes on the shoulder of the arm holding it.

"Don't shoot!"

The face of the paratrooper above the carbine registered astonishment. "How the hell did a spick like you learn to speak English?"

"I'm a lieutenant in the US Navy. I'm Danny Crivello from New York!"

My captor spat disbelievingly: "Yeah. And I suppose your buddy comes from Yonkers."

Falco was standing with his hands above his head whilst a large sergeant, having taken his gun, frisked him for hidden weapons.

"I'm on an undercover mission. He's my contact. He can help you."

"Don't believe him, Harold. It's just a con." A third soldier had risen from the ditch at the other side of the road. "He probably went to the US once on vacation to visit his aunt. He's just a dirty little Fascist like all Mussolini's boys."

"Jesus. This here place is full of cactus! It's worse than Texas." Another figure had pushed through the prickly pears. "We can't take prisoners. Let's just shoot the sonsofbitches and take their bikes. We need all the transport we can get." He eased the bolt on his carbine ominously.

"Wait. Don't be fuckin' stupid. I'm an American officer. I'm attached to Admiral Hewitt's staff. I was training in Oudjiida last month."

The sergeant took a step closer and lifted my head up towards what light there was.

"I was there then. Don't seem to remember you."

"There were thousands of us goddamit!" The sergeant's eyes were intelligent. I sought desperately for something that would convince him. "What did General Ridgway say we'd be by the time we finished?"

"You tell me."

"By take-off time for Sicily, we'd be so lean and mean, so tough and mad, that we'd jump into the fires of Hell just to get out of Africa."

"What does SNAFU stand for?"

"Situation Normal All Fucked Up."

The sergeant nodded. "We'd better take them to the captain. You two, get those bikes off the road and keep watch. Harold, you come with me."

Harold and the sergeant escorted us to a dried-up creek at the foot of twin hills, on top of which loomed the bee-hive-like shapes of three pillboxes. Crouched in the bottom of the creek were about a dozen men. An officer detached himself from the group and crawled towards us.

"What's the problem, Sergeant Blum?"

"Captain Sayre, this guy claims to be a lieutenant in the Navy. I've asked him some questions. He seems to know his stuff."

The young captain looked at me closely: "Who the hell are you?" He had a Texan accent.

"Lieutenant Daniel Crivello, US Navy. I'm here on a special mission for Admiral Hewitt. I landed near here from a British sub last week. I've vital information I've got to get through. Have you a radio?"

"I'd give my eye teeth for a radio. My radio unit must have been blown twenty miles away. What's so vital?"

"To start with, you've got the new Mark VI Tiger Tanks heading your way."

The captain whistled. "I was briefed we'd only face Italian formations."

"Well, we've been dodging Panzers all day."

He caught sight of my pack. "What are you carrying?"

"Explosives."

"We could certainly use some of that. Lay a few booby traps. We've only got grenades and two 60mm mortars..." He was cut short by a burst of machine gun fire from above. "Our orders are to take that strong point; at least I think it's that one. Hold off any counterattack coming from the north. We were supposed to do it with a full battalion – I've got about fifteen combat-green men."

I turned to Falco: "Can you do anything to persuade those guys to surrender?" Falco stared at me uncomprehendingly. "Use your imagination. Tell them we're a whole battalion and we're about to call down naval fire and wipe them out."

Falco got the idea: "Have you a white scarf or handkerchief?"

Captain Sayre understood some Italian and undid a silk scarf from his neck. Falco took it, tied it to a stick and began to climb up the slope. I followed him instinctively but he pushed me back. "If they shoot me, you still must get your message to your Admiral." He disappeared into the darkness. A few more paratroopers had appeared. We all crouched and waited. We didn't have to wait long before two bursts of machine gun fire erupted above. Shortly after, Italian was yelled from the pillbox to the left. I was relieved when I recognized Falco's voice, but couldn't make out what he was saying. More Italian was shouted across to the other pillboxes. Then silence again, before men slowly began to emerge from the pillboxes and come down the hill with their hands above their heads. In a few minutes, the paratroopers were in complete possession of all three strong points, together with twenty machine guns and countless boxes of ammunition. Forty Italian soldiers sat on the road under the watchful guard of Sergeant Blum.

Falco returned Sayre his scarf. The Captain wound it back around his neck. "What did you tell 'em? It sure as hell worked."

"I told them they could go home. For them the war is over."

Sayre nodded and turned to a private: "Tell Sergeant Blum to make sure they're disarmed and let 'em go." He then smiled at me: "I don't know who the hell he is, lieutenant, but I sure am grateful. He's saved the lives of half my men."

"We've got to get to Gela. Is it OK if we take back our bikes?"

Sayre laughed: "You sure can, Lieutenant. I wish I could spare you some men. Just one thing before you go," he took a silk invasion map from his breast pocket, "could your friend tell me exactly where we are?"

Falco understood and took the map from him, rubbing the texture between his fingers before studying it by Sayre's lighted torch. He frowned at the inaccuracies before pointing to a road junction a few miles north-east of Gela. It was marked – Piano Lupo.

We ran back down the hill. More paratroopers were arriving as Captain Sayre began to organize his defence. The Italians had already vanished into the night, but Falco picked up one of their discarded guns. We found our trusty machines in the ditch and headed southwest towards Gela. Shells from the fleet passed over our heads in arcs of solid flame before exploding to our right. Searchlights perpetually swept the sky. We rode unchallenged past small parties of lost, disorganised Italian troops, and saw dead paratroopers hanging from trees, until finally, the sea appeared between a fold in the hills. Falco pulled up, awed by the magnitude of the dark shapes upon it. They stretched to the horizon and beyond. I watched beside him as flashes of fire broke from the biggest ships and salvo after salvo hammered into the coastal defences. It looked like the end of the world, divine retribution.

Falco shook his head: "How can a man live under that?"

I had no answer and kicked my tired bike back into life. We'd gone a mile or so when an incendiary shell bathed the road ahead in light. I made out a long high wall with an ornate gateway. As we drew closer, in the flashes of shellfire, I could see it was decorated with grotesque stone faces, depicting devils or gods. They looked as if they were grimacing in horror at the war exploding around them. A red and white barrier pole lay discarded on the ground at the gateway and the sentry boxes on either side were empty. Falco stopped and briefly looked around. He nodded to me, turned his bike towards the gates and rode through. We sped up a single-track road as poplars began to loom out of the night. The trees grew thicker and thicker, forming a comforting tunnel, before we burst into an open space, perhaps a parade ground. At the far end was another crenellated wall. Falco drove along the wall to where double gates gaped open. We past another deserted guard post and came into a stone courtyard. The water in the basin of a broken fountain reflected the turmoil in the sky above. A four-turreted castle, like something out of a fairy tale, towered above us. Its main door was half open and papers were blowing out into the wind.

Falco turned off his engine and unslung his gun. He listened for a moment.

"Anyone there?"

The only response was the rustle of windblown paper. We looked at each other. We were both exhausted. Our faces were white with dust, our nostrils black with grime;

our eyes were circled with red. The fountain looked cool and inviting. I swung my aching crotch from the saddle, plunged my head under the water and drank gratefully like an animal. Falco did the same. We washed away some of the dirt and dust, then Falco listened again before crossing to the entrance of the castle and gently pushing on the iron-studded door. It opened onto a black and white marble floor. We entered a large hall, lavishly furnished with heavy gilt furniture and portraits of aristocrats, who I guessed had enjoyed a life of pampered indolence within these very walls. Their armour and weapons hung from the walls together with the heads of the deer and boar they'd slaughtered. The most recent occupants had left in a hurry. Discarded pieces of military equipment and uniform were all around. Half-eaten food covered a long oak table. Empty bottles lay on the floor in puddles of red wine. I looked out for booby traps as we crossed the hall to a heavy door, which had been left slightly ajar. There was a sign hanging from it:

ADMIRAL MARIO ARISIO.
202ND COASTAL DIVISION.
PORT DEFENCE GROUP N.

Falco pushed the door fully open with the muzzle of his gun. A larger than life picture of Mussolini pouted down at us from behind an ornate desk, on which were yet more papers together with a photograph of a smiling blonde, a red telephone, a bottle of Johnnie Walker whisky, and an exquisite cut-glass goblet, half-full of amber liquid. The air was heavy with the scent of cologne. A large safe was set in the wall. Had the Admiral evacuated in such a hurry that he'd left important secrets behind? I began to slip off my pack. "Keep watch outside. I guess I'd better try my explosives again."

The noise of the bombardment outside was increasing in intensity as the invasion fleet drew ever near. I'd just attached explosive to the safe with sticking tape when the telephone rang. Falco appeared in the doorway. We watched it ring several times before I picked it up.

"Hello?"

"Hello, you speak German?" The voice was cold and officious.

"No. Can I help you?"

"Who am I talking to?"

I checked the sign on the door: "Admiral Arisio's duty officer."

"This is Field Marshal Kesselring's headquarters at Taormina. Where is the Admiral?"

I looked at the photo on the desk: "In bed with a friend"

"That is no way to fight a war. We have received reports there is large scale enemy activity in your area."

"There's nothing going on here apart from the weather." I prayed the barrage wouldn't carry down the line. "Not even those British and American idiots would risk an invasion in weather like this." I covered the receiver with my hand as a shell exploded outside.

"What was that?"

"I told you, we are having quite a storm here."

The German didn't sound entirely convinced. "Well, let us know immediately if the situation changes."

The line went dead. I wiped my lips then returned to the safe.

Another five minutes and I was ready. I lit the fuse; made sure the heavy door was fully closed behind me, and then joined Falco in the hall "We'd better get under that table." We crouched under the thick wood with hands over our ears. I found myself studying the carved legs and wondering who'd laboured so long to produce such convoluted patterns. A fly buzzed and settled on the wood a few inches from my face. I was about to blow it away when there was a deafening blast. The heavy door flung open. Shattered glass flew from the windows. Clouds of dust and plaster rained down from ancient rafters above. Through the dust, through the open doorway, I could see into the Admiral's office. Mussolini's portrait was awry and the door of the safe was hanging open – papers and documents were floating down onto the thick pile of the carpet. I got up and ran inside. At first, I was disappointed. I found only routine orders, the report of a deserter's court martial, which had resulted in the defendant being shot. Requests for new equipment and extra supplies, ordinary mundane stuff, then, just when I thought there was nothing of value – I had to read them twice before I could believe it – was something that would more than make up for allowing Luciano to escape. There in my hands was the enemy order of battle, showing the complete disposition of the Italian and German naval forces in the Mediterranean, together with a navigational chart clearly marking the minefields and safe passages around the entire coast of Sicily. They were priceless.

I looked up at Falco and grinned: "We've hit a home run."

He stared at me uncomprehendingly: "Please?"

Lt. Frank Dunford:

A full moon had emerged from behind the storm clouds, the wind was dropping and the turbulent sea was beginning to rest. The port of Gela was burning and even bigger orange flames were illuminating the sky from the fuel dumps to the east. Not all the Italians had fled. Some brave men or fools or fanatics had survived the terrifying barrage and remained at their posts. Streams of tracer came in a withering fire from strong points along the coast, backed up by deadly German 88mm guns from further inland. Searchlights swept the shoreline seeking men struggling through the shallows with their heavy equipment, easy meat for machine guns.

Our landing craft was now awash with vomit as the beach grew nearer and nearer. Twenty-odd yards of sand beyond which I could see a wall and above that a road that climbed up through tall buildings into the heart of the town. The Rangers were in the dead centre of the attack, leading the assault of the entire 1st Division. Our Commanding Officer, Colonel Darby, was speeding up and down the line in a small motorboat, cajoling or swearing at the inexperienced helmsmen to keep in position. But I could see gaps in the line: some craft had stuck on sandbars; one or two had struck mines. To our right, a large coastal battery was keeping up a steady crossfire, sending huge spouts of water as it tried to find our range. Our boat shuddered; I could feel the steel keel scraping beneath my feet. Our speed was dropping markedly. We'd struck a sandbar and were a sitting target. The shore was still a tantalizing fifty yards away.

The ship's captain – I'd never found out his name – went forward to the 22mm cannon at the blunt prow, and addressed the anxious boys in the hold. "It looks like Coney Island on a lousy night. You guys will just have to make your own way. I'll cover you as best I can." With that he swung the gun round and opened fire on the battery.

The Ranger Lieutenant climbed on to side of the craft. "You heard him, men. We'll make for that wall. That'll give us cover from the town. Keep together and follow me." He leapt into the water, which reached above his waist, and holding his semi-automatic M-1 rifle above his head, started to strike out for the beach. The other Rangers began to follow, some more reluctantly than others.

I touched Sue's crucifix still hanging by my throat, praying I'd be spared the terrible wounds and disfigurements I'd seen at Casablanca and in Tunisia. A shell erupted in the sea twenty yards away, soaking me with its deluge. I couldn't put it off any longer. I nudged Wilson, who was making final adjustments to the straps of his bulky radio, clambered over the side and dropped into the choppy sea. I felt cold water swirling around my private parts, and prayed God would cure me of the pox as well as keeping me safe and unharmed. I could see bursts of machine gun fire being directed towards us from the buildings on the waterfront. I tried to forget my bowel-curdling fear and concentrated on the buildings. As I got closer, I could see they were little better than slums: filthy, run-down and neglected. Was this shitty dump worth dying for? My concentration was broken by a soft sigh to my right and a young boy from Kansas, who'd won a medal at El Guettar, sank under the waves. His helmet bobbed on the surface as his blood rose in bubbles from beneath. Somewhere ahead someone was screaming. More men were being hit. A body floated by, its limbs still kicking. But the damn fool Rangers kept going and Wilson and I were swept along with them. The water became shallower, it was below our knees and we moved faster. A few more yards and it was barely over our boots. Then firm wet sand before we finally reached the sanctuary of the dry soft stuff below the wall. We were almost there, almost safe, when Wilson, just ahead of me, gave a gasp, almost of surprise, and fell sideways into the sand, a dark stain spreading from his heart. I fell down behind him, desperately trying to use him for cover, reached out and frantically un-strapped the radio. I tore it savagely from

Wilson's lifeless arms and scrambled to join the Rangers under the wall.

They had lost almost half their number. I looked back and could see the dead scattered on the sand and floating in the ocean. As I watched, a searchlight fixed itself on our beached landing craft. In its beam I could see the captain still firing his cannon, still trying to give us what protection he could. He looked like a star actor spotlit on stage, but at that exact moment, the battery to the right finally found the correct range. There was a burst of brilliant light. A brave spirit had been extinguished and the landing craft was no more. Fragments of metal and men rained down into the sea.

The lieutenant looked along the wall. The guns were turning, seeking further victims. "OK men. You know the drill. We'll put those bastards out of action."

My numb fingers were fumbling with Wilson's radio. I was frantic for any excuse to stay under the protection of the wall: "I'll get the *Moravia* to take care of it. I'll work out the co-ordinates."

"No. It'll take too long. We'll handle it ourselves."

The Lieutenant signalled two men. They followed him closely as he ran in the shadow of the wall towards the gun emplacement. Twice they were obscured by bursts of machine gun fire, kicking up sand and blasting fragments of cement from the wall; but each time they reappeared, three dark bent-over shapes, moving doggedly towards their goal. They were finally beneath the guns, which swept above them like huge angry serpents stiff with venom. The Lieutenant took out a stick grenade. The others did the same. At a nod from the officer, they stepped out from their protection and hurled their grenades into the gun slits above, before diving back into cover. The force of exploding grenades in such a confined space was deadly. Furious flames leapt out with the terrible blast. The men inside were blown apart. The guns shuddered like mortally wounded beasts, and then were still.

The Rangers around me cheered: they'd struck their first blow. Their dead and the captain of our launch had been partly avenged. Along the beaches, to the right and left, wave after wave of infantry were now coming in behind us. The normal combat units faced only sand dunes and then open country. I cursed my luck that I was with the Rangers, the elite – they had to take the town. The Lieutenant, having left the other two to secure the battery, returned. I watched in trepidation, as he began to send his men over the wall in sections, to begin a deadly house-to-house battle. I picked up Wilson's radio and followed reluctantly, as far behind as I could.

Lt. Danny Crivello:

Our bikes ran out of gas again a couple of miles outside Gela. We left them in a ditch and hurried towards the coast through streams of retreating Italian troops. They paid no attention to us, even though we were the only ones going against the tide. We could hear the battle raging around the port and made our way towards the heart of it. I intended to put ourselves into the custody of the first American troops we encountered. The road was littered with debris and abandoned vehicles, and at first I didn't recognise the old red Fiat truck. Then I saw a girl crouching beneath it, desperately waving at me; the same girl who only yesterday I'd given lire to buy a new dress. She was still wearing her old one. It had become even filthier and more torn. She was terrified: her flirtatious assurance gone. How had she got here? What had gone wrong? Falco and I ran over and joined her under the truck. She was so distressed and spoke so quickly in her local dialect that I barely understood a word she said. I kept watch whilst she fervently told Falco her story.

Soon after we had departed, two SS officers arrived at the farm in a staff car. They were seeking routes along the minor roads to convey their Panzers south. They saw our bike tracks in the dust and became suspicious. They took her into the house and questioned her. She'd hidden the lire I'd given her inside her drawers. One of Nazis wanted sex. He put his hand up her skirt to pull down her drawers and discovered the money. They began to hit her, demanding who'd given it to her. She screamed – her father, who'd been hiding in the barn rushed in with an axe. They shot him between the eyes. She fought them, but they were too strong. They laid her on the table. One got on top of her whilst the other held down her arms. Then the door opened and a man came in. He had a pistol. He shot dead both of the Germans before they even knew he was there. The man had a scarred face and a drooping eye. She thought for a moment he was going to rape her as well. He told her more Germans would soon come, looking for the dead officers. He asked if the old truck had enough gas to get to Gela and did she know the way? He said she must go with him. He abandoned her and the truck when it ran out of gas. She'd no idea where he'd gone or what she should do now.

Before Falco could proffer any advice a troop of Rangers came round the corner...

Lt. Frank Dunford:

The Rangers captured Gela by mid-morning, fighting off counter-attacks by Italian infantry and light tanks. I was

exhausted and soaked in sweat even though I'd contributed very little – indeed nothing at all. I'd followed in the
Rangers' wake from house to house, using every conceivable bit of cover, to the very edge of the town, but because
of the proximity of the enemy I'd been unable to call down
supporting fire from the fleet. I decided I'd done enough,
and surreptitiously made my way back to the beach as the
First Division's second combat wave was coming ashore. All
was frenzied activity. Bulldozers had been brought in by
tank landing craft, and were towing sleds loaded with sections of prefabricated metal beach matting. Engineers were
struggling to form it into a causeway for tanks and trucks to
pass over the soft sand.

In the shadow of the harbour wall, where I'd left
Wilson's body only an hour or so before, were now a large
group of Italian prisoners, sitting huddled and dejected
under guard. Two were standing apart from the rest. One,
short and squat, stood proud and silent with folded arms,
disdainfully watching the chaos of the invasion. I couldn't
understand why his companion was shouting frantically in
English to every unit that went by. The passing men were too
intent on the ordeal awaiting them to pay any attention, but
I thought I heard him yelling he had vital information for
the Admiral, and something about German units equipped
with Tiger tanks. I thought the young guy must be hysterical
or was deliberately trying to undermine American morale. I
went closer to catch exactly what he was saying.

"Frank! For Chrissake! It's me! Danny Crivello, goddamit!"

It took me a moment to recognize the dirty, unshaven,
Italian soldier.

"Danny!"

Though we'd never been close, something seemed
to overwhelm both of us. To the amazement of the other

prisoners and watching guards, we fell into each other's arms.

Danny was the first to break free. "Tell these guys that I'm on their side you sonofabitch."

"How in blazes did you end up here?"

"It's a long story. Some Rangers captured me and my partner as we were trying to get into the town," he gestured towards the fierce-looking man at his side. "They took our packs and weapons, but I've got vital documents hidden in my boot that Admiral Hewitt's got to see as soon as possible."

I turned to a wide-eyed guard. "It's alright, soldier. I know him. He's a lieutenant in the Navy on special duties."

The soldier was about to nod his assent, when a thin-faced major and a group of battle-stained men came up with yet more prisoners. The major looked astonished and his tired grey eyes were angry. "What in the Devil's name is going on here?"

I attempted at a salute: "It's OK, Major. I know this man. We were in Naval Intelligence together. He's here on an undercover mission."

"Tell that to the birds. Can he prove it?"

"I'm on Admiral Hewitt's staff. I'm carrying top secret information for him." Danny bent down impatiently and drew some papers out of his boot. The major went to grab them but Danny held them out of his reach. "These are for Admiral Hewitt only. If you hold me up there'll be hell to pay."

"We've been through hell already. I've lost nearly half my company. I couldn't give a monkey's ass what hell the Admiral tries to raise."

I sensed an opportunity to escape further action for the day. "Put him in my custody, Major. I'll radio the *Moravia* and get verification on him."

The major, not wishing to lose status in front of his men, took his time before nodding to the guard. "OK. Let him go."

Danny's pal went to step forward as well, but another guard pushed him back with his rifle. The Italian knocked it away. The major drew his revolver in a flash.

"He's with me." Danny thrust himself between his pal and the weapon.

At that moment the major hated all Italians and especially those wearing Mussolini's uniforms. His revolver remained pointing at Danny's breast. "Who the fuck is he?"

"He's my contact. I'd never have got through without him."

"As far as I'm concerned he's just another greaseball. He's staying with his buddies."

"No way! He's staying with me... I've been through more with him in the past week than any pal I've ever had."

I stepped between them. "Take it easy, Danny. We'll get your pal out later. Let's get this information to the Admiral."

Danny squeezed the Italian's arm, "Don't worry. I'll be back soon."

The major lowered his gun and signalled the guards to move the prisoners towards a stone warehouse.

"Tell your Admiral this is disrespect for Don Calo. You will not win without us," Danny's pal called out as he was taken away.

I'd no idea what he was talking about, but pulled Danny away before he could reply. DUKWs – two-and-half-ton trucks, designed to both swim in water and roll on to land – were being used that morning for the first time. I looked at them approvingly as they doggedly battled to and fro, transporting troops and supplies through the flotsam of war. They offered a way of escaping further from the action. "Forget the radio. We'll take one of those back to the *Moravia*. That'll be the quickest way to get you to the Admiral."

The beaches were rapidly becoming ever more chaotic. From every conceivable direction came the moan of puttering engines, the sound of spinning wheels, the cursing of drivers and the shouts of NCOs, as jeeps and heavily loaded vehicles strained and sank hub-deep in soft sand. A confused mass of men swarmed aimlessly around, whilst huge dumps of artillery and ammunition, together with all types of supplies were sprawled along the shoreline, sitting targets for enemy air attack. We made our way through this bedlam to where a DUKW was approaching. It stopped in front of one the webbed causeways the engineers were struggling to lay. Most of the engineers were misfits and rejects from combat units, and they seemed little better than a rabble. They were arguing vehemently as the ramp of the DUKW lowered and a small group of officers stepped ashore, accompanied by the whirling newsreel cameras of two sergeants of the Signal Corps. An old guy with three stars on his helmet led the way. His shirt was perfectly tailored and form-fitting; a gleaming hand-tooled belt with a pair of ivory-handled colt revolvers was strapped around his trim waist. He carried a riding crop and was wearing pink whipcord riding breeches and highly polished riding boots, and had a pair of huge binoculars hanging from his neck. He surveyed the chaos in disbelief. He turned crimson with rage before yelling at the nearest Beachmaster:

"Get those yellow-bellied bastards working. Brave men are dying up ahead. The tanks and the guns have got to get through."

He'd hardly got the words out before a lone Messerschmitt 109 came screaming out of the sun, strafing the beach. The engineers scattered and dived for cover, as did most of the General's party. I threw myself down beside Danny and tried to bury myself in the sand, pulling my helmet over my head. I only peeped out when I thought the danger had passed. The old General nodded to the ashen-faced cameramen before walking, stiff-backed, towards the cowering engineers. "These causeways must be laid. We've got to take the airfields outside the town so we can get our own fighters here. I will only leave this beach as a conqueror, or a corpse." Shamed by this awesome display of courage, the men began to return to their tasks. The old guy motioned the cameramen to stop filming.

I pushed Danny forwards: "It's Patton. Tell him what you know."

Patton turned and was flabbergasted to see a lone Italian soldier approaching him. An aide, a well-fed major in an immaculately pressed uniform, drew his revolver as if to defend his general from some attempt at assassination.

Danny came to attention and saluted: "Lieutenant Crivello, US Navy, reporting General."

Patton stared at him in amazement: "I hope you've a damn good reason for wearing that fucking uniform, Lieutenant."

"I'm here on a special mission for Admiral Hewitt, gathering information to aid the invasion, General. You've got two German Divisions in front of you: the Hermann Goering and the 15th Panzer. The Italians are just holding you until they get here. The Krauts have got some of the new Mark VI Tigers. I've seen them – they're real monsters. They could drive you off the beaches before you establish a bridgehead."

Patton shook his head. "My boy, I've been aware of those facts for the past month. I've planned my campaign with that information in mind."

I guess Danny thought he'd been misheard or that the old fella was deaf. "I'm sorry sir, but did you understand? They have new Mark VI Tigers!"

At that moment a shell came screaming in from the west and landed twenty yards away, covering us all with sand.

"What sonsofbitches did that?"

Patton forgot Danny completely. He raised his binoculars and scoured the road to the left. I could make out a group of black painted Italian tanks attempting a counter-attack. They were light tanks, small, and out of date. There were just over a dozen of them.

"Holy cow! We've no goddamn artillery or tanks ashore. Even those ancient tin cans are capable of sweeping us back into the ocean." Patton turned to me and pointed to my radio: "If you can connect with your goddam Navy with that goddam thing, tell them to drop some shellfire on that road, for God's sake." He noticed Danny again and turned to the pink-faced major, brushing sand from his knees: "Get this young fella back to the *Moravia* on that DUKW, so he can have a bath and change out of that goddam uniform!"

The plump major, who looked as shit-scared as me, gratefully took Danny's arm. To my horror, my sanctuary on the *Moravia* was being snatched away. I couldn't believe my luck. I was about to protest, but caught Patton's eye and thought better of it, and nervously undid the straps of the heavy radio on my back. The Italian tanks advanced in line with gay pennants flying, almost as if on parade, Patton focused his binoculars as a platoon of Rangers moved to meet the attack.

"Our men are taking rocket launchers and hand grenades into the upper storeys of those houses that line the road. Looks like some are dragging blocks of TNT up on the roofs. That's what I like to see – use the enemy's own supplies against him."

My heart pounding fit to burst, as I radioed hastily calculated co-ordinates to the gunnery officer on the *Moravia*.

Patton fretted beside me: "Kill every one of those goddam bastards!"

The lightly armoured tanks continued their steady progress towards the houses. I was nearly crapping myself again as I called down my first salvo. It was short and landed in the sea lapping the road. The tanks were drenched with water but suffered no damage. Patton fumed. I became even more nervous, but adjusted the range. The head of the column had almost reached the houses when the great naval guns roared again. Their aim was too far left and only the rear two tanks were hit. One stopped; the other began to burn with black smoke rising from its turret. I was about to adjust the bearings again when Patton impatiently snatched the radio microphone from my hand.

"This is Patton speaking. Range correct. Adjust your aim one point five degrees east."

The leading tanks had entered the sanctuary of the buildings when the third salvo hit the middle of the line. It disappeared in a flash of fire and smoke. As the smoke cleared I could see a gap, where four tanks had been blown apart, blocking the road for the remaining vehicles behind. But the head of the column was now in the town, being blasted from all sides with grenades and rockets from the Rangers on the roofs. Patton yelled approvingly as a Ranger hurled down a block of TNT. There was an explosion and more black smoke. Another two tanks had been destroyed. A mortar platoon had disembarked from an LCI and was beginning to give support. They quickly found the range while the naval guns slowly dismantled the immobile tanks on the road. The Italians had been cut to pieces.

Patton was beside himself with pride and satisfaction. "It's always been my luck to be at the right place at the right time."

Though my own binoculars I could see leather-coated Italians climbing out of their burning tanks and running for safety. "Shall I order cease fire, General?"

"Hell no! Our object is to kill more of those bastards than they kill of us."

The bombardment continued until there was no movement under the black pall of smoke hanging above the road. Patton clapped me on the shoulder. "Well done, young fella. If you weren't in the Navy, I'd make a soldier of you." A company of the 16th Infantry Regiment was passing on their way to the front. "You go along with those men, Lieutenant. Give 'em all the support you can. Remember, you'll soon be meeting German Panzers and that'll be a different ball game altogether."

I could have howled at the injustice of it, but saluted and joined the column with heavy heart. We marched up the hill through the ruined town, avoiding dead Italian soldiers lying in the dust, whilst thin shabby people began to emerge from their cellars, staring at us questioningly with hollow eyes.

The leading Italian tank was still burning as I passed the town hall. The commander, in resplendent uniform, sat weeping on the steps.

Lt. Danny Crivello:

I'd had no time to shower or change and was still wearing the tattered Italian uniform as I stood in the State Room, while Vice Admiral Hewitt vigilantly studied the navigation chart. The guns were still booming intermittently above, violently rocking the giant battleship with the force of their mighty recoil. The Admiral was plump, grey-haired and had a double chin. They wobbled in appreciation as he read. He looked like a genial college professor enjoying a particularly good student essay.

"Apart from allowing that hoodlum, Luciano, to abscond – he should never have been let out in the first place – you've done an excellent job, Lieutenant. If this is genuine, which I am pretty sure it is, it'll be invaluable. It will shorten the war; here in Sicily at any rate. I will certainly recommend you for some sort of decoration. You've saved many lives." He pressed a bell on his desk and an executive officer entered. "See Lieutenant Crivello gets everything he needs: food, rest and the best quarters available." He smiled at me kindly. "Now if you'll excuse me, I have to get on with this invasion."

In spite of my tiredness, two things were gnawing at my gut. "May I ask a question, sir?"

The Admiral gave the slightest hint of irritation. "Certainly."

"Why was I led to believe we'd no knowledge of the strength of the German forces in Sicily? I allowed three men to be killed to ensure the information got through to you, but General Patton told me you knew it already. You'd known for weeks."

The Admiral's steely blue eyes now glinted with annoyance. "There are many things in this war that are not in the province of a lieutenant. We all have to accept somebody senior to ourselves has all the answers."

I was beginning to feel like a patsy. I tried to control my anger. "What will happen to Giuseppe Falco? He's been taken away with the Italian POWs. I could never have managed this without him, and he's the representative of Don Calo Vizzini. The meeting with Don Calo was the main objective of my mission."

"That mission was always questionable and it went up in smoke the moment Luciano defected. Besides, this so-called Don Calo is just a local hoodlum. We already had the information he gave you. Now we're ashore we've no further use of him."

"If you'll excuse me, I don't agree, sir." I was tired of being treated as green young kid. "I've seen the power and effectiveness of these people. Even without Luciano I'm sure we can use their help."

"Really?" The Admiral pondered whilst shuffling the papers in his hand "Very well. Get some rest, make out your report, and when things have stabilized, when the beach-head is secure, I'll give you my letter of authority for the prisoner's release. Perhaps I may have further use of those gentlemen and you."

❦❦❦

Lt Frank Dunford:

It was early afternoon when, alongside two battalions of the 16th Infantry, I joined Captain Sayre's parachute force defending the main approach road to Gela at Piano Lupo. From the high ground we occupied I could see the parched brown earth of the flat plain of Gela with its air-field to the west, but my attention focused northwards, up the road along which I presumed the dreaded Tigers would come. It was just within the range of the naval guns. I'd seen how easily they'd destroyed the light Italian tanks, but would they be as effective here, at their extreme range and against such heavily armoured monsters? On either side of the road, dense olive groves were carved out of the hills in terraces, each supported by a low drystone wall – difficult terrain for 60-ton tanks to manoeuvre in. They'd find it difficult to evade fire if I could give the Navy the exact range. Whilst the 16th dug in alongside the paratroopers to fight off any infantry attack, I worked out bearings and established radio contact with the cruiser *Boise* and the destroyer *Beatty*. When I'd double-checked everything and was satisfied I'd done all I could, I jumped into a foxhole alongside a friendly-looking sergeant.

"I thought that Africa was bad, but this place is really the pits." The sergeant handed me a tomato. His helmet was full of them. "Have some. It's all we've managed to find for chow. They quench the thirst too. Now I know why Italians have tomato sauce on their spaghetti – over there, to the east, there's fields and fields of them growing as far as you can see. Don't eat too many, though, some of the guys have got the shits already."

I sucked on the sweet juicy fruit as I looked towards the first line of hills, little more than half a mile away. The only movement was the tall grass moving in the light wind. I'd survived the morning. What would the afternoon bring? In spite all my efforts, I'd ended up in a life or death situation. I wasn't a hero. I felt inferior to these dog soldiers around me, who had marched uncomplaining towards death. Every time I thought of death I remembered George – and his mother. I'd received a letter from her in Oran, a letter like any mother would write to her son's best friend. Was she ashamed of what we'd done? I tried to feel contrite, but couldn't. Life was cheap and short and every second had to be lived to the uttermost. Any pleasure, any experience that was offered had to be savoured and enjoyed. But did I really care for anyone? Was I capable of love? I felt the warm crucifix at my throat and thought of Sue. Where was she? Working in some naval hospital, somewhere on the East Coast? Perhaps she was being fucked at this very moment by some convalescent captain or home-posted commander. Whoever the bastard was, I sure envied him. I thought of her mouth, the sweet wetness of her pussy. The little noises she made when I went to work with my tongue. To my surprise, my pecker was stiff.

There was a burst of gunfire to the right. It had begun. Grey-clad German infantry appeared from behind a stone wall. The troopers and GIs on that flank met them with a withering fire of rifles and carbines, together with the machine guns in the pillboxes. At almost the same time huge lumbering shapes began to rise out of the hills ahead. The Tigers were on their way. The Germans certainly knew their tactics – armour was most effective when infantry supported it. My stomach churned as the Tigers approached, throwing up clouds of dust, their tracks cutting deep into the dry Sicilian soil. The roar of their engines and the clank of metal on rock mingled into a terrifying sound. I wanted to call the naval guns and fire immediately, but the tanks were still well short of a clump of cypress trees I'd calculated as the limit of my range.

"It needs two to operate this. Can you load?"

To my consternation the sergeant had climbed out of the foxhole and was carefully aiming a bazooka at the leading tank. Every fibre of me wanted to refuse, to remain in what flimsy safety the foxhole provided, but reluctantly I found myself clambering out. Remembering the drill, I picked up a 38lb shell and gingerly slid it into the rear of the launcher. I made sure it was secured and then tapped the sergeant on the top of his helmet. There was a deafening blast. The sergeant's aim was good. The rocket struck the

Tiger on the front, just to the right of the machine gun, but bounced harmlessly off the thick steel.

"Shit!" The sergeant shook his head in frustration before rifle bullets kicked up the dust around us. We both dived back into the foxhole. He picked up his carbine and returned the fire of some German infantry, sheltering behind a group of large white boulders over to the left.

The first Tiger had arrived at the cypress trees. It was now time. I squatted in the foot of the foxhole and radioed the gunnery officer on the *Boise*. The gun crews were standing by; the guns already loaded and laid. I fearfully raised my head and looked over the edge of the dugout. I waited until the tank reached the second tree. My voice was hoarse as I ordered the *Boise* to fire. It seemed like eternity, but only a few seconds later a deluge of five-inch shells began to rain down on the approaching Tigers. Like great beasts trying to avoid the darts of puny hunters they tried to take evasive action, but slipped and slithered on the terraces. Some tried to drive through the olive groves, but the trees were so thickly planted even Tigers couldn't smash their way through. They seemed uncertain what to do; they veered left and right, vainly seeking a way forward. It was time for me to call in the extra guns of the *Beatty*. A moment later an even greater barrage began to explode around the tanks. The shells weren't enough to destroy them, but sure as hell they were inflicting damage. One Tiger turned, then another, in a moment they were all in retreat, like cowardly bullies, towards the safety of the far side of the hill. I forgot my fear. I followed them with my fire, lengthening the range. My buddy yelled in triumph as the German infantry, seeing the failure of the almighty Tigers, also began to withdraw.

The way to the beaches was still barred.

✤✤✤

USS *Moravia*
Ensign Danny Crivello:
I'd made out my report omitting any reference to the girl's
story. I had no proof the guy with the droopy eye was Luciano
and I didn't want to open another can of worms. I followed
the soldier's routine and shit, shaved and showered, before
lying on my bunk in an officer's cabin. I felt bitter and
betrayed. My superiors had known about the troop dispositions and the new Tigers, and hadn't felt fit to tell me. Why?
If I'd been captured, before I bit on my cyanide pill, I would
have tried my upmost to endure agony to prevent the enemy
knowing what I knew – but what I knew was of no import
since it was known already. I remembered Captain Sayre's
surprise when I'd told him the airborne troops would be
facing Tigers. It was obvious they'd also been kept in the
dark. Why? Why not disclose such vital information to your
own men? Were they scared the Airborne would refuse to
face such odds with their lack of heavy weapons? I thought
of Falco and my heart warmed. I felt closer to him and whatever cause he followed, than to these smart-assed officers,
for whom my death or survival was just another entry in the
ledger of war. Falco's war was plain and straightforward. I
could understand it, or at least most of it, even if it repelled
me. I could still see the dead eyes of the young Italian soldier, staring at me as if in accusation. But if I'd not shot him,
maybe we would never have discovered the navigation chart
and the location of the mines. Surely that was worthwhile?
Admiral Hewitt was right – it could save countless lives. A
decoration? Maybe Ma and Uncle Tony would be proud.

I dropped into an exhausted sleep, which even the thun-
dering guns above could not disturb.

❧❧❧

11 July, 1943
Piano Lupo
Lt Frank Dunford:

I'd spent a fearful, fitful night. It was nearly dawn and my turn to keep watch whilst Sergeant Blum slept. The hills in front remained black against the lightening sky. Behind them, I could hear the roar of the great motors, which I took to be the Tigers, deploying for the coming attack. I guessed their fitters had been busy with repairs. Occasionally, on the faint wind, I could hear orders barked in guttural German. I could even their smell their food. I'd had nothing but tomatoes. I longed for a hamburger with plenty of onions. A homemade hamburger, like mother made me on that last leave. When was it? Last October – nine months and two campaigns ago.

There was a crunch on the stony ground to my right, and Colonel Gorham crawled out of the night. He'd turned up the previous evening with thirty more paratroopers and taken command. His headquarters were in the central pill-box further up the hill behind.

"You guys OK?"

"Sure, Colonel." Sergeant Blum was awake immediately.

The Colonel's keen eyes and boyish smile were visible in the starlight. "Is this a private war or can anyone join in?"

Blum laughed. "Be our guest."

The Colonel's smile faded. "Keep a sharp look-out. Under no circumstances will anyone pull back. We've got to hold this position until enough of our own tanks and artillery get ashore. We're staying on this goddamn hill till Hell freezes over."

"You betcha!" Blum watched the Colonel crawl to the next foxhole then lit a cigarette, cupping the match with his hand to hide the light. "Did you ever read Shakespeare?"

I shook my head bemusedly.

"He's my favourite writer. I've read all his plays. It's part of my job – I teach English at Abraham Lincoln High School in Brooklyn." He inhaled reflectively. "The great thing about Shakespeare is that he understands everything. He'd seen it all – all those hundreds of years ago. He even understood us Jews. You should read the *Merchant of Venice*. That's a great one to start with. I've seen many Shylocks among the Jews in Brooklyn – but Shylock's not all bad, Shakespeare gives the old guy many reasons to act the way he does."

Blum broke off and gazed towards the hills. He cupped his cigarette in his hand and dragged on it, before declaiming softly in a rough but clear voice:

"From camp to camp, through the foul womb of night,
The hum of either army stilly sounds,
That the fix'd sentinels almost receive
The secret whispers of each other's watch.

That's from my favourite, *Henry V*. I've appreciated it even more since I joined the Army. The soldiers in it are no different than us. They're tired, screwed up, scared shitless of dying – but something makes 'em fight. Know what it is?"

Again I shook my head.

"Leadership. A good leader makes you fight: gives you a cause. Henry V goes round his army the night before the battle and sees how they're doing. Shakespeare has a nice way of putting it – *a little touch of Harry in the night*. That's what the Colonel's doing. *Upon his face there is no note how dread an army hath enrounded him."* He laughed, pleased with his comparison. "See what I mean? Old William S. knew it all."

Engines were revving up beyond the hill. We both looked in the direction of the sound, but still nothing came.

Blum bit into one of the few remaining tomatoes. "I can't wait to get back stateside. Get back to teaching and the kids. I really feel I can be a good teacher – I only taught for a few months before I was drafted. What did you do before the war?"

"I was already in the Navy. I was a cadet at Annapolis."

"Will you stay in when this is over?"

"I enlisted to get a free college education. I don't really know what I want to do."

"Are you married?"

"No."

"Have you got a girl?"

I rubbed the crucifix with my thumb. "There was one, but I let her go. I think now it's too late."

"You've got to get a girl; gives you stability. That's what my mother always said. I found one. A nice Jewish girl, just like my Ma. Wanna see her picture?"

He flipped open his pocket and handed me a well-worn photo of a homely-looking girl. "We got married just before we embarked last November; a real wedding under the *huppa*. Y'know what a *huppa* is?"

Yet again I shook my head.

"It's a canopy made of white silk or satin, under which we Jews take our vows. It's like a royal ceremony, and for that one-day the bride and groom are king and queen. Except all Jewish women are princesses every day of their lives. My princess is having our first baby any day now. I didn't waste any time."

I handed back the photo and envied him. Blum was happy and knew what he wanted from life. He was about to continue but I held up my hand. To the north a distant drone was coming from the dawn sky. The drone grew louder and then we saw them. I identified squadron after squadron of Dorniers, Junkers and Italian Caproni Ca-135s, on their way to pound the beaches and our ships at sea. This was it. The real counter-attack was about to begin.

This time the Germans put down a savage barrage from their deadly 88s before the tanks appeared. Blum and I huddled in the bottom of our puny foxhole, while all around us the very earth was blown to pieces. The bombardment lasted no more than twenty minutes but seemed an eternity. Blum's ears began to bleed; my eyes were smarting with the smoke. I pressed myself against Blum's back even though my pants were warm and wet where I'd pissed myself with fear. We could do nothing but lie there and endure. The shelling ceased at last.. We raised our heads from the earth and looked around at the other foxholes. Every face was white from the rock dust, with dark slits for eyes. Miraculously, there had been few casualties. Some men had been injured by shrapnel; the medics were taking the most badly hurt to the primitive medical station the Colonel had established in one of the pillboxes. The medics had barely got the last of the wounded inside, when the rumble of tank engines roared angrily behind the hills, and then the monsters were lumbering towards us again.

But the Germans had learnt from the bloody nose they'd suffered yesterday. Today, they sent the lighter Mark III and Mark IV Panzers against us. They were still terrifying opponents with accurate and powerful 75mm guns, and there were dozens of them. Some came the same way as yesterday but, as they were slightly smaller and more agile, they managed to manoeuvre across the terraces and through the olive groves. At the same time, more were attacking from the west, across the Plain of Gela.

I immediately called down the naval guns, using the same bearings and ranges as yesterday. Within seconds the Panzers were advancing through a torrent of shells. A few were hit but most came on – weaving, lurching, clambering relentlessly towards the outlying foxholes. Colonel Gorham left his command post and crawled across. "These Mark IVs have less armour on their backs. Let 'em roll over you and then give it to 'em with your bazooka up their ass. It should be lethal at that range."

Blum nodded as the Colonel crawled over to the fox-holes to our left.

The leading Tiger was little more than fifty yards away.

Blum shouldered his bazooka. "Fancy having another go?"

It was the last thing I wanted to do, but I found myself picking up our last shell.

We crouched together in the trembling earth as a Panzer drew ever nearer; its machine gun spitting fire. I was almost frozen with fear. For a moment a gigantic dark shape eclipsed the bright morning sun – the Panzer passed over us like an angel of death. It emitted black fumes like a flatulent beast, choking our lungs. But in an instant, the sun was shining again. We scrambled from the foxhole, ignoring the bullets and shells exploding all around. Blum immediately crouched with the bazooka on his shoulder. The Panzer was only a few yards away. I again slipped the shell into the breech and slapped the top of Blum's helmet, falling backward as it fired. Again Blum's aim was true. There was a blinding flash as the 4.5-inch shell pierced the armour on the Panzer's rear end and exploded inside. I could hear the screams of burning men as I scrambled frantically back to the safety of the foxhole. I glanced back and saw Blum lying face down in the dusty earth. He had a wound in the middle of his back – red blood mingling with dark sweat. Certain I was about to die, I forced myself to crawl back and feverishly pulled the big man into the hole. I laid him on his chest and applied an emergency dressing to the gaping wound, trying to staunch the flow of blood. I then took out the morphine from my first-aid pack and gave him all I had. He wasn't dead. His eyes flickered.

I returned my attention to the battle. The naval guns were still raining shells. Two Panzers had been put out of action and were belching black smoke. But I could see four more had broken through the outer defences and were lumbering up the hill towards the centre of our position. Then I saw Colonel Gorham crawl out of a dugout and make towards the back of the leading tank. He was alone but had a bazooka in his hands: he must have managed to load it himself. He crept from rock to rock, as if he were stalking a deer. Sometimes he disappeared in smoke and I was certain he'd been hit, but he reappeared, doggedly making his way across the baking hot hillside. He got within a few feet of his quarry, knelt and lifted the cumbersome weapon to his shoulder. He fired: hunter and hunted vanished in flames and smoke.

There were more explosions. The Panzers were coming under fire from an artillery unit that had just come ashore and was deploying along Route 115. The range was short and their howitzers inflicted heavy damage. The Panzers stopped dead in their tracks. They wavered, then turned, and were in retreat. I radioed new bearings and chased them with naval fire. Then all was quiet. The line had held, but it was certain the Germans would come again.

I knelt down beside Blum. His eyes were no longer flickering. Forgetting my fear for the briefest moment, I stood up and yelled: "For Chrissake, I need a medic here! A man is dying." I knelt down again and took him in my arms. I could feel his still beating heart. It wasn't right this man who loved life, who'd had so much to live for, should die. I yelled again. Still no one came. In desperation I emptied my revolver into the cordite laden air.

"OK. Hold your water. I'm coming."

A spotty-faced boy, no more than eighteen, crawled out of the smoke. His round glasses were covered in dust and splattered with blood. It was a miracle he could see at all. He did no more than give Blum a cursory glance. "There's nothing I can do. His lungs have been shot through. He's lost too much blood. We can't give him a transfusion here."

"You've got to do something. He's still alive. His wife's gonna have a baby."

The boy squeezed at an angry pustule on his cheek. "I'll give him some more morphine. At least he won't be in pain."

Blum's eyes opened. He recognised me and smiled: "Did we win?"

I nodded. I realised my cheeks were wet with tears.

His smile grew wider. "*Some must go off, so great a day as this is cheaply bought,* the old boy had a word for everything." Blum died within the hour.

I buried him at Piano Lupo alongside Colonel Gorman.

USS *Moravia*
Lt. Danny Crivello:
I'd spent the day trying to rest while above the naval gunners pounded the shore and fought off wave after wave of

enemy aircraft. The gunners' ears were deafened and their gun barrels scorching hot when darkness and comparative peace finally descended upon the Mediterranean. I was claustrophobic in the small cabin and desperate for fresh air. I put on a helmet and climbed up to the top deck. About a mile away an ammunition ship had taken a direct hit several hours before and was still burning brightly. I leant on the rail and watched flashes of fire erupting all along the shore and wondered if Captain Sayre and his paratroopers were still alive.

"It's been a helluva day." A major with clean-cut, rounded features and immaculate uniform had joined me. It was Patton's aide who'd accompanied me on board. "You're certainly looking more civilized than you did on the beach yesterday."

I nodded. In Africa I'd grown to despise staff officers, or ninety-day wonders, as the enlisted men called them. They usually came from families with the right connections, hoping to have either a comfortable war or one that would further their military careers. No stinking foxholes for them, but luxury hotels or palaces way behind the line, where headquarters were usually situated.

"We've taken heavy casualties. But the beachhead seems pretty secure." As if to explain the authenticity of his information he added: "I'm Major Powell by the way." He raised powerful binoculars to his eyes. "That Gela place is the pits. And the population! Did you see them? General Patton said Sicilians are the most destitute and god-forgotten people he'd ever seen." I was about to reply to this insult to my homeland, but the major continued: "I hear we certainly gave hell to those Tigers you were so worried about." He said this with a tone of admonition, as if reproving me for doubting the wisdom of a plan for which he'd personally been responsible. But I was no longer listening to him. I could hear a heavy drone in the sky behind. I turned and looked up apprehensively.

My companion laughed and looked at his watch. "Don't worry. That's Patton's reserve. Bang on time: 504th Paratroop Regiment. We've called them up from North Africa to reinforce the centre of the line. It should be quite a show."

The night was clear with a glorious moon, and we could see the flashing lights of the first wave of C-47s flying slowly overhead. The second wave had barely passed when some gunner, on a ship to our left, perhaps having fallen asleep at his post and being wakened by the noise of aircraft coming yet again, automatically let loose a few rounds of flak. Only a few rounds of tracer crossed the sky, like the fireworks I used to make as a kid, but it had the effect of a lighted match dropped into can of gasoline. Immediately, savage and devastating fire erupted from ships around us and the Army gunners all along the shore, all aiming at the slow-moving targets above. Coloured tracer crisscrossed again and again, as shells ripped through the fuselage of the Dakotas, like harpoons tearing at the bellies of clumsy whales.

Major Powell's expression had gone from complacency to horrified disbelief. "The crazy, stupid, brainless, idiots! For God's sake stop them! Stop them!" But his screams were engulfed in a deluge of sound and fury as the friendly fire took its fearful toll. We watched helplessly as the pilots attempted evasive action, trying to steer a course between the shells, scattering like chaff in the wind. Unfortunately, the naval gunners had had plenty of practice that day and plane after plane plunged into the sea. I could see paratroopers jumping from their blazing transports. Some parachutes caught fire as they jumped and fell like Roman candles into the sea. Others fell among the pitiless rocks on the Plain of Gela.

Major Powell was already covering his ample rear. "We informed all units. They knew the time and the route. They acknowledged. There was no possibility of a mistake. Somebody has screwed up in a big way."

I turned in disgust and went back to my cabin.

7

An Offer is Made

13 July, 1943
USS *Moravia*
Danny Crivello:

"Lieutenant, I've read your report and you've done well. I've also given consideration to your comments on the Mafia." The Admiral fussily tidied the papers on his desk. He looked at the dark-haired army captain, dressed in plain fatigues, who was standing under a signed photograph of Roosevelt that hung on the wall. "I passed them on to Captain Limo; one of the few people to know about the Luciano fiasco. It must remain top secret – even Patton doesn't know about it. It would be bad for morale back home if they thought the Navy had to stoop to seeking aid from a public enemy to win this war."

"But what will you do if he's seen? Or captured?

"Deny it's him and produce his body at Great Meadow, where he'll have suddenly died of a heart attack. We've injections that can simulate anything." The Captain had a hawk-like nose and his voice was high-pitched and nasal. "I've agents ready to bring the bastard in dead or alive as soon as we get up there."

I'd taken an instant dislike to the captain, but Admiral Hewitt broke in: "We needn't concern ourselves any more with Luciano now you've made contact with his Sicilian colleagues. Captain Limo and I have been discussing the situation." He smiled at me paternally, "I'm afraid I'm going to have to ask you to go back..."

Limo's nasal whine interjected. "Our problem is if we want to control this island we must have some sort of civil authority. We can't work with the Fascists – they're completely discredited; the Communists are definitely out. That leaves your friends. They helped Garibaldi the last time this place was invaded; at least they've been opposed to Mussolini..."

"But do they have the organization and any sense of moral duty? What is your honest opinion?" the Admiral enquired.

I looked at Limo uncertain how much I should disclose. The Admiral smiled apologetically. "Captain Limo is with the OSS – they have a more general view of the situation. How we intend to run Europe after the war..."

Limo broke in impatiently. "As soon as we liberate an area we're going to bring in AMGOT." I registered incomprehension. The captain smiled condescendingly: "Allied Military Government of Occupied Territories. Some of their people have landed already. Their job is to re-establish the political, economic and administrative machinery of this godforsaken place. To promote a temporary form of local government representative of the local people, free of Fascist influence, and ready to support the Allied war effort. It won't be easy. Sicilians have a long tradition of political indifference and have just had twenty years of Fascist bureaucracy."

Admiral Hewitt came to the point. "Do you really think these people you've met will be suitable?"

"I was brought up by my mother and uncle to think the Sicilian Mafia were nothing better than a brotherhood of criminals. Now I'm not so sure. They're not hoodlums and gangsters like Luciano. I've seen how close they are to the people. Could be, they're the only protection the Sicilians have ever had."

The Admiral nodded and rolled a yellow pencil with the tip of his index finger. "I'm inclined to agree, although many would say we're sullying the proud tradition of the US Navy by merely talking to them." He gave Limo a disparaging glance, as if regretting the pragmatic tasks he was being called upon to perform. He thought silently for a few moments before picking up a sheet of paper. "But we're in a nasty business, facing an even nastier enemy. Here is my letter of authority. Go and find this Falco guy; the prisoners are in the warehouses by the docks. We haven't got much time. I've somehow got to win this war and feed and govern the population at the same time."

Limo took over impatiently. "We've taken some airfields at last, and I've a small plane standing by at Ponte Olivio; a Lysander from the RAF. I've borrowed one from a colleague in British Intelligence. They're much more used to this sort of thing than we are. They've been dropping agents into occupied France for years."

The Admiral continued: "I want you to parachute into the country where this Don Calo is hanging out – where exactly is he by the way?"

"I've no idea. He's moving around, he's still a wanted man. Falco will know."

"Very well, you will both go back to him with my proposals tonight. Namely: does he want to work with us? If so, what are his terms? But remember, this is still top secret. I'll have to disown any knowledge of this if things go wrong."

I nodded. I'd expected nothing better. I knew now I was in a dirty game.

I saluted and turned to leave but Limo called me back. "By the way, Lieutenant, did you have anything to do with that operation in the fish market, when you were with that counter intelligence section in New York?"

"No sir. Why?"

"I thought we'd do the same thing here. Get the fishing boats organized to bring us information about the movements of enemy shipping, knowledge of the coasts of southern Italy – we may well be going there next. Besides, we've got to feed these people, and I'm told the mobsters ran the New York Fish Market very efficiently."

"Frank Dunford went there nearly every day."

The Admiral looked up quizzically: "Who?"

"Lieutenant Frank Dunford. He was in F Section but he was transferred to ship/shore gunnery. He's here in Sicily; I met him on the beach the other day."

The Admiral checked his papers. "He did quite a job at Piano Lupo: helped to destroy any number of Panzers. He's been recommended for a Bronze Star." The Admiral gave me one of his rare smiles: "He's here on the *Moravia*, in the sick bay. He needed urgent treatment. You'd better see him before you go."

I went below to the hospital deck and passed men with terrible wounds and burns. Some were nothing but huge swathes of bandages, some had had limbs amputated, some were in a drugged sleep; some groaned in pain, others were calling for mothers or sweethearts. I looked from one wrecked human being to another, pitiful remains of proud fighting men, but couldn't see Frank. A sour-faced orderly, bearing a noxious bedpan, came down the aisle between the beds. He looked at me questioningly.

"Can you help me, please? I'm looking for Lieutenant Dunford."

The orderly's face broke into a malicious grin. "Well, he's not in this ward. With what he's got we had to put him in isolation. He's at the end on the left."

I followed his directions with great foreboding. What terrible wounds had poor Frank suffered? I fearfully pulled aside a green curtain: a seemingly unscathed Frank was sitting up in bed reading a thick book.

"Where did they get you, pal?"

Frank looked up and sadly shook his head: "I survived three days with the Tigers, but came down with the most virulent dose of clap west of Suez."

I hitched a lift on a DUKW going ashore with ammunition, and half an hour later was walking through a sweltering warehouse, packed with thousands of forlorn-looking Italian prisoners. The air was fetid with stale sweat and urine. Some men looked up at me with soft, sad eyes, like penned cattle. But these men had been treated worse than cattle. Led for the most part by cowards, and given the oldest and most inefficient weapons and equipment with which to fight, they'd been sacrificed and betrayed.

"What unit was this Falco guy with?" The white-helmeted military policeman surveyed the heaving mass of humanity with distain.

"It wasn't a regular unit. He was with me; we were wearing old uniforms to get through enemy lines."

The MP gave a little sniff, as if smelling a false alibi. "What does he look like? These greasy spicks all look the same to me."

I was beginning to dislike him. "I know what you mean. Take me, for instance, my name's Crivello. I guess I'm pretty greasy too."

He sniffed again and walked on towards the far end of the warehouse, where a glass partition had served as a rudimentary office. I could see a few prisoners sitting around a small table within, enjoying some sort of comfort and privacy from the rest of the herd. One of the prisoners, despite his surroundings, had an air of authority about him. Falco looked up as I pushed open the door into the partitioned area.

"It's taken you a long time."

"I'm sorry, but there is a war going on, you know."

Falco nodded and looked at his companions who were regarding me suspiciously, and said by way of explanation: "We know. That's why we are beginning to organize things here."

"I will not go in that!" Falco looked at the small plane in abject terror. It stood in one of the few surviving hangars on Ponte Olivo airfield.

Even I was taken aback by its odd design. It had the appearance of a WW1 biplane with its wings supported by two pairs of sturdy struts and bulbous fixed landing gear. "It's the only way. We've not got time to go by road, even if we could get through."

The RAF pilot, a red-faced young man with handlebar moustache, looked on with amusement. "Don't worry about old Lizzie. She may look and fly like an old duck, but she can land anywhere, not that we'll be landing anywhere tonight." He patted the odd looking plane as if it were his MG Roadster. "They've cut a special hatch in the floor for you. They've also taken out the cannon so there's room for two in the back cockpit. By the way, the name's Stiles: Pilot Officer Raymond Stiles at your service. Where would you gentlemen like me to take you?" He had a large map of Sicily in his left hand.

I shook his right. "I'm Danny Crivello, US Navy, and this is my associate – just call him Falco. He doesn't speak

English anyway." I turned to Falco who was still staring at the flimsy aircraft and said in Italian: "You must show him on the map where you think Don Calo will be."

Falco's eyes filled with even greater terror. "There is no landing field there. No place even this little plane could land."

I steeled myself before saying very softly: "The plane will not be landing, but we will."

"What do you mean?"

"We're going to have to jump." I pointed at two parachutes lying nearby, together with a pile of rough-looking clothes.

"Jump?" Falco looked at the parachutes as if they were the most barbaric implements of torture. "A man does not jump from the sky. He is not a bird. It is not natural."

"It's no big deal. Jumping may not be natural, but there's nothing to it. I've done it many times. It's just like jumping off a ten-foot high wall."

"I get scared even on a wall. I will not do it."

"Have a shot of this. It's very good for the nerves. I always have a good swig on take-off." Stiles gave Falco a leather-bound brandy flask. Falco drank greedily. "Now ask him again to show me where he wants us to go."

Falco stared at the map miserably before pointing, with a grubby finger, to a mountainous area east of the small of town of Prizzi, about fifty miles due south of Palermo. "You will find Don Calo there."

"Wacko!" Stiles studied the map then looked at his watch. "May I suggest we wait until 22.00 hours to avoid the attention of the Luftwaffe? There's a heavy bombing raid planned tonight on the German units around Caltanissetta. It's just to the east of our flight path. They'll be too busy chasing Flying Fortresses to bother about us."

It was quite dark when, dressed once more in rough peasant clothes, we crouched beneath the back cockpit of the frail-looking Lysander. Stiles opened the hatch and I climbed aboard and then pulled in the reluctant Falco as Stiles pushed from behind. Falco was even bulkier with the parachute harness and it took both of us to get him inside. Though he'd finished all of Stiles's brandy, it had failed to ease his terror. The cockpit was designed for observation and had windows the entire length. Falco crouched cowering on the floor to avoid the view. "All right, chaps. Let's get this show on the road." Stiles shut the hatch and went forward to the front cockpit, as I sat down opposite Falco and smiled reassuringly. A minute later the single engine roared into life. Falco gave a canine howl of anguish, which continued as the propeller spun ever faster and the Lysander began to speed along the uneven runway. The darkness of the Sicilian night sped past the windows above us, and then we could feel the wheels leaving the ground as we started to climb. It was then that Falco involuntarily evacuated his bowels. He was past all shame and began to whimper softly.

"Everything all right back there, chaps?" Stiles's voice came through the radio headphones I was wearing. I wasn't sure if he was referring to the stench.

I clicked on my speaker, "Sure. He's going to be just fine."

"Whizzo! It should take us about thirty minutes to drop off, that is if Jerry behaves himself. Just get a bit of shut eye while you can."

I looked at Falco and tried to recognize the cool, resourceful companion who'd got me across Sicily and back again. Everyone had a particular terror. I wondered what was mine. "You come from Villalba?"

Falco nodded mournfully.

I was tempted to ask if he'd ever heard of Ciro Crivello, but thought it better to give nothing away. "What do you do there?" Falco looked at me uncomprehendingly. "What's your job?"

"I have no job. I refused to wear a black shirt. I am not a Fascist. If you are not a member of the Party there is no work."

I realized I knew nothing about him, apart from his closeness to Vizzini. "Why do you follow Don Calo?"

"I told you, I am his nephew. That is, among the younger men I am the one he considers the most promising. Besides, there was nothing else." Falco looked down at his large, hairy hands as if ruminating what other purpose they might have followed. "*Cosa Nostra* is our religion as much as the Church. It is a code of life. It demands humility with manliness. It has been our only protection since the days when the Spanish ruled here. The Spanish lords owned all the land and lived in luxury in Palermo or Madrid, whilst the estate managers, the *gabelloti*, worked the Sicilian people to death. When Garibaldi came in 1860, we fought for his cause of unification because he promised us land reform: land for the peasants who worked the soil. But it never came. We were even worse off. The big estates got even bigger. They even took away the common lands and we starved. Hundreds of thousands of us were driven across the seas to your country. The *Fratellanza* was the only justice we ever knew. It gave a man the right to avenge his own wrongs and not to trust fat lawyers or crooked policemen." Falco lifted himself with his hands so that his soiled behind was raised from the floor and leant back against the canvas fuselage. "The Fascists were no better than the Spanish, and the French, and all the others that came here to enslave us. It is time we Sicilians ruled ourselves – broke away from Italy.

We never gained anything from the union. A Sicilian would rather pay for protection to the *Fratellanza* than pay taxes to a corrupt official in Rome."

"Why pay for protection? My uncle is a Communist; the Fascists drove him from Sicily. He believes all men are equal, no one should pay others to protect them."

"The Communists are just as bad. Within a few years it would be the same, only we would be governed by corrupt officials in Moscow."

"My father organized a strike to get better conditions at the sulphur mines, the *Fratellanza* helped to break it. They were on the side of the owners then."

He shook his head dismissively. "That was before Mussolini. Now even the Church supports us. Don Calo's brother is a priest." Falco's dark eyes narrowed: "Why would your father organize a strike? I heard you tell Don Calo your father belonged to the *Fratellanza*?"

"He only joined when he got to America. He wanted money to get a good life for my mother and me. It was the only way he could find."

Falco shrugged. "So, you see?"

The small aircraft shook as anti-aircraft shells began to explode in the air around us. Stiles's reassuring voice came over the radio: "Sorry, chaps. It's the flak at Caltanissetta; I'm taking the kite higher and veering off a bit to the west. Don't know where your Flying Fortresses are – the blighters should've been around by now."

Falco's terror returned. "I am not afraid of being shot at on the ground. There I can take cover and take my chance, use my cunning and strength. But here, I am just floating in this flimsy little machine waiting for a shell to explode up my arse."

I strove to divert him: "Are you married?"

"No."

"Have you a girl?"

"There is one. But she is not ready. Have you?"

I shook my head. I could feel my cheeks blush.

"I see American movies. All you Americans have plenty of women. I like this – what is her name – Betty Grable. I like the blondes, but not of course to marry." Falco stiffened as another shell exploded nearby. "Why do you have no girl?"

I wondered myself. I'd watched the other guys collecting their mail, showing their photos, boasting of the steamy sex they'd had and their plans for the future. But I received no letters apart from a few from my mother. I recalled Uncle Tony's words that morning aboard the *Normandie*. I hoped I wouldn't die a virgin. "I guess I've not met the right girl." I changed the subject. "You told me Don Calo was betrayed. Do you know who betrayed him?"

Falco's face became hard. "I will find out when I get back to Villalba."

Villalba contained so many secrets.

Stiles's voice came through again: "We're back on course. In France we land in the fields and drop chaps like you off in comfort. The Resistance mark out runways for us with flares and we take away out-going passengers, or sometimes a couple of crates of brandy, sometimes both. We even land in clearings in the forest, but this place is far too rough and rocky. Besides, the mountains are in the way. I'm going to drop you off at about two thousand feet. Is that all right with you?" I decided not to translate this for Falco, but Smiled at him instead. Stiles drawled on as if he were discussing his sports car. "The great thing about the Lysander is that it can fly so slowly. The wings bend slightly, a bit like the wing of a seagull. They're thickest at mid-span but shrink by nearly half at the wing roots. It's got trailing edge slats and leading edge slats."

I put the speaker to my lips, grateful to distract my mind from what lay ahead. "What do you mean?"

"It means I can drop my speed to little more than fifty miles an hour and still stay airborne. It gives it great manoeuvrability and will be much more comfortable for you when you jump."

Falco had been watching like an old dog awaiting his master's decision to be put down. I spoke to him firmly as if addressing a child. "We'll go in about ten minutes. I will open the hatch in the floor and then you drop out." I lifted the ripcord on my own chute. "Once you are out count five slowly and then pull this. The chute will open at once and it will bring you down gently. When you see the earth approaching brace yourself, as I told you, with your feet clamped together, as if you were jumping off a ten-foot wall. When you touch the ground, roll over. I will be coming right behind."

"What if it doesn't open?"

"Don't worry, it will. But you have a back-up chute here." I patted the bundle on Falco's heaving breast. "There's another ripcord there, see? This red one." Falco examined it suspiciously and nodded. "But don't pull it unless you are absolutely sure the first is not going to open."

"I won't be sure until I hit the ground. Why can't I pull both cords at once to be sure?"

"You'd probably turn upside down. You'd be blown all over the place and you wouldn't come down for hours. Trust me. You'll be OK. I'm going to need you down there."

"I reckon this is as about a close as we'll get." Stiles's voice crackled cheerfully in my ears. "We'll have a couple of large G & Ts together when you get back. Tell you the honest truth, I could manage a large one very easily just now. Got to be very careful, there's lots of bloody mountains round here."

"Thanks." I took off the headphones and crawled over to the hatch and began to unlatch the clasps, Falco watched in horror. I reached out and took his hand. "Don't worry. I will see you down there in a couple of minutes. I will light a flare as soon as I land so you will know where I am." I opened the hatch. At that altitude, even at fifty miles an hour, the full force of the wind rose up and hit me like a blow. Mysterious shadowy shapes of land were passing beneath. Falco had backed away on his knees, but I grabbed his wrist and pulled him towards the dark void. "Come on, Falco. You are the bravest man I know."

Falco looked at me, with his dark terrified eyes, as if for the last time, then kissed me passionately on the lips. "I loved you as a brother." He dropped out into the emptiness with a terrified scream.

I followed immediately. I watched the flat shadows below becoming closer and closer, until I landed with a breath-taking wallop. I lay for a moment before easing myself up. I felt feverishly for the quick-release box, and scrambled out of the harness. To my relief, Falco's grounded chute was wafting in the wind a few yards away. I hurried over and released him. We had landed in a dry naked field, and we buried our chutes among the dark shapes of small poppies that had sprung up in the stalks of the recently reaped wheat. Falco's courage and resourcefulness returned with his feet on terra firma. He soon found a poverty-stricken farm, where a peasant provided him with a clean but ragged pair of trousers, an emaciated horse and cart, and the location of Calo's latest hideout.

Two hours later, just after dawn, we found the Don sitting in an old chair outside a grey stone shack, fondling the soft ears of his dog, gazing over empty brown mountain ranges that seemed to stretch to infinity. Before I could speak, he wiped his greasy moustache with the back of his hand and nodded as if he had been expecting us.

"Salvatore!" He leant over his great belly and shouted into open door of the shack:

"Hi kid. How ya doing?" Luciano came out of the darkness.

I couldn't believe my eyes. He'd managed to acquire some slightly smarter clothes. His stubble had become a thick black beard which, unlike his hair, showed no trace of grey. He smiled making his teeth seem whiter:

"Where the hell did you go? You're down to be shot for desertion."

"I couldn't face another fuckin' boat trip and I got pissed off with being bossed around by a smart-assed kid. Besides, I wanted to check that your fuckin' invasion was going to work before I stuck my neck out. I went down to Gela and saw that the entire caboodle had started. Things were too hot there, so I reverted to my original plan. Used some of that government cash you gave me, to persuade a guy to get me to Palermo in his car. I wanted to case the joint, and meet up with a few old friends." He shot a glance at Calo, "I've got a hell of respect up there. Let me tell you, the city is wide open. All the fuckin' Krauts have gone. They're grouping around Etna waiting for the British."

I turned to Calo, "Is that true?"

The fat man nodded enigmatically.

Luciano was more assured than I'd ever seen him: "The Don and me are pals now. I've convinced him I ain't intending to muscle in on his territory. I'm a city boy and I hate being out in the sticks. But I know cities, and Palermo is a huge city and it's there for the taking. Tell the Admiral to stop fartin' around and make for Palermo at once, tout suite. He'll have a smacking great victory served up on a plate."

"My friends will guide you through the minefields and show you the safest routes." Calo seemed anxious to reassert his supremacy. "They will also point out the traitors."

I stared into his calculating eyes. "I have learned in Sicily nothing comes for nothing. If this succeeds it will help Luciano gain his freedom. What is in it for you?"

"Make me mayor of Villalba. Make my friends mayors of all the towns here in the north. They have been jailed under the Fascists and will be completely loyal. We have contacts throughout the rest of Italy. When you invade the mainland, we will counterbalance the Communists. The people are near starvation, the Germans have taken everything, you Americans will have to feed them. Let us administer whatever aid you give."

I was forced to smile: "Do you have friends aboard the Admiral's ship? Those were the exact terms I have been ordered to offer you."

"Then waste no time. Go back and tell him I accept."

"How will I find you again?"

"Go to Villalba. My brother, Salvatore, is the priest there. He will bring you to me."

8

ON TO PALERMO

July 16, 1943
Lt. Danny Crivello:

Villalba, the town where my father spent those final weeks in Sicily; where something happened that changed him for ever. What secrets could it hold? It seemed as if fate was leading me relentlessly towards solving the mystery, but I forced myself to concentrate solely on my mission. My duty as a US officer came foremost. I had no radio with me. It would have been a fatal give-away if we'd been stopped, and Don Calo's response to the Admiral's proposals had not been considered urgent in the current situation. I therefore decided to go straight to Patton at Agrigento – he was closer, only thirty-odd miles away, and I figured the information about Palermo was more pertinent to him. If the way was indeed clear, he'd have to move as soon as possible. I left well before dawn, with a guide and bicycle provided by Don Calo, and reached my destination six hot hours later. I'd been issued with fresh security passes, but still had great difficulty being admitted into 7th Army HQ, where I was finally ushered into the office of Major Powell.

The Major sniffed in disapproval at my Sicilian attire, "I wouldn't advise you to see the General today, especially dressed like that. He's having one of his headaches. The red mist, as he calls it, has descended. The old boy played too many games of polo, had too many falls, and was concussed too many times. It affects his temper. He's fretting that Alexander is giving precedence to Montgomery's Eighth Army, and has relegated the Americans to guarding the flank."

"But I have vital information for him on that score."

Powell sighed and eased his fat ass out of his chair: "Very well. On your own head be it. I'll take you to him."

We found Patton standing on the esplanade of Agrigento, gazing through his large binoculars at what appeared to be distant ruins.

Major Powell gave a polite cough.

The General continued to focus his binoculars: "The Valley of the Temples. Isn't it a magnificent sight? The ruins of the Greek city of Akragas, described by the poet Pindar as the fairest city inhabited by mortals. Greek, Carthaginian, Roman and Arab have all worshipped in those golden temples. We've taken them intact and 6,000 Italian prisoners, with hardly a casualty." He swept his glasses to the east. "But over there at Catania, that little bastard Monty has got the bear by the tail. He attacked with a whole Division yesterday and only made 400 yards – he's stuck. It's back to the trenches of the Great War. This army is not being put to its best use. I should be over there, hitting the Krauts with a flank attack."

Major Powell coughed again. "Beg pardon, General, but Lieutenant Crivello insists on seeing you."

The General took the glasses from his eyes. It took him a moment to recognise me. "A few days ago, I told you to have a bath and get into your uniform. You look even worse today."

"I'm sorry, General. I've been on another mission for Admiral Hewitt. I have important information for you."

He exchanged a quizzical look with Major Powell. "Make your report, Lieutenant."

I decided to omit all reference to Luciano. "I've been in contact with Don Calo Vizzini, the leader of the Sicilian Mafia. He says there's nothing between you and Palermo. I've just come down from the area around Prizzi, and didn't see anything but the odd Italian tank and small groups of demoralised troops. I barely saw an officer. As far as Palermo goes – it's there for the taking. The Germans have moved out, and gone east to fight the British."

Patton whistled. "If Palermo falls, Mussolini falls with it and Italy will be out of the war."

"The Mafia want to help us," I continued. "They say they'll provide guides – mark out booby traps and mine-fields, and persuade any Italians who still feel like fighting to surrender."

The General sucked his lower lip. "If it were true, we would be the first Allied army to liberate a European capital. Palermo isn't Paris, Rome or even Brussels, but it's a name that will resound around the world." He contemplated further. "It would also prevent Monty and the damn British taking all the glory. But can we do a deal with mobsters? What sort of men are they?"

"They've their own code of honour," I replied. "I think they're men who'll keep their word."

"If we go north, we will be moving further away from Montgomery, unable to offer any assistance when he comes up against Kesselring's defensive lines around Etna," Powell protested. "Surely our objective is to take Messina and cut off the Germans? Prevent them from retreating onto mainland Italy."

"But Palermo is on the north coast. We could take it, then advance swiftly eastwards, and take Messina behind the Germans' backs." Patton rubbed his hands eagerly, like a young boy about to go on a treat. "It would also demonstrate the full capabilities of swift armoured warfare to the American public."

Powell was still unconvinced. "Surely we should consult with General Montgomery?"

Patton silenced him with a furious glance. "My mind is made up. Monty can go fuck himself: I'll fly to Tunis tomorrow and have a showdown with Alexander. I will lead the Seventh Army north and cut the island in two."

⚜⚜⚜

Lt. Frank Dunford:

I felt soiled – unclean. What decent girl would want me now? I was recovering from my morning treatment, which had involved a small shiny metal instrument being inserted in the eye of my pecker by a sadistic orderly, who then opened it like an umbrella, before scraping out the remains of the pus I'd picked up in Algiers. The doctor had told me that tomorrow's scrape would be the last. The prospect frightened me almost as much as the Tigers at Piano Lupo. Whenever I thought of Piano Lupo, I thought of Sergeant Blum. I reached over to my bedside table and picked up the complete works of Shakespeare I'd requested from the ship's library, and flicked through the pages until I came to *Henry V.* I'd read it several times during the past few days. I found I was stirred by the resounding language and could begin to sense the beauty of the poetry, but it was distressing to read so many references to the pox. I'd learnt from the notes at the bottom of the page that it had reached epidemic levels in Shakespeare's London. 'The Malady of France' they called it, and in the play Mistress Quickly even dies of it. I hoped the M&B pills and the agonising treatment I'd suffered would prove more satisfactory.

"Lieutenant Dunford?" I looked up from the book and saw a hard-faced army captain at the foot of my bed.

"Yes, sir?"

"Captain Limo, of the OSS; you've heard of us?"

I nodded.

"May I have a word?" He didn't wait for a reply but sat in the chair by the bed. "I don't think we'll be disturbed here in the isolation wing." He smiled cruelly. "How's the treatment going by the way?"

I felt nothing but abject humiliation. "The doctor says I should be fine in a couple more days."

"Good." The cold smile remained. "You'd better stay out of those places in future. I heard you went inside the black hole of Calcutta." He made an unsuccessful attempt to suppress a sneer.

I tried to ignore it. "Why do you want to see me, Captain?"

"You've proved yourself a competent gunnery officer, but now we've got tanks and artillery ashore, there's not much more for you to do, at least not until we move on. I'm told you organized intelligence in the fish market in New York?"

The mere mention of the fish market put me into denial. "I didn't organize anything. I just took the subway there each morning, and collected any information that might have come in."

"Nevertheless, you're familiar with the procedure, which is more than anyone else I have in my team. As soon as you're fit, the Admiral wants you to get to grips with the fishermen at Gela. You speak Italian, I gather?"

I nodded thoughtfully. Fish suddenly didn't seem so bad. At least I would be out of harm's way.

"Good. The Admiral has issued special orders. My office is on the waterfront, at the end of the breakwater. Report there immediately you're discharged."

⚜⚜⚜

Lt. Danny Crivello:

I related the information again to General Truscott, as Patton spread the map across the table, holding it in place with his glass.

"Bradley will go due north with his division and head for the sea. You'll advance north-west to Palermo and beyond. We'll cut Sicily in two."

Truscott, a white silk scarf around his neck, bent his dark head over the map.

"How on earth will you persuade Alexander?" He enquired in a gravelly voice.

"The only way to start something is to start, so I'll give him the 'rock soup' treatment."

"What do you mean?"

Patton lit his pipe. "It's an old story my father told me. A tramp once went to a house and asked the lady for some boiling water to make rock soup. The lady was intrigued, so she gave him the water, which he poured over two polished stones in the bottom of his pot. He then asked if he might have some potatoes and carrots to flavour the soup a little, and after she had given them to him, he finally asked for some meat to give it some substance."

Truscott chuckled and traced a line on the map with his forefinger. "But it makes more sense for us to advance here, north of Etna. We can fight and hold the Germans there, and then the British, when they eventually take Catania, can move on Messina through the corridor east of the mountains by the sea."

Patton's smile had gone. "Continuous attack is superior to Monty's system of stop, build up, and start again. Death in war is incidental; loss of time is criminal. The essence of this campaign is speed. You should be in Palermo within ten days. It's going to be a cakewalk."

Truscott frowned. "It won't be that easy. I've sent out reconnaissance patrols; they tell me a few Italian tanks are still active, and I see from aerial photography there's a concentration of Italian troops about thirty miles from here, around Santo Stefano. Besides, it's difficult country: mountains all the way – some above 4,000 feet, and the roads, if you can call them roads, are full of hairpin bends, ideal for ambushes. We've got aerial photographs of bridges over high gorges just asking to be demolished. If they want to resist they could slow us down no end."

"Don't worry about resistance; this young man assures me we've got new allies among the Sicilians who will make things easy for us. Once I get the go ahead from Alexander, you won't stop until you get to the outskirts of Palermo."

The following morning, an hour from dawn, I swung gently from my parachute as the moon-bathed Sicilian landscape came slowly up to meet me once more. Admiral Hewitt, with Captain Limo's enthusiastic approval, had agreed to give Don Calo his complete support and backing, and had promised food supplies would follow behind the troops as closely as possible. I was to be the Admiral's special representative until more senior figures arrived. I had also informed the Admiral of Luciano's return: my orders were to give him a free rein whilst he proved useful; if he transgressed again I was to shoot him, or hand him over to the first Military Police I encountered. A south-west wind was wafting me off course. To my left, I could see a white-walled, hilltop town, dominated by a huge turreted castle, like something out of a fairy tale. I remembered from my briefing, that the ancient fortress of Mussomeli lay ten miles south-west of Villalba. I stiffened in my harness as a searchlight flared up from the castle battlements and began to sweep the sky. Small batteries of anti-aircraft guns, stationed in the amphitheatre of the surrounding hills opened fire in response to the light, but they aimed far away and I dropped unseen into a rock-strewn plateau. I covered my chute with stones, checked my bearings from the stars, and began to walk north-east in the direction of Villalba.

The night sky had lightened into dawn when I came to a rugged pass, on each side of which huge lowering rocks stuck out like jagged teeth. As I made my way through the dark rocks, I spied an unexpected a flash of colour. Someone had laid a posy of wild flowers in a dim cavity, like some sort of pagan offering. As I reached in for the flowers I heard a jingle of bells, and through the half-light white forms began to appear on the hills around. I then heard another sound, like the rattle of pebbles being thrown up at the wheels of a car. I sensed someone was watching me. I turned my head and saw a shepherd lad sitting on a rock. He was thin and pale, with large protruding ears. He was holding a pile of small stones, which he was throwing at a tin can set on a rock above him. I nodded a greeting but the boy didn't respond.

I tried again: "What are you doing?"

"I am throwing stones at my can, to try to knock it down. It passes the time. You speak with a strange voice. You do not come from here?"

"I came from here once. Now, I come from America."

"I have heard of such a place, but don't know where it is."

I smiled again. "How far am I from Villalba?"

"That is a very big town and is very far away. You will have to walk in that direction for two hours or more." He pointed to the reddening eastern sky. "Would you like some milk? It will give you strength for the journey." Before I could reply the boy jumped from his rock and knelt beside the nearest ewe. He groped amongst the dirty wool of her belly and began to squeeze milk from her teat into his battered can. I'd never tried sheep's milk and had no desire for it now, but the lad was so eager to please I couldn't refuse him. The boy talked continually he milked. "If you squeeze too tight they stiffen and nothing comes out. My father says women are the same. I love sheep and my sheep love me. I watch them, follow them, and pick berries for them to eat from the branches they cannot reach. I help them when they drop their lambs – I make the hole bigger with my hands when they cannot come out. They never forget it and are always grateful. This one is a *pecore* – she had her first lamb this year."

The can was now full of warm white liquid. I took it and gulped it down. I was surprised how good it tasted. I reached into my pocket before remembering it was empty, and wished I'd risked bringing a Hershey bar.

"I am afraid I've nothing to give you in return."

"Why should you? My sheep have plenty of milk."

I handed him his can and tapped my thanks on his shoulder. I turned back as I made my way down towards the valley: the boy was still watching me.

Morning broke: the soil became more fertile; small red poppies and the aquamarine of thistle covered the black earth. Swallows swept the skies, seeking the first flies of the day. I passed small farms with dilapidated pantiled roofs, surrounded by olive groves and the stubble of wheat fields. I walked on until, set in a fold of the hills, I could see a clock on a church tower in the middle of a small town. It little more than a village; a poor-looking place. It had to be Villalba. Mussolini's carabinieri were still in nominal control. Their flag was flying from the barracks just beyond the church. They would question the identity of any stranger.

I entered the town, with pounding heart, and made my way down Corso Dante, a street descending a steep hill towards the one and only square. The stone houses on both sides were built on steps and reeked of poverty and neglect. The only trace of colour came from a few wilted hollyhocks that had rooted themselves in the angles of walls. Dust was everywhere. Scrawny chickens, their tails void of feathers and pecked red raw, scuffled amongst the refuse piled up outside each dwelling. It was already hot and the stench of the sewers made me glad I'd not had breakfast. Some doors were open and old men sat on their thresholds, staring at me with cold, questioning eyes. Others looked down from rusty iron balconies. I couldn't see any women, only old, suspicious men, who seemed to be guarding a secret they would never disclose. It was a sad, unwelcoming town. What could my father have been doing here?

I reached the square. The church, the only substantial building, was on the east side, next to a pile of rubble. On the other side of the square were two run-down cafés. Sitting smoking at a table outside one of them I could make out the dark blue uniform and red-plumed Napoleon-style hat of a Maresciallo of the Carabinieri. A girl came out and served him what looked like a cup of coffee. She was pretty. He began to engage her in conversation. She went to move away, but he grabbed her arm and pulled her towards him. I decided to take my chance while he was distracted. I looked toward the dark door of the church. I prayed it would be unlocked. Once inside, I'd find sanctuary and hopefully Vizzini's brother. Once I'd made contact I'd be safe. I felt eyes watching me as I stepped onto the bright sunlit square and quickly crossed to the church. The door was carved in a pattern of roses and leaves. I put my hand on it and pushed: it swung open to reveal a cool interior. I entered thankfully. Inside, in contrast with the stark poverty of the town, all was lavish decoration. The walls and ceiling were covered with finely painted pictures of prophets and saints. Gold leaf adorned the interior of the dome above the altar; the floor was laid in intricate patterns of black and white marble, but I had little sense of God's presence. In spite of the heat outside, the stones smelt damp as if exuding cold sweat. I looked around: two black-clad women were chanting at their rosaries, there was no sign of a priest. A shrine to the Virgin was to the left of the altar, and beside it was an elaborately carved confessional. I made towards it, drew the heavy black curtain aside and sank gratefully into the worn seat.

"You have a confession, my son?"

Through the screen was a heavy, shadowy form. "I seek the brother of Don Calo Vizzini."

There was stiffening behind the screen. "Why do you seek him?"

"I wish to speak with him. I have returned with a message."

"My son, you have sinned, but God with his infinite mercy will forgive you. Follow me and do not speak another word."

Sunlight flashed on the other side of the screen as the curtain was pushed aside. I got up and followed a burly, black-robed figure to a door on the right of the altar and then down steps to a musty cellar. It was only then that the priest turned and revealed his face. It was Don Calo's face, slightly younger and a little thinner, with a mouth like a slit, which looked as if it would never smile.

"Wait here. I will bring you food. I will send word to my brother."

Father Salvatore Vizzini returned within the hour. I followed him back up the stairs to a door at the back of the church, where a horse and cart were waiting. A familiar figure was at the reins. Falco gestured to a tarpaulin that half-covered a pile of straw.

"Get under there. The carabinieri are watching. Don Calo will seal his treaty with you tonight."

MY SICILIAN CAMPAIGN by General George S. Patton Jr:

I was up at first light to watch the beginning of the advance. One of Truscott's crack units, Lt Colonel Doleman's 3rd Battalion, 15th Infantry, were in the van: their first objective the Italian garrison at Santo Stefano. On the outskirts of Agrigento, Doleman encountered a motley collection of armed Sicilians, led by a dark-bearded peasant. He informed Doleman in English that the best way into Santo Stefano, avoiding the strong points and remaining artillery, was a fifty-four mile march over the mountains. The Sicilians were shepherds and knew the swiftest, safest trails. The bearded man said they could get us there in thirty hours. Doleman accepted his offer. Each section was assigned a guide and the march began. The mules, which General Truscott had insisted on bringing, followed with the ammunition and supplies. It was almost like the Wild West.

By mid-morning the armour was pushing along the main road, meeting little resistance. The Italian tanks were no match for my Shermans, so I decided to cut back across country and see how the infantry and the mules were progressing. The four-wheel drive of my jeep and the skill of my Negro driver, Master Sergeant John Mims, negotiated the mountain trails with little difficulty. I soon caught up with the column and made my way along it, encouraging, reprimanding and occasionally blaspheming. I was much impressed by the speed of Truscott's infantry. He'd been training them to march as fast as the ancient Roman legions or the foot cavalry of Stonewall Jackson in the Civil War – moving the marching rate up to five miles an hour from the standard two and a half. The troops had even given it a name: 'Truscott's Trot.' They were indeed marching cavalry. A few months ago these men had been rabble, now, thanks to leadership and training, they had been transformed into warriors. The line stretched up over the mountain in front of me, ant-like files of advancing troops.

I have an instinctive genius in understanding my men. By looking in their faces as I passed, I knew how much they could do and how much they could take. I stood up, held onto the windscreen for support, and shouted: "Now, I want you all to remember that no sonofabitch ever won a war by dying for his country; he won it by making the *other* dumb sonofabitch die for *his* country." The men within earshot cheered. I felt like Caesar leading his legions across the Rubicon. But then I noticed the line was slowing down; for some reason the soldiers at the front of the column had come to a halt. I couldn't understand why. Sergeant Mims stepped on the gas and we sped past stationary infantry until we came to a narrow stone bridge over a fast-flowing river, running down from the mountain. In the middle of the bridge was an ammunition cart. In the traces, stubbornly ignoring the urging of his driver, a mule stood with its four damn feet firmly planted on the bridge. It looked as if it would stay there till Hell froze over.

I told Mims to stop and stormed onto the bridge towards the offending beast. The mule's driver turned and gave me a weak smile. I saw red and drew one of my ivory-handled pistols and shot the mule between the eyes. The animal gave me a look of shocked surprise and collapsed in a heap. There was a murmur of unease from the watching men. I turned and glared defiantly: "Cut this beast loose and throw it in the river. No fucking mule is going to stop me getting at Mussolini and that paper-hanging, sonofabitch, Hitler."

Someone shouted "Good old Blood and Guts!"

The tension broke. A cheer spread down the line. The advance surged forward again.

Lt. Danny Crivello:

I'd fallen asleep but woke when the motion of the cart stopped. Sunlight shone into my eyes. Falco's face glowered down from behind the tarpaulin.

"The woman will take care of you. I have other things to do."

Falco had gone before my feet touched the earth. We were high up in the mountains outside yet another lonely farm. Calo's sad-looking woman was waiting by the door. I nodded a greeting but she gave no sign of recognition. She led me to a simple room under the pantiles. She left without speaking and I sat down on yet another flea infested bed. After a few minutes the stairs creaked, and a girl came up with a bowl of water, bread and some hard cheese. She was the most beautiful girl I'd ever seen. Her hair was as dark and shiny as a raven's feathers; she had huge soft brown eyes under thick lustrous lashes, and firm breasts that were almost bursting from her simple black dress. I smiled my thanks but her eyes remained fixed on the floor. She also left without saying a word, though the smell of her body lingered. I remained in the room throughout the rest of the afternoon, sometimes catching sight of her as I watched from the small dormer window. Women were preparing food and carrying it into a large stone barn at the back of the farm. The girl moved among them with a grace that set her apart. Once she lifted her eyes towards me as if aware of my watching. Our eyes met for an instant then quickly looked away, as if each felt we'd been found out by the other.

As dusk descended, men began to arrive on bicycle and horseback: hard-faced men, who did not greet each other, but went silently into the barn. Some had their hair cropped short and bore the pallor of recent incarceration. Many had *lupare* – sawn-down shotguns – slung from their shoulders. One man carried a *zampogna* – a form of bagpipe made from a sheep's bladder; others carried guitars, mandolins and even a tambourine. Some were dressed like peasants, but others, mostly those that came on horseback, were smartly dressed, defying the heat in well-cut velvet hunting jackets, corduroy trousers tucked into highly polished riding boots, and with fedora hats pulled down over their eyes. I could see no sign of the women or the girl. Night had fallen when a car, without headlamps, came slowly up the pass. As it drew nearer I recognised the ancient Fiat. It drew up at the farm and Falco got out. He checked all was clear, then opened the rear door. Don Calo heaved himself out, followed by his dog and his brother, the priest. There was no sign of Luciano. They spoke for a moment and then the two brothers and the dog went into the barn. Falco came towards the house. A moment later he joined me in the little room. He avoided my eyes.

"Come with me. They are ready."

I followed him down the stairs and across to the barn, from which traditional music was drifting into the warm night air. Falco pushed open the big door to reveal tables, lit by wax candles and laden with food, arranged into the shape of a large U. At the top table sat Don Calo, his brother, and two of the better-dressed men. There were two empty seats at either end. Falco indicated that I should take one while he took the other. Once we had sat down the men began to eat. Nothing was said. I looked for the girl, but there were no women to serve the food: huge bowls of pasta of every conceivable variety, flavoured with ricotta cheese, fried eggplant, meatballs and pork; together with – despite the distance from the sea and the inaccessibility of the location – huge dishes of mussels, clams, octopus, prawns, sliced tuna, cuttlefish, fresh sardines and anchovies. It was hard to believe that people were starving in Palermo and Catania. The guests drank copiously from the huge earthenware jugs of strong dark wine that seemed to stand by every elbow. The musicians struck up a melancholy tune as an old man sang:

"*I spent my youth in a cell; I know a hundred jails,*
But I am resolute and will never betray my friends."

Calo looked up from his food and saw the bemused look on my face. He stopped chewing for a moment and listened. "You have never heard a *musseta* before? They are the songs of prison, *canzoni di carcere*, songs of *miseria*, of sorrow."

Don Calo returned to his *caponata*, but I listened with greater attention. The music seemed to stir something deep inside me. The singer's voice was distorted but I could just make out the words:

"You can imprison a man's body but not his soul.
I killed my friend because I loved his sweetheart."

All around me the men were eating and drinking unconcernedly, but I sensed that someone else was listening as intently as I was. I looked towards the half-open door. Calo's woman stood in the moonlight. She was looking at me with tears running down her cheeks. She caught my eye and disappeared.

They had done with the food at last. Don Calo pushed his plate aside and put it on the floor for his dog. He gave a nod to the musicians. They changed tempo into a tarantella. Calo rose, wiped his greasy hands on the sides of his stained trousers, and ponderously made his way to the middle of the barn. The men watched silently from the three sides of the table. Calo paused, listened for the rhythm, and then placing his hands on his wide hips, began a nimble footed dance. The others stood up and clapped their hands to the increasing tempo of the music. It developed into a dance of joy, of wild exhilaration. Calo's pace became more frantic, sweat poured down his face. His damp shirt clung to his chest, revealing flabby breasts, flapping like a woman's. He danced on and on until, with a final whirl and triumphant shout, he stopped exhausted and leant on the table for support. His face was blotched and red as he nodded to me to take over. I'd done a little dancing at the Unione Siciliana when I was a kid in New York. I gave a little bow and began to take up Calo's frenzied pace. I could see the watchers nodding their heads approvingly. I let the music engulf me. I felt ecstatic, immortal: I'd survived the war so far and I would make the world a better place. I sensed I'd come home, this was where I belonged; these were my people, my new-found friends. I saw Falco watching me. I paused in front of him and gestured him to dance. Falco's eyes sparkled and he accepted the challenge. We circled around each other cautiously, like two boxers in the opening round of a fight, before quickening our pace. We whirled in a frantic two-step, hands on hips, eye to eye, daring the other to be first to break off. My heart was pounding, the food was churning in my stomach, my head was spinning with the dance and the wine – but I would not stop. Falco was in no better condition, he was heavier and less nimble, but he continued to match me step for step. It was the raw fingers of the musicians that finally brought our dance to an end to cheers and wild applause.

Don Calo came forward, offering a bottle of amaretto. I raised it to my lips and took a long draught before handing it to Falco. Don Calo embraced me. His body smelt ranker than ever and his breath was foul as he kissed me warmly on both cheeks. "You are now our friend. We will go together to the death." He nodded to Falco, who produced a crumpled card from his trouser pocket. Falco carefully laid it upon the table, smoothing it down. It bore the image of some saint. He then took a sharp thorn from another pocket and held it for a moment between his fingers, testing its sharpness. When he was satisfied, he took hold of my right hand and pricked the tip of my thumb with the thorn. A small crimson bubble appeared. Falco then pressed my thumb upon the picture of the saint and smeared it with blood. I watched mesmerised as he picked up the bloodied card and put a match to one corner of it, whilst Don Calo began to intone in a deep and soulful voice:

"*I swear on my honour to be faithful to the Fratellanza just as the Fratellanza is faithful to me, and as this saint and these drops of my blood burn, so I will shed all my blood for the Fratellanza, and as this ash and this blood cannot return to their original state, so I cannot leave the Fratellanza..."*

It was only then I understood the true meaning of the words. I pulled my hand violently from Falco's grasp. "No. I wish to be your friend, but I will never be a *Mafioso!*"

Exclamations of surprise and concern came from all around the table. A look of terrible anger crossed Don Calo's face. "You have refused my offer of brotherhood. You have made me lose respect."

He turned on his heels and stormed out of the barn.

The following morning, word was that the Americans were only a few miles away. The Fascist HQ in Villalba had already been looted as we drove past in the ancient Fiat. When we reached the piazza, American flags and red white and blue bunting had appeared as if from nowhere and torn-up leaflets with portraits of Mussolini were blowing in the wind. As the car stopped, I could see a platform had been erected in front of the church, around which a band had assembled, mostly made up of the musicians who'd been playing at Don Calo's banquet the night before. They were now performing every Yankee tune in their repertoire. The citizens of Villalba filled the square and erupted in rapturous cheers as Don Calo Vizzini, wearing an American officer's jacket and with a yellow handkerchief around his neck, clambered out of the Fiat followed by his dog. I brought up the rear, still dressed as a Sicilian peasant. Don Calo made his way across the piazza towards the platform like an overweight messiah. The crowd parted before him, some even kissing his hands. They didn't care if the sleeves of his jacket were too long, or his pants were as stained and soiled as ever. He stopped as he neared the platform and looked triumphantly at a group of better-dressed men who were clustered about it. One was deliberately trying to avoid his eye. Calo stared at him triumphantly.

"It is good to see you, Prince Alonzo. You have come to welcome the Americans as you welcomed Mussolini, when he came here to extirpate the *Fratellanza*. You supplied Mori, his Prefect, with many names, and you rejoiced that you would no longer pay your rightful dues. You were a magistrate, an instrument of the pure white flame of Fascist justice, and you signed the warrants that sent many of our friends to the penal islands. What have you to say for yourself today?"

The Prince's mouth seemed devoid of saliva, but he forced himself to make the greeting of obeisance. "*Bacio tua mano* – I kiss your hand."

Calo didn't respond. He glanced at his dog, scratching for fleas at his feet, before taking a thin piece of rope from his pocket. Alonzo stared at it fearfully, thinking he was about to be garrotted. Calo saw his fear and enjoyed it. He flexed the rope as if testing its strength. "Look after my dog," he whispered, tossing the rope into the Prince's nervous hands. Alonzo made to protest, but thought better of it. He knelt down, to the jeers and laughter of the populace, and tentatively endeavoured to tie the rope around the animal's neck. The dog, sensing his master's dislike for this man, who smelt of cleanliness and sweet cologne and fear, growled threateningly, showing his yellow fangs. Alonzo looked up beseechingly, but Calo's face was stone. The citizens of Villalba crowded eagerly around; Alonzo looked imploring towards his fellow landowners, but they backed away. Some even smiled as if they were enjoying his humiliation. He vainly sought for the black uniforms of the carabinieri, but the Maresciallo had surreptitiously taken his men to the other side of the piazza. The Prince tried again. His hand was trembling as he attempted to put the rope over the dog's head. This time the brute moved faster than his seeming ancient appearance suggested, and, to the cheers of the people, sunk its front teeth into Alonzo's white hand. Aristocratic blood spilled into the dust of the square and over the Prince's silk shirt and cream trousers.

Tears were welling in Alonzo's eyes. "I can't do it. He won't let me."

"But you are a prince. Your will must be obeyed. Surely a dog cannot defy you? A mongrel dog at that."

The crowd laughed louder. They were now a pack of animals, like the citizens of Paris around the cart carrying Marie Antoinette to her doom. They began to chant, "Try again! Try again!" A stone was thrown and caught the Prince above his right eye. He raised his hands to cover his face and began to weep.

I'd had enough: "Stop. We're here to enforce some sort of government, not mob rule."

Calo's eyes, which had been burning with excitement, became cold. He ignored me, but raised his hands to quieten his fellow-citizens. "Let him go home. My dog can take better care of himself." They jeered and laughed even more raucously. Some looked as if they wanted to exact a bloodier revenge, but Calo's word was enough to calm even the most ferocious. The Prince rose to his feet and ran through the cheering crowd, sobbing in shame, his face buried in his hands, his coat drenched with spittle and phlegm.

Don Calo nodded his satisfaction, before heaving his unwieldy body onto the platform. I clambered up behind. The whole town was now chanting: "Don Calo! Viva Vizzini!" He basked in their acclaim, like a provincial Napoleon with his hands clasped firmly behind his back. Father Salvatore, dressed in his finest robes, came out of the church and stood beside him. When he had had his fill of their adulation, Calo raised his hand and the mob fell silent. "Citizens of Villalba, we are about to be liberated by our glorious American allies. The days of the tyranny of Mussolini and the foreign oppressors are over". He undid the dirty yellow handkerchief from his neck and waved it above his head. "Yellow is the colour of an independent Sicily. The Americans have given me their word they will allow us to govern ourselves. They will provide us with food and the basic needs of life, and will help restore Sicily to prosperity."

There was an even louder cheer. "Viva America! Viva USA!" Calo waited for it to subside. I looked around the screaming, animated faces. I recognized some of the old men who, only yesterday, had suspiciously watched me from their doors; today, their features were contorted in delight and greedy anticipation. Then, among the ugly old faces, I saw the girl. She stood among a group of other girls, staring at me, looking even more serene and lovely than she'd looked the previous night. Our eyes met. This time she did not look away. I reluctantly turned my attention back to Calo's oration.

"But you must have some sort of government in place to distribute the aid. Some authority you can trust: a man with no connection with the Fascists; a man who has suffered under them; a man who will establish a new order, but who will still uphold the traditions of the Holy Catholic Church. I say to you, I am that man. Make me your mayor, and I will ensure justice, work, and fair shares for all."

The piazza erupted once more. Even the landowners joined in. Calo acknowledged the universal acclaim, clasping his hands above his head, like a boxer who'd knocked out the champ. I sought out the girl's eyes again. To my surprise, they appeared to be fixed on the front of Don

Calo's pants. I leant forward to see what had so captured her attention: the effort of raising his hands above his head had raised Calo's tunic, his fly was completely undone revealing grubby underwear. I looked back at the girl. She saw I'd noticed too. Her face broke into a shy smile. I smiled back and her smile widen. I winked and she began to laugh. Unfortunately she laughed at the precise moment Calo stilled the crowd to continue his speech. Her peal of girlish laughter echoed across the piazza. Others noticed Calo's predicament and nudged their neighbours. Soon the entire populace was aware of it. Vizzini looked down and was aware of it too. He looked up to see who had ridiculed him, and fixed a terrible look upon the girl. She stared back at him transfixed. She opened her mouth to apologize, to explain, but no sound came. Don Calo's face was black with rage, throbbing veins stood out on his brow and on the sides of his neck. It was as if he was exuding a terrifying malevolence towards her. The girl was still trying to speak, to explain, but in spite of every effort, she couldn't. She broke away from Calo's stare and sought my eyes, as if imploring me to explain for her. But the effort was too much, her eyes shot upwards as if disappearing into her forehead. She collapsed onto the flagstones. Before I could jump from the platform and comfort her, a young boy came running into the far side of the piazza yelling: "The Americans are coming! The Americans are coming! They are here! They are here!"

The citizens of Villalba immediately forgot Don Calo's embarrassment and began to greet their deliverers in joyous acclamation. The band struck up its own version of *The Star-Spangled Banner.* Father Salvatore nodded to an acolyte who ran inside the church. Within seconds, the bells in the clock tower were pealing their welcome, adding to the cacophony, as a solitary Sherman lumbered into the piazza.

Sitting on the turret alongside the tank commander, triumphantly waving his yellow handkerchief to all and sundry, was the black-bearded Luciano. He saw me and raised his right hand in a flawless salute. I shook my head in disbelief. I turned back to where the girl had fallen. She wasn't there.

Within the hour, five more Shermans and a dozen jeeps of the 82nd Reconnaissance Battalion were parked in the piazza. The two bars were packed with GIs, buying wine and amaretto at inflated prices, with bundles of dollars and the special lire the Allies had distributed to all troops. The Americans were also distributing fistfuls of Raleigh's and Lucky Strike, which the men of Villalba, having been starved of tobacco for years, resorting to dried vine leaves or worse, were smoking with sublime appreciation. Boys were chewing gum for the first time, while the young and not-so-young women of the town enjoyed attention and appreciation such as they'd never experienced before. The Maresciallo, the last vestige of Mussolini's power, had surrendered himself into protective custody; his men had been disarmed and been marched with him to their barracks, accompanied by hoots of derision and promises of revenge.

I pulled Luciano from the throng and took him to the quietest corner of the piazza. He smiled at me with new-found warmth. "See kid, I kept my word. That's the one thing I've always done. I've always kept my word."

I was reluctantly responding to his undoubted charm. "I'll inform the authorities when we get back to Gela. It'll help your parole."

Luciano looked enviously at the party going on outside the cafes. "I ain't ready to go back yet. Give me a few more days, a week at the most, and I'll help give you Palermo and all the towns around."

I thought quickly. A few days would make no difference. "Can I trust you this time? You will only deal through me."

White teeth flashed against the black beard. "I give you my word. Besides, I kinda like being a hero." He caught the eye of a smiling woman and pushed his way towards her.

Twenty minutes later, Don Calo, having recovered his good humour, had taken over the Fascist party headquarters. His followers had used crowbars to gouge Mussolini's insignia from the front of the building, and it now lay in the dust, having been pissed on by every small boy in Villalba. Calo sat behind the desk of the departed political secretary, whilst Father Salvatore made out a list of the food and medical supplies the town urgently needed. Falco and I looked on, together with Captain Limo, Major Vincenzo – the AMGOT liaison officer, and Colonel Birtles of the 82nd Armoured Reconnaissance Battalion. The only sound in the room came from the scratching of the priest's pen.

"My brother is a man of learning," said Calo, by way of explanation. "I had no patience for it. Reading and writing I never mastered, but I solve problems faster in my head than other men can on paper. We have urgent need of even the simplest things: cereal and flour, cooking oil and salt. When winter comes, we will want clothes and blankets and fuel. The Germans took everything."

I began to translate, but Major Vincenzo, a fleshy, seemingly easy-going, native of Detroit, replied immediately in Italian, "Don't worry about a thing. It'll take a week or so, armour and ammunition must have priority. But as soon as we get some ports operating smoothly and have established secure lines of communication and supply, you'll get whatever you want."

Calo smiled, revealing the full decay of his black and yellow teeth. "If you have any problems, '*e cosa mia*' – 'it is my thing'."

This time I was allowed to translate.

Limo spoke for the first time. "Your people are already assisting us in Gela, and Licata, but only the harbour at Palermo can take the really big ships. It will have to be in use almost immediately. We cannot afford any sabotage."

"You can be sure that the port employees will be completely trustworthy."

"We still have a helluva way to go," Colonel Birtles, a lean, tall man from Montana, took off his helmet and wiped his forehead. "Can we expect the same level of co-operation all the way?"

"I will give you names of heads of families, '*gli amici*' – 'friends of friends', who will be able to run all the towns from here to the Bay of Castellamarre. Many of them are in the Uciardone prison in Palermo. Falco will go with you and identify them."

Falco nodded morosely as I translated.

The Colonel laughed. "I was going to take him with me anyway, we could never have got through that minefield without him and that bearded guy. There's another thing. I've received reports from my reconnaissance patrols that there's a heavily defended position on Mount Cammarata – dominates the entire route of our advance. They say there's motorized artillery, anti-aircraft guns and batteries of 88s up there, enough to hold up an entire Division for days."

Calo smiled. "It is truly an impregnable position. They are in ravines and caves that can only be reached by secret paths. Slaves defended it at the time of Spartacus. They held out for months against a full Roman legion."

Captain Limo looked at him sharply. "I was given to understand you assured us there would be no resistance."

"There will be none. The commander, Colonel Salemi, is a Fascist fanatic and is prepared to hold out to the death, but most of his soldiers are Sicilian. My people will go up the mountain tonight and speak to them. Tomorrow morning, you will take Mount Cammarata without a shot being fired. I give you my word, as a man of honour."

Captain Limo was still weighing Calo up. "We plan to set up Committees of Liberation in every town. Their main concern will be food, transport and sanitation. We'll have to have some form of police force. The simplest solution will be to disarm the carabinieri, give 'em new armbands and let 'em continue in the job." Don Calo's eyes narrowed at this and made as if to speak, but the Captain continued: "As far as local officials go, I'll let you have whoever you want as long as they're not Communists."

Calo laughed with derision: "The Communists and the Socialists are the enemies of religion. They hope to degrade the Church and put their parties at the head of the State. My people will be completely trustworthy. Is not my brother a priest?"

Father Salvatore attempted a benign smile.

Limo ignored it. "We want to make sure things run smoothly. But everything must be done according to law. If not, we'll enforce martial law until we can put a proper civilian administration in place." He looked out of the window at the citizens who were now dragging the Fascist insignia towards the piazza. "We want no mob recriminations – physical or pecuniary. We'll form a Committee of Liberation and establish courts of justice as soon as possible."

Calo studied Limo's features. "You are Italian are you not?"

Limo replied in Italian for the first time. "My father came from Rome. But I am an American. There are over a million men of Italian blood in the US Forces," he glanced at me and Vincenzo by way of affirmation, "but they think themselves Americans first."

"Here, we are Sicilian. The Government in Rome has always been indifferent to our needs."

Limo reverted to English. "Things will change from now on. As long as things run smoothly, and you provide us with assistance and intelligence information, we will let you do things your way – as long as it is within the law."

Calo smiled. "Of course, my people have administered justice here for hundreds of years."

Limo was anxious to move on. "I almost forgot," he looked towards Birtles for confirmation. "We're taking far too many prisoners. They're slowing us down, besides we can't feed them all, and we don't want to end up by giving them all free trips to the USA. Can you spread the word that all Sicilians in the Italian army should just go home? Quit their units and go back to their native villages. If they're plain enlisted men we've no quarrel with them."

Calo nodded again. Each request was an added infusion of power into his veins.

Limo continued, "I'll leave a provost sergeant and piquet in charge of law and order. It'll just be for a few days, until the AMGOT officers arrive and reorganize your cara-binieri." He turned to me: "Lieutenant Crivello, I'm going back to Gela tonight, you'd better stay here and go on with Colonel Birtles to Palermo."

Calo dropped his aura of self-satisfaction. He'd virtually ignored me throughout the meeting. He gave the slightest of frowns and turned to examine me more closely. "Crivello? I did not know your name was Crivello."

That evening, Colonel Birtles established his temporary headquarters at Alonzo's castle, a few kilometres from town. The Prince was only too glad of the protection, even though his manicured lawn became a tank park, and his cellars were emptied of fine wine by thirsty GIs, bivouacking in his orchards. I arranged for one of Colonel Birtles' jeeps to pick me up outside the church at dawn, and bedded down in the old Fascist building that was now officially the local AMGOT headquarters. Although I considered myself a free agent, only answerable to Admiral Hewitt, I decided to go along with Limo's instructions – at least for week or so – and give Luciano time to make good his promises.

I lay on the blankets I'd arranged on the floor of a storeroom and tried to rest. I wondered why Don Calo had started at my name; there was so much I wanted to ask him about my father, but my thoughts kept returning to the girl. Had she suffered harm or injury? I kept seeing her eyes, her smile, that firm young body. Music and laughter drifted from the piazza through the open window. A pang of jealousy, at least I thought it was jealousy: I'd never experienced it before, nagged in my gut. She could be out there now, enjoying the company of another guy. For one terrible moment, I imagined her sitting on Luciano's knee. I closed my eyes and tried to sleep. It was no good: I kept seeing her face. I got up, took a couple of boxes of K Rations from the pile Major Vincenzo had left and, still wearing my Sicilian clothes, went out to find her.

The heat of the night hit me as soon as I stepped into the street. The party was continuing in the crowded piazza, even though the troops had been ordered to vacate the town by dusk. Don Calo's musicians were now playing dance music of uncertain origin. Many couples were locked together, swaying in rhythm in the moonlight, while at the tables outside the bars, women and girls were sitting on soldiers' knees, pouring yet more wine down their throats. Plain, fat, even dirty women were being sought after, flattered and cosseted like the finest ladies of Palermo. The atmosphere was heavy with lust. Hands were reaching up beneath shabby dresses to stroke naked thighs, wet with sweat. Other hands were fumbling at heaving bosoms, seeking nipples, which had only recently left babies' mouths. The men of Villalba watched and smoked American cigarettes, and on this one night appeared to sanction toleration, determined to suck these easy-going liberators dry.

I scoured the scene: hoping against hope I wouldn't see my girl locked in an embrace or sitting on a knee. Then something caught my eye among the crowd in the shadow of the café awning. I looked again and could see Luciano, engaged in earnest conversation with an American officer. The officer had his back to me but I could see his fat ass. I was sure it belonged to Major Vincenzo. But that didn't make sense: Vincenzo was supposed to have returned to Gela. The crowd swirled around and swallowed them up. I pushed to where they'd been and found Luciano leaning against the wall, a cigarette hanging from his mouth.

"Hi, kid. Still trying to get laid?"

"Where's Major Vincenzo? Why were you talking to him?"

"Major Vincenzo? Never heard of the bum."

"I saw you talking to an officer. I told you – you don't talk to anyone but me."

"Take it easy kid. Some fat guy asked me for a light. I gave him one – didn't say a word. Why don't you make a play for one of these broads and relax?"

Luciano grinned lasciviously and gestured towards the dancing couples. My eyes followed his hand automatically and at once recognized the young girl with her arms clasped around the neck of a burly, white-belted, provost sergeant, whose fingers were digging into her soft behind as they danced. She was the girl who had resisted the Maresciallo the previous morning. She'd stood next to my girl in the crowd. Maybe she'd helped her home after she fainted. Forgetting Luciano, I pushed through canoodling couples and tapped her on the shoulder: "Excuse me?"

The sergeant frowned, thinking I'd had come to claim his partner.

"I'm sorry, but the girl who fainted in the square this morning, where is she?"

The sergeant obviously didn't understand a word of Italian, and was even more convinced I was about to hustle him out of what he had in mind. He reached into his breast pocket and drew out a handful of dollar bills. "If she's your sister take ten dollars. If she's your sweetheart take twenty."

"It's OK, sergeant. I'm Lieutenant Crivello of the US Navy. I just want to ascertain the whereabouts of a young lady who was in your friend's company this morning."

The sergeant's pair of chins dropped in astonishment. "Would you believe it? The guy's an American?"

The girl smiled at me enticingly. She'd seen me in the company of Don Calo. Maybe she thought I'd be a better provider than the sergeant. "You mean Gina? She went home to her grandmother. They live at the end of the Via Bocetta." She pointed to a dark alley between the two bars. "Go down there. Cross over the Via Cavour and keep on. You will see a shrine to the Magdalene. It is the door opposite."

I nodded thanks. Gina! I knew her name at last. "Carry on, Sergeant."

The sergeant was raising his right hand by way of salute as I plunged into the darkness of the Via Bocetta. It reeked of a poverty and squalor even more dreadful than the slums of Syracuse. The younger inhabitants were in the piazza, but the white hair of frail old women caught the moonlight as they watched me from their windows. Here and there, I heard the cry of an infant, seeking the breast of its absent mother. I crossed over the Via Cavour, which possessed a couple of dusty, ill-nourished almond trees – the first trees I'd seen in Villalba – before plunging back again into the destitution of the Via Bocetta. The habitations here were the most destitute of all. Rags were hung up in place of curtains, the stench of urine and ordure wafted from every door. Once, I heard the sound of moaning and the thump of something heavy on wood, and found myself gazing into the pitiful eyes of a seeming idiot, banging his head against the windowsill. I knew inbreeding was rife in small towns as this. I thanked God my mother had forced my father to rescue us from such despair. I had the same blood as these people – I'd been born barely twenty miles away, but America had made me a breed apart. These people would never experience Macy's, Central Park, Coney Island, and the thrill of Ball Game. But did that make me superior? Falco had survived all this and had become a man I was proud to think of as my friend.

I finally came to a whitewashed wall. In a recess, behind stout iron bars, as if in perpetual imprisonment, was an image of a blue-robed Magdalene, a little lamp burning at her side. Opposite her was the meanest, poorest house of all. I rapped my knuckles on the ramshackle door. My heart was pounding, as it did when I'd been a kid just before I opened my presents on Christmas morning. I could hear movement and whispers on the other side of the thin wood. Then there was silence. I knocked again. This time the door opened a few inches, and I made out the anxious, wrinkled face of an old woman, framed by a black shawl.

"What do you want?" There was fear in her voice.

"I am sorry to disturb you. I wanted to know how Gina is. I saw her faint in the piazza this morning."

"She is sorry. She did not mean to insult Don Calo. She begs his forgiveness and pardon."

"I do not come from Don Calo. I am an American. I am here with the soldiers."

She looked at my clothes incredulously.

"I have been here on special duties. I will have a uniform shortly." I smiled at her encouragingly, as I peered over her hunched shoulders, trying to catch a glimpse of her granddaughter. My nostrils were repelled by the stench of the hovel behind her. I couldn't believe that something so beautiful could live in an atmosphere so foul.

I took the boxes of K Rations from my pocket. "I thought you might need these."

Her look was even more incredulous. She grasped them in her thin, bony hands. Tears began to well in her pale, glazed eyes. "You are too kind."

"I'm sorry it's only basics, but there is some sugar and a few candies – there will be proper food for you all soon."

The moon shone for a moment into the darkness of the hovel and its beam glanced on shining raven hair. The girl was standing there watching me with apprehensive eyes. I felt awkward and shy.

"May I speak with your granddaughter?"

Gina stepped fully into the moonlight: fear was still etched upon her face; her breasts heaved with anxiety. "You swear that Don Calo has not sent you?"

It was the first time I'd heard her speak. Her voice was as sweet as the rest of her.

"I am an officer in the US Navy – I do not take orders from him."

She looked up at me as the old woman backed away, clutching the K Rations to her scrawny bosom.

"How do you know my name?"

"Your friend told me. I met her in the piazza."

"You do not sound like an American."

"I was born in Sicily – in Lercara Friddi."

She smiled. My heart melted. "My mother was born there."

I shifted my weight nervously from foot to foot. "I wondered if you would like to go with me to the piazza. There is dancing there."

Her smile vanished as she shook her head. "No, it is better that I do not go there."

"Why? It is a special night. The town has been liberated."

"The women would not want to see me there. They would say that I am my mother's daughter."

"Why should you not be your mother's daughter?"

She smiled sadly. "That is an old and very long story."

"Will you at least walk with me? We will not go the piazza."

She stared at me intently before turning to the old woman. "I am going out for a while." The crone muttered something under her breath and retreated further into the darkness, ripping open one of the K Rations. There was a cackle of delight as she discovered the sugar. Gina wrapped a shawl around her shoulders and stepped into the street. "Let us walk down the hill. There is a path beside the river."

I fell in beside her. We walked in an awkward silence. I'd never walked with a girl before. I sought desperately for things to say.

"Gina is a pretty name."

"Thank you. What is your name?"

"Daniello."

"I have always liked that name. It makes me think of bravery."

"Why?"

"Did he not go into the den of the lion?"

I laughed. "I suppose you could say that I have been in the den of the lion these past days."

"What do you mean?"

We'd reached the river. I stopped under a tree. "I have been in the house of Don Calo, where I saw you for the first time."

"I know," she smiled at me again, "and I saw you." Her smile faded. "But Calo is not a lion. He is an animal, but not a lion. I have never seen one, but I know a lion has dignity." She stopped herself. "I am sorry I should not have said that."

Tall reeds and long grass grew all along on the riverbank. I took her hand and we sat down, making a snug nest as the vegetation sprang back up around us. For a few minutes, we silently watched the sparkling river. I looked up and saw stars shining brighter than I'd ever seen before: I didn't know if it was the clear Sicilian air or because this lovely girl was sitting beside me. The music floated down from the piazza. The war and Don Calo seemed far away. I reached out and tentatively touched her hand. It was warm and soft and malleable. It turned in mine and gripped my palm. The moment was perfect; I didn't want to break it. But I was desperate to know more about her.

"Why do you hate Don Calo so much?"

She took her eyes away from the flowing waters and gazed into mine. "Your eyes are blue. I noticed the first time I saw them."

"I am supposed to have Norman blood. You did not answer my question."

"He treats my mother worse than his dog."

"Your mother?" I understood. She was the daughter of the sad-faced woman. I could now see traces of her mother's worn features in her face. That explained why the women of Villalba didn't like her. "But Don Calo is not your father?"

She gave a bitter laugh. "Of course not. My father is dead."

"Then why does your mother..."

She put her hand to my lips. "Please do not ask me questions. It is a beautiful night. Tonight, let me pretend that I am like any other girl in Villalba, and you will remain with me for ever..." She broke off as a squadron of bombers thundered overhead on their way to Palermo. Some half-hearted anti-aircraft fire lit up the mountains over to the north. Her mood changed. "But you will not stay here will you? You will follow the war." She stared at me intently. I couldn't reply, but I was certain she wanted me. I clumsily slipped my hand around her waist and eased her backwards onto the ground. My mouth found hers; it was wet and sweet. Our tongues were mingling, twisting and exploring together. I sensed I would fulfil Uncle Tony's wish: I would not die a virgin. My right hand was reaching towards her firm breast. She began to moan softly as my left hand fumbled upwards along her smooth legs, sliding under the rough fabric of her drawers. Her hands fumbled with my belt. She undid it and shyly started to probe inside the front of my peasant pants. I gasped as her fingers found it, hard, throbbing and erect. I raised myself up, my hands pushing down onto the crushed grass, as she eased my pants down, exposing my white ass to the moon. I'd never believed I would feel such excitement and ecstasy. My blood was pounding through my veins. I thought I'd arrived in heaven. But then, at that supreme, indescribable moment, I heard a rustle and a snigger to my left. Something, or someone, was watching us. I raised my head above the grass and met the dark frenzied eyes of two urchins, feverishly rubbing their little peckers in their grubby hands. Gina sat up, saw them, and screamed. The boys fumbled with their short, ragged trousers, trying to push their upright pricks back inside, and ran away giggling.

Gina's cheeks were flushed with a ruddy fire. She looked even more beautiful than before. I raised her to her feet. "I have somewhere we can go. This is a precious time. It should not be spoiled. Trust me."

We were soon standing in the darkness of the old Fascist building. Moonlight shone through the flyblown glass of the window and illuminated her beauty. I tentatively reached out and began to undo the buttons on her shabby dress. It eased from her smooth shoulders and sank to the dusty linoleum on the floor. She stood there in her white shift – my very own vestal virgin awaiting sacrifice. I felt such love, such tenderness; hot tears welled in my eyes. She stepped out of her rough, baggy knickers and began to pull the shift up over her head. Her black hair tumbled from the white garment, struggling to be free. She stood before me naked: all that I could ever dream of, or yearn for. Desire was written on her face, her eyes never left me, and my blood pounded even more frantically than before. I tore off my own clothes and knelt before her. I threw my arms around her legs and passionately kissed her knees, her thighs, and her soft downy hair. I was unaware of everything but her. I reached up and clasped her breast. She gave a soft inward groan. Our bodies were aflame as we sank together to the blankets on the floor.

Bells were pounding inside my head. I was in the middle of a delicious dream. I was stiff as a ramrod and Gina's naked body was beside me. We were in New York, sleeping in Ma's apartment, and everything was safe and beautiful. I wanted to remain like this for ever. I would never let Gina go again. But why were bells ringing? I reached out my hand to feel her softness, but only found the roughness of an army blanket. It was damp and sticky. I opened my eyes. It was not quite dawn. I was on the floor alone. Gina had gone, but her blood was on my hand. Why were the bells ringing with such urgency?

I pulled on my pants, flung my shirt over my head and raced towards the church. The first streaks of day were lightening the eastern sky. Even at this hour, a small crowd had gathered round something in the middle of the piazza. They backed away apprehensively as I ran towards it. The thing they'd been looking at was pale and white, but streaked dark red. I slowly recognised the Maresciallo of the carabinieri, lying naked in the dust. He had a dozen stiletto wounds in his heart. His genitals were arranged around his neck, his mouth had been forced open and his tongue sliced in two.

The provost sergeant and a short young GI came running into the piazza from the police barracks below the town. It was the same provost sergeant I'd seen with Gina's friend. "Holy Cow!" He took one look at the bloody mess and promptly threw up.

"How the hell did this happen?" As the only American officer in town, I supposed I was nominally in charge.

The sergeant wiped his mouth and blinked uncomprehendingly. "We were just having a little fun that's all."

"I heard Colonel Birtles order you to lock him in a cell for his own protection."

"I did. We put him in one of his own cells. One of his men told me it was where he interrogated prisoners. There was blood all over the walls. If you ask me the sonofabitch deserved all he got. I left Private Futcher here, in charge..." He turned to the short guy, even younger than me, who was staring at the mess with tears streaming down his cheeks.

"The cells were all locked. I had the keys on the wall beside me. I wrote a letter to my mother and fell asleep."

I turned back to the sergeant. "What's your name?"

"O'Brian, sir."

"O'Brian, it was your responsibility. They'll have your balls for this. You disobeyed orders and left the prisoners."

O'Brian was also close to tears. "Give us a break, Lieutenant. If you report me I'll lose my chevrons. I've got a wife and three kids back home; I can't afford to lose the extra pay. I could even end up in the stockade. We were only doing what everyone else was doing last night."

I couldn't deny it; but found myself saying: "They were not ordered to safeguard a prisoner."

"Yeah, but they were told that the town was off-limits after dark, and no one took a blind bit of notice. If you'll excuse me saying so, Lieutenant, you, yourself, told me to 'carry on'." He attempted a smile. He had his fair share of Irish Blarney.

"I shouldn't need to remind you sergeant, that we're fighting a war. That prisoner could have escaped and released the others and committed any number of acts of sabotage."

"Yeah, but he didn't did he? He must have had a key hidden away somewhere up his ass, and just tried to run away. He met someone who didn't like him. We'd have probably shot the motherfucker in the end. Someone saved us a job. Please don't report me, Lieutenant. I've worked hard for those stripes. The guy was a bastard. I saw the stuff he kept in that place to soften up the prisoners – he got what was coming to him."

"He is right. Let it be. An account has been settled that's all." Don Calo and his brother had appeared out of the gloom. Calo's dog was licking the blood from the stones.

"I did not know you spoke English."

"There is a lot about me you do not know."

"That I do not deny."

Calo smiled. "Why stir the waters? We have our own code of justice. It is our ancient right to avenge our wrongs. It is ingrained in us. Mussolini tried for twenty years to wipe it out, but it is stronger than ever. We will dispose of the body and no one will be any the wiser."

Father Salvatore made one of his rare utterances. "I will see he gets a Christian burial."

I was moving on anyway. I turned back to O'Brian: "I've got no time to make a report – but no more indiscipline. Remember, you and your men are the representatives of the Allied powers. You're the only law and order they've got until AMGOT arrives. Dismiss."

O'Brian gave me a relieved, but knowing look: "Thank you, sir. I assure you from now onwards I'll be exemplary in my duty." He saluted, genuflected to Father Salvatore, thought about patting Calo's dog, decided against it, about turned, and hurried back to the barracks with Futcher at his heels. They passed some women with buckets and mops, en route to wash away the Maresciallo's blood.

I turned back to the brothers Vizzini. "There will be no more revenge killings. That is all past. The Allies will help you build a new society, based on freedom and justice."

Calo looked at his brother and smiled. "But of course."

He perplexed me more than ever. "Why were you surprised yesterday that my name was Crivello? Did you know my father?"

"Of course. He was a loyal member of the *Fratellanza*."

"He did not join until he came to New York. He led strikes here. He fought the *gabelloti*."

"Unlike his son, Ciro Crivello swore allegiance to me in this very town.

I was astounded. "Why?'

"The secrets of the *Fratellanza* cannot be revealed; especially an oath sworn in blood."

I heard the chug of an engine. A jeep drove into the piazza and braked beside us. Falco was sitting beside the driver.

"It is time to go."

I turned again to Don Calo. "I will come back and I will find out the truth about my father. I will also make sure you keep your promise. You will make this town a lawful place. It will break completely from the past.'

I caught sight of Luciano stumbling into the southern side of the piazza. I ignored him and climbed reluctantly into the jeep. As we drove past the church, Gina was standing in the shadows. My heart burned at the sight of her. She gave me a furtive wave.

I returned it, calling, "I will be back. I promise"

I didn't want to go. There was so much to settle here.

I noticed that Falco was frowning.

Falco and I rode in Colonel Birtles's jeep at the point of the column, spearheading the 2nd Armour on the eastern wing of the advance, whilst Bradley's division stormed up through the centre to cut the island in two. I was wearing a motley collection of Army issue clothing, donated from various officers in Birtles' command. All along the roadside, peasants waved us on our way with shouts of "Death to Mussolini" and "Long Live America". I should have been feeling elated, but my mind was troubled. I'd experienced the greatest happiness in my life but I was leaving it behind all too swiftly. Would I ever recapture it again? And could Luciano or Calo be trusted? I was beginning to doubt it in the clear light of day. My cogitations were interrupted by a noxious smell impregnating the fresh morning air,

"Phew. What a stink." Birtles studied his map. "We're approaching Lercara Friddi. There's a sulphur mine or something here."

And then, under a cloud of smoke, surrounded by yellow-stained land, a grey, drab town came into view. Even on this day of liberation, the fires of the *calcaroni* were burning, as the sulphur was separated from the limestone rock. The cartel that ran the mines would find a market for their malevolent product whoever won the war. The miners stood by the roadside, thin and pale from their hours spent beneath the earth. Their red-rimmed eyes were dead. They'd been worked like animals since they'd been boys. Once more my heart filled with gratitude. If my father hadn't taken me from this terrible place, I might well have been standing there this day among those broken men.

We met no opposition and by noon had reached Monreale, a hill town just eight kilometres from Palermo. I stood with Falco in the shadow of the massive Norman cathedral, alongside the Sherman tank from which General Keyes, Patton's second-in-command, was looking down on the huge city. All around us, in sharp contrast to the rocky, inhospitable and arid country we'd been traversing, were orchards and groves of oranges, lemons, almonds and olives, planted by Arabs centuries before. Palermo had been under almost constant attack from heavy bombers and fighters for weeks: smoke was still rising from the morning's raids. Whole areas, especially near the railway station and the docks, appeared to have been obliterated. The latest exodus of terror-stricken citizens were streaming down the roads out of the city; small, dark, ant-like shapes, pushing prams and carts loaded with the pitiful remains of their belongings

Keyes, an old cavalryman and long-time friend of Patton, pushed his goggles up on to his helmet. His face was black with dust except for two patches around his eyes, as he wiped his binoculars with the bandana around his throat. He focused his glasses through the midday heat-haze at a cloud of dust that appeared to be moving swiftly through the refugees. As it drew nearer, I could see that it was a black Maserati saloon flying a white flag. I became aware of rapid clicking, as if a safety catch was being switched on and off. I turned to see a photographer snapping away with a Rolleiflex, while a Leica swung from his neck. Keyes frowned, but ignored him. Generals never liked civilians around, even if they were accredited. He turned to me:

"Crivello, ask your pal what he thinks is happening."

I dutifully translated his request to the sullen Falco, who'd been more reticent than ever the entire morning.

"They are the Fascists who have been running the city for the past twenty years; they will try to make terms with you. Don't listen to them. They are pigs."

I translated back to Keyes, who was still watching the car, as climbed up the hill towards us. Its gears clashed and its engine groaned, it twisted and turned like an animal in death throes, laboriously navigating the dizzying hairpin bends and steep inclines until it drew to a halt before us. Three portly men in double-breasted suits and black trilby hats got out. The fattest took off his hat and half bowed to the General. His brow, beneath a fuzz of ruffled black hair, was pale as ivory and glistening with sweat.

"On behalf of the Prefecture, may we offer the surrender of our city to the illustrious American Army?"

Keyes listened carefully to my translation before exploding: "Like hell they will! Tell 'em we're occupying the city on behalf of the Allied powers and we don't recognize their authority. We'll requisition the automobile – let the sonsofbitches walk back home." He turned again to me: "I'll send in a couple of jeeps as a reconnaissance patrol. You and your pal go with them. Make sure there are no German forces left. I've reports there's an Italian battleship in the harbour. If all is clear, radio back, and we'll come in behind you."

I translated to Falco. His countenance changed from morose to incredulous. "And now you Americans want us to capture a battleship?"

The two jeeps descended the hill and headed for the city, along the same dusty road on which the Maserati had come. We began to pass pathetic refugees, their faces pale and strained from lack of sleep and their bodies weak from hunger. They carried bags and bundles of all sizes. Many were wounded, the luckier ones rode in wagons pulled by emaciated mules, but most either limped along painfully or lay wrapped in bloody bandages in hand-drawn carts. One mother carried a dead baby in her arms. Dirty-faced children walked morosely beside their parents, failing to understand the logic of war. Some looked wondrously at the two jeeps and their occupants: we were the first Americans they'd ever seen.

The photographer had jumped into my jeep as it began to move, and was snapping away furiously, a cigarette hanging from the right hand side of his mouth. "They always look the same: the people who've lost everything. I saw it first in

Spain, in China, in the Blitz in London, and then in Africa. The poorest suffer most." He looked like a Sicilian with his dark hair and hawk-like nose. There was intelligence and humour in his face.

"Where do you come from? I can't tell from the way you speak. What kind of accent d'you call that?"

He laughed. "It's never been officially identified. It's a sort of Hungarian, so I've got an equal chance of being shot by either side. I was born in Budapest deeply covered by Jewish grand-fathers from every angle. I guess I'm the original Wandering Jew." He threw the stub of his cigarette away and immediately lit another from the packet of Lucky Strike in his breast pocket. "I left Hungary when Horthy, the dictator, took over. Then went to Berlin until that bastard Hitler showed up. He's followed me to Vienna, Spain, and Paris. It seems like I've been taking pictures of his victims all my life." His smile faded. "Hitler's little buddies the Japs are just as bad. You should've seen what they did to the Chinese in Nanking. I'll tell you this; a Chinese city burns just as crisply as a Spanish one, and weeping women sound the same in all nations. Where are you from, kid?"

"I was born here, but New York is all I can remember."

"I had a studio on 9th Street. Wish I was back there now with a blonde and a large Manhattan."

"What's keeping you? You're a civilian."

He winked. "It's the dough, kid. *Colliers* pay 400 dollars a month, plus expenses. And my expenses are heavy. If I can't get champagne, it has to be Scotch, and I drink a helluva lot of Scotch." He spied a naked little boy was standing at the roadside waving a white flag and unslung the spare camera from his neck. "I'll need the Leica for him: light-sensitive film."

We entered the city along the main road from the south-west. Tank traps had been dug: great pits covered with wire

netting smothered with sand and gravel – but there wasn't
a defender in sight. Rubble was piled everywhere, littering
the pavements and adding to the omnipresent dust. We
came to the Corso Calatafina and passed blackened buildings with windows devoid of glass. The upper storeys of
some were crumbling apart, exposing their intimate contents, which were spilling pathetically into the street. My
companion's camera sought out every detail, but I found
myself turning away, as if I were seeing something indecent,
like dirty underwear. Falco was in the lead jeep, navigating the way through to the port. Now and again, we passed
ragged Italian soldiers, furtively scavenging through the
devastation. They looked up at the sight of the jeeps and
scuttled away, like jackals disturbed over offal. We swung
right across the vast expanse of the Piazza Indipendenza,
and made our way to the huge railway station that Mussolini
had built in the Piazza Cesare. The grandiose, three-tiered
white edifice at the front of the building was still in place,
but the tracks leading into it were a mass of twisted metal.
We drove down the deserted and shuttered Via Roma, where
the fashionable ladies of Palermo had once bought gowns
from Paris and Milan. A dappled horse lay in the middle
of the thoroughfare. A bomb had split it in two, its black
and red guts oozed over the cobbles. The hungry people
of Palermo had hacked its hindquarters to the bone, its
ribs had been pecked white, and crows were feeding on its
uncomprehending eyes.

Falco signalled and we turned right at the Via Vittorio
Emanuele, which led to the heart of the port. The destruc-
tion was even more severe, entire blocks of buildings lay
demolished, but through the dust, at the top of the street,
I could just make out the sparkling waters of the Gulf of
Palermo. I eased the safety catch off my carbine. My new

friend looked up from his camera and laughed: "Yes, kid, you'd better be prepared in case the battleship is still there." We burst from the shadow of the bomb-damaged street into the bright sunshine of the quay. There was no sign of a battleship, but all over the harbour, masts, funnels and hulks were protruding from the oily water. The Germans had attempted to render the port useless by scuttling ships of all types and sizes. Buildings around the jetties were still in flames and a pall of black smoke hung over the entire docks. On the quay, the remnants of an artillery unit sat or lay among their ruined guns, which were still smoking from the morning's raids. The Italian artillery had proved most dogged in their resistance and these men must have been under bombardment for weeks. Many were wounded; some had blood pouring from their ears, their eardrums shattered. They gazed with red–rimmed eyes as our jeeps drew up before them.

A corporal fixed me with a defiant stare before slowly getting to his feet. After a beat his fellows followed his example. The corporal took off his cap; his cheeks were stained with dust and streaked with tears. His nostrils were black and his lips cracked. "*Il gioco e finito* – the game is finished," he whispered. His men stared disbelievingly; unable to comprehend their agony was over. "*Il gioco e finito*," the corporal repeated, louder. The soldiers took off their caps and cheered.

Standing a little apart was a portly figure dressed in an elaborate uniform. He wore six rows of medals on his breast, and a highly polished Sam Browne belt was straining at his waist. His turnout was immaculate: I guessed he'd spent most of the past few weeks out of harm's way, in a requisitioned villa along the coast with his wife or mistress. His cap, with the gold insignia of King Victor Emmanuel, was set at a jaunty angle above the deep scar that ran across his podgy face. As the cheers of the artillerymen faded, he sauntered over and gave an elaborate salute: "Generale di Brigata, Giuseppe Molinero, Commandant of the Port Defences. Take me to General Patton. It is no disgrace to surrender to an American gentleman." He glanced disdainfully at the shell-shocked men behind him. "A General cannot fight without good men. Sicilians are not human beings but animals."

I didn't return his salute. "There are a couple of Sicilians over here. If you don't want to be shot, you'll surrender to us right now."

Molinero trust out his lower lip and gave a withering glance, worthy of Mussolini himself. He turned on his heels and walked back to the edge of the quay, where he stood looking out to sea, his arms folded across his be-medalled breast. Falco would have shot him on the spot, but I radioed General Keyes, who ordered me to bring him to the Palazzo dei Normanni, the ancient royal palace and seat of government, where he was going to officially accept the surrender of the city. Molinero condescended to agree to this, but insisted, in recognition of what he claimed to have been a gallant defence, on keeping his revolver. I consented, after Falco had removed its clip of bullets.

⚜⚜⚜⚜

MY SICILIAN CAMPAIGN by General George S. Patton Jr:

Keyes contacted me by field telephone and informed me that Palermo was open. No German forces were there. It would be ready for me to enter as soon as I arrived. I was sorely tempted. I'd read a lot of poetry, the words of Marlowe's Tamburlaine sprung to my mind:

"Is it not passing brave to be a king?
And ride in triumph through Persepolis?"

But it wasn't so simple. I was all too aware that many would hold it against me; accuse me of glory seeking. I'd heard from some old colleagues in Bradley's headquarters, that Bradley considered the whole Palermo venture 'a vain and useless exercise' and that there was no glory in 'the capture of hills, docile peasants and spiritless soldiers.' It was typical of Bradley. He would've made a better schoolmaster than general. He lacked aggression and was teetotal to boot! I have never completely trusted anyone who didn't enjoy a drink. Besides, I didn't want to antagonize Eisenhower. I knew I would have greater victories before this war ended. This time I decided to take no personal glory and let my conquests speak for themselves. I told Keyes: "Be my guest. You took it. You enter and I'll enter after you."

Lt. Danny Crivello:
We drove back through the city with General Molinero crouched on the floor of the jeep covered by a blanket. When arrived at the main thoroughfare, the Corso Vittorio Emanuele, people began to emerge from their cellars and shelters in ever-increasing numbers. At first, they tentatively waved white sheets and homemade American flags, but soon they were surging around the two jeeps, applauding, cheering and even throwing flowers in our path. The great

bells of the Duomo were ringing in thanksgiving; small boys climbed to wave from the tops of the palm trees – it was as if the entire population was assembling to give us their thunderous welcome. The Rolleiflex clicked relentlessly beside me and captured it all. At times the vehicles hardly moved. Every man wanted to shake my hand and every woman wanted to kiss me. I yelled back protests in Italian, but they became even more excited and took me as one of their own, shouting, "Siciliano! Siciliano!" An emaciated old man, in trilby hat and grubby singlet, yelling, "I have a cousin in Brook-a-leen", reached in and stole my helmet.

The Piazza Indipendenza, before the Palace, was an impassable sea of ecstasy, which Falco avoided by leading us to a side entrance. Once inside the quietness and security of the precincts, General Molinero came out from beneath his blanket. He fussily arranged his uniform and frequently applied a white silk handkerchief to his oily forehead, as we waited by the coolness of the fountain at the bottom of the Grand Staircase. Even in this sanctuary there were scars of war. Shrapnel had pockmarked some of the decorated walls, whilst damaged statues stood with their heads bowed, as if in pain from missing limbs. The comparative calm was shattered by the increasing roar of the crowd, signalling the arrival of the conqueror, before a horde of white helmets surged into the courtyard and Keyes stepped out of his Maserati, surrounded by a swarm of aides. Molinero stood to attention and rendered his elaborate salute. Keyes looked at him coldly before responding. He then gave a curt nod and led the way up the stairs into the sumptuous royal apartments.

The official surrender took place in the Hall of Roger II. The walls and ceilings were covered with bright mosaics depicting hunting scenes, designed by Arab architects for

the Norman kings. Leopards, centaurs, lions, deer and pea-
cocks looked down as I translated Keyes's terms. Molinero
was duly photographed, unconditionally surrendering the
city and surrounding military district. After Keyes had for-
mally accepted, Molinero asked me to ask Keyes if it would
be possible to take his 'wife', orderly and personal belongings into captivity with him. Keyes was non-committal, but
Molinero was alone, without belongings or orderly when he
joined the other 44,000 prisoners captured on the advance.
I was told that the lady claiming to be Molinero's wife
would not be paying her weekly visit to the coiffeuse. Her
head had been shaved by revengeful citizens in the Piazza
Indipendenza.

9

OCCUPATION

Lt. Danny Crivello:

"I wonder kid, if you could do me a favour?" The photographer was waiting at the foot of the Royal staircase.

"That depends. Who the hell are you by the way?"

"Sometimes I'm not sure myself. I was born Endre Friedmann in Budapest, but I'm Robert Capa right now."

He smiled and offered his hand. It was hard not to warm to him. He seemed to be the sanest man in Sicily. Patton had chosen the Palace as his official headquarters: I'd been attending a tedious briefing on the security arrangements for the General's imminent arrival, and welcomed the prospect of an enlightening diversion.

"What do you want?"

We walked over to a pockmarked stone bench under the shadow of some trees. Capa lit a Lucky Strike. "Well it's like this. When I told you I was working for *Colliers*, I wasn't exactly telling the whole truth. I was working for them and covered the entire North African campaign. I took some great shots, but the War Department suddenly changed the rules. They decided that all the folks back home should see how well their boys were doing. They insisted on pool regulations. All photographs they approved should be made available to all US publications, irrespective of copyright. My work was being published by the dailies before *Colliers* could use them. Last month they decided I was no further use and withdrew my salary, expenses and accreditation."

"Then how on earth did you manage to get here?"

"I had an old girlfriend, working for *Life* in London. She told me that if I could get out here and get some really good shots, she might be able to persuade her boss to put me on their books. I managed to hitch a lift to Tunis, and by pure luck a buddy of mine, who works for Associated Press, was down with C Ration diarrhoea. I took his place on the boat over." He lit another cigarette. "I've got to get those photos I've taken today developed at once and sent out by radio. That way, they'll arrive at *Life* just as the news hits that we've taken Palermo. The censors still think I'm fully accredited, but any moment now my loss of status will be published. I've got to find a darkroom tout suite."

"They've allocated me a room for my bedroom and office. It's little better than a cell – you're welcome to use that."

A few minutes later blackout material was covering the small window of my room, on which the late afternoon sun seemed to be concentrating its most powerful beams. The heat was stifling. Capa busied himself, arranging his developer and printing trays. "Can you get me some ice from somewhere, kid? I'll need to do high-speed processing."

I stared blankly. Photography was an art I'd never understood.

He smiled sympathetically. "I can reduce the processing time if I use sodium nitrate at an elevated temperature. I'll need some ice to put in the tray from time to time, or else the developer might boil over."

I was glad to escape the oven-like atmosphere, and found my way, through long dark corridors to the Palace's vast kitchens, where Patton's personal cook, Mess Sergeant Thue P. Lee, a Chinese American, was already in control. The guys told me Patton had discovered him at the beachhead in Casablanca, where he'd boasted that he was the 'best damn cook in the US Army'. Patton had taken him at his word, but today Lee's patience and ingenuity appeared to be severely taxed by the antique Sicilian equipment. His usually inscrutable face broke into a glare as I entered his domain.

"Waddya want?"

I decided to baffle him with science. "I'm Lieutenant Crivello, Military Intelligence. I must have ice. There are some vital photographs we have to develop."

Mess Sergeant Lee's suspicions of the inane workings of the US Army were confirmed. "What you fuckin' need ice to develop film for? You need ice for ice cream. General Patton like ice cream and all refrigeration units in this fuckin' place are fucked. Me, best cook in this whole fuckin' army, but even me cannot make fuckin' ice cream without ice. That's all there is in whole of this fuckin' town." He pointed to two large blocks of ice that were rapidly melting on a marble slab.

"I'll have to requisition them. The photographs are more important than even the General's ice cream."

Mess Sergeant Lee made to protest vehemently, but I signalled to a bemused kitchen orderly to wrap the ice in a large sack. I then heaved it on my back and with Lee's cries of execration ringing in my ears, carried it back to my room, leaving a trail of water over the rococo splendour of the marble floors.

Back inside the darkness of my room I found Capa, stripped to the waist, holding a negative up to a red lamp, as his sweat dripped into the developing trays. I peered at the picture and could make out weeping young women having their heads shaved by a jeering mob. Their bare skulls were cut and bleeding from brutally applied razors and shears. Capa lit a cigarette. "Last week they were sleeping with German colonels; tonight, they'd kiss the ass of the humblest GI. That's war, kid."

I glanced at other prints, which he'd hung to dry like washing on a line. One suddenly caught my eye. Falco was seated in the jeep in front. A grateful hand was slapping his back. A bespectacled GI stood next to Falco, smiling as he shook one of a multitude of eager hands reaching up to him. All around was a sea of happy, exultant faces, all reaching for a touch of their newly arrived saviours – all but one. My heart skipped a beat. One face was not smiling but looked questioningly past the camera towards where I'd been sitting behind Capra; a dark, swarthy face, well into middle-age. I could see only the face, such was the density of the crowd that I couldn't discern a uniform, but I was sure it was him. I'd no idea how he could have got there, but it was the face of my Uncle Tony.

The prints were ready as the last of the ice melted away.

My brain was still buzzing with the shock, as Capa persuaded the censor to stamp his approval on the photographs and then charmed a radio operator to wire them directly to *Life*. After the final shot was sent spinning across the Atlantic, Capa insisted he owed me dinner and led the way out into the rubble-strewn streets. He instinctively knew the best places and we were soon sitting on red plush banquettes in the elegant art nouveau restaurant of the Excelsior Palace Hotel, where the Nazi elite had dined but a few days before. Despite the acute shortage of food the black market was flourishing and, thanks to Capa's plentiful supply of dollars, we were served sirloin steaks and Spumanti, the nearest thing on offer to champagne. As we dined, Capa told me stories of his eventful life. How he'd changed his name to Robert Capa in Paris, pretending to be a rich American, as part of a hoax to get higher prices for his photos. How he'd become friends with Ernest Hemingway in Spain, and had gone to Russia with John Steinbeck. I was enchanted by his intellect, integrity and compassion. He was the complete antithesis to Luciano, Don Calo, and the corruption, parochialism and brutality they stood for. Capa seemed all that a man should be: idealistic, cosmic and compassionate.

My thoughts went back to Uncle Tony. "There's one thing I'd like to ask you."

He lit another cigarette. "Go ahead, kid."

"Does the camera ever lie?"

"Sure, kid. I can make it tell what story I want. One of my most famous photos in Spain was a set-up, a fake; but unlike the Nazis the message I tell is a good one. Why d'you ask?"

"There's a face in one of your pictures that looks just like someone I knew at home."

"Could be a trick of the light, a shadow..." He broke off as a cigarette girl approached bearing her wares on a tray attached to a red ribbon hanging around her neck. Her pretty face was anxious and distraught. "There's another one due for a head shave. I bet she was selling the Nazis more than smokes last week." His pockets were bulging with Lucky Strike, but he beckoned her over and bought a pack, adding a ten-dollar tip. He gazed hungrily at her swaying butt as she walked away. "That's what I call a classic Italian ass: round and sensuous – as wide as it's long." He turned to me. His eyes softened: "You got a girl back home, kid?"

"No. But I think I've found one over here. I only met her last night, but she's the most beautiful girl I've ever seen. I'm going back for her as soon as I can."

Capa raised his glass of Spumanti, "Let's hope she looks as good when you see her again." He grimaced at the sweetness. "It's not champagne, but at least it sparkles."

"Have you got a girl?"

"Kid, I've got girls all over the world: from Fifth Avenue to Bond Street and the Champs Elysees. If you're really lucky, you'll find one that's really special." For a moment the gaiety left his eyes. "I had a girl that was special. The bravest girl I've ever met; braver than most of the men I've known. Gerda Taro. What a dame, and she was almost as good a photographer as me." He lit another cigarette and reflected for a moment. "She was Polish. A blonde, looked like a perfect Aryan, an ideal example of Nazi womanhood. But she hated Hitler and all he stood for." He took another swallow of Spumanti. "We had a few great years together, living on the Left Bank in Paris. We were both dedicated Socialists, members of the Popular Front, and when Franco invaded Spain in 1936, we both went to aid the Republic. We decided that the truth of our photographs would be the best weapons we could offer." He paused again, whilst I waited, not wishing to disturb his remembrance. "I spent a year at the front, but she stayed on."

"What do you mean?"

"I had to attend to some business in Paris – she wouldn't go with me. The International Brigades were about to launch a new offensive and she wanted to cover it. The trouble was that Hitler had just supplied Franco with hundreds of new ME 109s and Heinkel 111s – the bastard wanted to try them out for his future wars. The Republicans didn't stand a chance. The equipment that the Russians had given them was way out of date. But Gerda wouldn't give up. She wanted to show the full horror of the war; she took even more risks than me. It all ended in a chaotic retreat a few miles out of Madrid. She was riding on the running board of a car, there was no room inside. A Nazi plane strafed the column. A tank went out of control and crushed her to death. She was six days short of her twenty-sixth birthday. I couldn't leave her in Spain. I brought her back to Paris, where we had our best times. She's buried in Lachaise, next to Henri Barbusse, her favourite poet."

He broke off and lit another cigarette.

I felt I had to say something. "I'm sorry. War is no place for women."

"It's no place for a dog. But you see, kid, there is now no safety for anyone, anywhere – even if you remain behind. Death is ingenious, and will find you from out of the sky. The more I see, the more I know people are the same all over the world. It's nations that cause wars. I'm an Internationalist." He took a scrap of torn and dirty paper from his breast pocket. It was stuck together with glue and tape. "That's the nearest thing I've got to a passport. It's an identification document from my days in Budapest. I'm an alien all over the world and I like it that way."

"What are you doing next?"

"I won't be farting around here. Patton has arrived and the old boy is a stickler for regulations. If anyone finds out that I'm not officially accredited I'll be put on the first plane stateside. Besides, I want to get to where the action is. I try to take pictures of war that look as if the photographer could not have taken them and remained alive. It's the only way to reveal the horror. There is no glory as Patton would have you believe, only tragedy and pain." He paused and a look of great sorrow passed over his face. He caught the anxious look in my eye and forced himself to smile. "I think I'll move over to the east and join up with the 1st Division. They are the closest to the Germans and they'll have to move against

Messina soon. Besides, Generals Allen and Roosevelt are old drinking pals of mine. What are your orders, kid?"

"My orders are secret I'm afraid. But I guess I'll be hanging around here for a few more days."

I returned to the Royal Palace, to Capa's erstwhile dark room, to ponder about Uncle Tony and dream of Gina, while Capa was more actively engaged with the cigarette girl in a double bed at the Excelsior.

MY SICILIAN CAMPAIGN by General George S. Patton Jr:

During the course of the afternoon, Truscott's 3rd Infantry Division, complete with mules, entered Palermo from the west, having advanced over 100 miles in seventy-two hours. I entered the city that evening at 1900 hours and took up my quarters in the Royal Palace. Dined in the great State Dining Room on china plates marked with the Cross of Saxony. No damn ice cream, but ate an edible omelette from powdered egg and tinned cheese, which Mess Sergeant Lee had somehow contrived to make from his K Rations. Discovered the Cross of Saxony was also on my toilet pan and practised my aim. Before retiring I wrote in my diary: '*I really feel like a great general today – all my plans so far have worked. I hope God stays with me.*'

Gela
Lt Frank Dunford:

The kid was waiting for me on the wall by the beach as usual. His head was shaved for lice and he had no shoes, but he sure had a cute grin. On the first day I'd given him a Hershey bar and seemed to have earned his life-long gratitude. I searched in my pocket for a stick of gum, threw it to him and walked along the shore. The kid followed behind.

I'd been ordered to quit the sick bay because my unique experience was urgently needed in Limo's operation at the fish market. Now, after barely three days, the fishermen were diligently reporting any movement of enemy shipping they'd sighted and passing on information they'd gleaned from their fellows in Sardinia and on the mainland. They were only too willing to co-operate. AMGOT was paying them top prices for their catches: food was desperately short and the fish was supposed to be distributed throughout the region as even-handedly as possible. Limo had found some English-speaking Sicilians, who had volunteered to make the port of Gela fully operational. It was only after some questioning that I established most of them had been deported from the USA on charges of larceny and coercion. It was almost as if I'd never left New York.

I'd finished for the day and made my way beyond the harbour to where the shore was rocky, the kid still following like a faithful puppy. I sat on a comfortable-looking rock and fumbled in my breast pocket for my pack of Camels. The boy grinned again then took a handful of colourful, crushed packs from his trousers and gestured for more: the kids in Gela were already collecting them avidly. I smiled and tossed him the near empty pack. The boy caught it and smiled everlasting gratitude. I lit my cigarette and watched the sun sink into the sea. Its dying rays caught the gold of Sue's crucifix, hanging outside my shirt. In my fancy, its gleam seemed to radiate love. I resolved there and then, that if I managed to get through this war and Sue was free, I'd beg her to give me another chance.

MY SICILIAN CAMPAIGN by General George S. Patton Jr:

The following morning, having received the Cardinal's representative along with other petitioners, I walked alone through the Cappella Palatina, and gazed at the Royal Throne with the Aragonese coat of arms. I was being treated almost as a king but, like my favourite Shakespearean character, Macbeth, my ambition was not allowing me content. Now that the first flush of triumph had passed, I realised Messina was still the real prize, and my 7th Army was now further away than it had been on that first morning at Gela. I was convinced Montgomery had blundered. In his haste to get round Etna and grab all the glory, he'd allowed himself to go against his usual safe but sure principles, and had broken his own rule of concentrating his forces. He was trying to advance on three fronts and was dissipating his strength. Moreover, he had shifted his campaign from the coastal plain, where tanks and naval guns could have been used to advantage, into the rugged interior. His troops had been fighting continuously for ten days against crack German units in well-ordered defensive positions. The Eighth Army was becoming exhausted and the reports told me they were fighting malaria as well. It looked like stalemate. It was then I spied a little spider scurrying sideways across the geometric tiles and recalled the legend of King Robert the Bruce. Perseverance is a general's greatest weapon. Now that I was established on the northern coast, there was nothing to stop me scurrying steadfastly eastwards.

❧❧❧

Gela
Lt. Frank Dunford:

The kid had bought other kids with him today. I sat on the sea wall surrounded by them, like some latter-day Pied Piper. They were all pitifully thin. Their ragged clothes hung from their skinny bodies as if they were three sizes too big. The boys were mostly shaven headed and without shoes, but several of the girls were pretty and even in the desolation of Gela, had somehow managed to keep their hair clean and their faces bright. I emptied my pockets of chocolate and gum and found myself smiling at the grateful little faces around me. The kid seemed to think that he had a special call on my affection, and spoke to me for the first time.

"Are you a cowboy?"

"No. There aren't many cowboys left anymore: especially where I come from."

"You come from New York?"

"No. But I have lived there for a while."

"I have a cousin who lives in New York. I will go there one day."

"I have two uncles and an aunt in the Bronx," one of the bigger girls said proudly.

"I have a brother there," said a small boy with a mouth full of gum. "He is rich – he has a car; a Chevrolet."

"Everyone has a car in America," said another girl.

"You are Italian?" asked the bigger girl.

"My mother is."

We were interrupted by the thunder of a squadron of Mustang A-36 dive-bombers on their way from Tunisia to pound the German supply lines at Messina. The American star stood out boldly on their wings. I looked up with the children and followed the planes until they disappeared behind some white cloud.

"Why do you bomb us if there are so many Italians in America?" asked the kid.

"You'd better ask Mussolini that. He is a friend of Hitler, who is a friend of the Japanese, and they started it by bombing us first."

"My father says that Mussolini is finished. He sent my brother to Russia and he never came back."

"The Germans are pigs," said the bigger girl."

"Have you killed any Germans?" The kid inquired.

"I think I have."

"How many?"

"I don't know."

"Did you shoot them with your gun?"

"No. I called on a radio for big guns to fire."

"You have a radio that can do that?"

I nodded.

"You Americans have truly wonderful things."

"My mother says that soon you will give us all plenty of food," said the bigger girl.

"We will, as soon as we have ships to spare to bring it."

"What sort of food?" asked the kid.

"Everything: wheat, eggs, meat: all the things you need to make you grow up big and strong."

"Is that why you Americans are so big?" asked another boy, who was particularly thin, "You have plenty of food and we are always hungry."

"Things will get better soon, and you'll all grow up to be bigger than me."

"What is your name?" asked the kid.

"Franco."

The kid's face flushed with pride. "We have the same name."

❖❖❖❖

Palermo
Lt. Danny Crivello:

"Unlike Gela and the other towns along the southern coast, Palermo is a deep-water port, capable of handling big ships direct from the United States. It is vital to the future course of the campaign, both here and on mainland Italy. We've got to get it up and running." The engineer colonel in charge of port operation cast his eyes around the devastated harbour. I counted the wrecks of 44 vessels blocking up the moles and channels. Men of the 504 Engineer Shore Regiment were already on the job, converting some of the larger sunken vessels into improvised piers and bulldozing new roads through the rubble. Compared to the bums on the invasion beaches at Gela, these guys were professionals, possessing an abundance of American ingenuity and know-how.

The colonel turned to Captain Limo, who stood alongside him, together with Falco and a well-dressed Sicilian: "We'll need every trained longshoreman, stevedore and crane driver you can muster." He looked further along the dock towards a large assembly of sinister-looking artisans. "Are you sure these fellas are up to the job?"

Limo nodded impatiently: "No problem; some of 'em spent time in the United States."

The colonel gave a wry grin: "Perhaps it's better I don't inquire what sort of time and why they decided to return home."

A PX van arrived. The Sicilians had immediately adapted to this ancient American custom, and everyone broke for coffee. I watched Falco break away and walk alone along the harbour wall. I couldn't understand why he'd avoided me

since we'd left Villalba. I took two tin mugs of coffee, thick
with condensed milk and sugar, and walked over to where
he was gazing out to sea.

"I thought you might like a mug of real American coffee."

Falco took the steaming mug without averting his gaze.

I tried again. "Is anything wrong? You've been avoiding me."

Falco sipped the hot liquid before turning his blazing
eyes on me. "I told you there was a girl I wanted, but she was
not ready. I have waited for her for years, and you came and
took her in one night. You have dishonoured our friendship. You have made her a whore."

I looked at him in disbelief. "You mean Gina?"

Falco nodded. His eyes full of pain and rage.

I was lost for words. My dreams and fantasies were suddenly threatened. "I didn't know you wanted her. There
were so many girls in the town. Does she want you?"

"It is not for her to decide. She has no family; she is
under the protection of Don Calo."

"This is the twentieth century, for Chrissake. We are
supposed to be fighting for freedom. Slavery was abolished
a hundred years ago."

"We are fighting for our honour. You are no better that
all the others. You come here and despoil our women and
then leave them with your bastards."

"I love Gina. I have never met anyone like her before in
all my life. I am going back to Villalba for her. I will take her
with me to America."

"If you try to do that I will kill you."

"Falco, I am your friend. I tell you again that I didn't
know you wanted her, but I love her now. I cannot stop that
love."

"What is love? You see a girl once – you use her as a whore
and you think you love her? A man has more important

251

things in his soul than love – his honour, his loyalty to his friends. You are not my friend. We still have much work to do here, but one day I will give you the kiss of hate, and we will settle this in the Sicilian way. Your coffee is shit as well."

He threw remains of his mug into the Mediterranean and rejoined the others.

Gela
Lt. Frank Dunford:

The *pupi* had returned. The old puppeteer had carved quickly. Instead of an armoured-clad Orlando fighting the dastardly black Saracen, an overblown little Mussolini, with paunch and jutting jaw, was kissing the ass of a mad-eyed Hitler, who continually farted, and then turned round to kick little Mussolini for his pains. The ill-fated history of the much-vaunted Pact of Steel between the two mighty dictators was encapsulated in that little scene. A few weeks ago such irreverence would have resulted in imprisonment or worse, but now the whole town gathered round and roared with laughter and derision. Crimi, the puppeteer, had learnt his ancient craft from his father, who had learnt his from his father before him. His expert hands manipulated his puppets by a combination of iron rods and strings, as if he were weaving some intricate spell, disguising his art, making his skill seem easy.

I sat with the kids, who were ravenously chewing on the hard tack biscuit I'd brought from the stores. They were screaming with pleasure and excitement, their hunger temporarily forgotten. I'd never seen puppets like this before. The figures were alive: Hitler grew more and more frenzied; Mussolini became more and more humiliated. I could have sworn I could see their expressions change. I felt at one with the children and the people around me. I forgot about the war; Captain Limo, Major Vincenzo, and the fish market; the villainous looking characters who seemed to be taking over the distribution; the chore of writing out the daily reports from the fishing boats. I even forgot I was recovering from the pox. I was happy.

Letter from Mussolini to his mistress, Clara Petacci:
Cara Mia,

I am sorry I cannot come to you this evening, but all of Italy is weighing on my shoulders. Five days ago at Feltre, on the Swiss border, in a bourgeois little room, decorated with mock antique tiles and hung with cheap prints of birds of prey, I endured a non-stop diatribe from my German friend. On top of that, his vegetarian diet and the drugs and pills his quack doctors prescribe, have made the Fuhrer's flatulence and breath unbearable. Two hours in close proximity to him in an enclosed room gave me nausea from which I have yet to recover. I, who had once been the senior figure, I, who had conceived the idea of Fascism, was forced to listen to a hysterical account of the abject failure of Italy's military might. The man, whom I had considered no more than a mad little clown, has dragged me to disaster. Although I never admitted it, even to you, I had known in my heart that Italy was completely ill-prepared to fight a major European war. Despite the Pact of Steel, I had never intended to march blindly behind the Germans. But after the Council saw the ease with which Hitler had swept through Poland and France, their incessant clamour for a share of the booty overcame my better judgement. I had hoped that it would be a short war; I had only needed a few thousand dead to be able to sit at the peace conference as a conqueror. But as you know only too well, the British, under Churchill – who had once admired me, who had once said that had he himself been born an Italian he would have worn the Black Shirt – did not give in. They drove me out of Africa, and now, with their American Allies, they are at my throat in Sicily. As ever, that accursed island is a nest of traitors. They are flocking to the Americans. I should have given my Prefect Mori more power to eradicate the scum, but now it is too late. Palermo has fallen. I know now I will not be able to resist an invasion of Italy itself without German support. When I stood on the balcony outside my office in the Palazzo Venezia and held the masses of Rome in the palm of my hand, I truly believed I was the heir of Caesar. I had only to thrust forth my proud jutting jaw and stare at them with my black fearsome eyes, and orate in my reverberating voice, which you think is the most beautiful in all of Italy. For years I proclaimed: "The Duce is always right" – but how will history judge me now? All I want is a little peace and a quiet life with you, my beloved Clara.

Your Benitito

Gela
Lt. Frank Dunford:
The sun had not yet risen from the sea but was already lightening the eastern sky and throwing crimson streaks across the water. The boats would soon be returning, and I was on my way to the fish market to gather their reports. In the half-light it was hard to make out the pathetic little figure sitting on the wall. Franco lifted his tear-stained face at my

approach, then lowered it and continued to cry, wiping his
wet nose with the back of his hand. I sat beside him and put
my arm around the little boy's thin shoulders.

"What's wrong?"

"My mother is weak. She cannot make milk. The new
baby is dying."

I took the boy's hand and led him to the harbour. It was
early; I wasn't sure if the depot would be open but there
would be a picket on duty. The large stone warehouse, that a
few days before had held the Italian prisoners, had reverted
to its original purpose. There was no sign of a sentry, but
the double wooden doors were slightly ajar. I sensed immediately something was wrong. I nodded to the boy to wait
and slipped inside. The comforting smell of fresh stores was
beginning to eradicate the stench of humanity. In the gloom
were stacks of crates containing K Rations, bully beef, powdered egg, powdered milk and sugar. I gazed down the long
lines of big cardboard boxes with the red and blue stamps
of the USA, which were as vital to victory as the ammunition
being unloaded on the docks outside. But these boxes contained the means of life, not the instruments of death. And
death was still stalking in Gela. It was waiting in Franco's
squalid home. A few cartons of powdered milk could keep
it at bay.

I looked around for the sergeant in charge, but nobody
appeared to be on duty. As my eyes and ears began to be
accustomed to the semi-darkness, I thought I could hear
whispers and movement coming from the distant corner
of the cavernous building. A light flashed onto the beams
high above. I made my way down a line of boxes and turned
right. Flashlights were flickering at an open door at the
back of the building. I thought I heard English being spoken. I unbuckled the revolver from the holster on my belt

and walked towards the sound. A sergeant was watching two Sicilians stacking boxes onto the back of an old truck, waiting in the alley outside. The bespectacled face of Sergeant Terranova swung round at my approach. The lens of his glasses reflected the torch in my hand.

"Good morning, Lieutenant," a hint of apprehension was in his voice, "we're just loading some special supplies for Major Vincenzo."

I was puzzled, "Why are military supplies being loaded on a civilian truck? Where are they going?"

Terranova gave a shrug. "I don't know; something to do with AMGOT."

"I thought I heard someone speaking English."

"English? No way. There's only me and these guys here."

The two Sicilians in the shadows smiled and nodded their heads. One had a thick black beard and a drooping eye. There was something vaguely familiar about him. The truck appeared to be fully laden: I made out dozens of boxes of cigarettes and enough supplies to feed a battalion. But they slammed the tailgate in place before I could ask any more questions, then hurried to the cab and drove rapidly away.

I turned to Terranova: "Did they have any documents? Any authorization?"

Terranova attempted a wink. "Why don't you talk to Major Vincenzo? He'll explain everything. Is there anything I can do for you, Lieutenant?"

I hesitated. I was reluctant to ask him favours, but remembered little Franco. "Yes. I wondered if you could let me have some cartons of powdered milk. There's a woman in town with a dying baby."

Terranova gave me a knowing, toothy smile. "Sure, Lieutenant, anything you want. We're all in this together."

❖❖❖

MY SICILIAN CAMPAIGN by General George S Patton Jr:
July 25, 1943

I received the following cable:

'*MANY CONGRATULATIONS TO YOU AND YOUR GALLANT SOLDIERS ON SECURING PALERMO. WOULD BE VERY HONOURED IF YOU WILL COME OVER AND BRING YOUR CHIEF OF STAFF. WE CAN THEN DISCUSS THE CAPTURE OF MESSINA – MONTY.'*

JULY 26, 1943

First thing in the morning, I piloted my personal Mitchell Bomber across this god-forsaken island to the airfield at Cassibile, just outside Syracuse. I have to admit it was a bumpy ride, despite the fact that my personal pilot sat beside me at the controls. As I exchanged pleasantries with the British, I was amused to see Powell and others of my weak-kneed staff making half-hearted efforts to recover their equilibriums. I sensed they were dreading the prospect of the return flight. Montgomery made no ceremony of my arrival; he hadn't even provided an honour guard. He led the way to his staff car, which was parked in the middle of the airfield, well away from the hangars and any eavesdroppers, and put the map of Sicily over the hood.

"You can have priority on the two main roads north of Etna." He pointed to the coast road from Palermo to Messina and the inland road that followed a tortuous route over the mountains from Nicosia to Randazzo. He looked up and smiled, "If things go well for you, and I am still held up south of Etna, you can push on past Randazzo and go on to the coast at Taormina. Then the Huns' escape route to Messina will cut off, and we'll have two whole German Divisions in the bag."

I gripped my swagger stick and stared hard down at the map before casting a glance at my chief of staff, Brigadier General Gay, who was standing beside me, with arms folded and a quizzical expression on his face. Not only was the path to Messina being laid open for the Seventh Army, but I was being given almost carte blanche to enter Monty's own sphere of influence. I looked incredulously at the august figure of Alexander, who had put on his glasses and was studiously studying the lines of advance Montgomery had suggested. The Deputy Commander in Chief had arrived late, and Monty had not bothered to brief him properly. Alexander became aware that all eyes were upon him; he cleared his throat and nodded his affirmation: "I'm certain Providence is looking after us. We'll soon be in Messina now."

Monty gave a condescending smile: "It will take another five weeks; September 1st would be my estimation. It will be hard fighting – everyone must go all out." His high-pitched, squeaky voice irritated me profoundly. It was the first time we three generals had met since North Africa and I was shocked at Monty's apparent lack of respect for his superior. His dress was not appropriate: casually rolled up sleeves, ridiculous shorts, bony knees and no tie. He reminded me of a scrawny chicken. Nevertheless, I was beginning to see through Alexander. I'd initially been impressed by his patrician bearing and reputation: Harrow, Sandhurst, and the Irish Guards. Thrice decorated in the Great War – he'd ended it commanding a Brigade at the age of twenty-six. In 1940, like Ney on the Retreat from Moscow, Alexander had led the British rearguard and was the last man off the beaches at Dunkirk. Two years later in Burma, he had successfully extracted British and Indian troops before the all-conquering Japanese. But the man had no imagination. He was intellectually lazy and seemed incapable of giving clear and firm decisions. He plainly didn't understand how to combine armour and air power in a mobile offensive battle. He appeared to have no plan of his own but relied on the suggestions of others, notably Montgomery's. I couldn't help suspecting that Montgomery had some secret stratagem: giving the Americans some bloody and unrewarding task, whilst taking the glory of capturing Messina for himself. But the little fella droned on, being positively friendly, which only increased my incredulity and suspicion. I looked across to Monty's caravan, where a trestle had been laid out for lunch under an awning. Some yellow canaries were singing in a cage and some very well-fed chickens were searching for crumbs under the table. It was a welcoming scene, but the pompous little bastard offered no invitation, and there were only two places laid at the table. He was obviously going to plot something with Alexander after we'd gone. What the hell? One day I would show the British how Southern Gentlemen behaved, treat them to warm American hospitality, and teach the bastards the respect that allies should show each other. I was more determined than ever to get to Messina first.

"I'll need landing craft. I'll make amphibious landings behind the German lines."

Alexander gave a worried frown: "We want to preserve them for the landings in Italy, but I'll inform the Navy of your requirements."

Montgomery sensed my restlessness. "Well, we mustn't keep you. I appreciate you must have a lot to do, but there is something I'd like to give you before you go. Even though I would never dream of smoking, people all over the Empire are sending me cigarettes by the thousands, which I distribute to my troops. It's excellent for morale; keeps me in touch with them. I received a box of these this morning. Please accept one with my compliments."

He reached into a pocket of his voluminous shorts and produced a cheap five-cent cigarette lighter. For once, I was lost for words.

❧❧❧

Letter from Benito Mussolini to Clara Petacci:
Cara Mia

I am glad you are safe in the country. It has been a sweltering day. Rome in the dog days of summer is insufferable and the meeting lasted seven hours. I counted the members of the Grand Council sitting around the long table. There were twenty-six of them, most of them nonentities who owed everything to me. They had called this meeting, the first for more than three years, for me to report on my meeting with Hitler. Such effrontery would have been unimaginable only a month ago. But now Rome has been bombed. Over 500 American planes have dropped over 1,000 tons of high explosives over our sacred city. Graziani's much-vaunted air defences only managed to hit two of the bombers. I caught the cold eyes of my son-in-law, Galeazzo Ciano, Conte di Cortellazzo. He had been a mere journalist on the make when he first attached himself to the Fascist cause. He married my daughter Edda out of pure ambition. I begin to envy Churchill, whose daughter married a damn Jew; an unfunny Viennese comedian to boot. At least he knows his place. Ciano is no longer content with being Minister for Foreign Affairs, he wants to make peace with the Allies and gain supreme power for himself. But the one I fear most was not there: Badoglio, the old soldier who stubbornly resisted the rise of Fascism. But in spite of his pride and attempted guise of an elder statesman, he is no different from the others. He accepted the title of Duca di Addis Abeba, following that easy victory in Ethiopia, when he was only fighting a primitive African. It was easy to be a hero then. I provided glory for them all.

My head was splitting: I was aware of someone shouting at me; incessantly. I could not believe anyone would address me in such a tone. It was that jackal Dino Grandi, Conte di Mordano: a two-bit lawyer, who in the early days made a pathetic attempt to challenge me for the leadership of the party. I turned and fixed my dark eyes upon him. Once that frown would have been enough to silence the bravest opponent, but today even Grandi defied me: "You believe that you have the devotion of the people. You lost it the day you tied Italy to Germany. You believed yourself a soldier – let me tell you, Italy was lost the very day you put the gold braid of a marshal on your cap. A hundred thousand mothers cry: 'Mussolini assassinated my son!'"

And then they called for a vote.

A vote?

I am the Duce, for twenty years my word has been law.

The motion?

That the King should assume effective command of the Italian armed forces?

That the responsibilities of both Crown and Parliament should be restored?

The hands went up around the table.

Nineteen votes to seven called for my dismissal.

My beloved, all I want now is to be lost in your soft arms.

Your Benito.

❧❧❧

Gela
Lt. Frank Dunford:

I'd spent a fruitless morning on the wharfs, attempting to gather information on sightings of enemy movements from the fishing boats. The Allied air forces had now almost total domination of the skies, and the German and Italian navies seemed to have vacated the southern coast of Sicily entirely, although there were rumours of great concentrations and movement in the north-east, across the straits of Messina. The catch had been bad, as it had been every day. The older fishermen told me the breeding grounds had been ruined. The war had caused such a shortage of basic foods, that the Fascist authorities had forced them to use dragnets, which had destroyed the roe and all the young sardines and anchovies. Nevertheless, to my surprise, I'd seen crates of fish being loaded into unmarked trucks, and when I'd questioned the sergeant on duty he'd told me they were special shipments going out with the authority of Major Vincenzo. It seemed that half the catch was going to these secret destinations and the quota for the local population wouldn't be met. Something stank – and it wasn't the fish. When I questioned the sergeant further, I learned that Captain Limo was back from Palermo and was in the cannery with the Major. I was tempted to forget it – let it alone – it had nothing to do with me. But I thought of Franco's hungry face and reluctantly made my way towards the smoke of the cannery.

The stink was even worse than in New York. The steaming vats, where tuna were being boiled, reminded me of a painting of Hell which had terrified me as a child. Blood was seeping into the earth floor, covered with decapitated heads and innards, thrown down by the women who were gutting and filleting anchovies and sardines and laying them in salt or oil. Girls, little more than children, and some of the younger women, their dark skirts caught up between their legs and tucked into their waists high above their sturdy calves, were standing in tubs of brine and pressing down fish with their bare feet. The brine, splashing up to their thighs, had dried white on their skin. A few were singing or humming snatches of sad songs. Yet more women, some of them old and haggard, were straining on ropes, hoisting heavy baskets of steaming fish from the vats, then stacking them in cases, one on top of the other. Many of the women's hands and feet were inflamed and bleeding from sores. Little Franco's mother had worked here before she got too big with the child. The boy had told me the brine ate into her flesh, causing it to sting and burn like red-hot coals.

I made my way through the smoke and fumes until I made out the bulky shape of Vincenzo beside the slim figure of Captain Limo. They were in deep conversation with a smartly dressed stranger in well-cut jacket, riding breeches and boots, with a felt hat, pulled rakishly over one eye. He had a pencil-thin moustache and cruel mouth.

Limo turned at my approach: "Lieutenant Dunford, just the guy I want. You'll have to lend a hand in here. We've got to get the fish processed quicker. Major Vincenzo has got urgent requests from all over the island."

I shot a glance at the desperate labour going on all around and thought of Franco's mother. "The women are working as hard as they can. It isn't women's work anyway. There are enough men in town desperate for a job."

Limo shrugged: "This work has always been done by women. Besides, the men would want more pay. We haven't got unlimited funds."

"The women are doing a man's work. They should get a man's wage. I thought this war was about bringing justice and democracy."

"It's about making sure that those Bolshevik bastards don't take over the rest of Europe. You sound like one yourself."

Something told me I should back off but I found myself pushing on: "Why not do a deal with the unions, like we did in New York? We are all in this together."

"These women have no union. In any case the Communists have infiltrated all the unions. They are corrupt, disruptive and would hamper your efforts to win the war." The stranger spoke English with hardly an accent. "You will get better results without them."

Limo looked closely at me, as if tabling my reaction: "What we call collective bargaining is unknown here. Any wage scale they had was buried under a mass of Fascist indemnities. Besides, as you know, we've just introduced our new currency: the Occupation Lira. We have to exercise extreme caution or else prices will become chaotic."

Major Vincenzo, shuffled uneasily, put on his most affable smile, and sought to lessen the tension. "Lieutenant, this is Signor Montelepre. He owns this cannery, and is advising me on the distribution."

I shook the proffered hand coldly: it was beautifully manicured. Again an inner voice cautioned me to keep quiet, but I couldn't hold back. "Perhaps you can tell me the destination of the distribution. The other morning, very early, I found an entire truckload of Army supplies leaving the warehouse. I have made some enquiries, it seems a truck goes out every night, but nobody can tell me where it goes; and just now I discovered that half of this morning's catch had been requisitioned and driven away. We have people going hungry here in the town. Every basic food is almost unobtainable. Children are dying."

The smile left Montelepre's face. He was about to reply but Limo cut in: "I think we understand the problems of food distribution better than you, Lieutenant. My people are working day and night to stabilize the situation and render whatever practicable aid we can to allay disease and unrest. Maybe you're not cut out for this job after all. The intelligence you've managed to gather is negligible. Perhaps it would be better if I recommend you return to your gunnery duties."

Letter from Benito Mussolini to Clara Petacci:

Cara Mia,

I pray this reaches you. There are so few now I can trust. I disregarded the vote of the Council and went to the King at the Villa Savoia. I had no doubt that Vittorio Emanuele would support me. I had always been able to dominate him and I knew the frail old fool had no wish to take up the burdens and responsibilities of the war. I addressed him in my usual manner, justifying my conduct and pointing out where the blame for the mistakes and disaster lay. But today, although he was agitated and frightened, he summoned up the courage to interrupt me. I will never forget his words: "Dear Duce, I should have opposed you years ago, but I was weak. I thought things would turn out for the best, but things don't work anymore. Italy has gone to pieces. We have suffered one ignominious defeat after another." The afternoon sun sparkled on the undeserved medals and decorations on his breast, momentarily dazzling my eyes. I shook my head in disbelief as the old buffoon continued:

"The morale of the army is prostrate – it is filled with saw-dust. The soldiers no longer want to fight. At this moment you are the most hated man in Italy. You must resign." He took a sip of Pellegrino and carefully wiped his mouth with a silk napkin, like an old woman. "But I do not wish to see your Government replaced by the Christian Democrats and Communists. I want to save the monarchy for my son. With the backing of the army, we can have gradual change and not sink into anarchy. I am going to ask Marshal Badoglio to form a government. He is popular with the masses and will be able to disengage us from this dreadful war."

I could not believe my ears. "You forget my sovereign that the power in Rome rests with my Fascist Militia. They will not allow the Fascist Government to be replaced."

Beneath his thick white moustache, he gave one of his rare nervous smiles. "The Piave and Ariete Divisions are already in the city. They have pledged their allegiance to Badoglio and the Crown. Mussolini, you will have to go. There is no other course open to Italy or me."

History was repeating itself. His grandfather had betrayed Garibaldi: now Vittorio Emanuele was betraying me. I struggled to find my voice: "Sire, this is the end of Italy's glory. It will be the end of the monarchy."

Vittorio Emanuele was already picking up the phone on his desk as I gave the Fascist salute and marched out of the room. Armed soldiers were stationed all along the corridor but did not salute as I passed. A flunkey opened the door and I stepped outside into the hot sun. Sweat was dripping from beneath my hat into my eyes, although my mouth was strangely dry. All I wanted now was to seek com-fort between your soft breasts. I looked for my limousine, with its bullet-proof windows and reinforced steel doors, and my faithful driver and bodyguards. They were not there. A captain of carabinieri was waiting at the bottom of the steps.

"It would be safer Duce, if you travelled back to Rome in this." The sun sparkled on the polished black leather of his Napoleon-like hat. I reflected bitterly that Bonaparte had also been betrayed.

The captain waved and a shabby Red Cross ambulance trundled forward across the crunching gravel. The double doors at the back were opened from within and rough arms dragged me inside. I, Caesar's rightful heir, have been bundled away to captivity. I do not know where they are taking me, my beloved. I have given a guard my gold watch. He swears this letter will reach you. I must finish now before the guard is changed.

Your Benito.

Palermo
Lt. Danny Crivello:

I made my way back from the harbour, peering into every café and bar, looking vainly for a trace of anyone who resembled Uncle Tony. I began to believe it hadn't been him in the photo at all. It was a trick of light or a shadow as Capa had suggested. Dusk was falling when I found myself in the Piazza Marina, one of the largest squares in Palermo. In the middle was a small park, the Giardino Garibaldi, in which stood huge foreign-looking trees. Their branches reached hungrily down into the earth, writhing like giant serpents. Beneath the branches, among the tortuous naked roots, I became aware of dark and furtive figures twisting and rolling. The park was surrounded by a delicate cast iron fence, decorated with bows and arrows, rabbits, deer and birds, symbols of the chase. There was plenty of hunting was going on tonight, but the game was of a different nature. All around the fence, men stood with their wives on their arms, waiting to do business with GIs, who walked up and down, window-shopping, before making their choice. Some shame-faced fathers were even offering their daughters; their destitution so great that their own flesh was the only commodity they had to sell. Many of the women looked ill and dirty, but the soldiers didn't seem to mind – a piece of ass was just a piece of ass. For five minutes they could forget their fears and homesickness. They handed over dollar bills, the only currency that mattered, the seeming panacea for all of Europe's ills, before fumbling with the women among the branches of the gigantic trees. A park keeper was offering the hire of filthy mattresses for an extra twenty-five cents from his little brick hut at the corner. A few Negro soldiers, who'd driven supply trucks up from Gela and had been allowed into town for the evening, were enjoying white women for the first time. I stared incredulously. This was different from that heady night of liberation in Villalba – this was sordid, degrading, animal coupling. I began to question the idealized image of Gina that had been occupying my thoughts and longings: was she no better than these women? Did she feel for me as I did for her, or did she only look upon me as a meal ticket, a way to escape from this terrible poverty and squalor? Was she even now lying by the river in Villalba with some GI for the price of a packet of cigarettes? A knot of jealousy twisted in my stomach. I hadn't seen Falco all day. Had he gone back to claim her? I couldn't even write to her. I had no address. I'd forgotten the name of the squalid street in which she lived, opposite the caged Magdalene. I didn't even have a name, apart from Gina – Gina, c/o Don Calo Vizzini, Villalba. Don Calo. Was he keeping her for himself for when her mother became too old to satisfy his desires? I shuddered at the thought of Gina's body contaminated by Calo's corrupt and filthy flesh. What was the power he held over her? I realized my hopes and happiness were hanging by a scanty thread. I wanted her so deeply; the image of her beauty, smell and touch was so vibrant in my memory; but would she prove less perfect if I ever saw her again?

Two ragged women came up and smiled at me revealing black and missing teeth: "Signor want good fuck? Uno dollar?"

I hurriedly shook my head. They sneered and sauntered away. It was hard to believe they were same species as Gina. If I didn't rescue her would she end up like them? The women were already being eagerly propositioned by a couple of fresh-faced GIs.

"Yankee pigs." A smartly dressed young woman was watching with derision stamped on her pretty face.

"We have come here to help you," I answered in Italian.

"You speak Italian?" There was a note of surprise, perhaps fear, in her voice.

"I was born here."

Her scorn returned. "Are you not ashamed?"

"Why should I be ashamed?"

"You fight against your own people."

"America is my country now. I am Sicilian. I believe in the power of an oath. I swore an oath to the American flag and I will honour it."

"Your honour has destroyed my beautiful Palermo with a thousand bombs and left it bleeding to death."

"That is war. We did not want war – but now we are here we will give you freedom and democracy."

"Freedom!" Her brown eyes flashed. "Your Generals Alexander and Patton issue proclamations that forbid us to be out in the streets after eight o'clock at night. We cannot speak against you; we cannot bear arms to protect ourselves even when your glorious soldiers enter our homes to loot." I found her eyes seductive in their scorn. "I am forbidden even to take a bath."

"You are lucky. Most of the people here have nothing worth looting – and baths are the least of their worries."

She gave a flicker of a smile. "That at least is true. When Garibaldi came to Palermo he gave the people soap and they thought it was cheese." A corporal had just made his choice and took a shamefaced woman by the hand and led her into a clump of bushes a few yards from where we were standing. Her husband shuffled past with tears in his eyes. The young woman watched his bent figure move into the shadows. "Not all Italians are cowards and pimps. Mussolini wanted to give them dignity. To give them an Empire like the British and the French. He made them proud of being Italians. You have taken away their pride."

"It will be different when the war is over. We will help you build a new Europe."

"How little you Americans know. My brother wears a Black Shirt and is still fighting here in Sicily, and even now my father is in Russia, helping the Germans defeat the Reds. You should be fighting beside them there, not against us here. One day you will realize the terrible mistake you have made."

She tossed her curls and walked towards the large undamaged houses on the north side of the square.

Pa was standing before me with my mother on his arm. I couldn't understand why they were dressed shabbily, like the citizens of Palermo around the Giardino Garibaldi. Pa was holding out one hand, like a beggar, offering my mother to me. My proud mother stared at the ground, fearful humiliation on her face. My father was now speaking to me, but I couldn't understand: it was so difficult, there was so much noise. Then, through the no man's land of half slumber I began to make out a loud and frantic banging on my door. Before I could respond, someone had entered my small, insalubrious chamber and was shaking me violently. My father's face dissolved through clouds of departing sleep; I smelt sweet-scented soap and then slowly made out the rounded features of Major Powell.

"Lieutenant, you're wanted urgently. Typhoid has broken out in the Cortile Cascino district; practically just across the road. The carabinieri are in a panic – they say we must impose a complete quarantine on the area."

"Why me?" I groaned, "I'm needed at the port."

"There's nobody else who can speak Italian and it comes under AMGOT's umbrella. Anyway, nothing is going into those warehouses until the Engineers clear the harbour, and then the first priority will be military. Patton wants to bring in the 9th Division as soon as possible, they're due today – there's nothing for you to do." I began to protest but Powell cut me short: "The General Staff are up to their eyes with planning the new campaign. I don't know why we couldn't just sit here comfortably on our prats and let Monty finish the goddamn war on his own, but Patton has his own ideas. As well as scheduling the disembarkation of the 9th, I've got to organize the visit of the British tomorrow. Patton is going right over the top." He shook his head contemptuously: "Honour guards and a state banquet! You'd think the King of England was coming, instead of that smug little runt, Monty. You're the only person we can spare. Take a detachment of medical orderlies and get your ass over there. That's an order. You're in charge."

The major turned and hurriedly left the cell-like room without waiting for my response. Powell, in the manner of all staff officers, was avoiding an unpleasant job and washing his hands of any responsibility. But in one way the fatass major was right. There was really nothing for me to do at the harbour. Limo had entrusted the hiring of the civilian workers to the smartly dressed Sicilian, who'd been contracted to do the work for a set fee. I got out of my cot, splashed water on my face and dressed hurriedly.

A three-ton Dodge ambulance covered in red crosses, together with a spotty faced, jug-eared, young corporal with white medic's armband, plus two orderlies, were waiting in the courtyard of the Palazzo. The corporal gave a casual salute as I descended the Grand Staircase. "Morning sir. Corporal Robb reporting for duty." He didn't stand on ceremony and immediately got into the ambulance behind the wheel. I returned the salute, noticing that the stripes on the boy's sleeve were new and badly sewn on.

"What's this all about?" I climbed up beside the corporal, who hit the ignition as the orderlies clambered into the rear.

"A case of typhoid has broken out in a tenement. The other occupants reported it to the local priest and he got in touch with the carabinieri. They reported it to us. Apparently they treat it like the plague – no one wants to come close to the infected."

Robb was not a good driver and the engine was shuddering as we drove out into the Corso Vittorio Emanuele, with the siren blaring. A policeman blew his whistle and directed us towards the next turning on the right: the Corso Alberto Amedeo. It was as if we'd gone back to the darkest times of the Dark Ages. Nothing that I'd witnessed in the slums of Villalba, or any other part of Sicily or North Africa, had prepared me for this. Swarms of little naked children were playing in the mud and filth that lay thick in the gutters on either side of the street. The stench made my empty stomach retch. I retched even more when I realized the mud was mostly compounded of human excrement and urine. Decrepit tenements, three or four storeys high, loomed overhead, cutting out the sunlight and the scant fresh air that had managed to invade the oppressive heat of the city. Lines of ragged clothes stretched from one side of the street to the other, like bunting, celebrating the triumph of destitution and despair. Carabinieri were stationed at every corner, saluting and waving us on, their cloaks and smart black uniforms in stark contrast to the poverty all around. Through the windscreen, I saw two carabinieri standing guard outside a three-storeyed tenement, which seemed even more dilapidated than all the rest. A young lieutenant stepped into the street, frantically waving his arms and blowing his whistle.

He saluted nervously as we drew up beside him. "It's on the top floor." He spoke with a Tuscan accent, not giving the victim the dignity of gender.

I got out, with the others behind me. "Lead the way."

The lieutenant hesitated. "There is no need for so many to go inside. It will only spread the pestilence. We are keeping the building and its inhabitants in complete isolation."

"What did he say?" It was the first time Robb had spoken. I translated.

Robb nodded. "He's a yellow belly, but he's right. Let's just you and me have a look see." He took a musty smelling bandage from his haversack. "Put this around your mouth – it's sprinkled with DDT."

The two orderlies gratefully remained outside, as I tied the bandage tightly and led the way into the hovel. The sweet sickly scent of the DDT helped eradicate the foul and rancid odours that permeated the entire building. The floor at street level was simply packed dirt. The windows had long been broken and boarded up, so that there was no source of light or air but that of the open door behind us. There were doorways, bereft of doors, on each side of the narrow corridor leading to the stairs. Each doorway was crammed with people: silent, spiritless men; exhausted, sick-looking women; and emaciated, almost naked children of all types and sizes. There appeared to be at least three families living in each fetid room. They watched with fearful eyes as we passed, looking like masked bank robbers from some Western movie, or the veiled creatures of Death itself. The pestilence, that had persecuted them and their forefathers through the ages, had returned once more to claim its pitiless toll.

Robb and I began to climb the cracked stone stairs. The walls were sweating damp as if exuding poison. Cockroaches were resting out of reach on the crumbling plaster of the ceiling, with last night's food stuffed tight inside them. There was no sign of running water or sanitation. Slop buckets, overflowing with the night's soil, were outside every door. A young man and woman were anxiously watching our ascent up the stairwell from the top floor. As I drew closer I could see traces of beauty in the woman's dirt-streaked face, and a glimmer of hope and expectation in the dark soft eyes of the man. The couple anxiously beckoned us into a room, which at least had some light and air. There was a gaping hole in the roof, through which I could see the azure blue of the Mediterranean sky. There was no furniture in the room – empty jerry cans served as chairs; a wooden box was the table. A black robed priest was kneeling by a filthy mattress on which lay a little naked child. It was a girl, dark-haired, thin, wasted, and whimpering with exhaustion. Attached to her almost skeletal little stomach were five dark shapes, wriggling as if in sensual pleasure, catching the sunlight on their shiny black flesh.

Robb stopped in his tracks: "Jesus! Leeches! Now I've seen everything."

The middle-aged priest who was applying the creatures looked up. Beside him were an empty jar and a saucer of red wine, in which more leeches were undulating slowly.

"What on earth is he doing?" I tried to remember my mother's old tales.

"He's giving them wine to drink so that they get drunk and throw up the bad blood they've sucked. Then he puts them back into that jar to use again. No wonder these people are sick." Robb had already taken his haversack from his shoulder. "How long has she been like this?"

I repeated the question to the priest. The suffering of his flock was etched in every line of his face: "It came yesterday: in the evening."

I translated. Robb shook his head in disgust. "It's a miracle any of them survive. I have seen animals live cleaner. They have no idea or concept of simple hygiene."

The priest understood some English although he still spoke in Italian: "These are the most wretched people in all Europe. They have no money for proper medicine or drugs, even if they were available. The leech is all they have. All they can afford." He glanced momentarily at the angry pustules on Robb's forehead, "At least they suck out the bad blood."

The mother's anguish overcame her natural timidity. "Last week was the feast of Santa Rusalia; she once saved our city from the plague. We prayed to her to protect us, but she has so many prayers to answer she cannot listen to them all." Her tears were washing the dirt from her gaunt cheeks. "She is our only child. I cannot have another."

"What did she say?" Robb was rummaging in his haversack as I duly translated. "Santa Rusalia – they might as well pray to Santa Claus! They're still living in the Middle Ages. If they were Americans they'd get up and help themselves."

A flash of anger entered the priest's grey eyes and he answered Robb directly in English. "The young man here has never had a job. He goes to the hiring market every day. He has no clock, so he gets out of bed as soon as he hears the cock crow. He dares not go back to sleep; he might be late and miss his only chance. He walks through the town in the pitch dark every day to look for work, but he has not got the money to bribe the men that hire and so is never chosen. His wife walks into the countryside; sometimes she walks fifteen kilometres in the blinding heat, looking for wild fennel, frogs and snails. That is their diet and their life, but they never despair. They trust in the bounty of God."

Robb nodded thoughtfully and produced a small packet of salt. He sprinkled them on the leeches and carefully removed them from the thin little body. Each leech left a small red ring where their sharp teeth had fastened, and a small hole through which the blood had been sucked. Once the child opened her eyes and cried out with fear at the sight of the strange masked man bending over her, but was calmed by her mother's touch upon her fevered brow. After Robb had removed the last leech, he took a box of pills from his haversack. He handed them and his own water bottle to the woman. "This is the bounty of Uncle Sam. Tell her to give the little girl these. I'll leave the box. Give her two every two hours. And make sure she only drinks clean water. She can have these water purification tablets as well." He took another box from his haversack. "Meantime, we will spray the entire building with DDT and fill all those slop buckets with disinfectant."

The dark eyes of the child's father were regarding Robb with the dumb faith and expectation of a dog. I asked the question I knew he was afraid to ask: "Will she live?"

Robb put his hand to his right cheek, just above his protective DDT bandage, and squeezed a red blotch. "She was suffering from malnutrition before she caught the typhoid. If she got decent uncontaminated food and pure water, she might have a chance."

I recollected that Powell had put me in charge of the entire situation. The decision was simple. "We'll see that she gets it, and so will as many of those other poor kids as possible." I turned to the father: "We will do all we can to help you. Keep the room as clean as you can. Burn those blankets and the mattress. We will bring you clean bedding and more medicine and food. And lay off with the leeches and the frogs and snails."

The priest permitted himself a wan smile: "God bless you, my son."

The child's father sank to his knees, grabbed my hands between his own and smothered them with kisses.

⚜⚜⚜

MY SICILIAN CAMPAIGN by General George S Patton Jr: The downfall of Mussolini had changed the military situation completely. Would the new Italian Government fight on? It was imperative that the Allies crossed over to mainland Italy as soon as possible. I was therefore not surprised to receive the following cable from Montgomery:

'WOULD LIKE TO VISIT YOU ON WED. 28 JULY. WOULD ARRIVE AIRFIELD 1200 IN MY FORTRESS. QUERY. IS

*THIS CONVENIENT TO YOU. WOULD BRING MY CHIEF
OF STAFF. WILL YOU PLEASE NOTIFY ALL YOUR ANTI-
AIRCRAFT GUN STATIONS I WILL BE TRAVELLING IN A
FORTRESS ROUND THE SOUTH COAST.'*

Eisenhower had jokingly offered Monty a Flying Fortress
in recognition of his contribution to the victory in North
Africa, not expecting him to accept it. I decided to make
every effort to provide a far more impressive reception than
he had given me, and a full parade, with honour guard was
lined up to greet him at the airfield. A Marine Band was
poised to strike up *God Save the King*, the moment Monty's
foot hit the tarmac.

"I would reckon that runway is too short for a B-17,"
someone murmured behind me, as the giant plane thundered down towards us. I noticed Major Powell nervously
adjusting his tie. I recalled telling him to check the length
of the runway. I hoped it had not slipped his mind. The
wheels of the huge aircraft hit the tarmac and began to race
along it, without any discernible loss of speed, towards the
hangars at the far end.

"Jesus Christ!" exclaimed another voice. "There's a
squadron of Mustangs being refuelled and rearmed over
there. If it doesn't stop, there'll be one hell of a bang."
Major Powell looked as though he might have to change his
underwear.

The gap between the Fortress and the hangars was
decreasing ever rapidly. As it raced past, I could see the
ashen faces of our British counterparts, sitting frozen in the
glass domes where the gun emplacements had been. Monty
and his entire staff seemed destined for a mighty confla-
gration. Then, when all seemed lost, the pilot, using excep-
tional skill, revved up the port engine in deafening roars
and somehow managed to swing away from the hangars by

applying all the brakes on the starboard side. The monster plane rose from the ground very slightly, as if it was a game bird being brushed by a wayward shot. It trembled for an instant before crashing down on one side.

"Oh, my God!" Major Powell uttered behind my ear.

Immediately bells and alarms were ringing at maximum pitch, as ambulances and fire engines sped to the succour of the British. It took courage as the fuel tanks could well explode, but the water hoses were soon in play and the staff and crew began to be evacuated to safety. But there was no sign of the famous black beret and beaky nose. I feared for a moment that the accident had robbed the Allies of one of our best generals. The loss could be crucial to the entire war. There would be certainly an inquiry. Powell had gone deathly white: his career could be ruined. Then, just as I was convinced Powell would suffer complete disgrace and ignominy, there was a stir of activity around the rear door, and a familiar figure calmly emerged with a pile of documents in his hand.

Monty and his staff were escorted into the city centre with an escort of white-helmeted military police in siren-screeching scout cars and motorcycles. Inside the court-yard of the Royal Palace another band greeted them with a second rendition of *God Save the King* and *The Stars and Stripes*. A second honour guard made up of three regiments awaited Montgomery's inspection, together with my entire staff in their Number One uniforms. I had made sure my own turnout was even more immaculate than usual. My personal orderly and driver, Sergeant William Meeks, a veteran cavalryman who had been with me for years, had pressed my bespoke brass-buttoned battle jacket, studded with four rows of campaign ribbons and decorations, to perfection. My shoulders, shirt collar and helmet were bedecked with stars. I felt every inch a general. Monty by contrast wore a plain khaki shirt, devoid of any mark of rank or distinction. He was wearing a new beret, perched like a rookie's, inelegantly on his head.

I had ensured that a bewigged and breeched attendant waited behind every chair in the state dining room. A banquet, especially prepared by Mess Sergeant Lee, was served off the finest china and everyone, apart from the teetotal Montgomery, drank champagne out of glasses of the purest crystal. The champagne had been supplied by a local black marketer, who had been released from jail on my specific orders. Once the champagne had been delivered, I ordered his re-arrest.

After the meal, Montgomery and I walked alone in the exquisite beauty and solitude of the Cappella Palatina. Monty was feeling very pleased with himself. "That was a great reception. You Americans really are the most delightful people."

I was not sure if I'd been given a compliment. "I must apologize for my aides not clarifying that the runway was unsuitable for a B-17."

"It didn't worry me in the least. I was too busy with my plans to notice, but it was a pity to lose the Fortress, I had begun to look upon it as my flying Rolls Royce. However, I appreciate that it is too large for strategic airfields. I will ask Ike to supply me with a C-47 and a jeep. That would be ideal for Italy. You Americans are magnificent Allies. You provide us with the best equipment and are so easy to work with." He stopped and gazed up at the archangels around the central apse. "But if I may say so, I would suggest that you look to your administration. There is obviously a hitch in your chain of command. I have noticed that American Generals do not seem to understand administration in the field."

I bit my tongue at what I considered a blatant insult. I had heard that when Monty had returned to England after El Alamein, he had been idolized by the victory-starved British public. When he went to the theatre the whole house rose to their feet to applaud him. It must have turned the little fella's head. The Romans knew what they were doing when they had a slave whispering, 'Remember you are only a man,' in a conqueror's ear when he rode in his triumph. I made a mental note to make sure it would not happen to me.

Monty was examining a white marble candelabrum, considered the oldest Romanesque work of art in all Sicily. "The one thing you do have is mobility. I think you should move as quickly as possible. Go all out with your four Divisions."

"I now have five," I found himself boasting like a schoolboy. "I've brought over my reserve Division, the 9th, from Tunisia. They began to disembark last night. But the others are not up to full fighting strength." I had received reports that very morning that my all-out drive on Palermo had wreaked havoc on the tracks of my tanks. Seventy-five per cent of them were at present out of action, but I was determined not to give Montgomery the satisfaction of knowing it. "You forget we have conquered over half the island. I need to garrison troops everywhere."

Monty flicked his superior smile: "Perhaps it was not such a good plan to take Palermo after all. I was against it from the start – a tactical but not a strategic triumph. I dread to think how many troops you will need to garrison it."

I could not resist a repost. "What's taking you so long? You've been stuck at Catania for weeks."

"I am laying down airfields on the southern edge of the Catania Plain for my Spitfires and Kitty Hawk bomber

squadrons. Then I have got to take the foothills around
Etna to build more airfields – out of range of the enemy's
long-range guns." He smiled kindly, as if explaining a
difficult problem to a slow pupil. "Americans don't seem
to understand the possibilities of airpower. It takes time
to set up a big air command. You cannot operate a tactical air force without a telephone layout. You miss all
the good opportunities." He smiled patronizingly before
adding as an afterthought, "By the way, I think you
Americans should establish an independent air force,
like the RAF."

"I think we are managing pretty well as we are. We must
have some qualities that you admire."

"Without question. As I said, I have been impressed
by American speed of manoeuvre and boldness. But you
can always learn to be better soldiers. I have been in this
war now for nearly four years. It took me many months
in Egypt to train my Eighth Army into the fine fighting machine it is, with my own set-up and technique."
He broke off momentarily and looked up to inspect the
carved coffers of the painted wooden ceiling. He nodded
his approval at the exquisite Arab workmanship, before
turning his bright beady eyes back to me. "And in spite of
the opposition from those Generals in England, who said
it would only work in the desert, it has defeated the Boche
here in Sicily as well."

"I think the Seventh Army has assisted you a little."

Montgomery smiled, his vanity not recognizing the
resentment in my tone. "Of course, and you can help me
again. It is imperative that my experienced veterans of the
Eighth Army should head the invasion of mainland Italy,
but they have been in the line now for more than fifteen
days. They need a rest before their next ordeal. You will

have to take the responsibility for finishing things off here. You must drive eastwards at full strength along the north coast whilst I advance from the south. Then, when the full weight of our power is turned on the enemy hemmed into the north-east corner around Messina, I don't see how he can get away. It will be a very bloody killing match. He will fight desperately, to gain time to strengthen his defences on mainland Italy and in the hope of early winter rains, but he is doomed if we act swiftly and properly."

I was convinced that Montgomery merely wanted the Americans to serve as a diversion to drive German formations from his own front, and clear the way for a swift British swoop on Messina. "What do you plan on doing after that?"

Monty gave a sharp laugh. "Once we have cleaned up Sicily, I will take a strong force and sail into the Bay of Naples, land there, capture the city, and cut off all the Germans in the toe of Italy..." He broke off and looked at me closely: "Are you feeling well? You look a bit off colour."

"I think I have a dose of fever coming on."

"Could be malaria. Look after yourself; we're going to need you. I would lay off alcohol. I drink gallons of fresh lemonade every day. Make use of the local resources. I am always at my fittest in the field. Active service seems to suit me. I am never better than when I am fighting."

I could hold back no longer. "Does it worry you that many people think you are a cocky sonofabitch?"

Monty shook his head in self-satisfaction, failing to detect any animosity. His relentless mind appeared to tolerate no shades of doubt. "I fight to get the big thing right. I have won too many battles to mind in the least any mud that is thrown. All I want to do is win this war. The Boche is a very good soldier; he is far too good to be left being a menace to the world. He must be stamped on."

Montgomery flew back to Cassibile in a C-47, convinced that he had me firmly in his pocket. That evening he penned a personal message to all his troops:

'On your behalf I have expressed to the Commander of the American Seventh Army on our left, the congratulations of the Eighth Army for the way American troops have captured and cleaned up more than half the island in record time. We are proud to fight beside our American Allies. The beginnings have been very good, thanks to your splendid fighting qualities and to the hard work and devotion to duty of all those who work in the ports, on the roads, and in the rear areas. We must not forget to give thanks to THE LORD MIGHTY IN BATTLE for giving us such a good beginning towards the attainment of our object. And now let us get on with job. Together with our American Allies we have knocked Mussolini off his perch. We will now drive the Germans out of Sicily.

Into battle with stout hearts, good luck to you all.'

I received Monty's message and stared down into the almost empty Piazza del Parlamento from the window of the State Bedroom, with a large cut-glass tumbler of malt Scotch in my hand. It was a relief to drink liquor without Montgomery's disapproving eyes upon me. Eisenhower would soon have to decide who would lead the American landing in mainland Italy. It would be a close call between me and Mark Clarke. Clarke was eight years my junior, but had got his third general's star before me. In my opinion, Clarke was a glamour boy with no knowledge of men or war. Nevertheless, he had established a close relationship with Eisenhower. I reasoned that if my Seventh Army could take Messina as swiftly as it took Palermo, the Press and the American public would make it impossible for Eisenhower to deny me. On top of that I would prove once and for all to that cocky bastard Montgomery, and the world, that American soldiers were every bit as good as the British, and that I was the better general. I had to take Messina on my own, without any help from the British. It would be a horse race with the prestige of the US Army at stake. I resolved to use every means – even those Sicilian gangsters that led us over the mountains.

10

TROINA

MY SICILIAN CAMPAIGN by General George S Patton Jr:

And so the campaign for Sicily moved towards its final phase, as Montgomery laboriously fought his way into new positions to the east and west of Etna, and I swung round the axis of my forces for an all-out advance. The Seventh Army was in a poor tactical position. Keyes's Corps had been scattered throughout Western Sicily during their rapid drive to Palermo; Bradley was endeavouring to turn some of his forces 180 degrees so that they faced east instead of west. Moreover, the mountain ranges divided his command into two separate lines of advance. The 1st Division had fought its way up through the centre of the island, taking the stronghold of Enna, but was already encountering stiff resistance at Nicosia. The 45th under Middleton, after three weeks of constant combat, was already in position to the east of Cefalu, but meeting strong German opposition all along the northern coastline, which was bisected by easily defendable streams and ridges, running from the mountains to the sea. Each stream and each ridge would have to be crossed at a price.

The German forces, now under the sole command of the skilful General Hube, had constructed an even tighter line of defence. The key positions in that line were two mountain towns: Adriano in the British sector and Troina in the American. They stood like armed sentinels, blocking the only road, through the highest and most rugged mountains in Sicily, to Randazzo and Messina beyond. To take those towns would cost a mighty effusion of sweat and blood. Nevertheless it had to be done – and quickly. I sensed Bradley, essentially an infantryman, had an innate dislike for my swift cavalry tactics. He tried to convince me that the strength and determination of the German defence would force him to advance carefully with outflanking manoeuvres and full artillery support. But I would brook no discussion, and told him: "I don't want you to waste time, even if you've got to spend men to do it. You must beat Monty to Messina."

He did not take it well. I had heard he considered me a shallow commander who never gave a careful estimate of the situation, a showman to whom the 'show' always came first. I was concerned that he might hinder the advance.

Palermo
Lt. Danny Crivello:
The longing for Gina's body never left me, but I became so completely engrossed in my new task that I temporarily forgot Luciano and Don Calo. After supervising the erection of field kitchens throughout the narrow streets of Cortile Cascino, I'd begged, borrowed and acquisitioned all the food I could find throughout the length and breadth of Palermo. When that proved insufficient, I'd driven over the

makeshift piers and gone on board the Navy ships, which were now gradually entering the harbour, to persuade the cooks to give me the waste and scraps from their galleys and mess halls. Army cooks then boiled anything wholesome in great metal pots in their field kitchens, and three times a day the carabinieri blew a blast on their trumpets to summon the hungry. The hungry came and waited patiently in great long lines, holding empty tin cans, bottles and jam jars: anything to carry away the glutinous mess that was their sole source of life. It was a modern re-enactment of the feeding of the five thousand, but these thousands were always hungry and one miracle of loaves and fishes would never suffice.

Returning from yet another scavenge of the ships, our jeep laden with overflowing bins of scraps, the mass of people was so thick in Corso Alberto Amedo that we were forced to grind to a halt. The clamour of voices was deafening. I was hot and tired. I cussed, stood on the seat and looked over the seething sea of heads towards the back of the truck that was the centre of the excitement. There was a glint of sunlight on steel-framed glasses. Standing on the tailgate I could make out the familiar figure of Corporal Robb. I raised my binoculars and saw that the medic was distributing boxes of pills and water purification tablets to all and sundry. I jumped down and pushed my way through the crowd. Robb saw me approaching and grinned: "This truck just arrived up from Gela on the way to the front. I thought these people would need it more. I persuaded our friend here to make a diversion."

A giant Negro driver, who was breaking open large packing cases at the back of the truck, gave me a happy smile. "First darn useful thing I've done since I joined this man's army."

I noticed that there was something different about Robb's face. It was clear of blemishes. He saw me looking and put a hand to his cheek: "Wouldya believe it? I decided to try out a few of the priest's leeches. And the funny thing is they worked. I never had a skin like this since I was a baby."

Gela.
Lt. Frank Dunford:

The order had come through that morning. There would be further ship-shore gunnery liaison required in the north. I was assigned to Bradley's Headquarters and must move up with a convoy that afternoon. I cursed myself for losing yet another soft posting. I'd thought of challenging Limo again, but figured there would be no point. All eyes and efforts were on winning the war; no one would waste time on investigating petty pilfering. All the same, I despised myself for making such puny efforts to alter the course of my life. Not that I expected to have much life left. I'd used up more than my fair share of luck. But there was one thing I had to do before I moved on.

In spite of the powdered milk Franco's baby brother had died. I found the boy on his usual place by the wall, looking out to sea. Today the sea was at its deepest blue; calm and placid without the faintest suggestion of a ripple or wave. Only the twisted metal of destroyed landing craft broke the surface. The ocean was already cleansing itself of the blood and carnage of the invasion.

The boy did not turn but knew I was there. "Why must you go?"

"Orders. We still have to fight this war. Drive the Germans out of Sicily and the rest of Europe."

"What is Europe?"

"It is all the other countries around you; Italy, France, Greece, Holland and Russia."

"Why did they let the Germans come in? So many countries like that should have been able to keep the Germans out."

"They were not ready. The Germans took them by surprise."

"But the Americans are ready?"

"Yes, we are ready now and so are the British."

"Who are the British? Do they come from Europe?"

"Yes."

"Why did not the Germans go into their country as well?"

"They live on an island like you. They had a navy and that stopped the Germans getting in."

The boy continued to look out to sea. "Why did not our navy stop them?"

"Mussolini was the Germans' friend. He invited them in."

"Mussolini is a stupid man."

"You can say that again." I put a knapsack full of rations on the wall beside the boy. "There's enough food there for you and your mother for a week or so. After that there will be more supply ships coming in. You will not be hungry again."

"Will I see you again?"

"One day, when the war is over, I will come back here on vacation."

"What is vacation?"

"It's a sort of holiday – not like the holidays you have here in the church, but a time when you do not have to work and can go somewhere else and be happy."

"A vacation is a wonderful thing."

"When you are bigger you must come and have a vacation with me in America."

I said the words but I had little hope of ever making them come true.

⚜⚜⚜

MY SICILIAN CAMPAIGN by General George S. Patton Jr:

A large map of Sicily was attached to the west wall of the Morning Room of the Royal Palace. Major Powell briefed my staff on the latest Intelligence reports whilst I looked on and sipped my coffee.

Middleton was making slow progress on the coastal road, because of the difficult terrain and the destruction of bridges and tunnels by the Krauts as they pulled back. But inland, the 1st Division was well past Nicosia, and was expected to reach Troina the following day. Indications were that it was lightly held. Powell had received reports that the 15th Panzer were in a poor state. They were very tired, had little ammo, had suffered many casualties, and their morale was low. Fog had prevented aerial photography. Nothing was ever right for those Air Force sonsofbitches. They hadn't been any goddamn use since we landed.

I got up, put on my glasses, and walked over to the map in order to study it closer. The map was a poor one but gave some indication of the locale. I remain at heart a simple cavalry-man, and have an excellent intuition for how my enemy will react. "Are you sure they won't defend Troina?" I asked Powell. "It looks like there are few avenues of approach and little cover in that terrain." I peered even closer, "If I was defending it I'd put artillery on those surrounding mountains. That way it would be pretty hard to encircle." Powell assured me that

Intelligence had fresh information from newly taken POWs. Troina would not be defended – we would just pass through.

Allen and his 1st Division had been going all out since we landed. I decided to take them out of the line, once they had taken Troina, and replace them with the 9th, which would be fully landed and fully operational by then. Truscott and the 3rd would take over from Middleton on the coast. Truscott knew how to move fast. I was convinced the 'Truscott Trot' would get me into Messina first.

Lt. Danny Crivello:

I couldn't get Gina out of my head. My heart felt as if it were burning and melting away at the thought of her. I wanted her more than a junkie needed his fix. I had to get back to Villalba. I'd finally sorted out the food distribution and Corporal Robb could manage the without me. Apart from Gina, there was the enigma of Don Calo and my father; and then, not least, there was Luciano. It was time to deliver him safely and secretly back to Admiral Hewitt.

These thoughts were whirling through my brain as I drove back to my quarters from the Cortile Cascino. Two men were waiting by the Palace Gate. I recognized Falco at once, but could not place the other: a well-dressed figure in suit and fedora hat, although I knew I'd seen him before. I motioned my driver to stop and got out. I'd not spoken to Falco since our confrontation at the harbour. My mouth became dry and jealousy churned in my gut.

"Have you seen Gina?"

He stared at me with fierce dark eyes. "I told you, we will settle that in the Sicilian way when we have finished what we have to do."

"Where have you been?"

"There are now new mayors in Marsala, Trapani and Mazara. The entire west is ours again."

The other man had been looking distastefully at the empty slop bins in the back of the jeep. "You have been very busy."

I recognized him now as the guy who had been supervising the labour force at the harbour. "The people here have nothing. I am doing what I can to help."

"You should have used our friends here in the city. It would be better if the help were distributed from one main source."

"Your friends in the city have done nothing for these people. Only a few priests seem to care."

"There are many Communists among the priests. Don Calo says that it is important that we are seen to be the providers."

"I do not take orders from Don Calo. I am an officer in the US Navy engaged in humanitarian duties and will act as I see fit."

The man shrugged. "Captain Limo will be here tomorrow and I will speak with him. It is important that you work only with us. It was agreed. As well as the Fascists and Communists, there are bandits who want to disrupt everything and create chaos."

✿✿✿

MY SICILIAN CAMPAIGN by General George S. Patton Jr:

The small town of Cerami lay five miles west of Troina. General Allen had taken it, with little opposition, early in the morning of July 30. The following day he had therefore confidently launched his attack with only one regiment – the 39th, from the newly arrived 9th Division, which had just been assigned to his command. The 39th was commanded by one of my oldest colleagues and friends, Colonel Paddy Flint. By noon, one battalion had taken possession of the high ground a mile to the west of the town, and were looking down at the twin towers of Troina's Norman Church. It was at that moment that the full weight of the 15th Panzer Grenadier, operating as a full Division, and with units of the 29th Panzer Division and the Hermann Goering in support, launched their counter-attack. Flint and his men had been driven back to their starting lines with heavy losses.

I received the news at Palermo and was furious. I would have willingly shot those goddam Intelligence sonsofbitches who had sent good men to their deaths. Moreover, I knew this setback would cost me more time, and I could not afford to waste a single day.

Lt. Danny Crivello:

I'd returned to the Palace and was on my way to my room to shower and change out of my grease-stained uniform, when a furious bellow erupted behind me.

"My God, what in the pig's hole is that?" I turned and beheld General Patton standing spread-legged, staring incredulously at me. The fat-assed Major Powell was in tow. "What in hell's name have you been doing, Lieutenant?" The General's face was even more florid than usual. "You look as though you've just finished a shift at a hamburger stand."

I came to attention and gave the smartest salute I knew: "I've been assisting AMGOT, General. Major Powell gave me responsibility for taking care of the sick citizens in the Cortile Cascino District."

Patton turned and eyed Powell suspiciously. Powell nodded a somewhat reluctant confirmation.

"We are keeping the typhoid in check but they have no food," I continued.

"You seem to have enough food on your uniform to feed an entire family." Patton peered beneath his shaggy eyebrows: "Haven't I seen you before?"

"Yes, General. We met at Gela and at Agrigento."

"Of course, I remember now. It's the first time I've seen you in uniform, Lieutenant, and it's the most disgusting uniform I've ever seen." A gleam came into his eye. "You're in Naval Intelligence, aren't you? You've worked behind enemy lines. I want you to forget all this AMGOT nonsense and come under my specific command. You seem unable to wear a uniform properly, so I want you to dress Sicilian again. You will report to General Allen's Headquarters at Cerami, and then get yourself into Troina. I want to know the exact dispositions and numbers of the German forces there. Find out their intentions and how long they are prepared to resist. Every defensive position has a weak spot – find it. Use those Sicilian sonsofbitches, like you did before. I want answers and I want them quick."

I was still officially under the command of Admiral Hewitt. I had to get back to Villalba and check on Luciano. But I couldn't tell Patton that; as far as I knew, Patton was entirely ignorant of the Luciano operation. I sought lamely for an excuse. "What about the people in the Cortile Cascino? They've been relying on me."

"Lieutenant, I am giving you explicit orders. We're here to fight a war, not wet nurse a bunch of dirty dagos ..."

"If we don't feed them they'll break out of the district to look for food. They could spread typhoid all over the city. It could infect the Army. It's only a few blocks from here."

A look of concern stole across the General's craggy face. He nodded and turned to Powell. "We cannot allow anything to affect the fighting qualities of the men. You'd better continue with his programme, Major Powell. Find out how he's been working it; use the people he has in hand."

"I would recommend a corporal in the Medics. Corporal Robb. He's the best man we've got."

"OK. You got that, Powell? Corporal Robb. Better make him a sergeant."

Powell nodded unhappily.

The prospect of more action began to appeal to me. But it would take me even further from Gina. I wanted to make sure she was out of Falco's reach. "May I take a Sicilian with me? He knows the island better than anyone."

"Sure, get hold of him and leave immediately. Powell, see to the paperwork and requisition a jeep."

"The Sicilian may be reluctant to go."

Patton's blood pressure rose at the faintest hint of insubordination. "Like hell he will. I'll give you a warrant in my own name."

Falco had been less reluctant to go than I'd imagined, and bowed to Patton's mandate. We drove out of Palermo along the coast road with the sun, a perfect red ball, sinking into the sea behind us. In that light, for a short while, the realities of modern war dissolved, and I found it easy to believe the legends and myths of the Mediterranean. The pointed peaks of Capo Gallo, silhouetted against the evening sky, looked like mountains of enchantment, waiting to tempt Ulysses with another Circe. Only the wrecked Italian tanks and smoking ruins brought me back to reality.

Just outside Bagheria the road became congested with wagons carrying the newly landed 9th Division towards the front. I flashed Patton's orders at the Military Police and was waved through. We'd driven halfway down the long line of trucks when, in the half light, I caught a glimpse of the face of a driver looking out from his cab. We'd flashed by in an instant; I stared into the mirror but the face had gone. I slowed momentarily, desperate to see the face again, but a MP blew his whistle furiously and ordered me on. Nothing was allowed to slow Patton's advance. My mind was in frenzy. The face had been half obscured by a helmet, but it looked like Uncle Tony's face. But could it really be Uncle Tony? I'd convinced myself that what I'd seen in Capa's photo had indeed been a trick of the light. But this time I'd seen the face with my own eyes. I turned to look at Falco, to see if he'd noticed anything, but he was pointing ahead. I looked back at the road: a soldier, with his helmet pulled down over his brow, was waving at us to stop. For a moment I thought I was going crazy, and would see Uncle Tony's face again. But as I braked I made out a younger, leaner face. Another GI was sitting in the ditch. Both men were battle-stained and had muddy Big Red One insignias on their sleeves. They looked pale and far from fit.

The one who'd stopped me made an attempt at a salute. "Y'all headed east, Lieutenant?"

I nodded.

"Can yah give us all a ride? We want to join up with the 26th Infantry." He turned and assisted his companion to his feet.

"What are you doing so far from your outfit?"

"We got invalided to hospital because of malaria but heard we were gonna be transferred to another Division."

The second dog soldier was leaning on his carbine for support. "We're under General Terry Allen, and we're in the finest regiment in the finest Division, the Fighting First. We won't fight with anyone else."

"You should be in hospital. In any case, without an official discharge you're technically AWOL."

"Shoot, y'all get us to General Terry. He'll sort it out. He's like a daddy to us Texican boys."

Falco was morose and silent and I needed company to take my mind off the seeming manifestations of my uncle. I also wanted to know more about the legendary General Allen before we met. "You're lucky. That's just where we are heading. Jump in." They regarded Falco suspiciously as they clambered in the back. I smiled. "Don't mind him. He's one of our glorious Allies." I drove along the newly liberated road, occasionally glancing at them in the mirror. They were every inch cowboys; their faces etched with squinting into the sun. "What's so great about General Allen?"

"General Terry Allen goes out to bat for any man under his command, colonel or private. He looks after us as if we were his sons, his own boys."

The guy who'd waved me down gave a cocky laugh. "He's only made us the greatest Division in this whole war, that's all. We whupped the Nazis in North Africa. We did more than enough there to have been sent home stateside, but those motherfucking featherbed colonels in the rear gave us the shitty end of the stick, decided they couldn't do without us."

His companion ran his tongue around his cracked lips: "We got lickered up and ran a bit amok in Oran to show our disapproval; we drank the whole coastline dry, but General Terry Allen, he's a good ole boy, he understood. He told us he was proud of us and considered himself privileged to command such courageous men." He scratched at his unshaven chin. "We've been at the spear point of this here invasion since Gela. We killed the Krauts at Enna, Mazzarino and Barrafranca; took on the Hermann Goering Division in hand-to-hand combat. You leave the fighting to the Fighting First. We'll find 'em, fix 'em, fight 'em. Yes sir."

"But General Allen don't like losing a single one of us, not like that bastard Patton," the other rejoined. "Inflict maximum damage to the enemy with minimum casualties to ourselves. Night attack, night attack, night attack! Take the high ground!" He unwrapped a stick of gum and then offered the rest of the packet to me and Falco. I took a stick and began to chew. Falco sniffed a stick warily with his dilating black nostrils and declined. "Teddy is a helluva guy as well."

"Teddy?"

"General Teddy Roosevelt. Theodore Roosevelt Jr., son of the old President hisself. He's second-in-command of the Division and also commands our regiment, the 26th Infantry. We call ourselves the new 'Rough Riders,' after that outfit his pa raised in the Spanish American War."

"Boy, can those two old ornery critters drink," interjected the other.

"They sure can and they're happy to see us drink as well, as long as we do our duty."

To the obvious discomfort of Falco, they both began to caterwaul,

> *"The infantry, the infantry*
> *With dirt behind their ears,*
> *They can whip their weight in wildcats*
> *And drink their weight in beers.*
> *The cavalry, artillery*
> *And the goddam engineers*
> *They'll never catch the infantry*
> *In a hundred thousand years."*

There was something indestructible about them. Their devotion was unassailable. They were the same men who'd followed Lee to Appomattox and beyond.

We continued along the coast road as far as Campofelice and then southeast through the mountains via Petralia, Gangi, and Nicosia to Cerami. Every small town had been bought in blood, every building and every wall bore scars of the conflict. It was dark when we reached Cerami. I showed my papers to the Military Police as the two Texans melted into the night to seek their beloved regiment. Within a few minutes I was ushered into Allen's Command Post, an empty schoolhouse still decorated with Mussolini's slogan, *Believe, Obey, Fight*. Falco remained outside under guard.

It was a simple stone building with low ceiling and thick walls, which preserved the heat of the day. Three men were sitting around a table with a bottle of Scotch. It had the atmosphere of a wake. Two of the men were wearing the drab olive woollen beanie caps that ordinary GI Joes wore under their helmets, their uniforms were rumpled and stained, but I recognized Allen and Roosevelt from the stars on their collars. The other was more difficult to place. He rolled a cigarette whilst Allen read Patton's orders. He was well into middle age, but sat bare-chested with a black silk scarf around his neck. He was still wearing his helmet. Stencilled across the front was *AAA-O*.

He looked up with blood-shot eyes and saw he'd aroused my interest. "Anything, Anytime, Anywhere – Bar Nothing: it's the 39th's motto." He stretched out his hand in greeting, "Colonel Paddy Flint. I told my boys this morning, that they'd nothing to be afraid of. The Krauts couldn't hit a mule's ass in the last war and they wouldn't hit anything in this one. They couldn't even hit an old buck like me. At least that was true ... we sure took a bloody nose today."

He drained his glass before continuing in a low voice, "But General Allen's gonna let us have another go at those Krauts tomorrow." He stole an anxious glance at his commander, "That's true, ain't it, Terry?"

Allen took off his beanie, ran his fingers through his unruly black hair, and threw an arm around Flint's bare shoulder. "OK Paddy, you and the 39th will attack again at 0500 hours with full artillery support. My gut instinct tells me I should attack with more than one infantry regiment, but that would mean using my boys from the 1st. They've had more than twenty-one days in the line and are about to be relieved, and it hardly seems fair to put 'em in again." He passed the orders to Roosevelt before scrutinizing me closely. "If you can get me any of the information Patton requests, I'll be damn grateful. I reckon the Krauts have pulled back already. There should be only a couple of guns left." He glanced at his watch. "It's 23.30. That gives you just over five hours to get there and back."

"Anything you need, son?" Roosevelt spoke in a bullfrog voice for the first time. He had a rubbery face and looked more like a vaudeville comedian than a president's son.

"Just find me some old Sicilian clothes, General. My buddy outside is already fixed up."

Allen stood up and offered me his hand. His eyes were soft and warm. "You're a brave man, son. Its guys like you who will win this war. Make sure you come back."

Roosevelt, chomping on an unlit cigar and disdaining to put on his helmet, took it upon himself to lead us to the most forward position, a mile or so up the valley. I became aware of the smell and rustle of horses before seeing a group tethered behind a wall. Around the horses moved dark figures in long robes. Apart from the weapons they carried, they looked as if they'd stepped out of the Arabian Nights.

On closer inspection, I saw they were wearing British-style steel helmets over their turbans, and American combat uniforms under their brown and gold striped *djellabahs.*

Roosevelt noted my wonder and chuckled. "They're Goums, son: native Moroccan irregulars, from the Berber Tribes of the Atlas Mountains. Their specialty is the knife. They cut the ears off any prisoners they take – not that they take that many. Best cavalry troops we've got; but even those critters can't infiltrate the lines around Troina."

A pale blue *kepi* came out of the gloom. "The Free French. Leave this to me, son," Roosevelt whispered. "This is where we'll get you fitted out. As ex-governor of Puerto Rico, I've got plenty of diplomatic skills."

He explained our mission to the Goumiers' commander in perfect French. A tattered pair of trousers and a black shirt, reeking of stale sweat, was soon produced. Falco, probably remembering the indignities his ancestors had suffered under the Arabs, glared at the Goums with deep distrust, while I stripped and changed. The foul-smelling shoes that were offered were too small, so I decided to wear my own boots and also keep my army-issue wristwatch. It was imperative to be aware of the time. I declined the offer of machine guns. We'd have no chance in a firefight – our only hope of getting back was to remain undetected. We blackened our faces and strapped combat knives to our belts.

Roosevelt made a final inspection. "You'd better give me your dog tag, son. I'll keep it safe until you get back."

I slipped it over my head and put it in the General's hand.

"It's about four miles from here. Want a shot before you go?" Roosevelt took a hip flask from his pocket. I smiled and shook my head. Roosevelt seemed reluctant to let us go. "Some people think I'm a damn fool, but I never take an unnecessary chance. It's a matter of calculated risks. Calculate them extremely carefully and only if your intelligence tells you to take them, then by God, take them. But come back safe, son."

I smiled at him again, nodded to Falco and climbed over the wall. We entered a cup-shaped valley almost devoid of cover. Falco led the way as we tortuously crept through a sparse moonlit terrain, using every wall, shallow ditch and small rock we could find. Here and there we passed dead GIs, those the medics hadn't been able to recover from the previous day's attack. What vegetation there was had been burnt by phosphorus shells and tracer bullets. One ditch contained many burnt bodies. One completely blackened, sat upright, staring sightlessly at us as we slunk by. Falco Moved stealthily, continually stopping to sniff the night air like an animal, until he found the bed of a river. We waded through the shallow water for a mile or so, passing beneath two blown bridges. Then hills began to tower over us, throwing down fast-moving streams, which swirled into the placid waters around us. We were wading through the turmoil of one such stream, when Falco squatted down and thrust his hands into the racing current. I crouched beside him, not understanding what he was doing. Falco took my hand and placed it gently in the cold swirling water. I recognized instantly the feel of a round metal mine. Falco gingerly felt his way forward and discovered another. The riverbed was strewn with them. We crept out of the water and made even slower progress along the rocky banks. We caught sight occasionally of the only road that led up to Troina, a white ribbon over the barren landscape. Anything on that road would be a sitting duck if there were artillery on the hills above, where faint lights occasionally flickered. Finally, on a high and dominating bluff ridge, Troina loomed ominously above us.

I lay beside Falco in the shadow of a clump of olive trees and took stock. German soldiers seemed to be everywhere. Their artillery was in position just below the town, behind a wall on the road that ran halfway up the hill, before turning left and disappearing into a sort of pass. It would give perfect cover for an orderly withdrawal. I could see sentries patrolling it. The houses in the town were built of stone. They looked solid and well built: good holding positions for defending infantry. On the cliff to the left, a thin wisp of smoke was emerging from a round feudal tower, a perfect observation post for artillery. There were signs of activity on all the encircling hills, ideal for the positioning of an interlocking grid of machine gun nests, impossible to outflank. The remaining ground beneath the town was devoid of any cover, and even more rugged than that which we'd traversed. Any attacking infantry would need the agility and speed of mountain goats and the courage of lions.

"It would be suicide to attack from this side." Falco whispered. He'd hardly spoken since we'd left Palermo. "I used to hunt around here when I was a boy. I have a cousin in the town. There is a small dirt road coming over the mountain to the north, it would not be on your maps. The Germans would not expect you to come that way. My cousin will know if it is defended."

The moon had momentarily disappeared behind the cloud. Etna glowed in the darkness little more than twenty miles to the east. Great clouds of smoke and ash were silhouetted against its flaming crown, falling impartially upon both of the armies fighting desperately beneath it. I looked at my watch. It was a quarter to one. We still had time to get into the town, find Falco's cousin and get back with our report. I already knew the Germans had sufficient artillery and intended to defend Troina. No attack should be made without full air support. But if General Allen knew the other road was undefended, it would save innumerable lives. I remembered Roosevelt's advice. It was a calculated risk. I had to try to get that information to him. My mouth was dry with fear, but I forced myself to whisper in Falco's ear. "OK. Let's go in. Find your cousin."

Falco quickly found a large sewer pipe emptying into the river: "Follow me. It leads into the town." I crawled into the pipe behind him and struggled upwards through a turgid stream of stinking water.

I was clinging to the shadow of the wall that ran along one side of Troina's main street, which had been virtually carved out of the cliff face itself. Falco had slipped away, what seemed like hours ago, to seek out his cousin down the narrow street to the left. If he didn't return within half an hour, we'd agreed I would attempt to go back without him. On the road beneath me, behind the thick stone wall, the moon glinted on the cruel barrels of a battery of 88s, covering every inch of the land we'd crossed and over which we'd have to return. Stationed on each side of the 88s were several odd looking contraptions that I recognized as Nebelwerfers: a new and terrifying German weapon. I remembered being told the godawful thing could fire six rocket-propelled shells in five seconds. I pitied any troops advancing within its range. On top of that, a dozen tanks, hidden under camouflage netting, were in position for an instant counterattack. The crews of the batteries were bivouacked beside their weapons. I could just make out the tops of their tents and hear the whispered guttural of German voices and the crunch of jackboots on the gravelled road. I also made out the softer tone of Italian voices. Further away – towards the square beside the church. I couldn't distinguish what they were saying, but they were definitely military orders. It could only mean more soldiers. I looked up again at the hills surrounding the town. I was convinced there were more guns up there. The position was almost impregnable.

I looked at my watch and saw that Falco had been gone for less than fifteen minutes. Could I trust him now? What was to stop him going back to Cerami alone and leaving me, his rival, to my fate? But I remembered the mines. If Falco wanted me dead, it would have been the simplest thing to let me step on one. I waited fearfully, straining every sense. I looked at my watch again. Another five minutes had passed. What if Falco had been captured? Surely I would have heard something? I stepped out of the shadow and peered in the direction that he had gone.

"Halt! What are you doing out in the street? Do you not know there is a curfew?"

I turned and saw a young Italian officer with two soldiers; their rifles were trained on me. I cursed my carelessness. As they drew nearer I could see the black shirts beneath their pale green uniforms. I put on my simplest smile, although my heart was pounding. "I am sorry. I have been up in the hills with my sheep. I did not know."

The young officer, I could see now he was a lieutenant, came closer and peered into my face: "You do not look like a shepherd. There has been a curfew for the past three months. It is impossible that you did not know. What are you doing?" The insignia on his collar told me he belonged to the 171st Black Shirt Battalion, part of the Milizia Volontaria per La Sicurezza Nazionale: the Italian equivalent of the Waffen-SS.

"I told you. I have been up in the hills. I am going home."

"Where do you live?"

"Over there." I pointed vaguely in the opposite direction to where Falco had disappeared. The action caused the moon to sparkle on the steel of my watch.

The officer noticed immediately. "It is unusual for a shepherd to have a watch. Let me see it."

I shrugged and unstrapped it, trying to look unconcerned as I handed it over.

He examined it carefully. "What does a shepherd do with an US Army issue watch?"

"I took it off a dead soldier in the hills."

I could see something moving in the shadows over the lieutenant's shoulder. The officer gestured to one of the soldiers to search me, whilst the other kept his rifle levelled at my breast. The knife was found immediately. I could now see a figure moving towards us, silently and stealthily. I knew it was Falco before I saw his face; Falco with his knife in his hand, edging ever closer and closer.

The Lieutenant inspected my knife and ran a finger along its blade. "This is a combat weapon. Why do you have it?"

"I found it on the same dead soldier."

Half of me wanted Falco to go back into the shadows, to escape back down the pipe. He'd have an outside chance of returning to Cerami and informing Allen and Roosevelt of the daunting opposition they were facing, and perhaps guide them to the unprotected road over the mountain. The other half wanted him to come on and free me from this terrible trap. I caught Falco's eyes. I knew what he expected me to do. He sprang and viciously implanted his knife between the shoulder blades of the soldier with the rife. At the same instant I kicked at the groin of the other soldier with all the force that I could summon, and swung my right fist into the face of the lieutenant, knocking him back against the wall. Falco nodded and then raced over to the other side of the narrow road and leapt over the low wall. I followed blindly and flew down after him. Almost immediately my feet struck against the taut canvas of a tent.

It broke the force of my fall, before collapsing beneath the impact. I could hear shouts and whistles above and felt violent movement beneath me, as the sleeping gun crew we'd landed on fought to escape from the canvas. There were more shouts, closer now. Torches shone in my eyes. I could just distinguish the shapes of German helmets and the glint of MP38 submachine gun barrels. There was no way I could escape. I reluctantly raised my hands.

MY SICILIAN CAMPAIGN by General George S. Patton Jr:

At 0500 hours, Sunday, August 1, having received no further intelligence, and despite the fact that much of our artillery had not been brought far enough forward, due to roads being clogged with the traffic of the 9th Division, Allen launched his second attack on Troina. This time he gave Colonel Flint some support by throwing forward the Goums on his left flank. By mid-morning all the troops were back at their starting lines, having encountered heavy mortar and machine gun fire, and a furious German counter-attack. Moreover, the Luftwaffe made one of its rare appearances on the battlefield, and a squadron of Dornier 217Ms strafed what artillery Allen had in place. It was another bad day.

Troina
Lt. Danny Crivello:

A bucket of foul-smelling cold water brought me to my senses. I fought against it. I wanted to return to forgetfulness. To be unaware of the pain that wracked my body and the dread of what I knew was yet to come. I felt with my tongue to the spot where the cyanide capsule had been fixed, and wished that I'd not discarded it in those heady days at Villalba. I opened a swollen eye and saw again the hook hanging from the thick wooden beam that ran across the ceiling of the cell: the hook where I'd had hung from my wrists, whilst paratroopers had beaten my ribs with rubber truncheons. My kidneys were pulp; the urine that stained my trousers was streaked with blood. I forced my eyes away from the hook and saw the German captain was back, sitting on the wooden chair, with the black-shirted young Italian lieutenant behind him. The German watched me impassively with his watery blue eyes, turning a leather-covered swagger stick between his hands, as the Italian spoke.

"Your friend killed a soldier. That is enough for you to be shot. I would kill you willingly. The man that your friend stabbed in the back was a good soldier. He wore his Black Shirt throughout Africa and served his country well. He has a wife and children; he did not deserve to die in such a fashion." The Italian took out a cigarette and lit it, before offering one to the German. He shook his head without taking his cold, cruel eyes from me. I noticed for the first time the Iron Cross at his throat. He was still wearing his tropical uniform from North Africa. His peaked cap on the table was bleached almost white with the sun.

The Italian returned his attention to me: "We cannot understand why you acted as you did. You are not simple partisans; your companion maybe, but not you. You were wearing American Army boots that fitted you perfectly. They were worn to the shape of your feet. You did not take those off a dead man. My colleague here," he nodded towards the passive face, pale despite its exposure to the African sun, "suspects that you might be an American agent. If you are, you will have information that will be of interest to us. If you co-operate, we will make things easy for you, if not, you will wish you had never been born."

"I told you I am just a shepherd. I know nothing about Americans. The other man is not my friend. He is a bandit. I have never seen him before. He will tell you. Where is he now?"

"He is even more stubborn than you. He will not be able to answer questions for several hours."

The German spoke in his harsh language. The Italian translated: "Where are you intending to invade next? Even a junior officer will have heard rumours."

"Invade? What do you mean? Invade? I am a shepherd, I know nothing about invasions."

The Italian translated again. After a moment's deliberation, the German rose and savagely struck my swollen face with his swagger stick. I could not prevent myself whimpering with pain.

The Italian spoke once more. "I am a soldier. I do not like to see you suffer like this. Answer his questions and you will be treated well."

I gave full vent to my anguish and fear. Tears streamed down my face. "Please understand, I am a simple man. I cannot answer your questions. I wish I could."

Again the Italian translated and again the German spoke, this time in an even harsher tone. The young man, smiled somewhat apologetically: "My colleague wishes me to inform you that you are fighting a war that you can never win. There are only three German Divisions here in Sicily, but they are easily holding more than ten American and British. When Hitler decides to turn his full power upon you, he will drive you back into the sea from where you came. You are throwing your life away in a hopeless cause."

MY SICILIAN CAMPAIGN by General George S. Patton Jr:

I had received reports that Montgomery and the British were bogged down by malaria and strong German defences around Etna, but I would brook no delay. The following day, at my urging, Allen sent Flint forward yet again, but this time backed him with a full complement of artillery. In a barrage reminiscent of those I remember in the Great War, almost sixteen battalions of Long Toms and light artillery, 165 guns in all, pounded the town and the hills around it, but as the 39th approached Troina they were driven back once more by a seemingly impregnable German defence. Truscott had taken over from Middleton on the coastal road, but his advance was, as yet, just as slow. He was forced to contest every habitation, every bend in the road, as well as negotiating the thousands of mines and booby traps the retreating Germans had strewn in his path.

Troina
Lt. Danny Crivello:

The artillery barrage had pounded the buildings around me all morning, but although my very cell shook under its fury, I sensed the attack had failed again. *"You are throwing your life away!"* The words of the Black Shirt Lieutenant spun round in my head. I was beginning to believe it was true. I would never see Gina again: never know if she really loved

me. Tears welled in my eyes as I thought of my mother praying for me in our little apartment in New York; her hopes
and sins had all been in vain. I prayed to God that at least
Uncle Tony, wherever he was, would be spared and get back
to comfort her old age. I'd achieved so little in my life and
would never do the things I'd intended. I'd never be an
engineer, never marry, never have kids, never discover the
truth of Don Calo and my father. Never find out what had
really happened in Villalba all those years ago. And what
of Luciano? He would never return to Great Meadow. I'd
let him loose, like a contagious pestilence to melt into the
corruption of Sicily and wreak havoc on an unsuspecting
world. But what did the fate of one gangster matter besides
the death and destruction all around? And did my own fate
matter any more than his? I looked up again at the ancient
wooden beam above me. It was my cross, where I'd hung
and suffered anguish. The tree it had been carved from had
matured long before Columbus sailed across the Atlantic;
it had been a sapling when the Arabs had governed Sicily.
My life was a pinpoint in time by comparison. But under
torture a moment seemed eternity. I wasn't sure if I could
hold out for another day, another hour, or even another
minute. What would it matter if I confessed to being an
American officer? What information did I have that would
be of use to the enemy? The code! Of course, the Allies had
the German code. My superiors were willing to let me die
at Gela to preserve that secret. But if the Germans didn't
know the Allies had cracked it, would they even think to
question me about it? No. All they were interested in was
where the Allies would invade next. They'd asked me that
countless times already, and each time I'd pleaded igno-
rance they'd inflicted terrible pain. I'd heard rumours in
the Palace at Palermo that it would be Italy, but had no idea

where. Naples? Or further up the boot nearer Rome? Or Southern France? It still could be Sardinia; there had been a plan to fool the Axis powers into thinking we'd be going there before the landings in Sicily. Or even Greece? I didn't have a clue. What if I fabricated an entire invasion plan? But where? I might by chance choose the correct place and be the unwitting cause of its failure. Greece was the least likely. It was closer to the eastern front and the Russians, but it was further away from Germany. I didn't believe the Allies would invade Greece. Greece would be my answer. It might give me a few hours, or even a few days, relief from pain.

The door was wrenched open. Two burly German paratroopers dragged in a body and threw it on the filthy stone floor beside me. I could hardly recognize it as Falco. His face was swollen; his mouth black and bleeding; his eyes just two purple slits. He looked as if he had done fifteen rounds with Joe Louis with his arms tied behind his back.

The Italian lieutenant had also entered. This time he was alone. "I thought you would want to see what our German allies have done to your friend. I hope you now realise that it is not worth holding out any longer. One of you will soon die. Be sensible. I will let you have a quiet talk together. I am sure you will then agree to co-operate." He bent down and tried to look into my eyes. There was a hint of pity in his face: "You have been very brave. You have endured far more than could be expected of you. You have suffered enough."

He went out. The door slammed behind him. We lay side by side, united in pain. I looked up to where the sun had somehow contrived to hit the beam from a vent near the ceiling. It gave just enough light for me to differentiate Falco's battered features. I was certain that whatever conversation we had would be listened to. I painfully turned my head and tried to wink with my swollen eye. Falco peeped through his own disfigured face and painfully struggled to understand my meaning. I put one finger to my lips and then to my ear. Falco continued to look at me quizzically. I repeated the gestures. He nodded at last and I spoke. "I think it does not matter if they know I am an American officer. I am thinking that I will tell them what I know, in exchange for our lives. You know nothing, I am sorry that I forced you to guide me here."

Falco's dark eyes gleamed beneath their bruised lids. He reached out his hand, with bloody stumps where his fingernails had been, and held mine in silence. In spite of the passionate jealousy that had passed between us, I felt a strange love for this savage, stubborn man, my sole companion in hell.

"You could have got away whilst they were questioning me. Why did you come back?"

Falco continued to stare at the dark ceiling; a fly had found its way into the fetid cell and buzzed above our heads. I envied it. It had more freedom than either of us could ever hope for again. When the Sicilian eventually spoke it was as if the very act of utterance caused him profound agony. "I came back because of *omerta*." He turned his battered face and sought to look deeply into mine: "I had to try to save you. If I had not, you would have thought I abandoned you because of the girl. You might have died thinking that. I told you, one day we will settle that in the Sicilian way."

I did not ask him about the mountain road.

MY SICILIAN CAMPAIGN by General George S. Patton Jr:

General Allen finally resolved that nothing but a full-bodied assault with his veterans of the Big Red One could take Troina. He therefore threw forward the 16th Infantry Regiment in the early hours of August 3. It advanced along the riverbed to within a mile of the town before becoming pinned down by relentless machine gun fire. The protagonists were too close to each other for Allen to call down artillery support. To create a diversion the 18th Infantry attacked and took a ridge to the west, but then suffered a vicious German counter-attack of tanks and infantry. Only dogged fighting prevented the 18th from being overrun. Casualties were so high that some companies were down to one platoon strength. It was only the timely arrival of six RAF Spitfires, who strafed and bombed the German artillery positions on the surrounding mountains, which enabled the 16th and 39th Regiments to move into positions nearer the town at the end of the day. General Roosevelt informed me that Allen looked across the barren landscape, littered with the bodies of their men, and wept.

Troina
Lt. Danny Crivello:

We remained silent in our agony throughout the night. We knew our captors were listening through an air vent in the wall. The shelling had resumed in the morning, when the paratroopers took me out of the cell and dragged me along the corridor to a room lined with sandbags. There, as dirt and plaster scattered down from the explosions above, I told them everything I thought they wanted to hear. I admitted I was an intelligence officer and described the layout of Patton's Headquarters in the Palace. I said I'd seen reports that two more American Divisions were on their way across the Atlantic bound for Palermo. They would unite with the 1st and 3rd Divisions and sail in a task force under Patton for Greece. Once a bridgehead had been established, Montgomery would follow with the British Eighth Army, and they would push up through Yugoslavia to link up with the Russians. It would be the main focus of the Anglo-American war effort. There would be no second front in France. The German had listened impassively whilst the Italian, seemingly impressed, wrote down all I revealed. When I'd finished, they spoke to each other in German before the paratroopers hauled me back to Falco. Some bread and water had been left in the cell. I realized with profound relief that they would not torture me that day. In spite of all my resolve, all my training, I began to cry like a child.

Falco looked at me piteously but assumed hatred and contempt. He knew they were still listening: "Once a man has betrayed his friends he has lost everything. He is no longer a man."

❖❖❖

MY SICILIAN CAMPAIGN by General George S. Patton Jr:

That morning I received good and bad news. To my bitter disappointment, I was informed that Clark's Fifth Army had been chosen for the invasion of mainland Italy, but Ike's cable had added: *'I assure you if we speedily finish off the Germans in Sicily you need have no fear of being left there in the backwater of war.'* That could mean only one thing. Ike was saving me for the big one – the invasion of France. I was even more determined to demonstrate what I could achieve.

❖❖❖❖

Troina
Lt. Danny Crivello:

Several hours passed. We continually heard machine-gun-fire and the thunder of artillery. Then later, we made out the drone of aircraft engines and the scream of bombs, under which the very town seemed to shake and tremble. Sometime after that the Lieutenant returned. I turned my head towards the wall, in pretence of shame.

This time the Italian spoke softly with warmth in his voice. "I have transmitted what you have given us to Abwehr Headquarters in Rome. You will be sent there shortly, when transport is available and the road is clear. They want to interrogate you further. You are lucky; I have managed to keep you out of the hands of the Gestapo."

At this Falco raised himself on one elbow and spat in my face.

I wiped the spittle from my cheek with the back of my hand.

"What about him?"

"I would gladly shoot him as a traitor. He killed one of my best men; but they want him as well."

"He knows nothing. He followed me here because I had fucked his girl. Let him go and I will tell them everything."

The Italian smiled, somewhat sadly. "You will tell them everything my friend, whatever they do to him."

There was something familiar about his face: "Do you have a sister in Palermo?"

"Yes."

"Does she live opposite the Giardino Garibaldi?"

For once he seemed taken aback. "How do you know?"

"I met her. She is brave. Like you she has not surrendered."

"Now she will have to be even braver. I only heard yesterday; our father has been killed at Kharkov."

"I am sorry."

The young man gazed at me intently before replying, "I believe you are."

❧❧❧

MY SICILIAN CAMPAIGN by General George S. Patton Jr

Allen's advance had stalled yet again. I was not in the best of humour and decided to visit him personally to find out why. On my way, I called in at an evacuation hospital and discovered a malingerer: the only arrant coward I'd ever seen so far in this army. I naturally threw him out. It's shameful to put sulkers and brave soldiers together. Cowardice spreads like rottenness in apples. I was even more enraged when, on arrival at Allen's headquarters a few miles outside Troina, I found it surrounded by slit trenches. I demanded to know what they were for. General Allen informed me they were for protection. The Luftwaffe had strafed them badly two days before. I told Allen that only yellow bellies hid in trenches and asked him to point out which foxhole was his. When he did so, I unbuttoned my fly and pissed in it.

That evening my Headquarters issued the following order to my Divisional Commanders. '*Some men pretend that they are nervously incapable of combat. Such men are cowards and bring discredit to their comrades whom they heartlessly leave to endure the danger of battle while they themselves use the hospital as a means of escaping. You will take measures to see that such cases are not sent to hospital but are dealt with by their units. Those who are not willing to fight will be tried by Court Martial for cowardice in the face of the enemy.*'

The following day, having been informed that the Canadians were beginning to advance on the Adriano flank and Montgomery was at last at the gates of Catania, I ordered Allen forward once more. He tried a pincer movement with the 18th attacking from the south and the 26th in the north. The Germans, although they had lost many men, were still strong enough to launch yet another ferocious counter-attack and drove us back yet again. At noon Allied air power was finally available. Two squadrons of A-36s, a dive-bomber version of the Mustang, battered Troina and its surrounding mountains with their 500-pound bombs and 20mm cannons.

Troina
Lt. Danny Crivello:
We had been lying in our squalor hoping we'd been forgotten when, around midday, the first of the heavy bombs fell. Almost immediately, the whole universe seemed wracked with the terrible scream of the dive-bombers and vivid blasts of fire. We crouched trembling against the wall with our hands pressed to our ears, while the cell shook like a small craft upon a tempest-tossed sea, until the very earth seemed to shatter around us and the ceiling came crashing down on our heads. For a few moments we lay together, stunned and choked with swirling dust and debris. I rubbed the dirt from my swollen eyes and looked up to see the beam, on which I'd suffered such agony, was still above us, but closer. At the far end, its massive weight had fallen from its setting in the outer wall, but above us it was wedged firmly in place, protecting us from the heavy masonry which was still crashing down. It was brighter – the sun was fighting

its way in, giving the dust a golden glow. Through the dust, below where the beam had been, I could discern a fissure in the outer wall. It looked just wide enough for a man to slip through. I rose painfully on my bare feet and pulled Falco up beside me. The inferno of the air attack continued outside. The Germans were all preoccupied with anti-aircraft fire or simply taking cover. There was just a faint chance we might be able slip away unobserved.

I looked at the fissure and back at Falco. He understood immediately.

We stepped gingerly, hand in hand, over the fallen masonry towards the crack in the wall. The rough stones cut into my feet, like the pebbles on the beach on Long Island when I'd been a kid. I felt giddy and weak, but Falco's firm grip gave me strength.

Falco peered into the fissure. A squalid street was just visible. "You go first. You are smaller. I do not think I will get through."

I reached out and stretched with my right arm as I'd never stretched before, until I could just make a purchase on the exterior wall. I took a final glance at Falco's bloody, battered face, and then turned my head towards the light. I breathed in until my belly was almost flattened against my spine and began to squeeze into the crack. The stones felt cold and rough against my fevered, tortured body. They seemed to be pushing vindictively against the widest part of my rib cage – the ribs that had been pummelled so efficiently by the paratroopers' rubber truncheons. The pain returned in all its agony, I was sure my long-suffering ribs had cracked within me. I tried to make them close together, like the shell of a clam. Blood rose up in my mouth, but I sensed that I'd edged a fraction forward. I took an even firmer grip, dug my nails into the outside wall, and strained again. The pain made me cry out, but I'd moved further in. My head was almost through, one eye could see down the deserted street – everything was wreathed in dust. It was almost as if a smoke screen had been laid for our benefit. I could feel Falco's strong bleeding hands, on my hip and shoulder, desperately pushing me forward from within. I fought and twisted and pulled – like a helpless, bloody infant struggling to emerge from a stone womb – until, at last, in one final agonising effort, I burst through and fell upon the rubble outside. As I hit the stones, the terrifying scream of a Mustang's engine, fighting against the dive brakes, signalled the beginning of another attack. Within seconds a fiery blossom of an explosion erupted on a roof barely twenty yards to my right. I leapt up at once, my pain almost forgotten, and looked furtively around. The air stank of cordite, but apart from the furious sound of anti-aircraft fire, there wasn't a sign of a single living soul. I turned back and reached in for Falco.

He pushed my hand away. "It is no use. You will waste your time. I will never get through. Get away while you can."

"No. I will not leave you now." I desperately grabbed hold of Falco's hand and tried to tug him out towards me.

He shook me off again. "You are a fool. It is impossible. Go."

I looked the wall: with a crowbar or heavy hammer it might be possible to knock out more of the heavy stones. "I also have *omerta*. I will be back."

There was another scream as another Mustang dove in to attack at three hundred miles an hour. I looked up and for an instant saw its drab olive fuselage with yellow rings around its stars and empty cannon shells casting from its ejectors. I began to hobble along the road as fast as my abused feet would allow me, supporting myself with one hand on the wall. Another Mustang banked overhead. I couldn't go far. I had to get back before the raid stopped. But where could I find help? On the other side of the street was an iron door, dented with bullets. A child's toy, a crudely carved animal of some undistinguishable variety, lay in the dust outside. I guessed it to be the habitation of a Sicilian family. I ran across and beat on the door with my fists.

"Open up; for the love of God!"

There was no reply. I picked up a broken piece of stone and pounded even louder. I stopped and listened and thought I heard movement inside. There was a small hole in the door about head height. A bright eye was on the other side looking at me.

"Who are you?"

"I am a friend. I need help, quickly."

"You do not come from Troina."

"No, but please let me in. I have so little time. You can see I can do you no harm."

After a further moment's hesitation, a key began to turn and as soon as the door was ajar, I forced myself inside. An old man, gazed up at me in bewilderment. An unlit cigarette hung from his toothless mouth. He was dressed in a straw hat and stained double-breasted suit, giving him the appearance of a member of the bourgeoisie who'd seen better days. In a corner sat an old woman in a dark polka dot dress. She had a tattered rag tied around her head from which wisps of iron grey hair protruded; her sunken eyes were anxious with fear. Her gums were as toothless as her husband's; her chin seemed to reach towards her thin nose. I noticed the sandals on her dirty feet. They were similar to the ones Ma had worn on Coney Island when I was a kid. Behind her cowered a little girl, obviously their grandchild. She'd a crude bloodstained bandage around her right leg and a piece of bread in her hand. Her dress was torn.

The old man took the cigarette from his mouth. "Who are you? What do you want?"

"I am a friend of the people of Sicily. I need a hammer or a crowbar, something strong with which I can rescue my friend." My eyes scanned the bare, impoverished room. By the empty fireplace was a sturdy-looking axe. "That will do. Let me borrow that. I will return it."

I didn't wait for refusal; I knew the A-36s only carried two bombs each. The raid would soon be over and the Germans would return to the streets. I hobbled across the little room, grabbed the axe, and then ran agonizingly back along the street to the fissure, as another Mustang came in at low level for a final strafing run.

"I have come back. Stand clear!"

I judged where the widest part of Falco's body would be, and then began to attack the mortar of a big stone at breast height. The axe bounced of it. The mortar was harder than cement. I would have killed for my explosives. I took a firmer grip and hit again. A piece of mortar flew away. Another bigger piece came off with my next stroke. Five more pieces and the stone was beginning to loosen.

"Stop!"

Falco's bloody fingertips were through the wall, gripping the stone, in spite of the agony it caused him, wrestling with it, straining to prise it away. After a few seconds it began to move. I could hear it shifting and became aware a silence had fallen over the town. The raid was over.

"What are you doing?"

I turned and saw the young Italian lieutenant gazing at me incredulously. He was alone. As he stepped towards me, unbuckling the revolver on his belt, I swung the axe at his skull with all my remaining strength. It cleft through the ornate black forage cap and cut into his brain. The young man crumpled and fell with a look of hurt astonishment as Falco scrambled through the wall.

I stared sorrowfully at the dead man before I grabbed Falco's arm and raced back up the street, towards the sanctuary of the old couple and the little girl.

MY SICILIAN CAMPAIGN by General George S. Patton Jr

Despite their battering, the Germans still held their ground. At 1700 hours the re-armed planes returned and resumed the assault. By now the German losses were enormous, the 15th Panzer alone had lost more than 1,600 men, but Troina remained in their hands. That evening the Canadians took a stretch of the Troina – Adriano road, which meant they would soon be in a position to cut off the defenders' escape. Meanwhile Flint's 39th Regiment, after five days of bitter fighting and repulses, had managed to position itself to the east of the town. On the southern front, after twelve hours of fighting, the 18th regiment had finally taken Mount Pellegrino, which gave their artillery complete domination of the entire area. It was only then that General Rodt began to make an orderly withdrawal, leaving behind a rearguard, enabling his still formidable defensive forces to regroup, and to edge his valuable panzers and guns nearer to the sanctuary of Messina and a safe crossing to Italy. Allen, unaware that the bird had almost flown, made plans for yet another assault.

Report accompanying photos wired to Life Magazine 8 June, 1943 by Robert Capa:

A Piper Cub artillery observation plane reported at first light that the Germans had finally abandoned their defences. I'd been with the 1st Division throughout the battle, but so far my camera had captured little of note. I'd only been able to take long distance shots of Troina, shrouded in the smoke of artillery and bombs. Whatever soldiers I saw, friend or foe, appeared no more than black dots on the bare, harsh landscape. I moved forward at noon with the first wave of the 16th Infantry as it scaled the steep slopes into the town. The air was thick with smoke, cordite and the nauseous odour of death. The hot sun had baked the rubble almost like an oven, beneath which were buried defenders and civilians alike. I'd smelt that smell before at Teruel in Spain, where 20,000 Republicans perished. The living Germans, apart from the seriously wounded, who lay in the streets, had retired to their next defensive line, but the surviving natives of Troina were slowly emerging from their holes: some in their nightshirts, some in their Sunday best. As you can see from the photos, some are hysterical, some too dazed to comprehend, and many are wounded.

I reached the main piazza and my cameras caught a bespectacled young sergeant, with a medic's white armband, attending a blue-eyed German with a shattered leg. Both were little more than boys. A wizened old woman lay amid the crumbling plaster and smoking timber of what was once her home. She stretched out her scrawny arms towards me, moaning a heart-rending cry of agony and loss. I snapped a weeping woman holding a torn photograph of her children, buried beneath the ruins of her pitiful home. Before the twin-towered church, which still stood defiant at the onslaught of modern warfare, a priest knelt and gave thanks that the 500-lb bomb, which lay in the centre of the nave, had not exploded. I photographed a sturdy peasant woman carrying her entire worldly possessions in a basket on her head and in a bucket in her left hand. In her right hand she clutched a staff, her only protection against the world. She symbolized the spirit of survival that has sustained the poor of the earth throughout the ages.

Three generations of women sat barefoot on the threshold of a shell-scarred house, having dared to leave their cellar for the first time in days. The oldest was little more than thirty-five; she wore the traditional black scarf around her head. Her face was still beautiful, but drawn and seared with anguish. Her daughter was about eighteen. Her long chestnut hair hung over her shoulders. She stared in awe and suspicion at the strange soldiers, from the other side of the world, passing by on the other side of the road. Her child, a curly haired toddler, gazed at a discarded German helmet, as if it were some rare but unexplained toy. The greatest painter in the world could not capture the emotions of those women as perfectly as my camera did at that moment.

I then noticed a young Sicilian staggering towards me over the rubble with an emaciated child in his arms. His feet were bare and bleeding and his blue eyes spoke of extreme suffering and pain. His black hair was grey with dust and fallen plaster. The child was a girl with a fragile, beautiful face, framed by wild black hair. There was a crude bandage around her right leg. She was shivering and obviously shellshocked. I continued to take shots as the young man came ever nearer. Through the lens, his face looked vaguely familiar. He was begging me to stop taking pictures and help him find a medic for the child. He even seemed to know my name. How in hell's name could a Sicilian in this godforsaken hole know Robert Capa? I took the camera from my eye and slowly recognized Danny Crivello, the young Lieutenant who'd helped me get my photos out of Palermo – the photos which have put me on *Life's* payroll as an accredited photographer with the official silk US Emblem on my shoulder. I immediately ran back to the main piazza to find the bespectacled medic and dragged him to where Danny was sitting amongst the rubble with the little girl trembling in his arms.

Satisfied they were both in safe hands, I sought out more subjects. A few GIs were sitting, unconcerned, having their chow beside a plinth on which stood a statue of the winged Victory: the little town's memorial to the previous war. Victory's sword was still upraised defiantly, unvanquished by the utter destruction around her.

Lt. Danny Crivello:

Sergeant Robb didn't recognise me and automatically knelt down to examine my mangled feet.

"Forget me," I rasped. "Do something for the kid."

Robb puffed his cheeks in astonishment, but was too good a medic to ask unnecessary questions, and immediately turned his attention to the wound on the child's leg. After a cursory inspection he fumbled in his haversack and brought out a hard tack biscuit and gave it to his patient. The child clutched it in both hands without attempting to eat, and continued to stare with listless eyes, making no movement or sound of pain as Robb began to clean her wound.

"Why aren't you in Palermo?" I noticed the blemishes on Robb's face had returned.

Robb shot me the briefest of glances and shoved a thermometer in my mouth. "The main AMGOT detachment arrived a few days after you left. Some bastard called Captain Limo appeared and said that we had to let the

Sicilians look after their own affairs. He had these rough-looking guys with him and told me that all the supplies and administration were to go through them. I didn't like it, but there was nothing I could do. I heard they needed medics up here so I put in for a transfer." He finished tying a clean bandage round the child's matchstick-thin leg and removed the thermometer. "As soon as the ambulances get through, you're heading for hospital. The kid's not the only one with a fever – you've got a temperature of 103 and will get gangrene in those feet if they're not properly attended to."

I suddenly remembered Falco. We'd spent the past two days cowering in the cellar with the old man and his wife, until a shell scored a direct hit on the house above. The old couple had been killed in the blast; I'd managed to struggle out with the child, but hadn't seen Falco since. I wasn't sure he was alive.

"I'm not going to hospital. Just put some dressings on my feet."

Robb was now gently probing my bruised and blackened ribs with his stubby chewed fingers. "You've got at least three broken ribs as well. I'm giving you a shot of morphine to ease the pain."

"What about the kid? Her grandparents were killed. I don't think she's got anyone else."

"Don't worry," he stuck a large jab of morphine in my arm. "There's a convent in Nicosia. I'll tell an ambulance to drop her off with the nuns."

❖❖❖

Wired Dispatch by Robert Capa to *Life* Magazine:
I drove in a jeep with Generals Allen and Roosevelt, up the zigzag road to Troina, passing clusters of dust-covered

ginestra, the yellow flowering shrub that survives even in the rockiest and most inhospitable ground. Allen, despite regulations that make the wearing of a steel helmet obligatory, was bareheaded. He sat beside his driver in the front seat, his helmet between his legs as a faint breeze ruffled his unruly black hair. Roosevelt, alongside me in the rear, was wearing his habitual woollen beanie. In spite of the victory, both men were disturbed and upset. The casualty reports confirmed that nearly 1,600 of their soldiers had been killed, and so many wounded that the 'Big Red One' was down to forty per cent of its allocated strength. Moreover, the order of their relief from the command of their beloved Division had arrived this very morning in the daily mail pouch from Bradley's Corps Headquarters. They had been directed to go immediately to Algiers to report to Eisenhower for future assignment. Bradley, their direct commander, had not even given them the courtesy of an explanation.

At an almost right-angled bend, where the road has been practically blown away, our driver pulled over to allow a party of German prisoners march down under armed guard. One of the prisoners, a pale-faced captain in desert uniform, with an Iron Cross at his neck and a leather swagger stick stuffed into his boot, scrutinized the generals from under his sun-bleached cap and raised a hand in acknowledgement. Roosevelt gave him a sloppy salute in return. My camera clicked as I captured the moment.

Allen heard it and sighed. "You know Frank; we get along a helluva lot better with the Krauts up front than we do with our people back in the rear. I phoned George Patton and asked why the hell we'd been relieved? He claimed the decision was Bradley's, not his; but said we'd borne the brunt in Africa and had seen more than 28 days of action here. He said as an old cavalryman I should know a horse can be raced too much and the time comes when he has to be put out to grass, after which he'll come back as good as ever. I guess I goofed here. I should have committed the whole division sooner."

I snapped some of the enlisted men of the 47th Infantry making their laborious way up the hill. A little more than year ago they'd been living quiet civilian lives in small towns all over America. They'd worked in hardware stores or gas stations. Some had been graduating high school. Now they'd become part of the hardest unit in the US Army. Generals like Patton can talk of victory and glory, but these guys die and leave no mark of their existence on the world. They've lived like animals for months. They're filthy dirty, they eat if and when they can, and sleep on hard ground without cover. They live in a constant haze of dust, pestered by flies and heat, deprived of all things that once meant stability – things such as walls, floors, faucets and Coca-Cola, and even the little matter of knowing whether they'll be alive to go to bed in the same place they left in the morning. And this is only the beginning. We're paying enough to take this god-forsaken little island. After that we have to fight through the whole of Italy, then the whole of Europe and at the end of the road – Japan – island after island across the entire width of the Pacific. It'll take years and cost millions of lives. We passed another platoon of infantry, bent down with heavy packs, moving inexorably up the hill, their eyes fixed to the ground. A weary young private looked up and managed to give Allen a cheery smile. Allen waved back to him and was strangely moved. Throughout the ages, all the great civilizations have depended on the fortitude and heroism of the common soldier; once that fortitude has gone civilization will fall. Already in this century millions of the best men have uncomplainingly fought and died for freedom and democracy: in Europe, America and Russia. How long they can endure? Any victory the Allies achieve will belong to them.

A white-helmeted Corps MP was already on duty at the top of the hill. He'd waved us down before he noticed the stars on Allen's collar. He saluted with extreme embarrassment. "I'm sorry, General, but my orders are to ticket anyone riding without a helmet. My captain would give me hell if he saw you go by."

Allen, naturally, took it in good part.

The Germans had planted a time bomb in the mains before they'd quit the town, and precious water was flowing in torrents along the gutters. In the shadow of the twin-towered church, the severely wounded were lying in rows. It reminded me of that scene in Atlanta in *Gone with the Wind*. There were not enough ambulances and some men were being lifted into Transportation Corps trucks. Some had blood plasma attached to their arms, many were already in a drugged sleep. Among the soldiers sat a boy of about 13, naked save for a pair of drawers. His body was covered in burns and the medics had no salve for them. The little boy gazed up, shivering, as our jeep drove into the piazza. The two generals got out and walked down a line of wounded men...

Publication refused by US Army Censor.

Lt. Danny Crivello:

I was lying in the square. They'd given me more morphine and I'd sunk back into welcome oblivion. I don't know how long I'd been there before I heard a soft voice drifting down from above.

"Lieutenant Crivello."

A dark shape had come between me and the sun. I wanted to remain in my safe and secure cocoon, but struggled to open a heavy eye-lid. Through the mist, General Roosevelt's rubbery face was staring down compassionately.

"I took your advice, General," the mere effort of speech caused me pain. "There was another road into the town, over the mountain to the north. I took a calculated risk to find out if it was unguarded. I thought it was worth getting that information back. Sorry I didn't manage it." My chest heaved with uncontrollable sobs. I felt hot tears streaming down my blackened cheeks.

"That's OK, son." Roosevelt felt in his pocket and produced a dog tag. "I said I'd keep it safe for you."

11

BROLO

MY SICILIAN CAMPAIGN by General George S. Patton Jr:

The Canadians finally took Adriano on August 7; and the British now had the railways working on their side of the island, supplying their advance. I was bitterly frustrated at Truscott's fitful progress along the coastal road. Water was scarce and the heat was appalling – over 100 F. The retreating Germans fired on us relentlessly from their artillery positions in the mountains above, continued to blow up bridges and roads, and had laid thousands of mines, which the iron content of the lava and rock made extremely difficult to detect. I therefore decided to leapfrog my way along the coast by means of amphibious operations with the Navy.

Lt. Danny Crivello:

I lapsed in and out of consciousness. The smell of ether mingled with incense, shit and piss. I opened my drugged eyes and beheld a serene statue of the Madonna, smiling beatifically down on me; but I heard screams and groans not prayers. Suffering men were all around me. I thought for a moment I was in Hell. I heard a boy crying for his mother and I found myself calling out for mine. I called for her again and again and again, until she came at last, with Gina beside her. I felt a hand gently brushing my cheek. I turned my head, thinking it was Gina, but only made out a dark face. Strong arms lifted me up and took me out into clean night air; then a rough and bumpy ride, with my stretcher sliding around the floor of a truck; then blackness and peace, before soft, cool hands touched my fevered body and gently unwound the bandage around my ribs. Someone smelt clean and fresh – I'd forgotten how sweet a smell could be. I saw a pretty face hung with wisps of blonde hair escaping from a nurses' cap, before yet another needle was put into my arm and I drifted into unconsciousness yet again. I don't know how long it was before I opened my eyes and saw brown canvas above me and felt fresh cotton sheets. I glanced right and left, wounded men were lying quietly in neat rows of beds.

I lay for several minutes, contemplating my lucky survival, when the flap opened at the far end of the tent and a short little GI came in. When she took off her helmet and blonde hair fell about her shoulders, I realized it was my pretty nurse. She took a deep breath, pushed the stray wisps of hair under her cap and smoothed down her overall fatigues. She came slowly down the line, checking charts and medical requirements, but became aware of me watching her as she drew near. She took the chart from the foot of my bed and compared it with her notes.

"I guess I'd better see how those ribs are doing".

She unwound the bandage and tenderly laid her palm upon my naked ribs. I sensed a surge of excitement in my loins. I remembered Gina's touch and couldn't prevent the blood flowing within me. In a thrice my dick was standing erect beneath the thin blanket. She gave it a cursory glance before continuing her task.

"I'm sorry, nurse. It's been a long time since a woman touched me," I lied.

Her smile was warm. "Don't worry, I'm used to it. Wait till I give you a blanket bath." She had rewound the bandage with great care. "How's that feel? Someone gave me special orders to make sure I took special care of you."

I was poleaxed. "Who did that? General Roosevelt?"

She smiled, which made her face even more pretty. "My! You must be important. But I'm sorry to say it was only the buck private that brought you here. Took you out of the back of his truck and carried you in. Said you weren't getting the proper treatment in the place where he found you; made me promise to look after you. He had quite a way with him."

"What did he look like?"

"Just like any other soldier; maybe a bit older than most. Didn't really see his face – he'd pulled his helmet right down."

Uncle Tony. It had to be Uncle Tony. I felt strangely secure. Uncle Tony always seemed to be there: watching over me, even here amid this tumult of death and destruction.

"How on earth did they get in that condition?" She was looking at my mangled feet

"It's a long story. I'm in Naval Intelligence."

She flinched. She saw I'd noticed and attempted to pass it off with a laugh. "I thought you guys used your brains, not your feet." Our eyes met. "I knew someone in that outfit once."

I gazed hungrily at the trim figure that her overalls failed to conceal. "He must have been a lucky guy. What was his name?"'

"Oh, I don't suppose you'd know him. He was always looking out for himself. I'd bet he still has some soft posting in New York."

"I was in New York this time last year."

"That's funny. So was he."

'What's his name?"

"Frank Dunford."

"He's here in Sicily. I saw him at Gela on D-Day."

8 August, 1943
Sant'Agata Beach
Lt. Frank Dunford:

We disembarked late in the afternoon, nine miles west of Monte Fratello. I'd been appointed shore fire-control officer to the 2nd Battalion, 30th Regiment, which together with a platoon of tanks and a battery of field artillery had been code-named Task Force Bernard, after Lieutenant Colonel Bernard, our commander. Assisted by the covering fire I called in from the light cruisers *Savannah* and *Philadelphia*, our small force succeeded in killing or capturing 250 Germans, disabling four tanks and throwing back the Axis defence line to the Zappula River, bringing Patton almost twenty miles closer to Messina.

I'd come through once again without a scratch, but how much longer would my luck hold?

93rd Army Hospital,
Nicosia, Sicily
Lt. Danny Crivello:

Major Powell, with clipboard in his hand, eased his soft but-tocks into the small canvas campstool by my bed, and gave me a cold smile.

"You're looking very fit considering." He looked around the tent to ensure that he couldn't be heard, but the men were too preoccupied with their wounds and pain to notice. "Colonel Hardiman, Patton's G-2, has sent me here to debrief you. Did you manage to pick up anything of interest whilst they were interrogating you?"

"Only a couple of broken ribs, damaged kidneys and a few lost toe nails."

Powell forced a more kindly smile upon his smooth fea-tures. "I'm sorry. But I suppose you must expect that sort of thing in your kind of work. But what I meant was did you hear anything about their plans, their morale? Patton is set on getting to Messina as quickly as possible. Are they going to evacuate or fight to the bitter end?"

I shrugged. "I heard nothing, but those Germans are pretty tough soldiers. They'll fight you all the way and beyond."

Major Powell paused and pondered before writing some-thing down on the report sheet attached to the clipboard. He then looked up and seemed a tad embarrassed. "I'm afraid I have to ask you this, it's merely routine of course. Did you give any information to the enemy?"

I felt the bile of anger and resentment rising in my mouth. I'd held out for two days and given them nothing – suffering unimaginable pain whilst brown noses such as Powell played at being soldiers in the Palace at Palermo. "On the third day of interrogation I admitted to being an officer in Naval Intelligence."

Powell nodded and wrote something down. "I don't sup-pose that would do any harm. Was there anything specific that they wanted to know?"

"Their main question was where we were planning to go next. I told them I was only a junior officer and had no idea. They said I must have heard rumours. They kept asking me what rumours I'd heard."

"And did you tell them?"

"I didn't know how much longer I could hold out. I decided to give them the least likely scenario – give them a red herring."

A more serious expression had come upon Powell's face. "So what did you say?"

"I said that we were going for Greece. Patton and Montgomery were going to form a bridgehead there, and then push up through the Balkans and link up with the Russians. It would be our main effort – there would be no second front in France."

Powell shook his head: "It is a pity that you said so much."

"What does it matter? It wasn't true."

Powell slapped at a fly that was buzzing at his cheek. "They have experts who will be able to deduce all manner of information from that. It would have been better to have stayed silent."

"Silent? Have you any idea what they do to you?"

Powell was already on his feet. "There shouldn't be any trouble – you've an excellent record. When you're fit, we'll decide whether to send you back to the Navy, or keep you to help us with AMGOT. Your Sicilian friends seem to be managing rather well." He glanced at his expensive watch. "I must go. Patton has a large party of journalists arriving from stateside – CBS, NBC, *Newsweek, Saturday Evening Post* – you name it. We are putting on a special show for them; a combined operation."

Powell got up and walked back down the tent. I watched his large, fleshy butt shimmying up and down inside his freshly pressed pants. His after-shave lingered with the smell of bedpans. I lay back and closed my eyes and tried to make sense of the war.

MY SICILIAN CAMPAIGN by General George S. Patton Jr:

Following the success of the landing at Sant'Agata, I decided to repeat the operation a few miles further up the coast at Brolo. To ensure that all back home were aware of the efficiency and élan of my army, I arranged for a handpicked party of journalists to accompany the mission. I was only days from Messina, and as yet Eisenhower had made no mention of what new command he had in mind for me. Another successful operation would force Ike to show his hand.

93rd Army Hospital, Nicosia, Sicily.
Lt. Danny Crivello:

"How are you doing?"

"Haven't been so comfortable since I left New York."

Sue sat on my bed and despite regulations took out a pack of cigarettes. "Would you like a smoke?"

"I was the only kid in my class at school who didn't. They make me cough, give me a sore throat."

"You don't mind if I do?"

"Be my guest."

She lit her Chesterfield and inhaled deeply.

I sensed why she'd come. "I was never close to Frank, but I always thought he was a swell guy."

She smiled gratefully. "I can't believe you saw him here in Sicily. Last time I heard from him he was intending to stay in New York for the duration. He never struck me as being the heroic type."

"He's a ship-shore gunnery officer. When I left him at Gela, he was about to call down some naval guns on a bunch of advancing Italian tanks on the orders of Patton himself. He looked pretty heroic to me." A distant naval gun thundered out in the Tyrrhenian Sea as if in response. It was as if Frank was close and still alive.

That evening, I got to know plenty about Lieutenant Sue Martin, of the Army Corps of Nurses. Her unit had embarked from Camp Stark, New York, on April 4th, and landed at Casablanca on May 25th. From there they'd moved eastwards along the coast to Oran, to deal with the casualties from the Tunisian campaign. They'd crossed to Sicily on July 13th and had followed the advance ever since. She'd become as hardened a veteran as the men she nursed. The most intimate and sacred parts of a man's body and soul had been laid bare before her every day. She'd had more men than she could remember: some out of pity; some out of interest or desire; others merely as a means to forget her own terror and despair. She'd held the hand of countless boys in lieu of a mother, wife or sweetheart, and had whispered words of love, hope and comfort to them as they died. But these past few days even her resolve was beginning to crack. It had never been as bad as this in Africa, even in the days following Kasserine. How many more boys would die before this terrible war was won?

10 August, 1943

Caronia
Lt. Frank Dunford:

We'd been moved back westwards along the coast to Caronia and were now bivouacked on a small peninsula, by a shingle beach that would provide an easy embarkation. It was perfect holiday weather. The Tyrrhenian Sea was as calm as a millpond and at its deepest shade of indigo. A soft breeze came off it and cooled the sweat on my brow, as I sat on the pebbles with the rest of the men. We were sitting, like schoolboys, in a large semi-circle around Colonel Bernard and a Major Powell from Patton's staff, who'd brought with him a large blackboard and easel. The Major was plump and his immaculate uniform contrasted with the worn battledress hanging about Colonel Bernard's lean frame.

Major Powell cleared his throat and referred to his written orders. He gave a self-satisfied smile before speaking. "Well men, your action at Sant'Agata was highly successful. Normally you would be briefed through Corps Headquarters, but General Patton wishes me to give you all personally his warmest thanks and commendation. We have the Krauts on the run and you now have a chance – a chance few outfits get – to cut the rug and knock them all the way back to Messina. With support from the Navy and Air Force, you will embark this evening and cut off the enemy's line of retreat at Brolo." He turned, looked at his orders, and then drew a rough plan of the coast on the board with a piece of chalk. The chalk screeched and set my teeth on edge. "It's a small town about twenty miles east of here. We want to avoid street fighting, so you will land west of the town – here." He again consulted his notes before marking the spot. "Thanks to aerial photography, we have a very accurate knowledge of the terrain. When you leave the beach you will pass through lemon groves, crisscrossed with drainage ditches and stone walls. 100 yards inland you will cross a railway embankment, and then move through more lemon groves which rise in terraces for another 300 yards, until you reach the main coastal highway, which skirts the base of this steep conical hill of almost 1,000-foot elevation, which we will call Mount Cipolla."

He drew a cone and a few little trees, and then made two lines between them and the sea. One line represented the road. The other line, Powell diligently crossed with little horizontal lines to mark the railway. It looked like a child's drawing of a fairy tale. Behind me someone murmured: "How the fuck will the tanks get across the railway?"

Major Powell may not have been in the finest physical shape, but he sure had sharp hearing. He turned with a knowing smile. "Fortunately you have staff officers to solve those problems for you. There are passages under the railway embankment, here and here." He made two further marks on his plan. "They are large enough for the tanks and self-propelled guns to pass through. You will take Mount Cipolla, drive off any enemy forces that might be there, and establish your Command Post on the top. With radio contact, which will provide you with supporting naval gunfire or direct aerial bombing, you will be able to have complete control of the road and railway line, together with a four-mile strip of coastal plain. You will hold the position and thus prevent the enemy retreating towards Messina, until you are relieved." He turned once more and marked the positions on the board before facing us again. "I cannot underline how vital this operation will be. With luck, we should be able to cut off an entire German Division – one less for you to bother with when you get to Italy. To make sure that the folks back home appreciate what a great job we're all doing, General Patton has allowed a couple of accredited war correspondents to accompany you on the mission. Others will sail with me aboard Admiral Davidson's flagship, the *Philadelphia*, from where I will explain to them the purpose of the action. General Patton instructed me to tell you that he knows you will conduct yourselves with valour and uphold the honour of the Seventh Army and make all America proud."

During the afternoon two Heinkel He 177s managed to get through the air defences and strafed the beach. They damaged our only tank carrier beyond repair. The mission was delayed twenty-four hours until a replacement arrived from Palermo.

⚜⚜⚜⚜

3rd Evacuation Hospital, Nicosia, Sicily.
Lt. Danny Crivello:

That morning a young artilleryman, little more than a boy, was assigned the bed next to mine. He had no visible wounds and at first just sat shivering, hunched up on his cot wearing his helmet liner. He looked so desolate that I felt I had to try to share whatever was troubling him.

"How y'doing?"

The boy turned and looked at me. He had the same expression as the little girl in the cellar at Troina. He said nothing.

I tried again: "What's y'name?"

There was a flicker in his eyes; the words came out in a monotone: "Private Paul Bennett, C Battery, 17th Field Artillery."

I decided not to overawe him with my rank. It wasn't normal for officers and enlisted men to share quarters. "I'm in the Navy – Danny Crivello." I reached out my hand but the boy just stared at it. "What's wrong, pal?"

His eyes slowly focused on my face. "I don't know. My buddy, Chuck, we enlisted together, he was hit by a shell a few days ago: hurt real bad. Ever since I can't seem to stand the noise of the shells as they go over. I feel nervous and I can't sleep. A battery aid guy sent me down to the rear echelon and the M.O. there gave me some medicine, which made me sleep, but next day I was still nervous. Then the M.O. ordered me to be evacuated here – but I didn't want to leave my unit. I've been with some of those boys for four years." Tears began to well up in his eyes.

I leant across and patted his knee. "Don't let it get you down, pal. A few days in here and these beautiful nurses will make you feel as good as new."

11 August, 1943
Caronia
Lt Frank Dunford:

We loaded our vehicles and equipment aboard our small invasion fleet throughout the morning. Some of the men were uneasy as they went about their tasks. The delay meant the action had got off to a bad start and like me, they sensed we were pushing our luck, attempting a second landing behind enemy lines in three days. In the early afternoon, Colonel Bernard, whose little brush moustache bore a faint resemblance to Hitler's, explained the plan to us in greater detail. The force would land in four waves. The first wave would be Easy Company and the naval beach marking party. The rifle platoons would destroy any beach defences, block the entrances to the beach from east and west, and clear the lemon groves between the railway embankment and the coastal highway. In the second wave, fifteen minutes later, would be five Sherman tanks and a platoon of combat engineers, who would prepare the ground for the two self-propelled artillery batteries scheduled in the fourth wave. After another fifteen minutes, the third wave would roll in, consisting of Bernard's Headquarters, the two war correspondents, and three more infantry companies: Foxtrot, George and Harry. Foxtrot and George would pass through the lemon groves and make their way to the top of Mount Cipolla. Harry would provide a machine gun section for each of the rifle companies and send a section of 81-mm mortars to join the party on the top. The final wave consisted of two field artillery batteries, the naval gunfire liaison team, which was just me and my radio operator, Burton, and the ammunition supply train, consisting of fifteen mules and their handlers.

Our mission was to dig in and prevent the eastward withdrawal of German forces from the Naso Ridge. We were to hold and defend until relieved by the 15th Infantry Regiment, approaching from the south, and the 1st Battalion of the 30th Regiment, advancing from Cape Orlando, about three miles to the west.

⚜⚜⚜⚜

MY SICILIAN CAMPAIGN by General George S. Patton Jr:

I had spent an irritating morning explaining to the collected war correspondents, that despite all our meticulous planning and overwhelming supremacy at sea and in the air, a chance Luftwaffe raid had delayed our proposed amphibious operation by one whole day. I had then had been further enraged by a BBC broadcast, implying my American soldiers were eating grapes while Montgomery was doing all the fighting. I was also feeling remorse at the manner in which Allen and Roosevelt had been replaced. They were fighting Generals, a rare breed – like me. I decided to visit the hospital at Nicosia to calm my mind. I knew it contained casualties from the battle at Troina and wanted to give them my personal gratitude and sympathy. The suffering of men under my command has never failed to move me. I consider a wounded soldier one of the noblest of God's creatures.

93rd Evacuation Hospital
Nicosia, Sicily
Lt. Danny Crivello:

There was a godawful disturbance outside. I turned my head and saw nurses and orderlies running to and fro, like chickens with a fox in the coop. There was more commotion, the tent flap blew open and the bright sun outside sparkled on golden stars and highly burnished leather. General Patton swept into the tent, with Sue and Major Etter, the Receiving Officer, at his heels. Patton looked down the long lines of wounded, came to attention, slowly raised his hand to the three stars on the front of his helmet, and then began to make a reverential progress through the ward. In the first bed was a boy from Nebraska with an amputated leg; in the second lay a bandaged figure with terrible burns. He nodded his homage to them both and wiped away a tear.

I was in the third bed. He paused and stared at me. "Don't I know you, soldier?"

"It's sailor actually, General. Lieutenant Danny Crivello, US Navy."

Patton's craggy face smiled in recognition. "You can't blame me. You are so rarely in uniform." His smile faded. "I read Powell's report. I heard those Nazi bastards gave you a tough time. Don't worry, Lieutenant, we'll pay them back a thousand fold. I salute you. You are a brave man."

He then turned to the next bed where Bennett was sitting fully dressed. His helmet liner was still upon his head. Tears were rolling down his cheeks. Patton's expression changed immediately. "What's wrong, soldier, are you hurt?"

Bennett slumped even lower on his bed and began to whimper like a child. "Oh, no, I'm not hurt, but, it's terrible...just terrible...it's my nerves..."

Any trace of respect or concern vanished from Patton's face. "What did you say?"

Bennett continued to sob, "I can hear the shells coming over, but I can't hear them burst."

Patton turned to Major Etter; his eyes wild with anger. "What's this man talking about? What's wrong with him, if anything?"

Etter fumbled with his notes, Sue was about to speak, but Patton glared down on Bennett and yelled, "Stand up!" The boy got to his feet. Patton lowered his voice as if he were sharing his shame. "Why don't you act like a man instead of a damn snivelling baby?" He looked back towards me and the amputee from Nebraska, "Look at these severely wounded soldiers, cheerful, not complaining a bit, and here you are, a goddam cry baby."

Through his sobs Bennett managed to blurt out: "It's my nerves, I can't stand the shelling anymore."

Patton now shook with anger. "Your nerves, hell, you are just a goddamn coward, you yellow sonofabitch." He began to flick at Bennett's lowered head with the leather gloves in his hand. "Shut up that goddamn crying! I won't have these brave men here, who have been shot and hurt, seeing a yellow bastard crying!" He turned again to Sue and Major Etter, who were staring at him, ashen-faced. "You will not admit this coward into this hospital; there's nothing the matter with him. He's not fit to be among these brave men." He swung back to the hapless Bennett. "You're a disgrace to the Army. You're going back to the front to fight, although that's too good for you. You ought to be lined up against a wall and shot." The very words seemed to enrage him even further. He pulled one of his ivory-handled revolvers from its holster and waved it in the boy's petrified face. "In fact, I ought to shoot you myself right now. Goddamn you!"

I struggled painfully to get out of bed, while Sue and Major Etter attempted to throw themselves between Patton and his victim. The fury of Patton's rage was now resounding throughout the hospital, and its commander, Colonel Currier, came running into the tent. Patton, still waving the pistol in his hand, saw him and screamed.

"I want you to get that man out of here right away. I won't have these brave boys seeing such a bastard babied. He's a no good sonofabitch."

He slapped the terrified Bennett across the face amid loud protestations of outrage, shock and pity. Patton turned from his prey to see that the tent was now full of horrified doctors and nurses. This calmed him somewhat. He was about to leave until Bennett began to sob even louder. Patton's fury returned in a trice. He leapt back and hit the boy with such fury that he knocked his helmet liner from his head.

"I won't have these cowardly bastards cluttering up our hospitals. We should shoot them, or we'll raise a breed of morons."

❖❖❖❖

MY SICILIAN CAMPAIGN by General George S. Patton Jr:

On the coastal road, the Germans were still contesting every inch of ground: holding their positions until the last minute and then retiring in good order. To the south, Truscott and his Donkey Wallopers, the 15th Infantry and their mules, were continuing to make slow progress over the mountains. The jeep carrying their radio had broken down, and I had not even been sure of their exact location until I received a phone call from Truscott. He was never afraid of voicing his opinion and came straight to the point. His supporting artillery was not in position and his infantry was too far west of Brolo to support the landing of the task force. He requested that the operation should be postponed for yet another twenty-four hours. I told Truscott I could not allow a further postponement. I had informed the press we would definitely go that night and reporters were already aboard the ships. Besides, I had heard rumours that Montgomery was going to mount his own amphibious landing on the east coast. If we did not move, he could still get to Messina first. Truscott prevaricated. He considered the force we were sending in was too small. I told him we could not send more than a battalion as we did not have any more tank landing craft (LCTs). When he continued to protest that he needed another day, I decided that I had better fly down to his headquarters and slap some fight back into him.

I flew down to Torrenova by spotter plane and then drove by jeep to Truscott's CP. I found my old friend pacing up and down, studying his map. I didn't waste time with any greeting. I told him, in no uncertain language, that I had no intention of losing the race to Messina on the end-run and that the operation would go tonight. If his conscience would not let him conduct it, I would relieve him, and put someone in that would.

Truscott could be as stubborn as his mules and replied: "General, it is your privilege to reduce me whenever you want to."

I had no intention of doing that. Now Allen had gone, Truscott was my most experienced commander. I tried a different tack: "Lucien, I need you. I know how good you are, but as an old football player you know you cannot postpone a match."

"I've played enough matches to know conditions sometimes make it inevitable for some games to be postponed. This campaign is dictated by the terrain and there's a bottleneck delaying me getting my guns up to support the infantry"

I shook my head. "This match cannot be postponed. The ships have already started. I will take full responsibility for failure, but I know your boys will get through." I put my arm around his shoulder, "Come on; let's have drink – open a bottle. Then go to the front and open up that bottleneck."

Truscott took his Old Crow out of the drawer, but I sensed our friendship would never be the same.

93rd Evacuation Hospital
Nicosia, Sicily.
Lt. Danny Crivello:
The strident chirping of the cicadas and the boom of distant guns mingled with groans and snores. I looked around: in the small pool of golden light by each bed, faces were in torment or repose. Bennett was sleeping peacefully, at least

while he enjoyed the effects of the sedative. It was unbear-
ably hot even though the sides of the tent were rolled up. So
many thoughts rolled round in my head, I couldn't sleep.
I got out of my cot and slipped beneath the awning. The
hospital was located below the old town of Nicosia, which
sprawled out over four hills. The ruins of an ancient castle and the outline of an ornate basilica were silhouetted
against the moon. In different circumstances it would
be one of the most romantic places on earth. A cigarette
glowed to the right. A slim, dark shape was looking up at
the stars. A wisp of blonde hair caught the moonlight. Sue
turned and recognised me.

"You're up. You must be feeling better."

"I can't sleep."

"Would you like a pill? I could put you out in a matter
of seconds."

"I want to think. We have so little time – and I have so
much to think about."

"Would you like to share your thoughts? I'd like it if you
did."

"I'm wondering what this war is all about. Why are we
fighting? Why do we blindly obey generals and risk our lives
for the bastards, when they're not worthy of respect?"

"We're fighting for freedom, for democracy. We're free-
ing the people of Europe from dictators and Fascism. It's a
noble cause, even if not all of us are noble. Anyway, Patton
won't get away with it. I've a close friend," she confided, "a
captain, in public affairs. I'll make sure he passes on what
happened today to all American correspondents attached
to the Seventh Army."

I found her hand in the dark. "You're quite a girl, aren't
you? I like talking to you. It's so easy. It seems like we were
old friends."

"I suppose we are in a sort of way. We both were friends of Frank."

"I think you were closer than a friend. How come he split from such a swell girl as you?"

"Ask him next time you see him. I did all I could to keep us together." She paused. I think she was close to tears. "Have you got a girl?"

"I thought I had."

"Back home?"

"No, here in Sicily; just fifty miles away." I looked towards the dark bulk of the Madonie Mountains, breaking the horizon like the backs of black whales. "She's on the other side of those."

"So why are you unhappy?"

"She's beautiful – the first girl I've ever been with. I thought she was perfect and pure. Now I'm not sure. I've seen how women behave in war – how cheaply they sell themselves. There's another man, a Sicilian, I think he's my friend, but he wants her as well. I'm afraid he's making love to her over there at this very moment."

"Don't let your imagination turn to jealousy. If you love her you should trust her until you've proof she doesn't love you. Love is rare and precious. Hold on to it – it's all that matters." She was squeezing my hand. "I've known so many men but I've only loved one. You say we have so little time – don't waste it. Why not go to her tonight?"

I turned back to her. "Are you serious?"

"All your ribs need now is time to heal. You're fit enough to walk, if you keep those feet clean and change the bandages regularly. I could ask Major Etter to make out a discharge chit for you to return to your posting in Palermo. There are spare jeeps in the pool. If you left now you could be with your girl by the morning and get to Palermo by the afternoon. No one would be any the wiser."

My heart beat fast with excitement – it seemed so simple. My special orders carried me anywhere, and I had to check on Luciano. "Wouldn't I be deserting?"

"I think you've paid your dues to Patton and Uncle Sam for a while. You deserve a furlough."

⚜⚜⚜

MY SICILIAN CAMPAIGN by General George S. Patton Jr:

At 0100 hours on August 11, covered by *Philadelphia* and six destroyers, with night fighters circling above, Bernard began to transfer his small force into the landing craft. At 0210 all was ready for the final run in, and at 0243, thirteen minutes later than scheduled, Easy Company splashed ashore with no opposition. They moved swiftly inland to cut passages through the double barbed wire fence around the beach, twenty yards from the shore. They then crossed the railway embankment and paused to reorganize before beginning their task of clearing the lemon groves. They accomplished this quickly without firing a shot, taking 10 German prisoners in the process. Then one rifle platoon and two weapon platoons swung right to block the crossing over the Naso River, whilst the remainder swung left to take the railway and highway bridges across the Brolo.

The second wave landed almost at their heels but immediately ran into difficulties when it was found, despite all previous assurances, the passages in the railway embankment were too narrow for the Shermans to pass through. The commander of the leading tank got out and departed on foot to search for another route. Meanwhile the third

wave, including Bernard's Headquarters and the two correspondents, from *Time* and *The New York Post*, had landed
in their DUKWs and driven inland until they too hit the
railroad.

Brolo
Lt. Frank Dunford:

As I came in with the final wave, I cursed myself yet again
for not keeping my trap shut and losing my safe job in the
fish market at Gela. I could at least have made sure Franco
and his mother were provided for. But I knew, deep in my
gut, that it would have been dishonourable. But what was
dishonourable and what was honour? Was honour just a
word on a war memorial; a mere 'scutcheon' as Shakespeare
said? Thanks to Sergeant Blum, I had been finding more
and more relief in the words of the Bard. They distracted my
mind from the horrors around me. I'd just finished reading
Antony and Cleopatra, who'd fought battles at sea not so far
from here. Antony had come to Sicily to deal with Pompey
and the Sicilian pirates; nothing much had changed, there
were gangsters here even then. My reveries were interrupted
by the loud braying of a mule. I smiled – and mules too!
Two thousand years ago, Antony went to war with mules.
What did Shakespeare call their handlers? 'Muleteers'? It
was a good word. Another mule brayed. They were restless,
as if they knew they were going into danger or worse. The
smell of their dung and piss, swirling around on the floor
of the craft, brought the sour taste of seasickness to my
mouth once more. I turned away and scanned the beach
through my binoculars. Ahead, was the prominent offshore
rock we'd been told to watch out for. The ruined Norman

watchtower was on a rocky outcrop on the edge of the sea to the left, just as it should be according to my map. I checked my watch – almost 0330 hours: so far all seemed to have gone well, not a shot had been fired. It was imperative we got into position before the Germans became aware of our presence. I checked Burton, my radio operator, was beside me. The shore was getting ever nearer; I could see the sailors of the beach-marking party waving us in. My heart began to pound even faster. I went over what I had to do for the final time: find Colonel Bernard, get to the top of Mount Cipolla, and establish contact with the fleet. It seemed simple.

The ramp crashed down, and I immediately ran forward towards the nearest clump of lemon trees; the gap in the wire was clearly marked. Ahead all was silence. All I could hear, apart from my rubber boots crunching on the gravel, was Burton, just behind me, panting under his load. Within a minute we were almost at the railway – but something was wrong. There was no movement forward. The tanks and self-propelled guns were stacked up, like traffic waiting to enter the Lincoln Tunnel. There was no sign of Colonel Bernard. I supposed he'd gone for the other passage, half a mile to the west. I pushed my way to the front of the line to find the engineer officer, a nervous little fellow, in whispered consultation with the major in command of the guns. The engineer looked up as I drew near.

"That fool from Headquarters who briefed us was talking through his fat ass. The passages in the embankment are barely wide enough for a jeep. I've found a possible way round if we go through the bed of the Brolo River – that's a few hundred yards to the east. I'm gonna guide the guns round that way. The tank commander went off in the opposite direction. Wait here for him. If he hasn't found a way through, bring him along after us."

The guns, like giant crabs, were already moving labori-ously to the right and clanking away into the dark. I wanted to push on, but knew the tanks were vital to the operation. I waited anxiously until the tank commander came running out of the dark, glistening with sweat. He was relieved to see me. "I've found a river; I think it must be the Naso, about a mile to the west. I reckon I can get the tanks over through the riverbed. Tell Colonel Bernard we'll do everything we can to get them through."

As the Shermans manoeuvred themselves to the left, I took Private Burton and ran through the passage into the lemon groves on the other side of the embankment. Through the trees, I began to see the cone-like hill Major Powell had sketched, silhouetted against the night sky. The hill had a nose on the north-east corner where the incline was not so precipitous. Our assault would be made from that side. I stole a glance at my watch – it was only 0345 – it seemed like we'd been ashore for hours. Another three minutes and we reached the embankment of the high-way, where men of Foxtrot and George were assembling. I searched for Colonel Bernard, but couldn't find him. Nevertheless, things seemed to be going well: all remained quiet; we hadn't been detected and we were below our objec-tive in our correct position. The men were looking towards me expectantly. I realized I was the only officer present. I had to act decisively. I looked around in the darkness and could just make out a sergeant's chevrons and crawled over towards them. The sergeant was a short man, with a mass of thick hair springing out of his shirt. He looked thankful that I was there.

"Begin to get your men across and up the hill," I ordered. "Move them over in groups of five or six."

The sergeant nodded, whispered a few instructions and almost at once men began to run across the road in small clusters and clamber up Mount Cipolla.

Less than twenty men had got across when the unexpected roar of a motorcycle broke the silence. The GIs hit the dirt as a German dispatch rider sped down the road towards Naso. I feared he might hit one of the prone bodies, but he was past them in an instant, the sound of his engine swiftly swallowed up by the night. The men rose and continued crossing. Burton and I went next. We were in the centre of the road when a German halftrack revved round the bend. I turned towards it and froze. Why hadn't we heard its approach? I guessed the crew had been having a surreptitious rest by the roadside and had only that minute started their engine. Burton made a sudden bolt for the sanctuary of the trees at the foot of the hill. His movement caught the driver's attention and he screeched his vehicle to a halt. As he rose from his seat to get a better view, there was a deafening explosion and the halftrack disappeared in a ball of flame. A GI had fired his bazooka. Every German would be alerted for miles.

I hurtled across the road to join Burton, and we clambered up the hill as fast as we were able, grabbing at clumps of grass and small bushes. We could hear the cobra-like hiss of Spandau machine gun fire and the swish and crump of mortars coming from the top, while flares exploded in the sky above. The German guns to the east were already in action, sending 20mm shells screaming towards our landing beach. We continued upwards until we reached a cluster of large boulders on a ridge. The little hairy sergeant and a dozen men were crouched under them. He motioned me to get down beside him.

"Judging by the rate of fire there can't be that many Krauts up there. We can't afford to lose you and that radio. Wait here, we'll smoke 'em out – I'll send back a runner when it's clear."

It made sense. I nodded to Burton and gratefully took cover in the shadow of the largest boulder, while the sergeant signalled one group left, another right, before leading the remainder straight on up. For a few minutes all was quiet, apart from the buzzing of insects, protesting at the disturbance of their domain. More shells, from the German 88s in the east, screamed down towards the beach. I stole a glance at Burton, who appeared to be murmuring a prayer. More men went doggedly past us up the hill. Then silence again. Suddenly, sharp as whip cracks, rifle shots rang out above, followed by bursts of machine gun fire and the explosion of hand grenades. Then all was quiet once more. We waited anxiously – looking for any movement on the slope above. A few pebbles rolled down before the dark shape of a GI slithered into view.

His young face was elated. "It's OK; we've driven the motherfuckers off. Those we didn't kill, skedaddled down the west side of the mountain and headed for Brolo."

The sergeant and his men had already occupied the foxholes by the time we arrived at the summit. Machine guns were being sited and fields of fire worked out. While Private Burton selected the best spot to site the radio, I went into the small dugout that had served as the command post, to find it strewn with documents and the telephone switchboard smashed. The documents naturally were in German. Whilst I was trying to decipher them, a shout outside signalled Colonel Bernard and his headquarters had made it to the top.

I found Bernard grim-faced. Three of the tanks had bellied out trying to get across the deep ditches by the river, and the other two had damaged themselves trying to knock down stone walls. They could be used as fixed guns but could not manoeuvre, and would be sitting ducks for the German 88s. However the artillery had been more successful and was even now getting into firing positions to the north of the highway. Ammunition would be a problem. The German shellfire on the beaches had killed fifteen ammunition bearers and all but two of the mules. I remembered the mules' anxiety and wondered if the poor brutes might indeed know more than we did. Without the tanks and with a shortage of ammunition for the guns, the success of the mission was even more dependent on me.

I looked out to where the ships would be. It was still night, but to the east there were already slivers of red in the sea.

⚜⚜⚜

Lt. Danny Crivello:

Sue had provided me with a spare army uniform and a standard Colt M1911 revolver, and I drove the jeep out of Nicosia like an excited schoolboy. On the main road I met, as expected, the dimmed lights of convoy after convoy, laden with supplies for the front, but when I branched off on the minor road to Villalba, solitary trucks, some with US Army markings, came out of the dark. I'd no idea what their cargo or destination could be.

Dawn was breaking as I came down the hill into the squalid little town. The outgoing traffic was so heavy that I was forced to pull aside to let the heavily-laden trucks lumber past, and when I drove into the piazza before the church, I was confronted with an extraordinary scene. Army wagons and battered civilian trucks of indeterminate age were strewn in long lines across the entire length of the square. All about them was frantic bustle and activity. Sicilians were unloading jerry cans of gasoline, boxes and containers of all shapes and sizes, stamped with the insignia of the US Army. Others were carrying sacks of grain, crates of squawking chickens, bloody sides of beef and carcasses of pigs and sheep. In some cases it was two-way traffic. Goods and produce were simply being carried from one truck to another. Other large crates were being taken to the ancient stone barns, once used for tithes, which lay behind the church. Some men prowled about as overseers with *lupare* slung across their shoulders. I recognized several as guests at Don Calo's feast.

I parked the jeep in a dark street beside the church and immobilized the vehicle by taking out the starter motor, which I put with some K Rations in a kitbag and slung over my shoulder. I then made my way back into the piazza. I found the Via Bocetta; yes that was the name, with the two squalid cafes on either corner. The Sicilian band had gone but even at this hour, Glenn Miller blared from the new radios on the counters. Both cafes were full of laughing women and American soldiers, who I presumed were the drivers of the trucks. My heart pounded. I half expected to see Gina with her arms around a soldier, with that look in her eyes I'd thought was only for me. I remembered the gentleness of her touch, the sweetness of her body, the damp hairs around her most secret parts, the soft moans she made in pleasure at my love. I ached with yearning and jealousy. But the only familiar face I saw was that of Provost Sergeant O'Brian, with his right hand thrust deep inside the skirt of a voluptuous woman of uncertain age, sitting on his knee. I was thankful that Gina was not there until I remembered Falco. Had he returned and claimed her? He may even have thought I was dead – that his rival had perished in the bombed cellar in Troina. Falco might be comforting her even at that moment. The thought was unbearable. For the first time in my life I cursed my hot Sicilian blood. How easy to be cool and unemotional like the Anglo-Saxons.

I made my way along the Via Bocetta towards Gina's hovel. The air still reeked of poverty but something had changed. Gaudy garments, gifts from grateful GIs, hung from the washing lines; their bright colours just visible in the early morning light. A faint wind was flicking them into a brilliant scudding sea. From some windows wafted the delicious smell of frying sausage and fresh bread, which helped to counter the foul stench of the sewers. At the end of the alley, the lamp flickered on the blue-robed Magdalene, still imprisoned behind the bars of her niche in the whitewashed wall. The hovel looked as miserable as it had before. American affluence had not advanced this far along the Via Bocetta. Was that a sign that Gina had not sold herself? That she was still pure and loved me? My heart was bursting, just as it had that wonderful night. When had it been? Only three weeks ago? I'd lived a lifetime since then. Only my love for her hadn't changed. My knuckles pounded on the remaining traces of blistered paint on the door. All was silent within. I knocked again, even more frantically. I stopped and strained my ears. Someone was moving inside. The movements sounded quick and frenzied. They weren't the movements of the old woman.

I knocked a third time. "Gina! It's me. I have come back!"

There was the sound of a key turning. The door creaked open and Calo's woman, Gina's mother, was looking up at me. There was fear and dread, almost hatred, in her face.

"She has gone. Go away! You must never see my daughter again!"

I was thunderstruck, bewildered and afraid. It was like those nightmares I'd had as a child, when all my worst fears seemed to come true. "I love your daughter. I want to marry her and take her with me to America. I will take you as well, even your mother. I want to take her away from all this – from Don Calo – this war – I will make her happy."

"She is promised to another. Go before there is trouble. She does not want you."

The words were more painful than the throbbing of my ribs and my raw toes rubbing against the wool of my socks.

"I will never believe that until she tells me so herself."

She tried to push me from threshold. "Go! You will only bring trouble for her and me as well as yourself."

"Don't you understand that I love her?"

"Love? What do you know of love? You are an American. You think you can buy anything with your filthy dollars. You want only to fuck, not love."

"I am a Sicilian. I was born here. I am not like the others. I am the right man for her."

There was movement behind and Gina came out of the shadows. She was even more beautiful than I'd remembered. "You must go. What my mother says is true. I am promised to a good man."

I moved closer to her. I could smell her body. Our eyes met. I was certain I saw the same love and yearning in them that I'd seen on that magic night. The only night of real passion I'd ever known. It couldn't be the last.

"I know you love me. I will not go unless you swear on all the saints that you do not."

Her lustrous eyes slowly filled with tears, like reluctant fountains. For a moment she looked back fearfully at her mother, whose face remained hard as stone. Her fingers reached up to the crucifix at her neck and entwined themselves around the thin gold chain. She stared at me as if for the last time, before whispering, in a soft vibrating voice: "I swear on my mother's soul I will never marry you. Go away."

I shook my head in disbelief. A gulf now separated us. Everything I wanted had shrivelled to nothing and was void. It hurt more than anything the Nazis had done to me in Troina. At that moment I would have betrayed any secret, committed any act of treason, to have her change those words. She was still looking at me as the door slammed. The lock groaned as the key forced it back into place. I staggered back into the dirty alley and couldn't prevent the salt tears smarting my eyes. The Magdalene was regarding me piteously from her little cell.

"I knew you would come."

I turned. Falco was leaning against the wall.

"You did not waste time. You must have made her mother a good offer. Or did Don Calo make the arrangements for you?"

"You are my friend. You will always be my friend, but you cannot have her."

I hated him. He would enjoy what was rightly mine. I would have killed him gladly. "What about your honour? Have you forgotten I took her virginity? How can a man of honour marry or respect a woman another man has enjoyed? I thought you said we would settle this the Sicilian way?"

A terrible light gleamed in the iris of Falco's eye and his hand reached for the knife in his belt. The combat knife Sue had given me was loose and ready in its sheaf. We glowered at each other; waiting for the other to make the first move. Then something softened in Falco's face. The light in his eye went out.

"I can never fight you. I owe you my life."

Mount Cipolla
Lt. Frank Dunford:

As daylight broke, the German guns switched their fire from the devastated beaches to our positions on the slopes of Mount Cipolla. Three nights ago, the radio had functioned perfectly, but today, despite all the checks, Burton had barely been able to establish contact. It seemed an eternity before we managed to call down supporting fire from *Philadelphia*. It brought some respite as the German artillery quit pounding us and began to exchange fire with the naval guns, but to the west, elements of the 15th Panzer Grenadiers were beginning to advance on our small force.

Villalba
Lt. Danny Crivello:

Don Calo, still dressed in his now badly stained US Army tunic, was sitting behind the desk in the AMGOT office when I came in. A jug of red wine with fresh lemons was at his side. He looked up and registered surprise. "Falco told me he had seen you get out of that cellar in Troina alive, but I did not expect you yet."

His dog, like that of Ulysses, recognizing the returning traveller, got up and wagged his tail. But my heart was full of rage and pain and I pushed its wet nose aside. I stared at the huge fat dirty man and hated him from the very depths of my soul. "Why did you want Falco to take the girl from me? Do you want her for yourself? Haven't you stolen enough?"

His wicked eyes flared beneath the shaggy grey eyebrows, curling up towards his brow. Power, anger and corruption radiated from the great bulk of his body. He sucked on the greasy ends of his straggling moustache, as if deciding how much of the honour and respect he was due had been insulted. At length he smiled cajolingly, exposing his yellow, fang-like teeth.

"She is not for you. Her mother is little better than a whore. It is always the same with young men when they have their first fuck. They think they are in love. They marry and regret it for the rest of their lives."

"That is for me to decide, not you."

The eyes grew colder. "You forget that now I decide everything in Villalba. I am the *sindaco,* the mayor. I also have a senior rank to you. I am an honorary colonel in the US Army." He put his grubby hands on the lapels of his tunic, fingering the insignia of the spread eagle. "Her mother has spoken to my brother, the priest. It is arranged; they will be married next week. It is better for everyone that you go away."

⚜⚜⚜

Mount Cipolla
Lt. Frank Dunford:

Our situation had become even more desperate. The Germans had made two attacks: one from the east along the bed of the Brolo River, and another, much stronger, from the west along the bed of the Naso. We'd beaten them off with the dwindling ammunition of the mortars and machine guns, but now a large truck-born infantry column was heading towards us from the west. The Germans had realized the trap they were in, and were making every effort to regain control of the road. I called incessantly into the shell-like mouthpiece of the radio, while Burton held up the aerial in every which way, but it was fruitless, there was no contact. The ships wouldn't bombard a coast where friendly troops were fighting except on specific call, and that specific call I could not make. I sensed the unspoken anger and scorn of the infantrymen around me; they'd done their job, many of their buddies had died doing it, but I was unable to do mine. I nodded to Burton yet again. He bravely got out of his foxhole, held the aerial as high as he could reach, and began to circle round once more. There was a faint crackle. Burton froze where he was, as the gunnery officer's voice aboard *Philadelphia* came through loud and clear. I instantly I gave him the co-ordinates of the approaching convoy: barely a minute later it disappeared in the smoke of a 15-gun salvo. As the smoke cleared, I could see through my binoculars that several trucks had been hit and the remainder of the column was pulling off the road to gain cover from the embankment. German infantry were jumping out of their vehicles and seeking safety among the lemon trees.

The GIs in the nearest foxholes began to cheer: "The good old Navy!" "Jeez, there ain't nothing like the sound of naval guns!" But almost at once, their cheers turned into howls of rage. I adjusted my binoculars and saw that for some inexplicable reason the *Philadelphia* and its escort destroyers were steaming away.

I frantically screamed down the radio for them to return. It was dead again.

Villalba
Lt. Danny Crivello:

I wandered through the streets of Villalba. Hatred for Don Calo had made me forget my broken heart. Calo had dominated my entire existence, although I'd only been aware of him during the past year. He'd exerted such power over my father that he had changed the purpose of his life and turned him into a criminal. Now, he'd ruined my life as well. Why? Was it perverse cruelty that didn't allow any happiness unless he'd sanctioned it himself? I found myself sitting by the river at the same spot where I'd kissed Gina for the first time. As I gazed at the water flowing placidly past, I remembered her glowing face, her exultant eyes, as our bodies burned together. I could not believe that I would never know such ecstasy again. Trucks continued to thunder over the ancient bridge above me. I watched their reflections in the water until a particularly large truck thundered above. I looked up. Beside the driver, I caught a glimpse of a familiar face. A face I'd forgotten in my grief and anger. I got to my feet and followed the truck to the piazza. I watched in the shadows as Luciano jumped down and supervised the unloading. He had lost his beard and was smartly dressed in well-cut army shirt and pants. Overseers came to him with papers, asking his approval and advice. It was as if he were still running his bootlegging empire during Prohibition.

My mind began to clear. I waited until Luciano had disappeared in the direction of Calo and the AMGOT office, and then walked across the piazza to one of the storage barns behind the church. Some miserable-looking peasants were waiting outside with heavily laden carts. They informed me they were delivering compulsory quotas of grain, cheese, eggs and olive oil, which they sorely needed for themselves, and complained bitterly they were being paid in the almost worthless old lire. I went inside, where a handful of Don Calo's men were stacking the latest deliveries. Heaps of cereal, flour, salt, pasta and cooking oil, reached almost to the rafters, together with Scotch and rye whiskey, boxes of cigarettes and huge amounts of gasoline. It looked like grand larceny on the most lavish scale; but everything seemed to be official. When I demanded what they were doing, they produced passes, stamped with the authority of AMGOT, giving them right of access to US Army supplies. Beyond question, Don Calo, thanks to the ingenuity of Luciano, was controlling the entire movement and transport of goods throughout western Sicily.

I cursed myself that I'd helped give them that power. I vowed it would not last. I was Sicilian – I wanted revenge – for myself and for my father.

⚜⚜⚜

MY SICILIAN CAMPAIGN by General George S. Patton Jr:

At 0900 hours, when Truscott failed to establish radio contact with Colonel Bernard, he immediately requested urgent navy and air support. He was told Admiral Davidson had returned to Palermo, thinking the situation on shore was in hand. Even sailing at his maximum speed of thirty-three knots, he would not be able to get back into position off Brolo until around 1400 hours. There would be air support, but it was impossible to give a specific time for the attack, or the number of planes that would be engaged. Once again I and my land forces had been let down by the Air Force and Navy. It was becoming painfully obvious to me that Truscott's instinct had been correct. The landing force had been too small. I was receiving reports that most of the 15th Panzer was making an orderly withdrawal over the mountain road via Ficarra to their next prepared positions at San

Angelo. The Seventh Army was paying a heavy price for whatever German remnants were caught in my trap.

Mount Cipolla
Lt. Frank Dunford:

Yet another German assault, the strongest yet, two infantry companies in armoured personnel carriers together with Panzers, attacked along the Brolo River. Burton and I had just re-assembled the radio after dismantling it completely and checking and polishing every part. We must have temporarily driven out the gremlins, for just then it whined back into life. I couldn't reach the *Philadelphia*, but managed to get through to General Truscott himself, who was with the leading units of the relief force. I gave him the approximate co-ordinates of the Panzers along the Brolo, and he reckoned he would just be able to reach them at the extreme range of his Long Toms, his 155mm guns. They fired within minutes and succeeded in driving the Germans back for a while. But our situation was worsening rapidly: more enemy artillery was coming into play from the west, and it would not be long before the Panzers returned. I made another attempt on Burton's fading radio, requesting urgent, immediate naval and air support. Nothing came. The remaining guns of our small artillery force were all that remained to save us from complete annihilation. During the next hour, the self-propelled guns heroically sacrificed themselves, while destroying two of the enemy tanks and forcing a third to retreat. But the field artillery, mortars and machine guns were coming to the end of their ammunition. Bernard ordered everyone up onto Mount Cipolla for a last ditch stand.

All the men were in foxholes, trying to find as much cover as they possibly could before the next round of shelling. It was hard to tell the living from the dead; except that flies walked unheeded on the dead. The skin on faces and arms was scorched by the sun. Heads were swimming with heat and exhaustion. The rocks were too hot to touch and so was the metal on weapons. I finally sighted the *Philadelphia* returning, but I could also see new German advances emerging from the west, along the coastal road, and from the town of Brolo itself. Without massive supporting fire our little force would be finally crushed between the two. I rapidly calculated the co-ordinates as Burton feverishly worked on his radio. He tuned every knob, polished and spat on every valve, and called and called again into the mouthpiece, but in vain. It was as dead as the GIs littering the slopes. I looked again at the faces of the men in the foxholes around me and came to a decision. I scribbled a second copy of the targets and handed it to Burton, telling him to forward them if he ever again achieved reception, and then crawled my way across the ridge to Colonel Bernard's foxhole.

The Colonel looked up as I approached; his face streaked with sweat and mud. His own wireless operator was beside him, calling in all our ever-decreasing units on his short range radio. I could see the contempt in Bernard's eyes. "Is that damn Navy radio of yours working yet?"

"Burton is still trying, Colonel." An incoming German shell from the west exploded just down the hill and showered us with dirt. I wiped the earth from my eyes. "Colonel, the DUKWs are still stationed at the bottom of the mountain. If I took one and managed to run the gauntlet through the lemon groves, I could take it out to the *Philadelphia* and give her guns the target co-ordinates personally."

Bernard's eyes lost a little of their scorn. "I can't ask you to do that."

"If I stay here, we'll all end up as dead as Custer at the Little Big Horn."

There was a beat before Bernard nodded. "OK son. I owe you a drink when we get to Messina."

I gave a half salute, rolled over and began to pick my way down, past shattered trees and blasted shrubs and smoking craters. The mountain itself was wounded and ruptured. Weary GIs raised their heads in their foxholes and regarded me with hostile eyes, as if I were deserting a sinking ship. An eagle, its great tawny wings spread out as if still in flight, lay dead among the stones, dark blood oozing from its yellow-banded beak. It was as if mankind had declared war on nature; but mankind was paying a terrible price. All around, twisted bodies of young men and boys lay frozen in death. Some had their innards spewing out before them; others lay with flesh blown from their bones. Everywhere, above the wounds and mutilations, flies and a myriad of other insects buzzed continuously, gorging themselves in the oven-like heat. I thought again of Shakespeare, not the heroic words of King Henry V, but those he put in the mouth of the common soldier: '*When all those legs and arms and heads, chopp'd off in a battle, shall join together at the latter day and cry all "We died at such a place;" – some swearing; some crying for a surgeon; some upon their wives left poor behind them; some upon their children rawly left. There are few die well that die in battle...*' Yet here and there, the aroma of broom and myrtle mingled with the stink of cordite and death. Bright yellow and blue mountain flowers sprung defiantly through the parched earth. Surely life would go on? The slope became steeper and I began to slide down through gravel and loose earth. The world, my life and death, seemed to be sweeping past me, like a movie at fast speed. Sue's crucifix glinted in the sun as it swung around my throat. In that brief moment I thought of her and of my mother, of what I might have been, or yet become.

Before I knew it I was at the bottom. The remaining field guns had already fallen back and were being dug into position. Grouped under the shelter of some tall black cypress trees, I could see five DUKWs. Crouching forward, almost bent double, I ran to the nearest. My sweat had stuck my shirt to my back. The salt had made it stiff as a board.

A red-haired, freckled marine of about twenty, was taking cover under the DUKW's high wheels. He looked up anxiously as I ran towards him.

"Can you drive this thing?"

"Ah'm only the assistant driver, sir. My buddy got hit on the way in."

"I said, can you drive this thing?"

"Ah reckon Ah can, sir."

"Right; you're going to drive it through those lemon trees and out to the *Philadelphia*. We're going to get some real naval support for the guys on the hill."

The young boy gulped as he realized the scale of the task, but leapt up into the driving seat. I was sitting beside him before he'd kicked his 6-cylinder GMC motor into life. The boy meshed the gears and the front-wheeled drives got all six wheels into motion. We were off. I failed to notice that three of the remaining DUKWs were following behind. Perhaps the marines that drove them assumed they'd all been ordered to withdraw, or perhaps one driver's nerve broke and he simply saw a way to escape, bringing the other two with him. I never did discover the real answer.

The red-haired boy forced his DUKW up the steep embankment of the highway and across the white cement of the road. Rifle and machine gun fire opened up instantly from some German positions to the right. I and the boy crouched low, as fragments and splinters of cement splattered against the side of the vehicle. We were over the road in seconds and plunging down the embankment on the other side. The impetus enabled the boy to swiftly move up through his gears to a top speed of almost fifty miles an hour. Almost immediately we were swerving through the lemon trees as shells began to rain down from the German 88s, who'd spotted us from the hills above Brolo. Like most American boys, the red-haired marine really knew how to drive, and the DUKW despite its odd shape was easily manoeuvrable. We soon were approaching the railway, slowing momentarily to seek out one of the narrow passages beneath it. An instant of darkness, relief from the sun and the deadly heat of shell fire, and then we were through, into the last of the lemon trees, with the beach appearing like a golden band before us, and beyond it the cool blue refuge of the sea. As the DUKW sped across the soft sand, passing the disembowelled black bodies of the unfortunate mules, and into the shallows, the boy was already engaging the double set of wheels and propeller at the rear. We were slowing down all the time as the hybrid machine reverted to its other function as a boat. We were now going little more than six miles an hour and shells were cascading into the water all around, throwing up great white spouts out of the cerulean sea; but the *Philadelphia* was reassuringly before us, and its fifteen rapid-firing 6 inch guns were already ranging on the German batteries.

My eyes were transfixed on the cruiser; already I could make out individual figures lining the decks, anxiously watching our perilous approach. Another minute and we were almost within hailing range. I picked up a cone-shaped hailer and screamed for the gunnery officer. The first face

I was aware of was that of Patton's podgy Major, who'd first briefed us on this godforsaken expedition. He was gesticulating wildly and pointing back towards the shore. I turned for the first time, and was astonished to see the three other DUKWs close behind. Furthermore, a fourth was racing across the beach and about to enter the water. I swung back to the ever-nearing cruiser. A ladder had been lowered over the side, and one of the white clad gunnery officers was clinging to it, just above the water line. He too had a hailer. His voice came through above the sound of the DUKW's motor and the surge of the sea.

"What can we do for you? What's the situation over there?"

"Colonel Bernard's just about hanging on. You've got to keep a continual fire on these co-ordinates." The marine had manoeuvred us to within touching distance. I reached into the breast pocket of my soiled shirt and handed the immaculate officer my scrappy piece of paper. "But whatever you do, keep off Mount Cipolla itself. The whole force has fallen back on it."

The gunnery officer nodded and was back up the ladder in seconds.

"Your radio contact has been extremely erratic. Are you sure your operator knows what he's doing?" The pink face of Major Powell was now at the top of the ladder. "We've been going back and forth like a goddamn yo-yo. It's very embarrassing. We've got war correspondents aboard. They've missed their lunch in Palermo. Why did you bring those other DUKWs with you?"

My temper was near breaking point. "I'm sorry about the lunch, Major, and I've no fucking idea why these other guys came along as well."

The first three DUKWs were now alongside, sheltering beneath the cruiser's high sides. The fourth was approaching rapidly. Standing up beside the driver I recognized Force Bernard's artillery officer, his face contorted with rage.

"You yellow motherfuckers! You've taken all my fucking ammo with you. I'll have your balls for deserting under fire. Get back over there at once, our to pieces are being blown." The three DUKWs began to turn, their shame-faced crews steeling themselves for a return drive through hell. They took a final wistful look at the safety the *Philadelphia* offered and were gone.

The Senior Gunnery officer was now at the top of the ladder. "You've done well Lieutenant, but we won't be able to hang on here for ever. The Admiral has no guarantee of air cover. He can't risk losing the ship. You'd best come aboard, there's no more you can do back there if you've no radio."

I looked at the young freckled face of the marine beside me and remembered the faces of Burton and the other boys on the hill. I was part of their unit. I couldn't abandon them.

"Have you any spare ammo for the field guns and mortars?"

The Gunnery officer nodded.

I licked the salt from my lips. "OK. Load me up with all that you can. Also any machine gun and rifle ammo you've got as well. I'm going back."

Villalba
Lt. Danny Crivello

I wrote a full and detailed report, noting the inconceivable amount of excess supplies in the town, the names of the officials who'd signed the orders and, whenever possible, the ongoing destinations. The whole thing stank. I decided to present my report to the AMGOT headquarters in Palermo; if they wouldn't listen I would go to Patton himself: the bastard was insane but at least he wasn't corrupt. I went to the office of the carabinieri and procured a set of handcuffs from the sleepy corporal on duty. I didn't want to involve Sergeant O'Brian and the provosts; I guessed they'd be up to their necks in it as well. There was only one other thing I had to do. The sky was black with an approaching storm, when I found Falco outside one of the cafes at the entrance of Via Bocetta, sitting disconsolately at a table with an untouched glass of brandy before him. He looked up at me with his great dark eyes, as liquid and sorrowful as a chided dog.

"I swear my friend it had nothing to do with me. Her mother came and begged me to take her. I asked Gina if that was what she truly wanted. I told her you had saved my life, that I loved you as a brother; that I did not wish to cause you pain or grief. She said she would rather die than marry you. Her mind was made up. She wept and implored me to make her my wife. I could not refuse."

I stretched out my hand. Falco took it gratefully, before rising and hugging me in his bear-like embrace. He was my only possible ally in the entire town.

"Falco, you once told me, that you followed Don Calo in the hope of building a better Sicily; an independent Sicily – with justice and prosperity for all. I must tell you, you will never achieve that as long as he has power. He will pretend to help the poor, but will make himself rich by taking money from the rich to keep the poor more wretched. Nothing will ever change." Falco shifted his feet uncomfortably and tried to look away, but I held him firmly by his thick upper arms, forcing him to listen. "You are a better man than him, Falco. Oppose him. Form your own party, unattached from the Communists, without ties to Russia; a new party for the people of Sicily. Free from corruption, free from the ways of the past; independent of the politicians of Rome."

Falco broke away from my grasp. "I cannot do that. I have tried to do things alone before – when I opposed Mussolini and the Fascists. Now, I can smell money and power, I am not strong enough to resist. But I swear that I will always protect Gina, and I will always be your friend."

"If you are really my friend, make sure that I leave the town tonight with whoever I take with me."

Brolo
Lt. Frank Dunford:

The *Philadelphia* provided some degree of protective fire, as the DUKW splashed through the waves back to the beach, but as the red-haired boy and I were handing out boxes of ammunition to the gunners at the base of Mount Cipolla, eight fighter-bombers, Focke-Wulf 190s, armed with torpedoes under their wings, came out of the northern sky. The cruiser and her escorts were immediately forced to take evasive action. I watched transfixed as a furious sea and air battle unfolded before me. Torpedoes hit the water and sped towards the pale grey flanks of the ships, leaving a thin trail of white across the face of the ocean. Some exploded short of their target, throwing up huge quantities of water, hiding the ship from view so that it momentarily appeared to have been hit. Other torpedoes raced directly under the hulls to explode on the far side. Some sped towards the bow to pass safely in front, within seconds of impact; others missed the sterns by the same margin. The three ships veered to port and starboard, throwing up clouds of smoke, as the torpedoes pursued them like hungry sharks. Mercifully, the 190s only carried one torpedo and the ships managed to evade all eight. But the planes were also armed with 20mm cannons and came back to attack again. The fighters were the best the Luftwaffe possessed, superior even to the Spitfire in their speed and manoeuvrability, but the naval anti-aircraft guns returned fire furiously and accurately. The men around me cheered, as if they were watching a football game, as first one and then another 190 went down into the sea. The German pilots were brave and returned again and again. There were only three left when seven A-36s arrived like the US Cavalry. The GIs continued to cheer as two of the remaining 190s were shot down, and the solitary survivor sped away to sanctuary in the north. But their cheers turned to cries of horror as the A-36s, elated by their success, swept back from the sea towards us, seeking fresh targets.

I watched in horrified disbelief as two planes attacked Colonel Bernard's command post on the mountain above, while the rest sped towards the guns around me. The white flash of a shell exploded into the DUKW; I had a vision of the red-haired boy flying into the air like a stringless puppet, before my body was blown apart.

Villalba
Lt. Danny Crivello:
The rain was falling heavily as I waited in the semi-darkness between two lines of trucks, and watched the lighted windows of the AMGOT office. The windows were open and I could hear laughter and the clinking of glasses. I recognised Luciano's laugh. I guessed they were laughing at me. I

cursed myself again for my naivety. I would never give them so much as an inch again. I undid the cover of my holster and eased the safety catch on the revolver. I'd waited for more than half an hour, the thunder was booming like gun-fire and the rain was pelting down, before Luciano finally appeared. He crossed the piazza unconcernedly through the trucks, towards the haven of the bars and the women. He was almost level before I stepped into his path.

His mutilated face broke into a lop-sided grin: "The Don said you were back. I thought you'd stay longer at that hospital I took you to. She sure was pretty – that nurse I left you with."

"You took me?"

"Sure. Found you in some crummy dressing station in a bombed church. Gone there to pick up some M&B tablets from a guy I used to know in Brooklyn. Would you believe it? I thought I'd been cured of the clap in gaol – the only thing I got out of all those years inside – but with half of the US Army fuckin' anything in skirts, you only have to look at a broad on this shitty island and she gives you a dose." He reached for a Camel from the pack in his breast pocket and lit it. "But let me tell you, that dressing station you were in was fucking primitive, even for Sicily. They were using the altar as the operating table for fuck's sake! The heat was unbearable, the doctors and medics, were almost naked but for their aprons and caps. Pity that pretty nurse wasn't there – I'd sure like to see her naked butt. But it was really disgusting: bloody rags and bandages, together with guts, piss and shit spread out all over the marble floor. They were so busy with serious cases I reckoned they'd never get around to you. They just kept dosing you with morphine. I decided to take you to a proper hospital; thought I owed it to your pa."

Yet more disillusionment: my saviour had not been my good and faithful uncle, but this corrupt gangster. He continued to leer at me through his drooping eye:

"Heard you finally got that piece of pussy I told you you needed, and you've come back like a kid begging for more candy."

"I've come back for you. I'm sending you back to Great Meadow in the brig of the first ship out of Palermo."

"Don't be sore, kid. You've had a disappointment in your love life – it happens to us all."

"I've been a sap ten times over. I even believed you when you said you enjoyed being a hero, but you'll never be anything but a lousy hoodlum. How'd you manage to set all this up?"

He winked. "That time I left and went to Palermo. I wasn't sure if the Don here could handle what I had in mind. I had a list of contacts from my friends in New York. I met with them and convinced them of the possibilities. I came back here and convinced the Don. Everyone has a price. I learnt that when I was a kid like you, during Prohibition. Senators, policemen, judges – you can buy 'em all. Here it was just a few captains and majors and the odd GI. It was a cinch." He took a thick wad of dollar bills from his trouser pocket. "How much d'you want kid? I reckon you deserve a cut. You'll be a rich man by the time this lousy war ends. Be able to buy your old lady a decent apartment in Queens or the Bronx."

The storm intensified. Its violence seemed to envelope the entire war we men were waging. The grip of my revolver was wet and slippery in my hand. I felt it quivering as I eased it out of the holster and pointed it at Luciano's belly. "All I want is to see you back in jail. You corrupted my father – but you'll never corrupt me. I'm taking you to Palermo tonight."

Luciano's smile faded, "Don Calo won't like that. He's seen how valuable I am and knows I'm no threat to him. His people will hide me away until the end of the war. I'll have enough dough then to disappear anywhere I choose – Cuba, Mexico, or South America – I'll never trouble Uncle Sam again." The trucks and heavy rain obscured our confrontation from the US soldiers in the bars, but some of Calo's overseers had begun to take an interest. Luciano could see them edging closer, taking their *lupare* from their shoulders. His confidence grew. "You'll never take me with you, you stupid little shitheel. The Don's friends will never let you."

All my pain, hate and frustration erupted in my arm. I took a firmer grip and swung the Colt with all my might at the side of Luciano's head. He saw the blow coming and slipped it with the skill of a professional. He slammed a punch into my newly healed ribs and followed it up by stamping on my damaged toes with his heavy boot. I doubled up in excruciating pain before sinking down into an oily puddle at his feet.

He looked down at me. His eyes were as cold as a snake's. "Thing I learned early on, kid – know your opponent's weak spots."

I struggled to get up but couldn't. I could hear American voices laughing in the bars. I looked towards them and remembered Sergeant O'Brian – but there was little hope of succour there, and anyway they wouldn't hear me. Calo's men came closer and formed a tight circle around me. Their faces were hard and vicious. An iron tipped boot kicked into my agonised ribs. I yelled out in pain, hunched up and clasped my knees. Two more brutal kicks thudded in. I was certain they were going to kick me to death. I looked up beseechingly, and saw Falco looming out of the darkness. The others backed off at his approach.

"Help me," I pleaded. "Remember what I asked. Let me leave and take Luciano with me."

He agonised before he shook his head. "You are my friend. You saved my life, but the bonds of the *Fratellanza* are stronger."

"The bonds of family are the strongest of all." Uncle Tony was standing in the shadow of a truck, a M3 submachine gun in his hand.

There was a moment of silence. The only sound was falling rain and distant laughter and music in the bars. My assailants edged further away.

Luciano whistled in amazement. "Jeez! If it ain't the Commie bastard, that shot his own brother-in-law in the back. How the fuck did you get here? I should have finished you off years ago."

I grabbed my revolver from the puddle and struggled to my feet. Luciano was still staring dumbfounded at Uncle Tony and this time didn't see the blow coming. I made sure I gave him interest for the agony in my toes. He hit the paved stones of the piazza like a sack of potatoes.

"Keep them covered," I rasped. "I'll get help from the soldiers in the bar."

"No!" Uncle Tony shook his head emphatically. "We will take him and go."

I didn't argue. "OK. I've got a jeep on the other side of the square."

My uncle hauled Luciano up by the scruff of his neck. The bastard who'd kicked me raised his lupara, but Falco gestured him to lower it. Falco's eyes were fixed on mine as I picked up the kitbag and slowly backed away. Tony dragged the senseless Luciano through the puddles to the jeep. I handcuffed him to the back seat and threw an army blanket over his head. I hurriedly put the starter motor back in place, Uncle Tony clambered beside me, the engine kicked into life, and we were away.

The sky was a black cavern, flashing with lightning and crashing with thunder, and torrents of water were streaming down the gutters, as the jeep sped up the Corso Dante. The same hard, suspicious faces watched impassively from the shelter of their open doors, as they had that morning I arrived, before my heart had been broken. I vowed I'd never return to this accursed place again.

Uncle Tony didn't speak until we were clear of the town. "I thought I would find you in Villalba."

"I'm sure glad you did."

"Did you discover what happened to your father here?"

How could I tell him? How could I find the words? Some things must remain secret.

"No. Only that he swore an oath to Don Calo."

"I am sorry." He squeezed my hand, resting on the gear stick. "I will leave you soon. You will not see me again. I am a deserter. I will be shot on sight."

"A deserter? Why? I thought you wanted to help defeat the Fascists?"

"I saw all too quickly what was happening. The Americans are giving power back to the right and the criminals. I will always be a Sicilian, this is my fight. I have been away from it too long. I will continue the struggle your father began; I owe him that at least. The left are regrouping. My old comrade, Di Causi, has been released from the penal colony on Ponzo. I am going to join him. You don't belong here; you are an American. Get home safely, and take care of your mother."

He got out on a windswept mountain slope and melted into the night. I was alone again. I'd come to Sicily with so many questions to ask; a burning desire to understand my past. I'd failed in everything. But one thing I was determined to do: I'd return the sodden gangster behind me to the jail where he belonged.

MY SICILIAN CAMPAIGN by General George S. Patton Jr:

Bernard had rescinded the order to withdraw and had held the remnants of his force, which had been battered alike by friend and foe, in place around the slopes of Mount Cipolla. They no longer had the power to hold up the German withdrawal. The 71st Panzer Grenadiers were in complete control of the highway and a narrow stretch of land on either side. The bulk of the German forces and equipment made an orderly withdrawal behind their new defensive line on the other side of the Angelo River. Thanks to the incompetence of the Navy and Air Force, the enemy had evaded my trap.

It was still dark when Truscott and the leading elements of the 1st Battalion crossed over the Naso River and entered the lemon groves from the west. At the base, under the shadow of some tall cypresses, lay some of the one hundred and seventy-seven dead and wounded. Truscott was offering the wounded what comfort he could, when Bernard, followed by the two correspondents, who had spent the past day and a half crouched in a slit trench, eventually descended from the mountain. Truscott saluted, taking in the state of Bernard's battledress, the haggard look of his face and the deadness of his eyes.

"Thank God, Colonel, I'm certainly glad to see you."

"General, you just don't know how glad I am to see you."

❧❧❧❧

93rd Evacuation Hospital, Nicosia, Sicily
Lt. Nurse Sue Miller:

My friend, the captain in public affairs, had done his job well. Major Etter and Colonel Currier had spent the morning with Al Newman of *Newsweek* and Merrill Mueller of NBC, giving a detailed account of General Patton's recent visit to our hospital. They'd hardly finished when the first of the casualties from Brolo were brought in. The two doctors immediately went to the operating theatres, while I began admitting the men, marking down the most urgent cases for immediate surgery. There were many: the butcher's bill had been even more bloody than usual. Over one stretcher, a red-haired, freckled-faced marine, held the plasma above a seriously injured man. It was impossible to tell the man's rank, his battledress was so soiled and torn. His head was swathed in bandages. A tourniquet had been tied around the top of his ruined right leg. His gold crucifix glinted in the sun.

"There's not much you can do for him," the marine said sorrowfully. "But Colonel Bernard says do the very best you can. He's a real brave guy."

I knelt down, pushed the crucifix away and reached for the dog tag to write his name on my file. It was covered with caked blood. I had to scratch it with my fingernail before I could read it clearly. I cried out aloud when I read:

LT FRANK DUNFORD US NAVY

12

LAST LAP TO MESSINA

Lt. Danny Crivello:
August 13, 1943

USS *Colorado* sailed out of Palermo on the early morning tide. I'd made double sure Admiral Hewitt's executive orders were clearly understood: the heavily bandaged prisoner in the brig was to be kept in the strictest solitary confinement throughout the entire voyage to New York. An hour or so later, after taking particular care over my turnout, I was admitted into Patton's office. My aching ribs were tightly bound and my toes were in agony, but my new uniform was immaculately pressed and my boots so polished, they reflected the sunlight streaming in through the long window. It took Patton a moment or two to recognise me yet again.

"Good to see you on your feet, Lieutenant. Please be seated." He waved towards a gilded chair, upholstered in red silk. I limped over and sat down. "What can I do for you?" I handed him my report. The General put on his heavy rimmed spectacles and peered into it: "Why have you brought this to me, Lieutenant?"

"You're the only person with the authority to stop what's going on." I pointed to the reams of typewritten papers in

Patton's hand. "You have documentary proof that Don Calo of Villalba is head of a vast black market organization. He's receiving vital necessities from the US Army and AMGOT and is passing less than half of it on to the Sicilian people. On top of that, he's requisitioning the peasants' produce and paying them with worthless paper money. He's accumulating a fortune and building a criminal empire before our very eyes."

Patton frowned, "I am not a policeman. I've enough on my hands fighting this war. Go and see AMGOT."

"I've been to them. They're only concerned with bureaucracy; as long as the forms are filled out OK, they're not interested."

Patton gave a dry chuckle: "The only sensible thing that little bastard Montgomery has done in this entire campaign was to prevent those AMGOT idiots coming ashore until the very end of his landing schedules. What was it he called them? He told me when he was here last week." He affected an exaggerated British accent, "*'Very poor lot of chaps, old school ties, the peerage, diseased guardsmen.'* He wouldn't let them have transport, said he couldn't spare it – told them to *'get cracking on a bike.'*"

I feigned a smile at Patton's attempted humour. "I informed Captain Limo and the OSS, and they didn't want to know either. They ordered me to 'zip my lip' – drop the matter. That's why I came to you. If we don't stop this now, the Mafia will take over the complete administration of Sicily when we move on."

"I do not see what concern it is of the Seventh Army if they do. The Sicilian peasant has always been poor and hungry. I have observed these people from the day I landed at Gela. They are the dirtiest, most godforsaken people in the whole of Europe. They glorify murder. It would be better not to concern ourselves with their affairs."

"But what about those US Army Officers and NCOs I've named? There's clear evidence of corruption and involvement in the black market."

"Listen here, young man; the last thing I want is a scandal. Messina is only a few days away. Nothing must be allowed to distract from the brilliant and heroic conduct of the 7th Army in this campaign. If there have been a few rotten apples in the barrel and the press gets hold of the story, every man will be dishonoured. Their valiant deeds and sacrifices will be overlooked, and they'll all be tarred as thieves and gangsters. My men do not deserve that. They deserve to be accounted as heroes. I will do nothing to tarnish their name."

"Would they want to sacrifice themselves for the benefit of gangsters?"

Patton rose from behind his desk, clasped his hands together in the small of his rigidly erect back, walked slowly to the window and looked down on his white-helmeted guards in the courtyard below. "This war is not a simple matter of black and white as you would like it to be. Sooner or later, we are going to have to fight those Ruskie bastards. Italy can easily go Communist now that Mussolini has gone; we may well need Sicily for airfields and naval bases. If we let the Mafia have power here, they will at least keep the Reds out."

A sour taste was in my mouth. Everything I believed in was crumbling away: "May I request a transfer back to regular service in the Navy? I feel there's nothing further I can do here now."

Patton took off his spectacles and gave a fatherly grin. "You're a brave young man. You've a fine record already." He picked up a single sheet of paper from his desk. "Admiral Hewitt is full of commendation of your efforts. There's a new campaign about to start in Italy, much bigger than this one. Your experience and knowledge of Italian will be invaluable. You may even be asked to rustle up the assistance of some more of your so-called friends." He noticed the crestfallen look on my face and made an effort to make amends. "In a couple of days, I'll lead the victory parade when we march into Messina ahead of that little bastard Monty. You've contributed to that victory. I want you at my side."

MY SICILIAN CAMPAIGN by General George S. Patton JR:

I have always loved competition, ever since my days as a competitor in the Modern Pentathlon at the Olympic Games in Stockholm in 1912. I was now in the final lap of this race and pushed on with the utmost strength. I still couldn't believe that Monty did not have a secret ruse or trick up his sleeve.

14 August, 1943
Lt. Danny Crivello:

It was my last night in Palermo. I'd received orders to hold myself ready for the invasion of mainland Italy. I guessed they'd been instigated by Captain Limo, wanting to get me out of his hair. I was to report to General Patton the following morning, to accompany him on his proposed entry into Messina; but there was one thing I had to do before I left.

I wandered back to the Giardino Garibaldi. It was dusk, and there was already some activity around the exposed roots of the giant trees. Shame-faced men were beginning to appear from the squalid side streets, leading their wives by the hand. But not all the women appeared apprehensive or downcast; some had a gleam of anticipation in their eyes. I sensed they were developing a taste and expertise for their new profession. As I walked towards the large houses on the north side of the *piazza,* I noticed they were overflowing with people. Barefoot children ran in and out of the wrought iron doors, in front of which sat old, toothless women and sullen-faced old men. There was no sign of the girl. I leant against a tree and waited. It wasn't long before she came around the corner out of the Corso Vittorio Emanuele, walking erect and proud, with an empty basket in her hand.

My heart beat faster and my mouth was dry as I crossed the road and blocked the pavement in front of her. She stopped, momentarily startled by the sight of my uniform, before she recognized me. Scorn came into her eyes.

"Are you still bringing us democracy and freedom? First you destroy our city, and now you have taken my dead father's house from me and given it to peasants and beggars." She gestured towards the biggest house in the row, which seemed even more crowded than the rest. "My family have lived here for two hundred years, and all you have left me is a room on the top floor. I curse you Americans – why did you have to come here and meddle with things you do not understand?"

The old people sitting on the doorsteps were listening attentively. I tried to take her arm but she pulled it violently away.

"Do not touch me. Where is the food you promised to provide? The Mafia are back and have control of everything. If you are not their friend and have no dollars, you do not eat." She pointed at her empty basket. "Mussolini knew they were evil; he kept them in check. I pray God the Germans defeat you when you try to land in Italy. One day my brother will return, and we will have revenge."

"Please cross the road, I beg you. I want to talk in private." She eyed me suspiciously, but followed me to the dark shadows of one of the giant trees. "Have you heard from your brother?"

"No. Not since I learnt that my dear father was dead. But I know the *Aosta* Division has crossed to Calabria. My brother will fight you there."

"I met your brother at Troina."

A look of shock stole across her pretty face. "How did you know it was my brother?

"He was a Lieutenant in the 171st Blackshirt Battalion, his father had just died in Russia, and he had a sister living by the Giardino Garibaldi."

Shock was turning into tears. She whispered, "Why do you say 'was' and 'had'?"

My mouth was drier than ever. I wanted to tell the truth, to ease my conscience by confession, but the truth wouldn't come. It was easier to evade it.

"I saw his body. He was killed by a shell."

She let out a heart-rending cry that came from the depths of her being: the cry of an animal in extreme agony. She dropped on her knees among the bare, tortured roots, the empty basket falling from her hand.

I felt a coward as I knelt beside her, putting a protective arm about her shoulders. "I am so sorry. We were enemies, but I liked him. If we had met at another time he would have been my friend."

She pushed my arm away and looked up at me with her large dark eyes. Tears streamed down her cheeks. "He would never be a friend to you. He had too much honour."

"That is the trouble with Sicilians. They care too much about their honour." I stared into her face. She was beautiful in her defiance and grief. I began to feel something more than pity, but stifled it. I would never care for a woman again; besides my hands were stained with her brother's blood.

MY SICILIAN CAMPAIGN by General George S. Patton Jr:

During the afternoon of August 16th Montgomery arrived in Taormina, complete with his menagerie of chickens, turkeys, canaries and a solitary peacock, and installed himself in Kesselring's magnificent villa overlooking the Ionian Sea. That evening, a battery of 155mm howitzers of the Royal Artillery reached the southern heights of Messina and began to fire the first Allied shells across the Straits to mainland Italy. At 2200 hours, a patrol of Company L, 7th US Infantry Regiment became the first Allied Troops to enter the devastated city. At 0700 hours the following morning, the Mayor of Messina and Colonel Michele Tomarello of the Italian Army Staff, the highest ranking officer remaining, came to Truscott's Command Post outside the city and offered its surrender. I had given Truscott strict orders that no US units were to enter Messina until my arrival.

17 August, 1943
Lt. Danny Crivello:

A column of jeeps and staff cars followed Patton's highly polished command vehicle, with its fluttering three-star pennants, up the hill to Messina. The pristine condition of Patton's vehicle was in stark contrast to the devastation around us. The hill was devoid of trees and grass. The relentless shelling and bombing from both sides had destroyed any touch of nature. Craters covered the brown earth like huge angry pox marks. The hood was down and Patton, in his best gabardines, sat in the back with me beside him, much to the annoyance of Major Powell, who'd been obliged to ride in the staff car behind. The General was suffering from sandfly fever and was shivering slightly. He seemed strangely morose, displaying no great elation at his triumph – if that was what it was. As we neared the crest of the hill, we beheld Truscott and his troops lined up in the dry ditches along the sides of the road. Patton ordered his driver, the ever-faithful Master Sergeant Mims, to stop, but as the car came to a halt, the scream of a shell came hurtling towards us. It seemed like an eternity before there was an ear-splitting explosion, a blaze of light, and pieces of debris rained down. The staff car behind had taken a direct hit. Patton looked back at the blazing vehicle. The shattered bodies of his staff were littering the road, their blood soaking up the dust. Major Powell had given his last briefing. His well-fed stomach was split open: his bowels, spleen and half-digested breakfast erupting from within.

I'd heard that shellfire made Patton extremely nervous, but he forced himself to ignore it. He glared at Truscott and yelled in his high-pitched voice, "What the hell are you all standing around for?"

Truscott held on to his temper. He wiped the mud and blood off his face with his white silk scarf. "I reckon we should cancel the parade, George. We're in range of their guns across the water. We're sitting ducks – I've lost some good men."

Patton put on an air of supreme confidence. "Nonsense; we have taken Messina and I will take the salute to acknowledge our victory." He scanned the sullen faces of Truscott's staff. "Where's Bradley? I telephoned him."

Truscott shrugged. "He said victory marches were not his thing. I think he's at Corps HQ."

Patton frowned, "I'm greatly disappointed. He certainly deserves the pleasure of entering the town beside me and this young fella."

I gazed ahead and kept my thoughts to myself. I'd had my fill of entering liberated towns.

Shells continued to fall intermittently as we drove towards the central piazza. The GIs who followed behind their General didn't look like conquering heroes; they were exhausted and filthy, many could barely walk. Nevertheless, townsfolk began to come out of their cellars or the rubble of their homes. Some greeted us ecstatically, throwing flowers and grapes in our path. As we passed through the Piazza Carioli, I spied Robert Capa taking yet more photos with his ubiquitous Leica. I thought of that day, barely three weeks ago, when we had entered Palermo. Then I'd been in love, and had faith and hope for the future; now my life was as devastated as the city around me. And Messina was truly in ruins, worse even than Palermo. I wondered how many other ruined cities I would see: Naples? Rome? Milan? Berlin? Would the line stretch out for ever? Even to Moscow?

Patton surveyed his conquest gloomily, "I have never seen anything so horribly destroyed as this. I don't think indiscriminate bombing of towns is worth the ammunition." He watched an old woman limping painfully out of her ruined hovel and wiped a tear from his eye. "It's unnecessarily cruel to the civilians."

MY SICILIAN CAMPAIGN by General George S. Patton Jr:

I had just finished making a brief victory address in the Piazza Repubblica, when I heard the caterwauling wail of bagpipes and Colonel 'Mad Jack' Churchill, armed with his favourite weapons, claymore and longbow, arrived on top of a British tank. I stepped off the pedestal on which I had been standing to offer my hand.

Churchill took it, "Well done. It was a jolly good race, General. I congratulate you."

The conquest of Sicily was complete. Organized resistance had ended. Not a single German soldier remained active on the entire island. It had taken 39 days.

Lt. Danny Crivello:

It was not the complete triumph that Patton or Montgomery had planned. The Germans managed to evacuate 53,000 troops, 50 tanks and 9,800 other vehicles to continue the fight on the mainland. Furthermore, the two conquerors had little time to enjoy the fruits of victory. The correspondents had flown to Algiers with their reports of Patton's visit to the hospital and had reached Eisenhower himself. Later that day, the Commander-in-Chief wrote to Patton: *'I clearly understand that firm and drastic measures are at times necessary in order to secure the desired objectives. But this does not excuse brutality, abuse of the sick, nor exhibition of uncontrollable temper in front of subordinates. I must seriously question your good judgement and your self-discipline, as to raise serious doubts in my mind as to your future usefulness. You will make in the form of apology or otherwise such personal amends as may be within your power.'*

Ahead of Patton lay the humiliation of public apologies to the massed ranks of his soldiers, and the pain and frustration of seeing the highest commands denied him. His rival Montgomery also received bitterly disappointing news. His proposed plan, *Operation Buttress,* in which the British Eighth Army would lead the invasion of Italy under his command, had been cancelled. Instead, the invasion force would be split into three, with precedence being given to a landing of Clarke's Fifth US Army at Salerno, to which would be attached one of Montgomery's prize British Corps. The Americans were taking over the war. The Eighth Army, as he knew and loved it, was no more.

The two best Allied Generals would never achieve the supreme office they so fervently desired. Bradley would eventually lead the American Armies in France, but the real victor of the Sicilian campaign was Don Calo Vizzini of Villalba.

13

DEPORTATION

February 9, 1946
Commander Haffenden US Navy Rtd:

I t was exactly four years to the day since the burning of the *Normandie*. I stood in the snow at the gate of Pier 7 on the Brooklyn Waterfront, puffing my pipe, searching for faces from the past. It was cold enough to freeze the balls off a monkey. A bitter wind was coming in from the East River, swirling snowflakes around, like white patterns in a gigantic kaleidoscope. Through the gate, I could see the weather-beaten Liberty ship, the S.S. *Laura Keane,* and the long lines of stevedores carrying sack after sack of flour up the gang-planks into her hold. Europe was starving and the Marshall Plan was in full force.

A noisy throng of reporters and other onlookers crowded around me, kept at bay by a phalanx of longshore-men, armed with sharpened baling hooks. Now and again, the longshoremen, like a well-drilled Praetorian Guard, momentarily opened their ranks to allow shining black lim-ousines through. Passengers got out, stared up at the shabby vessel, shook their heads, stamped their cold feet, and then made their purposeful way up the gangway. They were mostly middle-aged men, thick and heavy, with the collars of their expensive topcoats pulled up round their faces and their hats pulled sharply over their eyes. Other arrivals were more circumspect, soberly dressed as befitting Wall Street bankers and politicians. One Buick unloaded three expensively dressed showgirls, who were laughing and chattering with excitement as they skipped up into the ship, followed by three porters struggling with heavy trunks and suitcases. Occasionally a press photographer would step forward to focus his camera on the arrivals, but each time the heavy hand of a longshoreman covered his lens.

I had lost weight and my pre-war civilian clothes hung loose about me. I'd achieved the wartime posting I'd sought, serving as a Beachmaster in the Pacific, and had proved my worth. A Purple Heart ribbon was pinned on the lapel of my raincoat. I knew the commendation by heart: '*At considerable hazard to himself, he crossed the island of Iwo Jima, which was then under sporadic gun and mortar fire, and returned with very helpful and valuable information. His performance of duty was highly creditable and in the best traditions of the Naval service.*' But the day after I'd brought back the so-called 'helpful and valuable' information, I'd caught the full blast of an incoming shell. It had left me with severe internal haemorrhaging. I'd spent months in a series of naval hospitals across the Pacific and in Hawaii, only to be diagnosed with having a tumour in my stomach when I eventually returned to the States. I'd convalesced at the nearby Brooklyn Naval Hospital before being declared unfit for active service and discharged from the Navy. I was no longer even on the Reserve. The bustle of the waterfront around me rekindled memories of those early days of the war, when I'd held a post of national importance and had briefly savoured the intoxicating sensation of power and influence. Now, I was just an old sailor standing in the snow.

The crowd stirred as another limousine approached. As it swept past, I caught sight of Meyer Lansky's cold eye through the curtained window. But the little Jew's face gave no sign of recognition; it remained still, as if set in stone. I felt old and alone. I'd even have welcomed the fishy scent of Socks Lanza: I could just make out his old hangout in the Fulton Fish Market across the river under the Brooklyn Bridge. I could still savour those lobsters. But Socks was still serving his sentence of seven and a half to fifteen in New York State Penitentiary. I felt a twinge of guilt. Maybe I should have tried to have done more for him.

The reporters became more agitated. The flash bulbs of their cameras began to explode. Yet another limousine was approaching; a Lincoln, bigger and blacker and shinier than all the rest. A lone photographer decided to brave the hooks of the longshoremen and stepped into the car's path; his camera gave out a brilliant blast as it caught, for a frozen second, the face of the occupant within. Three longshoremen broke from their ranks and pulled the foolhardy cameraman to the ground. They stamped on his camera, destroying whatever picture was within, whilst placing well-aimed kicks with their heavy boots into the unfortunate guy's ribs and kidneys. In the brief seconds, while the driver waited for the mayhem to stop and his way to the ship to be cleared, I peered inside the Lincoln and recognised a drooping eye and scarred face.

Luciano looked back at me before he rolled down his window: "Hey, Commander, how you doing? Jump in." The heavy guy sitting next to the driver was about to protest, but Luciano tapped him on the shoulder, "It's OK, officer, he's an old-time colleague of mine. Move over Moses." He nudged the well-dressed, overweight guy sitting beside him. "Commander, meet Mr Moses Polakoff, my attorney. My old pals are throwing a farewell party for me before I sail. You'd better come aboard. I guess I owe you a drink."

I was aboard before I knew it. The *Laura Keene* was not the *Queen Mary*, but three large adjoining cabins had been converted into a ready-made stateroom for her notorious passenger. A spread of the finest cuisine had been prepared, together with magnums of French champagne, the best Scotch whisky, and wine of the most sought after vintages. My eyes fell hungrily on whole turkeys, great ribs of rare roast beef, heaped piles of Nova Scotia smoked salmon, huge bowls of seafood, Italian pasta of all shapes and sizes, drenched in the most exquisite sauces, together with salami and cheeses of every variety.

Around the swarming buffet tables, I recognised many of the most powerful figures from the days of Prohibition, now making even more dough out of the post-war black market. Lansky was nibbling ruminatively over a plate of smoked salmon with his old associate, Bugsy Siegel, who'd flown in especially from some crazy new project he was organising in Nevada. I spotted Albert Anastasia, who gave me a flicker of recognition, Frank Costello, Joe Adonis, Willie Moretti, and Tommy Luchese. The other men, some of whose faces I vaguely knew from newspaper photographs or newsreel reports, were minor politicians, the odd congressman, judge or representative, whose campaign funds, I suspected, had been swollen by the contributions of the hoodlums around them, in return for favours and protection. The three showgirls mingled and joked with everyone; they were real professionals. They endeavoured to make each man feel he was irresistibly attractive as well as incredibly witty and wise. They even had an eye for me.

I quietly followed Luciano around, as his guests acclaimed him like a returning hero. They hugged him, kissed him, some even managing to weep tears of joy at his deliverance. When the excitement had somewhat cooled, Luciano, after making sure I had a large glass of Johnnie Walker, took me by the arm and led me into an inner cabin. Polakoff followed us and shut the door.

Luciano motioned me towards a couple of easy chairs. We sat in silence while he stared at me intently. I knew those snake eyes were taking in everything: the state of my health, the worn collar of my shirt, the condition of my shoes.

"How are you doing, Commander?"

"Can't complain. At least I came back – many a good man didn't."

"I want to thank you." He stole a look at the chubby face of his bespectacled lawyer. "Moses here, tells me you put your neck on the line, writing that affidavit to the Parole Board, telling 'em how I did my bit in '42 and '43, and recommending my release. I didn't expect to be fuckin' deported, but thanks. I won't forget it."

I grinned ruefully, "The Naval authorities have been on my back. They're threatening me with court martial. They say I should never have done it. They want to keep the whole thing quiet and forget all about it now it's all over – don't want to admit they ever asked for your assistance."

"You're telling me! If I breathe a word about what I did for 'em in Sicily, they say they'll extradite me back, and this time they'll throw away the fuckin' key." Lucky turned and looked at four open wardrobe trunks, overflowing with well-cut bespoke suits, silk shirts, ties, underwear, pyjamas and handmade shoes of the finest leather. "I should never have trusted those sonsofbitches. They couldn't even run the fuckin' war properly. I naturally had a vested interest in wishing the whole fuckin' thing finished as quickly as possible. When I got back to Great Meadow, I put up a big map of

Europe all over one wall of my cell, marked all the advances and stuck in pins as we took town by town." He began to take off the clothes he had worn from prison. "Why didn't Eisenhower let Patton get on with it? He'd have finished the war in Europe in '44; at least a year sooner. So he slapped a few creeps – so what? Everyone has done it; it's no big deal. I'm sorry the old sonofabitch is dead."

I nodded. "Yes, it was a great loss."

Luciano, now down to his underwear, selected a pair of silk shorts and an undervest and walked into the bathroom, continuing to speak through the open door. "Patton would've have taken care of those Ruskie bastards. Stupid old fucker: getting killed in a motor accident whilst huntin' pheasant with a broad in Bavaria. I bet that wasn't all the old boy was huntin'. But it's always the broads, they distract your mind; they always get you in the end." He came out of the bathroom in his fresh underwear, and began to rummage through the shirts and ties strewn over the double bed. "What happened to that kid who went to Sicily with me?" He affected unconcern.

"You mean Danny Crivello? He went on to Salerno and Anzio and won a Silver Star. He was one of the best agents we had. They gave him the Legion of Merit for going behind the lines in Florence whilst it was still occupied by the Nazis. He got hold of plans for a new type of midget submarine that could have gone to the Japs."

Lucky frowned. "He's an ungrateful little bastard. I still owe him for a headache he gave me. Where's he now?"

I shrugged, "I dunno. I lost track of him when I was in the Pacific."

Luciano pondered before he turned back to his open wardrobe trunks and changed the subject. "Unlike you, Commander, I have friends that look after me. I've a suit here for every day of the month. Most of this came from my old apartment in the Waldorf Towers, but Frank Adonis has stocked me up with some modern stuff from Bergdorf Goodman's." He pulled up his under vest and patted his naked belly, thickly matted with wiry black hair. "I'm only about a size bigger than when they put me inside, I'll soon work it off on the boat trip; it takes this fuckin' hulk two weeks to get to Italy. I asked Lanksy to find a few dolls to keep me company on the trip. I thought afterwards maybe that was a big mistake; Meyer's taste in dames is nothin' to write home about. You should see his old lady! But luckily, he asked Frank Costello to pick 'em for me. Frank owns the Copacabana and those three girls out there look real class. Fuckin' is the best exercise known to man. I'll soon be down to my best fighting weight." He was buttoning up a crisp cream Sulka shirt. "I learnt how to dress smart from Arnold Rothstein. I've always got on with Jews," he winked at Polakoff, "ain't that so, Moses?"

Polakoff gave an indulgent smile.

Luciano continued, "Rothstein was the only guy I ever knew to make a fortune out of gambling. He taught me never to be flash – wear dark Oxford suits – always buy two of everything – look like a businessman." He carefully selected a tie from a rack that appeared to contain every colour and variety of pattern. "I always bought French ties – see the label – had 'em sent over especially from Paris." He was now fully dressed in a sober double-breasted suit, looking more like a senior executive than a gangster. A pair of shining, black, hand-made brogues from London completed his attire. He glanced again at my down at heel appearance. "I'd offer you a couple of suits, I always gave away clothes to my friends, I didn't have enough room in the closets, but I don't think that we're the same size. Would you like a few silk ties?"

I smiled and shook my head.

"Waddya gonna do now you've left the Navy?"

I shrugged. "I was hoping to serve as a Commissioner of Marine and Aviation for the City of New York, but certain people don't seem to like me anymore. I'll guess I'll go back into business. I'll have to – I've no personal resources. I've been offered a job with a company that makes industrial wheels; I'll probably give that a try."

"The bastards should give you a million dollar pension for what you did for 'em. But I've learnt one thing: never expect nothing from no one. See here." He threw open the porthole and beckoned me to his side. "That's the only place on earth I want to be – Manhattan; and they won't even let me put my foot on it. When those bum immigration officers drove me here, I begged 'em to let me get out for just one minute, and feel the sidewalk beneath my feet, smell the smoke coming up out of the subway; but the bastards wouldn't let me." His eyes moistened with nostalgia. "See over there – the Chrysler building. Walter Chrysler gambled at my clubs, and I'd give him my marker when he went over his limit. And the Empire State; John Rascob who built it, asked me to help his pal, Al Smith, run for President. And I did. Now they wouldn't even let me come in through the swing doors. Fuck 'em all. I'll be back."

There was a knock on the door, and Meyer Lansky looked in. "The guys are ready with their envelopes, Lucky. You want to come out, or take them more personally in here?"

"Send 'em in. I'll just take a leak first." He paused at the door leading into the bathroom, "Do ya know the thing I missed most in prison? Broads? Booze? Good food? Nah. Good toilet paper."

I followed Lansky into the main salon and sat on a bench seat beneath a porthole, nursing my Scotch, watching the

tributes going in and coming out, one by one. Thick envelope after thick envelope, from Buffalo, Chicago, Cleveland,
Detroit, St Louis, San Francisco and Los Angeles, as well
as every district of New York City. Luciano was like an
emperor exacting tribute from conquered territories, reap-
ing the benefits from the impenetrable organization he had
established.

Eventually the stream dried up, and Luciano came out
to join the politicians at the buffet table. My bladder wasn't
what it had been and I felt the need for a piss. The can in
the salon was occupied, so I went back into Luciano's cabin
to avail myself of his facility. I'd just finished and was buttoning up my fly, when I heard voices in the cabin. I recognised Luciano's immediately, but couldn't place the other.
I was about to flush the toilet and announce my presence,
when I caught the drift of the conversation.

"How you fixed for dough, Lucky?"

"At this moment, I'm not sure. I've paid out almost a
million dollars to the fuckin' lawyers; most of what I had
stashed away has gone. Luchese, Torrio and Scalise have
been running the businesses I set up, ever since I went
inside. I've no real idea how they run now, or what they're
worth. The boys have been very generous today, but I'm not
sure if the payments will continue, especially if I'm stuck in
Italy for a few years."

"What about Meyer?"

I peeped through the slit in the door and made out a
short, mild-mannered, little fella, about five years younger
than Luciano, with a sharp beak of a nose. I couldn't understand why Lucky was showing him such deference, until I
recognised him as Carlo Gambino. His family had been
leaders of the Mafia in Sicily for generations; Luciano was a
parvenu by comparison.

"It's Meyer I'm really banking on." Lucky continued. "He's on very friendly terms with Batista – the guy who runs Cuba. I'm convinced it's the place of the future. It's close to the States; people are beginning to take vacations there. Havana is wide open, no gambling laws, beautiful women and plenty of sunshine. We'll operate the casinos and give the Cuban Government a rake-off; we'll all get rich and everyone will be happy. Besides, even if they don't let me come back here, in a year or so, if I lay low, I should be able to persuade the Italians to give me a visa for Cuba. I'm working on it already."

"Can you rely on Meyer? All he seems to care about these days is raising money for that Jewish state in Palestine."

"Meyer is always interested in making money. He's the one guy that won't let me down."

Gambino paused, as if questioning his judgement. "You've been away, Lucky; it's a different world. Gambling, prostitution, and for a time, the black market, will still be good rackets; but there are new opportunities for making more dough than you've ever dreamed of." He paused expecting a reply, but like a good poker player, Luciano waited his call. Gambino was forced to make his bid, "What do you think about narcotics?"

"You know what I think about junk. I got bust tryin' to deal in heroin in 1923 – never dabbled in it since."

"It's a different ball game today. It's run like a legit import business, same as sugar and coffee. It's like oil – if you can tap into a new source you'll make millions."

Luciano sat on the bed and motioned Gambino to continue.

"Opium is a thing of the past – far too bulky to transport. Morphine is what they deal in now – two guys carrying ten kilos each of morphine could transport the equivalent of two hundred kilos of opium. Turkey produces great quantities of morphine. It can be smuggled through Lebanon, then run by small boats across the Mediterranean to Sicily – just like we ran the booze in the days of Prohibition. It's got to be refined, but it's relatively easy to turn morphine into high-grade heroin. You'd have to set up a laboratory – find some chemists, who want to make some easy dough. That should be no problem; I'll make sure that you're provided with funds. I've got plenty of people wanting to invest. It may be easier to run it over to France, somewhere like Marseilles, legal production of narcotics is permitted there without government supervision, and then ship it back to Sicily. The *Fratellanza* can settle things with the authorities, but it needs someone like you, Lucky, who is known and trusted both there and over here, to set the whole thing up. It'll be better than Prohibition. There'll be so much dough, we can pay off everyone and everyone will get rich. All you have to do is find safe ways of exporting it here."

There was a knock: Lansky's voice rasped through the outer door: "Lucky, some folks are leaving. They want to say goodbye."

They both went out. It was one of the few occasions in my life I didn't flush the toilet. I waited a minute or two before I went to join them. The party was winding down. Lucky was busy shaking hands. Most of the guests were making their way back to the lights and excitement of Manhattan. I sat on a bench beneath a porthole, munched on a smoked salmon bagel, and ruminated on what I should do. This was bigger than any information I'd managed to gather in all my days at the Astor. But I owed the authorities nothing. Why should I squeal on a guy I was beginning to like? But drugs were something else ... My ruminations were interrupted by Lucky sitting down beside me and taking my arm.

"I never forget a favour. It's part of my upbringing. I'd like you to have this."

I looked at the well-stuffed envelope, and for a moment was tempted. I smiled ruefully. "No Lucky, but thanks all the same. All I ever took was some lobsters and crab from poor old Socks. I'll never let them say I ever took a bribe."

Luciano shook his head sadly, "Everybody else does. That's why you'll die a poor man."

Millersburg, Ohio
Professor Frank Dunford:

'Time had gone round, and where I did begin, there would I end.'
It was my first term as Professor of English at Millersburg High, and I'd just got home from watching the Saturday football game. My leg was aching after standing so long in the cold; it was now resting on a stool before the fire while I read the evening paper. After scanning the sports results, I turned over to the front page and was immediately struck by the leading article.

"Do you remember me telling you about how we did a deal with Lucky Luciano, when I was with 'F' Section in New York?"

Sue came smiling out of the kitchen wiping flour from her hands.

"You never did tell me what 'F' was for."

"They've let him out at last; deporting him back to Sicily."

Sicily – it was another age, a world away from Small Town USA. I sensed a cloud coming over my scarred face; the primitive plastic surgery at the field hospital had pulled down the lower lid of my right eye, giving me a permanent expression of sorrow. I remembered something I had almost forgotten.

"You know, I thought I saw him one day in Gela..." I broke off and began to think of little Franco. I hoped he had survived.

Sue gently kissed my ravaged face. She knew me so well. "We'll go back one day."

I could feel my ravaged features breaking into a smile.

14

Funeral In Villalba

13 July, 1954
Sicily
Danny Crivello:

I had vowed I would never go back to that accursed island, but when I read in *The New York Times* of the death of Don Calo Vizzini, the Mayor of Villalba, collaborator with the US forces in the liberation of Sicily, and one of the founders of the new democratic state, and that dignitaries from the US and all over Italy, would be attending his funeral in his small home town, I knew I had to return.

I landed at Palermo in the mid-morning heat, and hired a small Fiat Topolino. The young Sicilian at the Hertz office had spent several years in Rome. He was polite and eager to point out the attractions of the island. There had been many changes since the war. Tourism was to be the future; hotels were being built everywhere, bringing employment in their wake. He explained the car's simple controls, supplied me with maps and a list of recommended hotels, and sent me on my way.

Leaving the airport perimeter, finding the car cramped and fragile compared to my '51 Buick back home in New Jersey, I drove past block after block of concrete apartments in various stages of construction. None of them seemed to be anywhere near completion. I knew the Mafia, having acquired unimagined wealth out of the black market and drugs, were now investing in the construction industry, receiving huge public financing and aid as part of the central government policy to build decent housing for the poor. It seemed, in Sicily at least, the poor would have a long wait for their new homes. Although it was spring, almost early summer, the once fertile fields outside the city were devoid of greenery and fresh growth. There was only cement and sand. The landscape had turned into one vast builder's yard. The few people I saw no longer looked hungry, the children had shoes, but their faces didn't smile.

I stopped the car at a bend in the road and looked back towards the centre of the city. Under the brilliant blue of the morning sky, the dome of the cathedral and the towers, spires and cupolas of the ancient churches and palaces still remained. I made out the solid bulk of the Royal Palace, Patton's old headquarters, where I'd helped Robert Capa develop his photos. He'd recently been killed, following yet another war in an obscure little country in Indo-China. He'd stepped on a landmine and died with his camera in his hand. I guessed that was the way he'd have wanted to go. I looked towards the big trees in the Giardino Garibaldi and remembered the defiant girl whose brother I'd killed. I'd been a coward not to have confessed it to her. It had remained on my conscience like a mortal sin. Was she still living there in the house of her ancestors? What were her politics now? Was her anger still as fierce? Could she find it in her heart to forgive me? I restarted the little car and began to climb upwards into the mountains. There at least the ancient beauty of the island remained. The vivid yellow of the broom and the aquamarine of the thistle grew abundantly at the roadsides; the terraces of vineyards and olive groves were being diligently tended, as they'd been since the time of the Greeks.

I was now thirty and had been a member of the FBI since my demobilization in '45. My war record had ensured my placement. I'd entered as a potential candidate for high office but my promotion had been slow. Nine years, and I'd not yet reached the rank of Senior Investigator. I was uncompromising in my attitude towards criminals. I refused to make deals. I'd heard it said I stuck too closely to the book and, despite my wartime exploits, I'd achieved disappointingly little.

Apart from a few postcards in the first year after the war, we had heard no more from Uncle Tony. We presumed he was dead. My mother died of cancer in 1949, mourning her brother, but thankful her son had returned unharmed. But I had been harmed – my heart had shrivelled up inside me. Most nights I lay alone in bed and thought again and again of Gina, and how she'd betrayed me. I still couldn't understand what I'd done to kill her love. I had thought in time my pain would heal, like the other wounds I'd suffered; but this pain was still as raw as that first morning in Villalba. I had remained cold and indifferent to the succession of wholesome Italian girls my mother, aware of her increasing sickness and desperate for a grandchild, arranged for me to meet. I had resolved never to give my heart again. When I needed sex, I paid for it in dark alleys and cheap hotel rooms.

The road signs brought back more memories: Lercara Friddi, where I'd been born and where my father and Uncle Tony had slaved in the mines. Sulphur was no longer the economic force it had been. That was good; men would no longer have to endure those infernal conditions. But what else could they do until mass tourism arrived, if it ever did? Mix the cement for those ugly blocks of unfinished apartments, still under the control of the Mafia's ruthless *gabellotti*? Or wait fruitlessly for work on the street corners of Palermo? I remembered the horrendous poverty of the young couple in the Cortile Cascino and their typhoid-stricken child. At least work in the mines, however terrible, gave men some dignity.

I passed a sign pointing towards Termini Imerese, where I'd sprung Don Calo from prison. All the old questions came flooding back into my mind. What would have happened if I'd left him there to rot? Would the Fascists have shot him before they withdrew? Even if they had the Mafia, like the Hydra, would have swiftly grown a new head, as evil and vicious as the former. But would I, Danny Crivello, have ever gone to Villalba if I'd not freed Don Calo? Yes. I would have gone to try to solve the mystery of my father; a mystery that even now I was no closer to solving. Don Calo had said my father had sworn a sacred oath to him in Villalba. Why would he have done such a thing; unless he'd been tricked, as I had so nearly been tricked that night of Don Calo's feast? Don Calo's feast – the day I'd seen Gina for the first time. I'd wished a million times that I'd never gone. But I would still have seen her in Villalba, and I would still have loved her. Without Calo's malign influence she might have returned my love. And Falco? Did she really love Falco? Were they happy? I knew Falco had been chosen to succeed Don Calo. He was to be the new *capo* of this huge organization, now larger, richer, and more powerful, than all but the biggest corporations in the US. What sort of man had Falco become? My thoughts turned to Luciano, who was now living under restriction orders in Naples. I'd kept a watch on his activities through my access to sensitive FBI information, and knew that he was suspected of masterminding the influx of heroin, that was rapidly polluting New York and other major US cities. But he'd always somehow managed to avoid prosecution. I wondered how many men had succumbed to his bribery and corruption and wished, not for the first time, I'd shot him that last night in Villalba.

My conjectures and memories made the journey go quickly, and I was soon nearing my destination. I began to pass painted Sicilian carts, their garish colours draped with black mourning ribbons. The carts were crammed with country folk: wizened peasants, dark from the sun, together with their wives and widowed mothers, almost hidden in their shawls. Grown-up daughters were looking demurely down at the dusty road, while children were noisily oblivious to the solemnity of the occasion. Sullen elder sons strode manfully beside the carts, with their *lupare* slung across their shoulders. They were all on their way to pay their final homage to their Don. As I came in sight of the town, nestling in its hollow among the mountains and hills, the road became almost a camp. The peasants, their families, and their animals were bivouacked at the roadsides; food was being cooked over fires, beds being prepared beneath the carts. They'd arrived in good time, like me.

I parked the little car above the town and walked down the steep Corso Dante with the houses descending in steps. It was as I remembered – the sewers still stank. The houses were somewhat less rundown, there was the odd flash of bright colour from small pots of flowers on the window sills, but the old unfriendly men were still sitting in their open doorways, their small dark eyes following me with the same hostile suspicion. But I was not the only stranger in town. The piazza before the baroque church was full of cars of every shape and variety. Tomorrow, would come the American

Ambassador, official representatives of the US Army, Navy and Air Force, leading politicians of the Christian Democrat Party from Rome, the mayors of Palermo, Messina, Catania, Agrigento, and many other Sicilian towns. Today was the turn of unofficial guests. Mingling with the peasants were small businessmen, who had dutifully paid for their protection since the war. Others owned vineyards and olive groves, who had sold their wine and olive oil year after year to Don Calo and his associates at his agreed price. Some were men who had simply sworn their oath and had served him blindly and profitably ever since. All waited in a solemn line to enter the church and file past Vizzini's open casket.

I queued with them in silence. As I drew near, I saw a photograph of a benevolent looking Don Calo, pinned to the great wooden door of the church. Beneath it was a handwritten notice: '*Wise, dynamic, tireless, Don Calo Vizzini was the benefactor of the workers on the land and in the sulphur mines. Constantly doing good, his reputation was widespread both in Italy and abroad. Great in the face of persecution, greater still in adversity, he fought against the Fascists and the invader. He was the father of his people. With both words and deeds he proved that his brotherhood was not one of delinquency but rather one of abiding by the law of honour, protecting every right. He had greatness of soul. He was loved. Now with the peace of Christ and the majesty of death, he receives from friends and foes alike the grandest of tributes: He was a gentleman.*'

It could only have been written by his brother, Father Salvatore.

Little had changed inside the church. The richly carved confessional box, where I'd made my rendezvous with Father Salvatore Vizzini, was still there along the north wall. Father Salvatore himself was kneeling at the altar, praying for his brother's soul, as the organ softly played and a choir of small boys sweetly sang, swinging their smoking censers. The painted frescoes of Christ and the saints were still above, gazing down, perhaps in forgiveness, upon Don Calo Vizzini, whose florid cheeks contrasted vividly against the whiteness of the satin interior of his open coffin, and the banks of white flowers that surrounded it. There were so many flowers that the air was heavy with their fragrance. Calo definitely smelt better in death than he'd ever done in life. A black cord had been placed in his lifeless left hand; the other end was held by a heavy grizzled man, who stood with bent head beside the polished casket. With a catch in my heart, I recognised Falco. The ancient Mafia ritual was being re-enacted: the vital powers from the dead *capo* were being transferred to the living body of his chosen successor. I shuffled past with all the rest; some women wept, every man's head was bowed. As I neared the door below the altar from which the mourners were exiting, I sensed someone was watching me. I turned abruptly and looked up to the gallery high above. In the shadow were the heads of two women. One was old, her grey hair falling from her black shawl, the other plump and matronly, although she couldn't have been more than thirty. I saw her frightened, startled eyes and knew it was Gina. We each looked away and then back again, as we had done that first day at Don Calo's farm. Before I could think of what to do, or make any sign of communication, the press of the crowd had pushed me through the door.

I was blinded momentarily by the harsh Sicilian sun but glad to be back in the comparative fresh air of the *piazza*. I stood stock still, collecting my thoughts as the people thronged out around me, before making my way towards the cafes at the entrance of the Via Bocetta. They were as busy as they'd been on that day of liberation, twelve years before, but were now festooned with the emblems of Coca-Cola and Pepsi and bright, gaudy advertisements for gelato and Peroni. I walked into a dark bar. Hard, distrustful faces looked up at me from the tables and from the men standing silently around. I gave them a nod, hoping I might see some face I'd once known, but received only stony silence in return. I ordered a beer and went back outside with the ice-cold bottle. All the tables were full so I sat on a nearby wall. I was hot and thirsty and drained the bottle in a single draught.

"Please."

I felt a tug at my sleeve and looked down to see a small boy.

"Please, are you the American from the war?" His voice was little more than a whisper.

I nodded.

He looked about fearfully before murmuring, "Please, follow me. Not too close."

The little boy slipped into the dark shadows of the Via Bocetta. I followed as casually as I could, although my heart was pounding as quickly as it had ever done in the war. Was I about to meet Gina again after all these years? Would she explain at last why she'd rejected my love? Or had Falco, or one of his goons, spotted me in the church? Was I now being led into a trap? Instinctively, I felt for my gun in my shoulder holster, but this was a private visit; it was not there.

The houses in the Via Bocetta were just as poor. Here and there was a splash of colour. Cartons of soap on a windowsill; freshly washed clothes, strung from lines that crossed and re-crossed above. Radio music blared from open windows, drowning the other sounds of life within. Sinatra was singing 'Three Coins in the Fountain'. Every now and then the boy would turn fearfully, to check I was still behind. The neglected almond trees still bore the last vestiges of blossom as we crossed over the Via Cavour. An old man sat beneath one and raised his head to watch us pass by. Then the road grew darker and narrower, until we came to the dirty, whitewashed wall with the little Magdalene behind her bars. The boy stopped and checked for a final time, before pointing to a door. A door I knew only too well; my heart had been broken before it.

The boy had run off before my knuckles rapped on the blistered wood. The old woman that had sat beside Gina in the church opened it immediately. I thought for a moment it was the aged crone, her grandmother, but then looked into the sorrowful eyes and realized it was Gina's mother. In twelve years she had aged thirty. Her face was furrowed with grief. She looked fearfully up the alley in both directions before pulling me inside.

"I feared you would come back one day."

The hovel now bore some traces of affluence. There was an upholstered chair by the unlit fire; an electric light bulb hung from a cord in the ceiling, a small refrigerator, its motor chugging over noisily, was plugged into the wall. Above the fireplace, framed in black, was a photo of Gina's grandmother.

The woman was following my eyes. "My mother died seven years ago. I live here now." She gestured to the Formica-topped table and two metal chairs, the seats of which were covered in shining red plastic, "Please, will you sit?"

I crossed over and sat down. "Where is your daughter?"

"My daughter cannot see you. You will soon understand. I can only tell you now that Vizzini is dead." She paused, as if gathering her courage, before asking, "Will you have coffee?" I nodded. She lit one of the hobs on a minute electric cooker, placed a kettle on it and put a teaspoon of Nescafe into a cup. The cup was white, with a red band spotted with polka dots around the brim. It had a matching saucer. She turned once or twice and studied me in the gloomy light: there was warmth in her eyes that I'd not seen before.

"You look just like your father, the last time that I saw him."

A knot tightened in my stomach, "You knew my father?"

A trace of a sad smile flickered across her face. She went to a dark recess under the stairs and took a painted wooden box from a shelf. The box was old, its colours faded. She laid it on the table before me and opened it. Inside were some yellowing letters and a photograph. She handed to it me. I recognized my father, younger than I'd ever known him, but just as strong and confident. His arm was around a beautiful dark-haired girl of about sixteen. Her face was radiantly happy. It was hard to believe that she'd become the tragic woman beside me.

The kettle boiled. She poured the steaming water into the cup and brought it to me. "Would you like sugar? We have sugar now."

"No I'll take it as it is."

She sat on the chair on the other side of table, searching for ways to begin her story. "I was born at Lercara Friddi; I knew your father and your mother from the day I was born. Elvira, your mother, was my best friend, Ciro, your father, I loved ever since I could remember. We played our first games together, went to school together, took Holy Communion by each other's side. Your father carved me wooden dolls with his knife. It was his most treasured possession; it had a leopard on the handle. He kissed me for the first time when he was ten; I used to tremble when he touched me. When he was twelve, Ciro went into the mines and soon after that, your mother and I went to work in the fields. It was hard, but we were happy, although your mother loved Ciro too and we knew that he could only marry one of us. I was certain it would be me. Then Ciro got mixed up in politics. It was just after the first war; we began to hear of a great revolution in Russia; how the workers had seized power and made a wonderful new society and way of life. Ciro said we should bring the revolution here. He saw how terrible things were in the mines, how the owners ignored the simplest safety regulations and paid the Mafia and their *gabellotti* to work the men to death for the smallest of wages. In 1920, he was nineteen years old, I was two years younger. I wanted him to marry me, I was ready for his children, but he would only think of the strike. He had become the miners' leader. He made speeches in the piazza at Lercara Friddi, organized the pickets at the entrance to the mine. The owners brought in more *gabellotti*. There were bloody fights and the carabinieri were always on the side of the *gabellotti*. In one fight Ciro hit a captain of the carabinieri. He was sent to jail in Palermo for a year."

She wrung her veined hands together and studied them for a moment.

"My father was also a miner but he was old, they had broken his spirit. He was against the strike. One of the *gabellotto* from Villalba had seen me in the town and wanted me. He asked my father if he could marry me. At first my father refused. It was dishonourable, even for him, for his daughter to marry a *gabellotti*. But the man was persistent, he offered money. He said he could arrange for my father to have an easier job in the mine, away from the *calcaroni* and the melted sulphur. He told my mother that he would give me a good life, and eventually she persuaded my father to agree. I was appalled, heartbroken. The man, his name was Luigi – Luigi Natoli, was ugly, his manners were coarse and brutal. But I was only a girl of seventeen, your father was locked away in Palermo, and I could not hold out against them. Luigi took me to Villalba and married me here in the church before Father Salvatore.

When Ciro got out of jail and heard what I had done, he married your mother immediately. It was his way of showing me his anger. For several years I did not see him or hear from him, or even from your mother. I was very lonely. I had no friends here. Luigi was a brute. He treated me as if I was something he had bought. He would drink and beat me, and then, when no children came, he accused me of being a whore."

She broke off and went to the sink and held a damp towel to her eyes. I realized I'd not touched my coffee. I lifted the cup and drank the tepid liquid in a single gulp. She returned to her seat and picked up the photo and gazed at it lovingly.

"I had almost given up hope, when one day your father came. It was pure chance that Luigi was away on a mission for Don Calo. Your father's beautiful eyes were red and swollen. At first I thought it was from weeping, as mine so often were. He told me that he had contracted a sickness in the mines – the owners had been forced to take him back because of his skill in explosives – and that you and your mother had already gone on to America. He would follow as soon as his eyes were better, but he wanted to see me for the last time. We walked by the river. He told me that he did not love your mother: she was a good woman but he could feel no desire for her. But he loved you so much; he was determined that you should have a better life in America. I told him of my unhappiness – our love reopened as a rose in June. I knew my husband would not come back that night. I thought that we could enjoy a few hours of happiness. And we did – up there." She pointed to the floor above. "The following morning, a neighbour saw him leave and told my husband. Luigi's anger was terrible. He beat me with his belt and with his club. My face was black and swollen; the women of Villalba stoned me and called me *puttana.*

Ciro heard of my misfortune and came back. When he saw what Luigi had done to me, he confronted him, spat at him, and challenged him to defend his honour. I wept and begged them not to fight, but they went down by the river and fought with knifes. Your father killed Luigi with his knife with the leopard's head. Luigi's friends demanded justice. Ciro was brought before Don Calo. He held his own trial at his farm up in the hills. According to every rule of the *Fratellanza,* the sentence could only be death. Ciro had dishonoured the wife of a 'friend' and then killed him. But Don Calo had heard of your father's skill with dynamite. It was the early days of Mussolini's power. He was testing his strength against the Mafia. The Duce was about to send a Prefect, who swore he would eliminate all opposition. Don Calo swore that he would kill him. He too wanted to show his power. He planned an ambush for the Prefect's car as it came over the mountains from Palermo, but the Fascists had knocked down the walls beside the road to the height of a man's waist. A man could no longer stand and fire his *lupara* from behind them. A bomb was the only answer and only your father could make it. Don Calo swore that he would give your father his life and spare me from shame, if he would join the *Fratellanza* and accomplish the task that he gave him. Ciro had no choice. What would have happened to you and your mother alone in that huge strange land? He knew what they would do to me. He swore his oath – a terrible one. They smeared his blood over an image of Christ himself, and forced him to fire a pistol through

Christ's heart. He became Calo's man. He made the bomb and killed the Prefect and left for America. I never saw him again." She broke off and turned away again as her tears flowed. "Calo took me to his farm in the hills, away from my shame. The next month I knew I was with child. It could only have been Ciro's. Luigi had not taken me within the time. A woman knows such things."

The truth was at last becoming clear. But it was too much for my frenzied mind to comprehend.

She looked at me pityingly before continuing, "When Gina was born I swore she was Luigi's, although I know Calo never believed me. My father was dead. Calo sent for my mother to come here, to this house, and raise the child. After that I rarely saw her, and Calo began to use me like an animal whenever he felt the need."

"And my father never knew?"

She shook her head. "Why cause him more pain? But he wrote me a letter the following year." She took a yellowing piece of paper from the box. She looked at it lovingly before passing it to me. It was written in fading pencil.

My one and only love,

I am sending this to my cousin in Lercara and I pray that he will pass it to you. Not a day goes by but I think of you. I have become what I always vowed I would not be. I now have blood on my hands here in this strange new country as well as there in Sicily. But each time I kill it is easier, and I now have money. It is strange how blood is rewarded far more than honest sweat. Daniello is a fine boy and Elvira is a good wife, but I am becoming a bad man. If you need money send word to my cousin and I will send it to you. My oath was that I would never see you again. A friend should not enjoy another 'friend's' wife. That is their rule – and I must never break it or you will die. Vizzini has sworn that he will protect you. I have new masters here to serve.

Fate has driven us apart but you will always be the one I truly loved.

Ciro.

I finished reading and looked up at her. She shook her head sadly, as if imagining what might have been. "He never wrote again. His cousin died and there was no way I could reach him, even if I had wished. I decided I would bear my pain and humiliation as a penance for my sin. I thought that your father was out of my life until that day I saw you at Calo's farm in the mountains. You looked so like him – at first, I thought you were his ghost come home at last. I sent Gina away but you found her here. I never imagined that you would both fall in love. You know now why I had to stop it. You would have been committing an even greater sin."

"But why did you not tell me then? I would have understood. It would have made the pain easier to bear."

"You would not have left your sister. Calo did not want you here. You refused his oath. He feared you. He knew you would not bend like all the others. He would have killed you if you had stayed. I had to be cruel to make you leave at once."

"Is Gina happy?"

"She is happier than I. There are sparks of goodness in Falco, even though his hands are drenched with blood. She has her children; he gives her money to shop in Palermo. He even lets her buy a few things for me." She gestured towards the refrigerator.

I reached out and took her work-worn hand, "All these years I have wondered why she refused me. I have never trusted a girl again. I was afraid." I began to weep.

She drew me to her and hugged me as if I were her own child. "Your father and I, and Gina, have sacrificed our happiness. Love, if you can find it is the most precious thing of all. Go and seek it out. You are still young; live a good life for those of us who remain in Villalba."

It was dusk when I left the house, my mind clear at last, and retraced my steps back along the Via Bocetta. I'd nearly reached the piazza when a small blob of red glowed in a dark doorway.

"Hi, kid, how you doing?"

A once-familiar figure was lounging against the wall. His hair was streaked with grey, but the disfigured face was the same. A Camel drooped as ever from the side of his mouth. All my antipathy flooded back.

"What in the name of hell are you doing here? I thought you were under restriction orders in Naples."

Luciano shrugged in the old easy way. "I'm small potatoes now. No one really bothers 'bout me, 'cept to make my life fuckin' difficult."

"The word is you're boss of an entire drugs network."

"That's all baloney. Gambino had some ideas before I left New York, but it never came to nothin'. Some shitheel tipped off the authorities before I even got to Genoa. I've been under fuckin' surveillance for years; can't have so much as a crap without the Immigration Department knowing. All that junk business has nothin' to do with me. It's the same old story; blame it on Luciano. There's even some story going round that I ordered the sabotage on the *Normandie* to persuade you guys to let me out of solitary in Dannemora. Will you do me a favour and tell your pals to lay off?" He ground the cigarette butt under his foot. His shoes were expensive and polished. "Dunno why, I don't owe you a thing, you little creep, but there's something I wanna tell you."

"Don't trouble yourself. I know already. I've just come from Gina's mother."

"It's not that. It's about that stupid Commie uncle of yours."

"Uncle Tony?"

"Yep. In the winter of 46/47 Calo did a deal with the Christian Democrats; said he'd back them and give up his call for Sicilian independence, if they gave the local government the right to raise taxes and control of all the aid money for the next 30 years. It was too good an offer to refuse. Only trouble was the fuckin' Commies. There was just a chance they might win the election. Don Calo put down a marker on Li Causi, the Communist boss. He was due to hold a big May Day rally at some crummy place south of Palermo called Portella della Ginestre. I'd been deported back from Cuba and was under restriction orders in Lercara Friddi. I'd heard Calo had something planned and went along to watch." He put a fresh Camel in his mouth and lit it. He inhaled and watched the smoke rise. "It all went fuckin' wrong. Instead of a nice clean kill, stupid peasant fucks started shooting all over the place. Women, children went down like skittles. It was like the fuckin' war all over again. Then I saw your Uncle. He was standing on the platform beside Li Causi. He stepped in front and shouted: "Why are you shooting? Who are you shooting? Can't you see you're shooting yourselves?" He barely got the words out when he took a bullet clean through the head." He pulled on his cigarette and looked at me with his cold eyes. "Guess that put a final end to that business with your pa. Funny thing is, I kinda envy him: going out on a high. Maybe I should have been more of a hero in the war."

Everything was finally in place. I couldn't speak. I turned and began to walk away.

"Okay, kid? Favour for favour. You tell those jerks in Immigration that I'm clean. Tell the pricks to get off my fuckin' back."

I left him and walked across the moonlit piazza for the last time. An ancient dog was lying mournfully on the paving stones in the shadows before the church; the only creature that truly mourned the passing of Don Calo Vizzini. It heard my footsteps and opened a blue eye and watched me climb back up the steep Corso Dante, past the gaze of the malevolent old men. Like Dante in the *Inferno*, I was climbing out of Hell. My heart was finally lightened. I now understood and loved my father more than ever, and was proud my uncle had died a brave death. I felt it was possible to find happiness, that somewhere there was someone with whom I could share my life. '*The truth is often the most painful thing*' – Luciano had told me that many years ago. But it was not true. There must be no more lies. Truth made sense of everything.

As I got into the little Fiat I thought again of the proud eyes of the girl in the Giardino Garibaldi. I decided I would try to find her there.

Lucky Luciano never returned to the United States. He always protested his innocence of any connection with the drug trade, although a quarter of the world's supply of heroin was processed in laboratories in Sicily.

Charles Salvatore Lucania died of a heart attack in the restaurant at Naples airport on January 26, 1962. He was on his way to discuss the script of a possible film of his life, in which he would reveal many secrets. Both his former associates in the Mafia and the US authorities were strongly against it. There has been some conjecture over the exact circumstances of his death.

HISTORICALCHARACTERSFEATUREDORREFERRED TO IN ORDER OF APPEARANCE.

New York

Pete Panto: longshoreman and union activist murdered by the mob in 1939

Albert Anastasia: head of Murder Inc. Shot dead in a barber's chair in October 1957

Joe 'the Boss' Masseria (1887–1931): Shot dead by Lucky Luciano

Benito Mussolini (1883–1945): Fascist dictator of Italy

Commander C. Radcliffe Haffenden (1892–1952)

Joe DiMaggio (1914–1999): Baseball player and one-time husband of Marilyn Monroe Vice Adm Adolphus Andrews (1879–1948)

Frank S. Hogan (1902–1974): District Attorney. of New York County for 30 years

Thomas Dewey (1902–1971): Governor of New York. Republican Presidential candidate in 1944 and 1948

Joseph A. 'Socks' Lanza (1904–1968): Labour Racketeer

Meyer Lansky, born Majer Suchowlnski (1902–1983)

Charles 'Lucky' Luciano, born Salvatore Lucania (1897–1962)

John 'Cocked-Eyed' Dunn (1910–1949): New York mobster; executed by electric chair

Vernon Morhous: Governor of Great Meadow Prison, Comstock, New York State

Maj Gen William 'Wild Bill' Donovan (1883–1959): Head of the Office of Strategic Studies (OSS)

Gen Bernard Montgomery (1887–1976): Later Field Marshal and first Viscount Montgomery of Alamein

Don Calo Vizzini (1877–1954): Mayor of Villalba

Gen George Patton Jr. (1885–1945)

Fictitious Characters

Danny Crivello
Elvira Crivello, his mother
Tony Lorenzo, his uncle
Fats Florino, a hoodlum
Ensign Frank Dunford
Sue Martin
Yeoman Mary Hampton
PRRJ, Haffenden's Captain in WW1
Mrs Kelly, mother of Frank's friend, George

Sicily

Gen Matthew Bunker Ridgway (1895–1993)
Cesare Mori (1871–1942): Mussolini's 'Iron Prefect'
Col William Orlando Darby (1911–1954): Founder of 'Darby's Rangers'
Adm H. Kent Hewitt (1887–1972)
Capt Edwin Sayre (1915–2014): Cdr 'A' Company', 1st Bn. 505th Parachute Regt
Lt Col Arthur Gorham (1915–1943): Cdr 1st Bn. 505th Parachute Regt
Father Salvatore Vizzini (dates unknown): Don Calo's brother
Gen Harold Alexander (1891–1969): Later Field Marshal and first Earl of Tunis
Gen Lucian Truscott Jr. (1895–1967)
Robert Capa, born Endre Friedmann (1913–1954)
Maj Gen Terry Allen Sr. (1888–1969)
Brig Gen. Theodore Roosevelt Jr. (1887–1944): eldest son of 26th President; died of heart attack on Utah Beach on D-Day
Clara Petacci (1912–1945): daughter of the Pope's personal physician, executed with her lover, Mussolini
Col Gen. Hans Huber (1890–1944): Killed in plane crash on the Eastern Front
Lt Gen Omar Bradley (1893–1981) Later General of the Army
Col Harry Albert 'Paddy' Flint (1888–1944): Died of wounds in Normandy.
Generalleutnant Eberhard Rodt (1895–1979)
Lt Col Lyle Bernard. Wounded at Anzio in 1944
Vice Adm Lyal Davidson (1886–1950)

Girolamo Di Causi (1896–1977): Sicilian Communist leader
Lt Col John Malcolm Thorpe Fleming 'Jack' Churchill (1906–1996)

Fictitious characters
Giuseppe Falco
Sgt Harold Blum
Capt Limo
Plt Off Raymond Stiles, RAF
Maj Vincenzo

New York
Moses Polakoff (1896–1993)
Joe Adonis (1902–1971)
Willie Moretti (1894–1951)
Tommy Lucchese (1899–1967)
Frank Costello (1891–1973)
Arnold Rothstein (1882–1928)
Carlo Gambino (1902–1975)

Acknowledgements

I am heavily indebted to the following:

BITTER VICTORY by Carlo D'Este. The finest account of the Sicilian
   Campaign.
WAR AS I KNEW IT by General George S. Patton JR
PATTON by Martin Blumenson.
THE ARMIES OF GEORGE S. PATTON by George Forty
MUSSOLINI'S ISLAND by John Follan
THE WAR IN ITALY by Field Marshal Lord Carver
SICILY-SALERNO-ANZIO by Samuel Eliot Morison
MEMOIRS OF MONTGOMERY OF ALAMEIN
THE LUCIANO PROJECT by Rodney Campbell. The original inspira-
   tion for this book.
THE LAST TESTAMENT OF LUCKY LUCIANO by Gosch Hammer
LUCKY LUCIANO by Hickman Powell
LUCKY LUCIANO by Tim Newark
THE MAFIA AT WAR by Tim Newark
THE SICILIAN MAFIA by Diego Gambetta
THE HONOURED SOCIETY by Norman Lewis
COSA NOSTRA by John Dickie
SICILIAN UNCLES by Leonardo Sciascia
REPORT FROM PALERMO by Danilo Dolci
MIDNIGHT IN SICILY by Peter Robb
BLOOD WASHES BLOOD by Frank Viviano
SLIGHTLY OUT OF FOCUS by Robert Capa
THE IMPERIAL WAR MUSEUM LIBRARY

53478088R00264

Made in the USA
Charleston, SC
14 March 2016